THE DEAD SAGA

ODIUM

By

USA Today Bestselling Author

Claire C. Riley

Odium The Dead Saga Series
Copyright ©2014 Claire C. Riley
Cover Design: Wilde Designs Elizabeth Constantopoulos
Editor: Amy Jackson
Formatting: Sarah Barton Book Obsessed Formatting

LOVE FOR ODIUM. THE DEAD SAGA SERIES

"A MUST READ for fans of The Walking Dead."
Amazon Top 100 Reviewer

"A terrifying and exciting ride through a brutal post-apocalyptic landscape."
Goodrcads Top 100 Reviewer.

"I cheered, I laughed with some very snarky characters, I saw some very original ideas, I got grossed out, scared, and happy. Claire C. Riley writes a pretty striking story, and hell, I'm still excited about it!"
Liz – Fictional Candy Book Blog

"This book is not about Happily-Ever-Afters. It's a suspenseful thriller full of action, sadness, angst, death and emotions!"
Lo - Crazies-R-Us Book Blog

"I would recommend Odium to anyone that isn't afraid of an accelerated heartbeat! I have never laughed so hard and been so scared all within the same breath!"
Liz-Crazies-R-Us Book Blog

Sometimes the best dreams are the ones we have to chase.

Red.

ONE

"RUN, NINA!" Mikey's voice roars from behind me, sounding far away against the rampant beating of my heart.

My feet pound through the wet soil of someone's lawn as we run through the front gate and around the side of the house. The overgrown grass sticks to my calves and makes me stumble and trip, but I continue to run nonetheless. I'm not stopping for anything—not with fifty or so deaders closing in and the fucking Forgotten chasing our asses down. Run? Please, I'm fucking sprinting at ninety miles an hour. I'm like a goddamned gazelle on the run from its predator. *Wait, doesn't the prey always get caught? Shit.*

I chance a glance over my right shoulder, checking that Mikey is close behind. My heart skips a beat when my eyes don't immediately land on him, and I slow down and start to turn, until he grips my shoulder and drags me forward as he comes up on my left.

"I said run, woman!" he yells into my face, and continues to drag me along.

1

I shrug him off, but don't have time to tell him to go fuck himself for screaming in my face like an old fishmonger's wife. The smell of the dead makes me retch, and the gunshots from the Forgotten make my blood run cold. I'll write a mental I.O.U. to kick his ass for screaming in my face—if we make it out of this alive, that is.

The fence at the back of the little yard has collapsed, giving us an easy way out through to the other side into yet another soggy, overgrown field. My breath is ragged and dry in my throat, making me feel like I've swallowed some crushed glass. Every time I gulp, another shard digs in and causes me to cough. We stumble and slide down the side of the embankment, both of us gasping as we slip into the freezing shallow river at the bottom. I'm sure at one point this house was Grade A real estate, with its own land and a river running past it, but right now it's a survivor's nightmare.

We begin to wade across, lifting our arms above our heads to keep as much of us out of the ice-cold water as possible, my Doc Martens thankfully giving me firm footing on the rocks. We half-climb, half-drag ourselves up and out the other side, my fingers clinging to the thick, wet mud and roots to get some leverage. I grip on tighter, my fingers blue with the cold, and as I lose my grip and begin to slip, Mikey's hand shoots down and grabs my wrist, heaving me up the other side.

I nod thanks and then I'm back on my feet and we're running again, with the sound of zombies falling into the water behind us. The empty field and the houses in the distance spur us both on, and I grab Mikey's hand as we push harder, willing our legs to run faster and our muscles not to cramp. To cramp up now could mean death for both of us; by deader or by gun, death will be a long, drawn out, painful experience, that's for certain. Fuck that.

With deaders in the surrounding field getting closer, the scene plays out in slow motion when I trip and fall to my knees, mud splattering up around me. Mikey turns and grips me under the arms, dragging me back up to standing.

My eyes bug out when a gray arm reaches up out of the mud and grabs at his ankle. "Mikey!" I scream.

He kicks away from the deader's reach and swings down with his fist, narrowly missing its rotten mouth, which is snapping at his leg. He hits it hard across its skull with his fist, and its head whips backwards upon impact before the deader quickly rights itself and fixes its cloudy gaze upon me. It stretches a rotten hand across to me as it slowly pulls itself free of the mud and grass, growling and gnashing its broken, blackened teeth. Mikey's foot stamps down on its arm, cracking the bone in two; however, the ligament hangs by the bloated and stretched skin. The deader pays the broken limb no attention, but continues to drag its decomposing body toward me. Mikey grabs it from behind and drags it backwards, putting some distance between me and it. The deader thrashes around, growling in anger in an attempt to get to me, until Mikey falls on his ass. I grab the nearest thing to me—a heavy rock big enough that I need to use both hands to lift it—and with difficulty, I launch it at the thing's face.

It crushes into the brittle bones, making an almost concave shape where the deader's features should be and releasing a toxic stench that I can taste in my mouth. It stops moving instantly and collapses into the gore-soaked earth around it. I look at Mikey as he holds a hand out to me.

"Come on, baby. We need to go."

My shaky hand takes his, and I climb back to my feet and together we run.

STOP...REWIND...

Four months earlier...

"I'm cold, Nina." Emily huddles into my side, and I drape an arm across her shoulders, snuggling her into me.

"I know, Em." I speak through a cut and swollen mouth. My eyes are closed—well, one eye won't open and the other thinks it would be better not to see right now and so is staying firmly shut in the hopes that I'll be able to fall asleep and wake up to this nightmare being over.

You think you know how you will react in an apocalypse—the whole 'I'll never give up and never surrender'—but when you've been continually tortured for weeks on end, your strength to never give up wavers. In fact, if it wasn't for Emily I probably would have tried to end it after what happened yesterday. I squeeze her closer, feeling her body shiver and her teeth chatter.

I'm that worn out, that broken down; I've even begun to feel pity for the deaders—the hunger they must constantly feel, Jesus. I wonder if they have any consciousness. I hope not, because I haven't been this hungry for a long time—and I'm used to be hungry, but this type of hunger, this type of desperation...it's something else. Not even life behind the walls compares. Jesus, those poor people are going to die if I don't do something. I should be concerned for myself and Emily right now. And I am—for her anyway. I'm in too much pain right now to think about my own needs. I just want it to stop.

Mikey, Emily, and I have been captured by the Forgotten. There were more of us, but they are all dead now, or reborn into the walking abominations I call the deaders.

Deaders are, well, *dead*, but they're alive again. I guess 'zombies'

4

would be a better term of endearment for them. Insert mock laughter and a sarcastic roll of my swollen eyes. Oh wait, I can't roll my eyes, can I? Well, deaders don't rest, they don't stop, they feel no mercy. They only have one thing in mind: killing. But wait, I was talking about the Forgotten, wasn't I? The Forgotten are not a bunch of merry men here to help. No, no, no. The Forgotten are a small army of desperate and twisted individuals that were kept out of the walled cities when the apocalypse erupted onto this damned earth. Refused entry into the so-called protection of the walled cities, they and their families were left to fend for themselves. And they failed...miserably. I think they all lost more than just their wives and children that day, and now they are intent on reaping revenge upon all the walled cities and their inhabitants.

They don't just want into these cities. They want to kill every last person behind those walls—the lucky ones, as they call them. What they don't seem to understand, or don't care about, is that those cities were no safe haven, for anyone. The cities were ruled by self-proclaimed assholes—sorry, leaders. And we did what we had to in order to survive, whether that was sell our bodies or sell our souls. I should know—that's where I was living prior to escaping with a young girl named Emily-Rose.

I promised to protect her, and I did—for a while, anyway. Now I'm failing miserably at the job. So send me down to the unemployment line, because I need a new job. Since I suck so bad at this one. I place a kiss upon her head as her breathing grows shallower and she slips into sleep. *Where's Mikey?* you might ask. I honestly don't know; however, I think he's dead. I should feel something more for that heartbreaking fact, but I can't grieve for him now—not yet. Right now I have to focus on Emily, and protecting her.

I must drift off, too, because when I wake, I jump. My eyes immediately open, or try to, and I yelp at the pain in my left eye. I have to force myself not to move my mouth too much for fear of ripping open the gash that runs from the corner of my mouth to my cheekbone. It's only just started to properly scab over after Fallon sliced me with a knife like I was a prime cut of beef.

The door opens, a drawn out scraping sound of metal upon concrete, and then the light from the doorway penetrates the room. Fallon's guards are back. I flinch, a whimper escaping through my cracked lips even though I want to be every part of the fierce, strong woman that Emily believes me to be. Emily stirs, and when I squeeze her closer she wakes up completely and starts to cry, her hands gripping at my clothing, her demeanor that of a small child, not a teenage girl. Actually she's more of a young woman than I want her to be, because that's a dangerous age to be around these men.

"Get away from us!" I spit out.

They reach for me, strong arms gripping me tightly, and I force my body to go limp and not fight them as they drag me from the room with the sound of Emily crying ringing in my ears. My knees scrape along the concrete floor, but the pain is nothing compared to what I know is coming next. As we exit the room, a cloth bag is forced over my head, blocking everything out and making it difficult for me to breathe. We turn left, we turn right, and then I lose which way we go because of the nausea rising in my gut. Fear trembles through me, and I can't hold back my resistance any longer. I struggle and pull at their grip, receiving a punch to the gut for my efforts.

I cry out, my body trying to curl up on itself. I hear the men snicker, and I swallow the sob that is building in me. I won't let them see me weak...they won't have my tears.

A cold draft washes over me and the room seems suddenly darker as I'm dragged to a chair and forced to sit on it, with the back of it to my front. My hands grip it tightly. Footsteps retreat and I sit frozen in panic, trembles shaking me from my toes to the top of my head. The more I try to contain them, the harder it seems.

I tentatively push up to my feet, wanting to move, to run, to do anything but just sit here. A hand grips my shoulder and pushes me back down to my chair. I whimper and comply without question, no matter how much I want to run. I know which battles to pick, and this isn't one of them.

"It doesn't have to be like this, you know." A male voice. Could be Fallon, but fear has tried to eradicate that voice from my memory, so I can't be sure. "He's making it all the more difficult for you, making your pain worse." A pause, and then: "Why do you think he wants to see you in pain, Nina?"

I flinch at the sound of my name on this man's lips. He's not a good man, and while I'm no Mary Poppins, I'm pretty sure there's a special place reserved in hell for this guy. He's the man I've come to hate the most, possibly more than Fallon, because this man is the one that has been torturing me every day for weeks.

"Well?" he prompts.

Oh, he actually wants me to reply. "Who?" is all I ask.

The man laughs. "Who? Who do you think I'm talking about?"

I swallow hard. "Fallon?" I ask, confused.

The man laughs again: a deep, gravelly sound, followed by coughing. "No, not Fallon. Your boy, Mikey." He pauses again, and I want to scream *'enough with the dramatic effects already!'* but instead I keep quiet. "Why do you think Mikey likes to see you in pain?"

"He doesn't," I snap. "And he would do everything he could to stop this."

Another laugh. I can feel the cool air shift around me as he walks behind my chair. I want to follow the sound but instead I stay as still as a statue, only flinching a little when his hands come to my shoulders and he slowly massages them.

"Really? You think so, huh?"

"Yes," I reply quietly.

A shiver works its way up my spine, the urge to peel this creep's fingers away from me becoming harder to resist. My ears perk up at another noise: a belt buckle being shifted, moved—or undone. I grit my teeth, trying to swallow the acidic bile in my throat. Fear clenches in my gut, and I open my mouth a fraction to take a deep, steadying breath, readying myself for what is to come.

A loud snap by my ears draws a short, sharp scream from my lips. A belt, his belt—leather, I presume—cracks in the air, and I scream again and flinch away from the sound, nearly falling off my chair in the process. The man laughs again and pulls me back onto my seat.

"Sit on your hands."

"What?" I whisper with a gulp.

"Sit on your hands," he orders again.

I comply immediately, his tone telling me that he's not fucking around anymore. My teeth chatter painfully, not from the cold that has worked its way into my soul, but from fear. I feel his hands near my head and then slowly he begins to lift the black cloth bag away from my face. My eyes open painfully, and I quickly squeeze them shut and then reopen them as my vision begins to focus. I take in my surroundings: a small shell of a room, barred windows, gray walls, dirty concrete floor. I look straight ahead of me and realize that I'm looking at my own reflection. A large wall is in front of me with a huge dirty mirror on it, reflecting back my own frightened image, and I'm shocked and scared by what I see. I'm pale and visibly shaking, my hair a rat's nest of black tangles. My one good eye wide and glassy, the other swollen closed. I look behind me to a large beast of a man standing and staring at me—literally a beast of a man. His face is ravaged, the skin sewn over his left eye, and part of his cheek missing: a deep gouge where his flesh once was. His hair hangs lankly around his face. He smiles at me and my breath snags. Horror lurks behind those eyes.

His hand reaches out and he lifts up the back of my top. I shiver again, my skin covered in goose bumps from his touch and from the freezing air. He smiles again, a throaty sound of satisfaction coming from the back of his throat. I squeeze my eyes closed when I see him raise a large brown belt, and I wait with gritted teeth for the pain to begin.

It's only seconds later when the first lash rains down on me, causing me to scream loudly. My back burns, pain vibrating from the red welt that is no doubt now standing to attention. Another crack of his belt sounds out right before it lashes across my back, almost like he's taunting me with the sound. The pain is worse this time, and I scream, gagging on the sound. After the fourth I beg for him to stop, the tears leaking from my eyes no matter how much I don't want to cry. After the seventh I struggle to breathe. After that I lose count.

Nothing happens for what seems like an eternity. My breath comes in great, wracking sobs from my chest as I heave and fight the pain. I hear him tut, and I wonder what the hell I could have done now. I haven't moved, I've done everything he told me to, so why the tut? A new sound makes my eyes open.

9

I stare straight ahead, watching him leering at me. My flesh is pure white and trembling, yet he looks like he's having the most fun he's ever had. I swallow and choke on a sob as his large meaty hand reaches for my hair, grabbing a clump of it roughly as he drags me backwards from my chair. I stumble and almost fall to the ground, only his hand on my hair keeping me upright.

It happens so fast.

I scream.

He laughs.

And he continues to pull me backwards as I claw at him, screaming and crying until he throws me forward against a dirty bed that smells of mold and filth. My face buries in the rank material and I can hardly breathe. I look back over my shoulder as he comes toward me, one hand working the button on his jeans, and he says, "Why does your boy want to see you hurtin', baby?" He smiles.

I spit at him. "Fuck you," I whisper.

He smiles again.

TWO

t's relentless. That's all I can think as the door screeches open and they come for me again. Not a day to recover or time to banish the memory of dirty, groping hands on me, causing me pain and making me beg for mercy. Emily cowers in front of me, but I jut out my chin and push her behind me. I can't imagine anything worse than this—than what they've already done to me—so fuck it. Fuck them. And fuck the world. I snarl as two men stand in front of me, the shadows from their bodies falling over Emily and me.

One of them chuckles and as their arms reach out, I brace myself for them to take me, brace myself for more pain and torment, but instead they reach for Emily. I'm stunned as she screams in fear, her eyes wide like saucers, and then I scream and grab for her also. They laugh at us and I kick out at them, grabbing for her again as she reaches for me.

"Not her! Please not her! Take me, take me, please."

A sharp kick to my ribs sends me sprawling backwards, but I'm up and moving for them again with the sharp taste of copper in my mouth and my breath burning through my lungs. The door shuts and I'm locked back into darkness again, with only my tears and my memories of what they previously did to me to fill the empty space left by her.

"No," I sob. "Please, God, no, not Emily." They're going to break her down, tear that innocence away from her, and destroy who she is. "Please, NO!" I bang against the door with my fists and scream, feeling the gash at my mouth pop back open with a painful pinch and fresh blood ooze from it. "Please!"

I slide down the door to my knees, and cry. I cry for her and I cry for Mikey. I don't understand why he would let them do this to us, but I have my trust in him. He wouldn't just abandon us. The worthless self-pitying part cries for me, because I know that if any of us make it out of this alive—which I doubt we will—none of us will ever be the same again, and that is the saddest thing of all.

THREE

Two days, I estimate, I've been here alone. Two days in the cold and the dark with no word from Emily or Mikey. Two days of pissing in a bucket and shivering in the corner—lucky for me, my bowels are empty anyway. I guess that's the bonus of being starved. My right eye has decided to open back up today; it's both painful and a relief to know that it still works. I want to be using this time to exercise and get strong—like in the movies, where the woman does a hundred pull-ups and builds up her body strength so she looks like a miniature wrestler—but every part of my body is bruised either externally or internally. I know my pride certainly is. I stopped worrying for Mikey when I returned and he didn't. In my head I've accepted that they have probably killed him, so imagine my surprise when the door finally opens and he waltzes in, looking every bit the comedy villain: dark stubble covering his chin, red, blood-stained knuckles, bulging biceps, and all wrapped up nicely with a cold expression.

I stumble to my feet, my eyes sore from the glare coming from outside. "Mikey?" I ask, even though I know it's him—I'm not fucking stupid or something. I may have been beaten to near death, but all my mental health is still in place. Or at least that's what the voices keep telling me.

"You're alive!" I run toward him. "I knew you were and I knew you wouldn't leave us. I fucking knew it," I sob.

He meets me halfway, striding toward me quickly and wrapping his arms around me as I bury myself into him. The heat and strength in those arms dissolves every bit of willpower I possess and I cry, tears pouring from my eyes while I wail like a banshee into his chest. The surge in emotions only lasts a minute but feels like an hour, and I pull away, embarrassed. His face is calm and collected, not an inch of emotion showing. Even his warm eyes seem cold as they look me over.

"They took Emily!" I trip over my words, my eyes glaring at the man in the doorway. I push away from Mikey. "What did you do to her?" I sob, heading toward the dick by the door like a protective mama bear.

"She's fine, Nina. She's working." Mikey grabs me by the waist and pulls me back to his chest.

I look up at him, fear gnawing at my stomach. "What?" The worst thought pops into my mind. "Working? What do you mean, working?" I spin to get at the guard again. "You better not have touched her!" I scream.

Mikey catches on to my train of thought. "No, not like that," he rushes to clarify. "She's helping out around here, cooking and cleaning." He strokes my cheek carefully. "She's fine, I promise."

I stand back to assess him. How does he know all this? How can he be so calm about it? Has he been lapping it up in luxury while I've been living in squalor? And what about Emily—working? Which more than likely means she's being looked after, fed, watered, and has somewhere other than the floor to rest on. I look down at myself, finally smelling the stench of both this room and me. I look him over, finally seeing the long scars up his arms and the shadows of bruises on his face, but even those are healing. "Where have you been?"

He shrugs his shoulders, like I've asked him the time and not where he's been the entire time I've been being tortured. He looks behind him at the guard and then back to me.

"I've been working—preparing." He looks away guiltily.

"Preparing for what?" Bile rises in my stomach, dreading what he's going to say next.

"Preparing to break into the walled city," he says calmly.

I shake my head at him, confusion and shock covering my features. "But…no, Mikey."

He backs away from me, turning to stare at the doorway, his arms folding across his chest. "I don't know why you want to protect those people, Nina." He turns back around, his eyes narrowed. "After everything they did to you." I hear the tremor in his voice, though; he's not tricking me.

I grind my teeth. "So what? I'm over that."

"No you're not, and you never will be." His own teeth are grinding now, the muscles working at his jaw line. "You don't understand, Nina." He shakes his head.

"I understand that you're siding with these animals, and you think that's a better option. Look what *they* have done to me." Tears spring to my eyes, but they aren't sad tears. I'm fucking angry—furious, even.

Mikey walks to the doorway, his shoulders hung low. "I didn't come here for to fight with you, Nina. I wanted to check that you were okay after…" He swallows without finishing and I know what he was going to say, but neither of us voice it.

"Well, I'm not okay. I won't be okay if you do this. You're condemning all those people to death if you help the Forgotten, Mikey. You can't do this."

"It's already started, Nina."

I run to him, looking up into his face. "What do you mean?"

"We…" He rubs a hand down his face and I see a crack in his demeanor, a sliver of the man I thought I knew, and then it's gone and his cold façade is back. "We've destroyed one of the cities already."

It takes a moment to comprehend what he's saying. "You've destroyed one already?" I whisper and he nods. "And what about all the people?" I ask as I grab his arms and try to get him to look at me. "Mikey, what about all the people? What happened to them?"

"What do you think?" He steps back, his eyes staring into my face, searching for something. He must not find what he's looking for, because he pushes away from me and walks toward the door. "I'm trying to protect you, Nina." He chokes on his words.

I shake my head. I can't think; my thoughts are scrambling for something to grip onto. "I think you're a murderer," I whisper. "You killed all those people! How could you?" I shout after him, my voice cracking on the last word.

He turns his head ever so slightly, not really looking at me but directing his words to me nonetheless. "Better them than us." He walks out the door as he says, "Better than you."

"I'll never forgive you for this, Mikey. Never."

We stare at each other and I know my words have cut him, but instead of saying anything else he shuts the door, and a second later I hear the key turn in the lock.

"Don't fucking walk away from me, Mikey!" I shout again, tears flowing down my cheeks. "We said we would help them, not kill them." I sob loudly. I feel sick, weak, and exhausted, and as the world spins around me and goes gray and then pitch black oblivion, I swear to myself that I will never forgive Mikey for this.

I turn over, pulling the covers over my head. I don't know what that annoying sound is, but I am not getting up. I'm staying right here until lunchtime. I pull my knees up to my chest, flinching at the pain in my ribs, and my eyes spring open. It's dark, but then I'm buried beneath a warm duvet so that's to be expected, I guess. The thought registers as my hand fumbles with the cover. A duvet? I struggle to find the exit to my comfy cocoon, and when I do, things are different.

Gone is my dark cell of doom. *Yes, of doom. Don't fucking judge me.* Instead, I'm in a real bedroom. Well, I'm in a room with a bed, windows, and books in it, so it's the closest to a real bedroom I've been in in a long time.

I slip my feet out of bed, wary about where the hell I am and how the hell I got here. I scramble over to one of the windows and look out, my eyes stinging by the brightness of the world. I'm in a little town of some sort, with people milling around. There are shops and trees, and there's even a fucking park bench! My stomach lurches, making me feel nauseous from hunger and more than a little confusion. I turn and look around my room in confusion, my eyes finally landing on a tray of food on a large, round, wooden table in the middle of the room. I jog to it, ignoring the pain in my ribs and ankle, and dive straight into the food: scrambled eggs and fresh fruit—slightly cold scrambled eggs and berries, anyway.

I start eating, grabbing two handfuls of the food and shoving it quickly into my mouth before realizing that there is silverware I could use. With a shrug of my shoulders I continue with my own way of eating. It's quicker this way, and I haven't eaten in days.

I belch loudly as I devour the last of it, gulping down the glass of water in one go, and then sit at the table and stare at my empty plate. I don't understand what's going on. Where is everyone? Where the hell am I? Am I not going to die now, or is this just a tease—another form of torture, maybe? A sliver of hope to be dashed from me at the last moment because their other forms of torture weren't working on me. I want to laugh; clearly they didn't realize how close I was to breaking.

The last thing I remember was passing out by the door, with my ass going numb on the cold concrete floor. I look down at my feet, seeing dirty socks with holes in them instead of my well-worn Doc Marten boots. Standing abruptly, I set about looking for them. I'll kill them if they've taken my boots. They're mine; they were my last gift from Ben. A sob builds in the back of my throat, and when I see my boots by the side of my bed, I let it out in relief. I quickly go over and put them back on, making sure that the fraying laces are nice and tight, and then I continue my search of the room, finding nothing but a bathroom and a closet with no clothes in it.

I stand back at the window, frowning out upon this strange new world. There are a couple of children running in the little streets, playing jump rope and kicking a ball. A woman is pushing a baby buggy, and I can see the small movements of an infant within it. I watch as the people go into the shops and come out with purchases, arms laden with fruit and packages. What the hell are they buying? I don't understand what's going on. How can things be like this? How are they living like this? I pull myself up to sit in one of the window boxes to get a better view of my surroundings.

When I look down from my window, I can see great stone steps leading up to large double doors. There's a sign out front, but from this distance I can't read what it says. My eye is still tender from being swollen, and I'm glad I can still see from it, even if the vision isn't what it used to be yet. Maybe it never will be. I guess I should be grateful to be alive.

Grateful? I almost laugh. Grateful is the last thing I am. A sob builds in me again. Watching these children, mothers, and fathers walking around free and happy makes me think of the old world. I'd do anything to go back to that world, that life. Things were so much simpler then. Not to mention I was never chased by deaders or fucking lunatics.

The sound of the door opening behind me makes me jump, but I don't get down; I stay exactly where I am, watching and ready. Ready for what? I have no idea, and as usual, there's nothing I can do anyway. I wear a snarl on my damaged face, my fists ready by my sides, ready to attack anyone that comes near me. So when Emily comes in, I nearly fall from my seat in shock.

"Emily?" Yes, this sounds like déjà vu, doesn't it? That's what I was thinking, as the image of Mikey coming in to the other room comes back to haunt me.

"Nina." She runs over to me, arms open, tears pouring, like a little lamb running to slaughter. I say that not because I'm mean, but because I'm bad fucking luck and I have only seemed to make things worse for her since we met.

I jump down and run to her, and it's a real movie moment as we hug and cry and I kiss her forehead. "Are you okay? Did they hurt you?" My hands move over her shoulders and down her arms, my eyes scanning her pale face, examining every part of her that I can see and touch.

She shakes her head and offers up a small smile. "No, not even a little bit." She furrows her brow, her hands reaching for mine to still my movements. "I didn't understand at first, but it was Mikey. He convinced them not to hurt me."

My heart is pounding in my chest. I'm so glad she is okay, so glad they didn't hurt her in any way, and even though I hate him, I'm so damn grateful to Mikey for protecting her. The selfish side of me rears its ugly head when I realize that I was so easily forgotten. The irony of my choice of words nearly makes me laugh. Nearly *Forgotten*—yes, I know what it feels like to be on the other side of it now. The lack of concern he showed me is soul-destroying. I let him in, I let myself care, and this is how he repays me. Fucking men! Not only has he now condemned all the people behind the walls to death, he left me to rot in here.

"Nina."

I look into her face, seeing a young woman and not a child looking back at me, and know that they may not have touched her in that way, but she's all grown up now and there's no going back and changing that. She's hardening like I did, and once those walls are built, they aren't ever coming down.

FOUR

HILARY & DEACON

"Hilary, baby, you gotta come inside." Deacon's arms wrap around my hunched shoulders.

My eyes stay fixed on the old couple, dead in the front yard, blood still dripping from the holes in their foreheads. "Did you really need to kill them, Deacon?" I turn to look up into his blue eyes. "We could have talked to them—explained."

He leads me back inside and into the dimly lit front room. "You know I had to, baby. It was them or us, and it will *always* be us." He guides me to the sofa and sits me down, coming to kneel on the floor between my knees. He looks into my face. "Maybe we could have talked them down, but the way grandpa was pointing that gun at you. . ." He shakes his head before continuing. "I know it's hard, but we can be safe here now. At least for a little while. You rest up here, I'll move the bodies—"

"Bury them," I say. "The last thing they deserve is to get eaten by those dirty flesh-eaters."

Deacon nods, seeing the fight coming back into my eyes at the mention of the flesh-eaters. He kisses my forehead. "I'll be right back. I'm going to lock the door. Listen out for me, okay?"

"I should come with you." I start to stand, but Deacon gently pushes me back down.

"We haven't seen anyone in weeks. I highly doubt that we're going to stumble upon anyone else for a while. If you want to help, see if you can scramble us something up to eat while I deal with the bodies."

"Don't treat me like your little woman, Deac." I glare up at him. At six-foot three, he towers over me. "I don't need you to look after me."

Deacon laughs. "I know you don't, Hilary, no need to get snappy." He laughs again, the sound seeming odd in our quiet surroundings, especially after what we just did. "I don't think you're a little woman either." He chokes on another laugh. "I just don't think there is any need for us both to be out there. You really want to go shoveling dirt around and burying dead bodies, you go right ahead. Or you can stay inside and cook us up something good so we can eat, and get some rest. It's been a long day, baby. I'm tired and I bet you are too."

I relent with a roll of my eyes. "Fine," I pout, "but be careful."

Deacon heads to the front door, stopping to look back at me before he goes outside. "Hey, if you can hunt out any ramen noodles, you know I'd love you forever, right?"

"You're going to love me forever, anyway, but I'll see what they have." I grin, all thoughts of the old couple that he just killed long gone.

It was their own damn fault for not letting us in, anyway. What did they think was going to happen once the flesh-eaters caught up and ate us? I turn and walk into the kitchen, listening as the front door opens and closes behind Deacon, and I begin searching the cupboards.

The cabinets are unsurprisingly empty, but as I search further I come across the old couple's food stash, safely tucked away in a small downstairs bathroom under some old towels. It makes me wonder if these people had been looted before, and that's why their things are hidden. I shake my head sadly, my spirits only lifting when I come across a box of mac and cheese. I smile, knowing how pleased Deacon will be, since he used to love this stuff. Only ramen noodles would make him smile more—well, that or maybe a chai latte.

I set the table in the front room, filling two flowery yellow bowls with the warm mac and cheese, and placing a bottle of water for each of us next to our food. It feels almost civilized when Deacon comes in with his shotgun thrown over his shoulder and a grim expression marring his face. That changes almost instantly once he smells the food, and a smile lights up his handsome face. He heads straight for the table.

"Um, oh no you don't." I hold up a hand.

Deacon stops with a puzzled expression.

"Take those dirty boots off before you come and sit at my table. Walking mud across my nice clean floor." I tut at him. "I've been scrubbing these floors all day." I tut again.

He stands there speechless, his eyes going from the bowl of food to me and then back again, until I burst out laughing.

"Baby, don't do that to me." Deacon heads to the table, leaving a trail of muddy footprints behind him, and sits down. He dives straight into his food without another word.

It's only when he's halfway through his food that he decides to start chewing some of the mac and cheese instead of swallowing it whole.

He looks up at me with a huge grin. "This is so good," he says over another mouthful.

I, on the other hand, am chewing it slowly and savoring every single morsel. It doesn't taste quite as good as when it's made with milk and butter, but it's still heaven in my mouth after what we've been surviving on recently.

This whole situation feels weird though, like a slice of normality, a memory of a previous life with every swallow. It's only as I look around, seeing other people's things, using other people's silverware, that I come back to reality. This is our life now, but it isn't really *our* life. Our life ended when the flesh-eaters burst in on my birthday celebrations back in Maine, killed our family and friends, and Deacon and I had to hide out in some caves down by the river for several months, living off the land and grieving for our families.

A hand touches my cheek and wipes away a tear that I didn't realize had slid down. I look at Deacon with a sad smile. His hand covers mine, offering me some of his strength. It's like this sometimes when the grief overcomes us both; but we have each other, and together we will get through it. We have to.

"Eat up." I pull my hand from his and continue eating in silence.

Morning light illuminates the bedroom, the sun shining in on us both lying on top of the bedsheets and creating a light sheen of sweat on our faces, despite the fact that winter is closing in on us. I move closer to Deacon, reveling in his smell and the feel of his arms around me. If I close my eyes, I am home, and I have everything that a woman could ever need.

Deacon continues to snore next to me—not a soft, wistful snore, but a deep rumble from the back of his chest to the back of his throat—and after two or three minutes, I peek a frustrated eye open. I turn over, giving him a nudge as I do and momentarily stopping the annoying caveman sounds he's making. I feel myself on the edge of the cliff, waiting to drop back off into la-la land, when Deacon's snoring starts up again.

I sit up with a grumble and decide it's time to start the day. I've probably slept in more than I have in months anyway. Stretching my arms out, I stand and head to the bathroom, looking at myself in the mirror with another grumble. I'm looking like shit these days: tired, worn down; the constant stresses of life are beginning to take their toll on me. I can't help but hope that maybe we can stay in this little house for a while, maybe fortify it and spend the winter here. I can only hope. I check out the cabinets in the small room, opening and closing the small doors. There's toothpaste and a toothbrush, but they were the previous owners' and there was no way I am using someone else's toothbrush. I'll never be that desperate. Instead I squeeze some of the toothpaste out onto the corner of a towel from a large pile in the linen closet and rub it across my gums and teeth until they feel clean. I smile at my reflection, feeling better already. It's amazing what clean teeth can do for a girl's attitude.

Breakfast is oats made with boiled water with some canned fruit mixed in. It is delicious. More than anything, though, it's the first fruit that we've had in several months.

"There aren't many supplies here." Deacon looks up from his food. "We're still going to have to do some supply runs if we want to stay here for the winter."

"I was thinking the same thing," I say.

"We'll need to do some perimeter security too. This place is pretty well hidden all the way out here, but we stumbled across it, which means others might." He shovels another mouthful in, looking thoughtfully out the window.

We eat in silence until both of our bowls are empty, and he helps me carry the dishes to the kitchen. I place them in the sink and automatically reach for the tap, twisting it for water. Old habits die hard, even after all this time. Frustrated, I twist the tap the other way to close it off, which only leads to me being more frustrated.

I turn to Deacon. "So, what's first?"

"Security, I think. While we're out we can get supplies if we see any, but let's not go out of our way for them today. There's a lot of game around here, and there's the little brook at the end of this field I can fish from. The forest should provide pretty good basics for mushrooms and berries, so it should only be canned supplies and essentials that we'll need." He rubs at his scruffy beard, deep in thought. "I'm thinking chicken wire with cans tied to it all around the place, and maybe a trench too. We could put panels on the windows, and we'll knock the steps to the porch off. If any flesh eaters get past all of that, they won't be able to get up to us and we can pick them off easily." He smiles, pleased with his plan.

"That could take weeks to do," I say.

"So we'll cover the hardest areas first. It can be an ongoing project. First we chicken wire the place, then we dig trenches. If we do it now while the ground is soft, I don't think it will take too long. We're going to need supplies first."

I hate having to go on supply runs—they're dangerous, and you never know who or what you are going to meet out there—but it isn't like we can order from the internet and have them home deliver anymore. "We better load up then and head out if we're going to get started on this project of yours."

We lock the front door on our way out, lest anyone think the place isn't taken, and trudge back through the woods. I look at the two graves marked by a cross of stones on top of each heap as we pass. I hate that we killed these people, but it's kill or be killed these days, and like Deacon had said, it will *always* be us that survives, no matter what.

FIVE

NINA

Emily sits with me each day while I eat, watching every forkful, insisting that I finish everything on my plate even when I say that I'm full. Our roles have reversed, and it seems that she is now the caregiver and I am the child in this unusual adoptive mother-daughter bond that we have. She brings first aid for me, antibiotics and painkillers, bandages and even another pillow for my bed. A guard is always stationed by the door watching us, making me feel uncomfortable if we're talking too much. But I'm not touched again, not harmed in any way.

My concern for her—for us—grows with each passing day. Every day I feel angrier at Mikey. He doesn't come to see me and explain, or to check that I'm okay. Nothing, nada, zilch. I know my words hurt him, but they were true words. He is a murderer and I expected more from him, but I'd be lying if I said I didn't want to see him—need to see him. Emily doesn't tell me anything about him, and I don't bother to ask, either, but only because I think I'll completely lose it if I do.

The oddest thing is that Emily doesn't talk about the Forgotten or where we are, and if I try to talk to her about anything she makes a quick retreat and I'm left to my own thoughts again. So I stop asking and try to bask in the glory of getting healthy again, healing, eating, and still being alive.

I watch the people from my window as I gain my strength back, my bruises fading but still vivid, my cuts healing yet still painful. I feel like I've entered the Twilight Zone: another world lives beyond the glass—another life, another existence. My jealousy of them grows. Why couldn't I be one of these lucky people? Why am I always on the run or at death's door? Being ordered around by assholes? On really dark days I think of Britta and Josie, JD and Duncan. Maybe even Crunch gets a passing thought—but then that bitch tried to kill me and *did* kill Britta. In the end, I guess she got what she deserved when she was taken down by the dead. Still, my heart aches for all of them.

It's by day five that it occurs to me that things might not be what I thought they were—a lightbulb being turned on in my puny little brain, kind of a halle-fuckin-lujah moment. As usual, Emily is sitting opposite me, watching every mouthful I take. I have questions to ask, reactions to garner, and I need to be sneaky about it.

I take another forkful of my beans. "So, heard any good gossip lately?" I appear as uninterested as possible.

Emily makes a noise and I glance up and catch the tail end of a shrug from her. "Nope."

"You must have something exciting to tell me. I'm bored shitless in here on my own."

She shrugs again and I look back down at my food. "Heard from Mikey recently?" I look up with my eyes to watch her carefully, my stare darting to the guard and back to Emily. He turns to look at us, and I know I've piqued his interest, if nothing else. It pains me to ask about him, but I need to know what's going on.

She picks at her thin sweater and shrugs again. "No, I don't see him." Her eyes dart to mine, and it's there—so small that I wonder if I've missed it before: a quirk at the corner of her eyes, a twitch almost.

"Winter's coming." I change the subject, sensing her discomfort.

"Yeah, it'll be getting cold soon. We have to get through autumn first—not long to go, though. Not long before it happens. Winter, that is." Her eyes catch mine again as she gathers my dishes. "Make sure to keep eating your food, keep your strength up. It'll help keep you warm." Her mouth twitches again, as if she's refraining from smiling.

"The food tastes like shit, though, Mom," I sneer, pushing back from my chair, feeling lightheaded with a small revelation that I'm still trying to work out.

"See you tomorrow, Nina." She smiles at me and I watch her walk toward the door. The guard—*Rick the Dick*, as I've decided to name him—looks bored out of his mind, yet he's definitely watching us closely. He unlocks it and lets her exit first, giving me one last look before he turns and exits himself.

"See you tomorrow." I fight the urge to ask her to stay for a bit longer. I know she can't. Something else is happening here, something bigger than me. I know, big fucking surprise, right?

The leaves are turning golden browns and oranges and falling from the trees. I stare for what seems like hours, watching them drift lazily toward the ground and land at the feet of the children playing. I wonder whether any of the people out there know that I am here, or if they even care. Their life seems so far removed from mine it seems like madness.

I watch, I wait, and I think.

Watching, waiting, thinking.

Watch, wait, think.

Tick, tick, tock. There's no clock in this room, and if there was one it wouldn't be ticking anymore, its batteries long since dead, but the weird ticking noise in my head helps me think. Like a piano player with a metronome, it helps me to keep my beat. One question keeps playing across my mind, one question I can't seem to land on an answer for.

Why am I still alive?

The heat of the days is still there, but the weeks are passing, and soon it will start to get cold. Autumn will pass and winter will come. I think of my last winter behind the walls—the things I had to do to keep warm—and a sadness creeps over me. I'm so glad to be away from there, away from Lee and his men; but those other people, the ones I condemned for being cowards, what did they have to do to keep themselves warm? To keep their children and wives warm at night?

A tear slides down my cheek. For them, for me, for this godforsaken world.

A scrape of the key in the door draws my attention away from my brain's incessant ticking. Emily enters, her tray in hand as usual. I wipe my tears away as my stomach growls in response to the smell of food, and I jump down from my little window seat to join her at the table per our usual routine.

She sits, I sit, I wait, she stares. I stare.

"Dude, gimme my food." I reach across and snatch the dish away from her, lifting off the silver lid as I dive straight into the food with my fork. After a couple of mouthfuls of the overcooked pasta I stop, my eyes fixated on what lies under my food.

My eyes flit to the guard standing watch by the door. He's young—barely seventeen by the looks of it—golden brown skin and dark brown hair. He's slender but strong-looking, and not paying either of us any attention. In fact, when I think about it, that's not the same guard that normally comes in with Emily. I look back at her, seeing her smiling, a mischievous look to her face, her eyes gesturing downward to the food. My brow furrows and I dive further into the pasta, still hungry yet not wanting to eat it anymore. I push it around the plate, moving it to one side and revealing more of the large knife hidden underneath. I look up at Emily with worry, my emotions a mixture of uncertainty about what she's expecting me to do, being petrified of getting caught and receiving another beating, and yet excited to kick some of the Forgotten's ass like I've been dreaming of doing.

"It's okay." She grins at me.

I swallow hard. "Is it?"

"We're getting out of here."

I reach for the knife, feeling the sharpness of it in the palm of my hand. My eyes look up at the guard coming toward us and my face blanches. Emily turns to look, her smile growing wider.

"It's okay—he's okay. He's with us. With me, actually."

He places a hand on her shoulder, and I realize it's with affection as their eyes lock and they smile at one another.

"I'm going to help you get out of here." He holds out a hand to me. "I'm Alek."

I frown at his hand. "Well, you know who I am." I shrug, holding onto my knife tightly.

"Nina." Emily rolls her eyes at me.

I roll mine back and huff, feeling like a teenager, but I'm out of the loop and I don't like it, and Mr. Hero over here has his hands on my girl.

"Take your hands off her," I snarl. Images of him and her flood my head. *Jeez, now I know what my mother used to talk about when she said she worried about me and boys.*

"Nina, stop it. He's helping us—helping you."

"You're still a child, Emily." I glare at him and his cheeks flush with embarrassment. "I don't think this relationship is appropriate." I'm a fucking hypocrite and I know it, but I swore I would look after her and I'm doing a shoddy job so far.

"Nothing's happened, and I'm not a child." Emily stands, placing her hands flat on the table. "He's trying to help us escape, Nina. Stop with all this crap."

I look at him and then her, and then away.

"I know that you're scared. I am too—"

"No you're not." I stand now, walking over to my window and looking out, never letting go of my knife. "Look at you, all grown up and brave with a big strong boyfriend to protect you, and here I am crying like a fucking baby." I rub away the tears with the back of my hand. What is wrong with me? My freedom is being handed to me—literally on a plate—and I'm crying over Emily growing up and getting a boyfriend. She comes to stand next to me.

"I *am* scared, Nina. I've missed you. I *need* you."

"No you don't. I failed you." Misery engulfs me. I am a failure.

"No you didn't! I'd be dead without you."

I turn to look at her. She looks so different from the girl I first met. I grab her and pull her into a hug.

"You nearly died, and they did so much to you, but we're going to make them pay," she whispers into my ear.

Tremors wrack me as I struggle to stop the tears, and I pull out of the hug; it's only making it worse. I've bottled it all in—every touch, every lash, every wound inflicted. I've bottled it and bottled it and now the cellar door is creaking, ready to burst the dam with my stupid emotions. And yes, I'm fucking scared too. Scared that we may get caught, and scared of living in fear of the deaders again. But most of all scared that I'll fail Emily worse next time and end up getting her or myself killed.

"I'm sorry, you're right, I am scared, but fear isn't something to dismiss. So grab hold of it and maybe it can stop us from making the same stupid mistakes as before, because Emily, I don't think I can take this again." And I mean it: I can't.

She nods, tears glistening in her eyes.

"So what's the plan?" I clear my throat. Fear hums through me like electricity, but she's taking a risk for me, and so is this other person—Alek. She trusts him, and I have to trust her. The tables have turned, and she's all grown up.

"Distraction, disruption, evade, and escape." She smiles.

"Come again?" I frown.

"Mikey is causing a distraction and some disruption right now, giving us the window of opportunity to evade and escape—a.k.a. get the hell out of here."

"Mikey?" I frown harder, anger running through me and drowning out my fear.

"Look, we don't have the time to explain everything. Just trust me—you have a weapon, and we have Alek." She turns and smiles at him before looking back at me. "Now let's get out of here."

SIX

I take a deep breath and look at Alek and then Emily. "Okay." I nod slowly, my brain working overtime as I think about all the things I need to do. "This isn't going to be easy, you know."

"It is. Mikey was right when he said that he still had friends here. He does, and they're helping too." Alek steps forward warily.

I hold out my hand, forcing a smile as I try to play nice.

He smiles back and takes my olive branch. "Great to finally meet you. Emily's talked a lot about you." He pulls a gun from his belt and releases the safety. "We really need to go right now, though."

I can't help but be impressed: fire power—exactly what we need. I look to Emily, who only has a knife like me—granted, hers is bigger than mine, though. She sees my worried expression and shrugs.

"We shouldn't need any weapons. Everything should already be in motion for us. Distraction, remember?"

I want to ask more questions, but they usher me to the doorway, Alek peeking outside and then motioning for us to follow his lead.

I grip my knife and we move into the hallway outside what has essentially been my prison. My strength still isn't what it was before our capture, but it's better than what it's been in recent days.

The hallway is bright and cheery, not what I was expecting at all. Paintings cover the walls, and brown wooden paneling. A smell from long ago fills my nostrils, but I try to put it to the back of my mind for now. A sound in the distance grabs my attention, like a foghorn sounding loud and clear. Emily turns around and smiles.

"That's Mikey," she whispers with a grin.

I nod, shrug, and roll my eyes. I hate being out of the loop.

As we come to the end of the hallway, a wide set of stairs opens up and I realize what the smell is: books. Lots of them. I reach over and tap Emily on the shoulder.

"Are we in a library?" I whisper.

She nods and mouths something I don't get, and I mouth back a *what*? Emily huffs and starts to whisper to me urgently. I still have no clue what the kid is fucking talking about. A simple yes or no, even a nod or a shake of the head would suffice. Instead I seem to be getting a running rendition of a musical the way her arms are flying all over the place. I raise an eyebrow.

"I have no idea what you're saying," I huff, possibly a little louder than I intended. *We're in a life and death situation here, mouth, keep it the fuck down!*

Alek turns around with a frown and hushes us both. Boy's got attitude. I like it. We creep down the stairs in single file as quietly as we can. Lucky for us, the steps are old stone and not wooden creaky ones like in most horror movies.

There's literally no one around, and I get a deeper sense of unease when I see a large wooden door as we make it to the landing. I tap

36

Emily on the shoulder and point to it. She nods and I frown further. They can't be serious that we're going to walk right out the front door.

My heart is pummeling my chest from the inside out; the constant rush in my ears nearly makes me miss two voices coming toward us. Alek gestures to a small door and Emily and I quickly slip inside. I keep my ear to the door, listening to the voices getting closer.

"What you doing here, man? Fallon said he wanted everyone covering the breach."

"I'm on guard duty," Alek replies. "You remember the chick upstairs? Fallon doesn't want to take any chances."

Take any chances? I wonder what he's talking about.

They must not believe him because a couple of seconds later there's a scuffle and grunting and a shot rings out. Emily's hand covers her mouth as another one sounds loudly, and when the door opens back up we both flinch, yet it's only Alek standing there, thankfully, with a fresh spray of blood across his uniform.

"Help me get them inside," he says grimly.

I grip the hands of one of the men while Alek grabs the ankles and we shuffle the body inside. The man's hands are still warm in mine, and it freaks me out, but I shrug it off and grab the second set of hands, walk backwards and drop the body next to the first one. He twitches, blood oozing from a gash in his chest, but he makes no sound.

I turn and together we back out of the room. I look at Alek in a strange new light; I'm in shock that he managed to take them both out without getting hurt himself. I guess I didn't realize up until now that I had been doubting him—his ability to get us out of here unharmed. I look down at my hands, the warm feeling of the other guard's hands in mine sending chills down my spine. I step out of the room and shut the door behind me with a new sense of confidence. We keep our eyes peeled and our ears on high alert as we continue through the winding corridors. Bookshelves down here have been stripped bare of their books, walls are free of their paintings, but the dusty echo of them remains on the pale walls. Wooden paneling has been ripped away, carpets pulled up—it's bizarre. I wonder why here is so different from the rest of the place. Here it's barren, yet upstairs it felt almost regal.

A set of doors is in front of us, light shining from underneath, and my heart skips a beat. We're so close, and it's been so easy that it doesn't seem right. I chance a look behind us, checking that we aren't being followed, but there's nothing and no one. Damn Mikey and his clever plan—whatever it may be.

Alek stops in front of the door, his hand resting on the handle. He looks back to us, determination etched across his face, and I'm guessing this is the decider, the part where this plan will either succeed or fail. I swallow loudly and grip my knife tighter as he twists and pushes the door open. Sunlight glares in at us, but I don't get a second to adjust as we're running straight out the door and blindly trying to follow Alek.

The air is cool on my face and smells fresh, clean; even in my panicked state, the chill in the air makes me aware that winter is on its way. We run cautiously, keeping as close to the side of the building as possible, not speaking a word. A courtyard area opens up to us, and Alek looks across it and then back to Emily and me.

"We need to get to the other side. Once we hit that small group of trees, we need to go left and follow it all the way around. The gate out of here is there. That's where Mikey is waiting for us." His eyes flit to me.

"What?" I shrug, knowing perfectly well what they are getting at. My heart did a leap and my temper flared at the sound of Mikey's name.

"Just, don't cause any shit with him, not until we're away from here," Emily says, taking the lead from Alek.

"Oh please, I'm not stupid," I snap.

Satisfied that I'm not about to lose my cool, Alek continues talking. "We walk. No running whatsoever—not unless someone calls us out." He glances back around the corner and then back to us again. "We should be fine—no one's around, everyone's locked inside."

I grab Alek's arm as he begins to turn the corner. "Wait…what?"

"What?" he replies.

"Why is everyone locked inside?"

Alek shifts on one foot, looking at Emily. I glance at her and see the small shrug of her shoulders. Looks like she's out of this loop too. "We had to have a breach."

"A breach?" I ask.

"Yeah, it's the only way to lock everyone away. We need to get you out," he says, pointing at me, "while keeping everyone else safe."

"Why do we want to keep them safe? They deserve everything coming to them," I snap.

"Not everyone." Emily shakes her head. "There's children here. A lot of people don't have a clue what is going on."

I huff in agreement. I don't want anyone innocent to get hurt because of me. Alek attempts to turn the corner again, but I think of something else and grab his arm. "Wait!"

"What?" Emily and Alek say in unison.

"There's a breach?"

"Yes, can we go now?" Alek says with irritation.

"No, wait, you mean, breached as in there are deaders roaming around here?" I shout-whisper, checking behind me for stray deaders.

"Yes, which is why we should really get going." Alek emphasizes his words, and for the first time I actually notice his nervousness.

I look across at the small gathering of trees, thinking of what could be hiding in them, and then to my stupid little knife. It seems I've come full circle: armed with only a crappy butter knife to save my sorry ass again.

"Damn it, fine. Let's go."

We head out across the lawn at a brisk pace, keeping our weapons low and out of sight. Alek does the looking around for Fallon's other guards while I keep my eyes on the prize—or the trees, anyway.

A short burst of gunfire sounds off to the right, but it sounds far away—or at least not in my line of sight. I flinch nonetheless: gunfire kinda does that to a girl. The low moan of deaders draws my attention away from the trees in front, and my stomach does a little flip as I see people moving over by a bench as if getting ready to take in some rays. The way they move and the breeze that's blowing my way tells me that it's deaders, not people, taking a load off in the sun.

What I can't fathom is why Fallon's guards haven't taken them out yet. These guys are armed to the teeth, and are more than capable of taking out one or two zombies, so why on earth the entire place is in lockdown and these body-munchers are roaming around, I can't fathom.

We duck under the shelter of the trees, and Alek leads us as far back as we can go before we come upon a six-foot fence. Six feet or so, maybe seven . . . Fuck, I don't know! I glance behind me, seeing a male deader doing a weird, half-jog, dead-man-running thing toward us, growling and gargling on his own black phlegm. Alek steps around me, takes out his gun, and shoots it directly in the forehead without giving pause. The deader drops to the ground, its face getting lost among the brambles. Alek jogs back around me and keeps moving along the side of the fence.

"Let's go," he says in a hushed voice. Why—considering he just fired an extremely loud gun—I have no idea, but apparently that's acceptable and talking isn't.

I open and close my mouth a couple of times before following after both him and Emily. I feel a little dazed by it all, and know I need to get my head screwed on right. Once again, I'm going back out into the dead world, feeling unprepared both mentally and physically for it.

"This is it," he says, a little out of breath as he fishes out a small bunch of keys from his pocket.

He slips one in the lock and pushes the door open wide, and we walk out into another wooded area. He locks the gate behind him and I turn to stare open-mouthed at him.

"That's it?"

"Not quite. We need to get as far away from here as possible before Fallon or anyone else realizes you're gone—otherwise they're going to come looking." Alek offers a small smile. "Hell, once they realize where the breach came from, they're going to come looking for us all."

"Why has no one done this before? Got me out of here? If it's so damn easy." Tears threaten to fall, but I keep them back.

"It's not that easy." I turn to look as Mikey comes into view. He looks older, tired, his boyish charm erased. "This took a lot of planning, and a lot of working out who was still on my side." He drags a hand across the back of his neck. "I got you out as quick as I could, I promise you, Nina."

Emotions swell in my gut: hate, anger, sadness, happiness. They build and build, making me tremble, and the floodgates open as silent tears spill down my cheeks. In his face—deep in his eyes—I see that he's telling the truth.

"I don't want to be a dick and ruin the moment or anything, but we really need to get going," Alek interrupts.

Mikey doesn't say anything else, but turns on his heel and starts to walk away. We all follow without saying a word.

We hear rustling up ahead, and we all pull out the crappy weapons we have—all right, all right, I pull out *my* crappy weapon. Through a gap in the trees to the left, I see movement of the lurchy, shambly variety.

"Deaders," I state quietly, not wanting to draw attention to us. As a group we head left, away from the deaders.

The trees open up on a yard with a dilapidated house in it, and I stop and take a breather in the cover of the trees. The sound of breaking branches comes from behind us and I turn to see deaders shambling in on our direction—a lot of deaders, actually.

"The truck's over there." Mikey points in the direction of a town in the distance.

"Mikey . . ." I start to say something, but know I don't need to finish it. He knows what I'm going to say and he shrugs.

"There's an old field we can cross. It's a ten-minute run, you up to that?" he says, though we both know I have no choice. If that's where the truck is, then that's where we have to go. Mikey glances nervously behind us as groans echo around. "Shit, they were all supposed to go inside. I left the gate open for long enough." He takes my hand, his deep brown eyes looking into mine. "We need to run."

He pulls me from the tree line without another word, and we start to run. The ground is slippy underneath us, drenched through from the weeks of rain. Emily and Alek are ahead of us, running hand in hand without looking back. I, however, am clearly an idiot, because I do look back, and what I see scares the ever-loving shit out of me. I stumble as I gasp. Deaders are bursting from the tree line, and beyond them I can definitely hear a truck, which means the Forgotten.

"Shit!" I hear Mikey say from behind me.

I hadn't realized that I had let go of his hand; I hadn't realized that I was still jogging forward while he had stopped completely. I swallow back my fear as Mikey's eyes meet mine.

"RUN, NINA!" Mikey roars out, sounding far away against the rampant beating of my heart.

And like that my feet pound through the wet soil of someone's lawn as we run through the front gate and around the side of the house. The overgrown grass sticks to my calves and makes me stumble and trip, but I continue to run nonetheless. I'm not stopping for anything—not with fifty or so deaders closing in and the fucking Forgotten chasing our asses down. Run? Please, I'm fucking sprinting at ninety miles an hour. I'm like a goddamned gazelle on the run from its predator. *Wait, doesn't the prey always get caught? Shit.*

I chance a glance over my right shoulder, checking that Mikey is close behind. My heart skips a beat when my eyes don't immediately land on him, and I slow down and start to turn, until he grips my shoulder and drags me forward as he comes up on my left.

"I said run, woman!" he yells into my face, and continues to drag me along.

I shrug him off, but don't have time to tell him to go fuck himself for screaming in my face like an old fishmonger's wife. The smell of the dead makes me retch, and the gunshots from the Forgotten make my blood run cold. I'll write a mental I.O.U. to kick his ass for screaming in my face—if we make it out of this alive, that is.

The fence at the back of the little yard has collapsed, giving us an easy way out and through the other side into yet another fucking soggy, overgrown field. My breath is ragged and dry in my throat, making me feel like I've swallowed some crushed glass. Every time I gulp, another shard digs in and causes me to cough. We stumble and slide down the side of the embankment, both of us gasping as we slip into the freezing shallow river at the bottom. I'm sure at one point this house was Grade A real estate with its own land and a river running past it, but right now it's a survivor's nightmare.

We begin to wade across, lifting our arms above our heads to keep as much of us out of the ice-cold water as possible, my Doc Martens thankfully giving me a firm footing on the rocks. We half-climb, half-drag ourselves up and out the other side, my fingers clinging to the thick, wet mud and roots to get some leverage. I grip on tighter, my fingers blue with the cold, and as I lose my grip and begin to slip, Mikey's hand shoots down and grabs my wrist, heaving me up the other side.

I nod a thanks and then I'm back on my feet and we're running again, with the sound of zombies falling into the water behind us. The empty field and the houses in the distance spur us both on, and I grab Mikey's hand as we push harder, willing our legs to run faster and our muscles not to cramp. To cramp up now could mean death for both of us; by deader or by gun, death will be a long, drawn out, painful experience. Fuck that.

With deaders in the surrounding field getting closer, the scene plays out in slow motion when I trip and fall to my knees, mud splattering up around me. Mikey turns and grips me under the arms, dragging me back up to standing.

My eyes bug out when a gray arm reaches up out of the mud and grabs at his ankle. "Mikey!" I scream.

He kicks away from the deader's reach and swings down with his fist, narrowly missing its rotten mouth, which is snapping at his leg, and hitting it hard across its skull with his fist. Its head whips backwards upon impact before the deader quickly rights itself and fixes its cloudy gaze upon me. It stretches a rotten hand across to me as it slowly pulls itself free of the mud and grass, growling and gnashing its teeth. Mikey's foot stamps down on its arm, cracking the bone in two; however, the ligament hangs by the bloated and stretched skin. The deader pays the broken limb no attention, but continues to drag is decomposing body toward me. Mikey grabs it from behind and drags it backwards. It thrashes around, growling in anger in an attempt to get to me, until Mikey falls on his ass. I grab the nearest thing to me—a heavy rock—and with difficulty, I launch it at the thing's face.

It crushes into the brittle bones, making an almost concave shape where the deader's features should be and releasing a toxic stench that I can taste in my mouth. It stops moving instantly and collapses into the gore-soaked earth around it. I look at Mikey as he holds a hand out to me.

"Come on, baby. We need to go."

My shaky hand takes his, and I climb back to my feet and together we run.

We walk for a long time when we get across the field and into the burnt-out shell of a town, but strangely I don't tire; freedom runs through my limbs and I feel like I could run a marathon right now. The chill in the air keeps my senses alert, but it's Emily's hand in mine that gives me the greatest comfort. I hadn't realized how much I had missed a friendly touch until she takes my hand in hers. Lucky for us, the Forgotten got stuck in the mud halfway across the field, and by the time they realized that they would have to get out and chase us on foot, they were surrounded by deaders and we were too far ahead.

We come out the other side of the town and keep on walking down a dusty highway. About a quarter of a mile later, we head down a small embankment and come to a gathering of trees. Mikey tells us to hold back for a minute and jogs on ahead. I hear a scuffle, but by the time we get there he's taken care of the two deaders that were surrounding the small green car. We climb inside, with me taking a minute to look down upon the rotten deaders at my feet.

Some things change and some things don't. My feelings toward Mikey have changed—adapted, almost. Emily has grown from a young girl to a woman. She's tough, and I feel confident that she could survive this nightmare without me by her side. But the deaders…shit, the deaders are still the same: dirty, rotten, mutilated walking corpses. They still smell, they still want to feed, and for some inexplicable reason, they are still up and walking around like it's the perfectly normal thing to do when you die.

I take a deep breath as I close the door of the car and wonder if there will ever be an end to their reign.

SEVEN

Mikey drives like a demon, ninety miles an hour down a dusty highway barren of life—and death, which makes a nice change. Nature still flourishes around us in its sick attempt to brighten the mood, but with winter on the way, soon even that small comfort will be abolished and then nothing will help with the blues.

No one talks. What's there to say? For Mikey, he's escaped the Forgotten's clutches once again—bravo to him, but for how long this time? And if they do catch him again, will he be so lucky?

Me? I know that if they catch me, I'm a dead woman. I have no idea why I'm not now. Truth be told, I have no idea how I'm still alive, or why I haven't gone insane after what's happened to me. But just like anything else, I've hardened and adapted to the world around me. A piece of me was taken, beaten into submission by domineering hands, but in its place is a new part of me. A harder, meaner part of me.

The car pulls over to the side of the road, and I'm dragged from my morbid thoughts when Mikey turns around to talk to us. He avoids my stare as he talks, but he does glance in my direction.

"We need to go on foot from here. A town's coming up, and I want to ditch the car before we get there. It's the first place they will look for us," he explains.

"Where are we going then?" I ask.

He shrugs. "Honestly, I don't know. My short-term plan is to dump the car into this ditch and head across this plain." He points to the left of us. "I say we head to those mountains—it should take us a good couple of hours, bringing us to nightfall. We can camp out there until tomorrow and make a decision then. Even Fallon won't risk hunting for us at night."

"Let's go then." Emily unclips her seatbelt and climbs out without the slightest hesitation.

Alek quickly follows, opening up the trunk and dragging out backpacks for us all. That leaves me and Mikey alone together for the first time. I watch him, and he continues to avoid my gaze. A minute or so passes, with the sound of Emily and Alek talking quietly, before Mikey turns to get out of the car.

"Wait…that's it?" I snap.

Mikey turns back around. "What do you want me to say?" He finally looks at me, looking right into my eyes, and I finally see what the problem is: a little part of him is dead. Lines are thick under his eyes, a grayness making him look tired. The sparkle is gone, the sparkle in his eye that was Mikey.

"What did they make you do?" I ask quietly.

He scoffs out a laugh. "You know what they made me do."

I look away because I do know. They made him kill—kill innocent people—but what I don't understand is why he went along with it when he didn't have to.

48

"But why, Mikey? You didn't want to harm anyone, that's why you left in the first place." I scoot forward in my chair, bringing us almost nose to nose. "Help me understand, why would you go against everything you believe in?" I try to wipe the anger out of my voice. "You're...not the man I thought you were, but I want to understand. Why?"

He reaches out a rough hand and strokes my cheek. I don't flinch from his touch. This is Mikey, and he wouldn't hurt me. And with that touch, with his finger trailing the scar on my face, it hits me: the reason why he did it, why he killed all those people.

"Because of me," I say. I don't ask. To ask would be stupid of me, because I know it to be the truth.

Mikey offers a sad smile. "I'm sorry that they hurt you, that I dragged you into my shit." He looks down. "I'm sorry that I couldn't be the man you wanted me to be. I guess Crunch was right, I guess I am like her after all."

I almost don't hear the last words, he says them so quietly. Aah, Crunch: the superbitch from hell. Yeah, she said they were alike, that they would both do anything to survive. But she was wrong. That girl was crazy mental. Without a doubt *she* would have done anything to survive, but Mikey? No, Mikey would die before he hurt innocent people. And that's his sacrifice—to me. I survived, and hundreds of innocents didn't. What he did is on my hands too now, and I should be angry with him for that, but as I look out the window and see Emily standing with Alek, I know that I can't be.

The pressure of the burden still weighs heavy on my heart, but how can I hate him—be angry at him—when I would have done the same damn thing to protect Emily? He did it to save me, not to hurt me, so maybe I'm as big a monster as he is.

I sob and lean into his touch before pressing my lips to his. I feel his body tremble as he tries to contain his own tears, his own pain. The guilt wars inside of me—of him. I'm grateful to be alive, but not at the cost of someone else's life. But I can't say that to this man—not ever.

"Thank you, Mikey," I whisper as my tears mix with our kisses.

"I'm sorry that—"

I put a finger to his lips. "Hush, you don't need to apologize."

He looks into my eyes again, and I swear I can see his broken, tortured soul. "I do. I saw the way you looked at me back there when I told you I helped the Forgotten. I'll never forget that look."

I shake my head. "I'm sorry, I'm a judgmental asshole. I didn't know all the details."

"It doesn't matter. You were right: I am a murderer."

"We'll get through this—together." I lean in and kiss him again, pushing my tongue past his lips and tasting tears—mine, his, who knows? They all mingle together as I try to soothe him, try to quieten his conscience.

"We need to go." Alek speaks up from outside, pulling both Mikey and I from the kiss.

"It'll be okay, we'll sort this out," I say softly.

With that statement he knows that I don't mean him and me; he knows that I mean the Forgotten. We'll sort them out. We'll fight them, kill them, we'll fucking end them any way we can so that no one has to go through this again.

Together, somehow, we'll get through it.

After pushing the car into a deep ditch with another rusted-out vehicle and covering it with grass and dirt, we begin our trek across the plains. They're sodden and thick with knee-deep mud in places, making it impossible to pass by, meaning we have to divert our paths to an even longer way around.

The day is long as the fields pass us by. The mountains are further away than any of us thought or realized. Not that it would have mattered—this is what we have to do, and the best way for the Forgotten to lose our trail is for us to cross multiple muddy fields and head out across rocky landscapes and hopefully up a small cliff.

As the day gives way to night, panic rises between us all. With no flashlights, the landscape is getting more and more difficult to travel on. I'm trying to bite my tongue and not yell at them 'great job saving me and packing backpacks for us all, but you fucked up not packing any flashlights!' We're growing tired and hungry, and the thought of not being able to see if any deaders creep up on us is weighing us down with more worry. Not that deaders tend to creep—they generally shamble aimlessly—but the dread of stumbling across a shambling zombie is still there regardless.

I'm more than happy to see the ground getting rockier as we travel until eventually, sheer cliff faces seem to pop up in the dark all around us. We stumble around until we're covered on all sides by mountains, and then we begin to climb as the smell of the dead rises around us.

"Shit," I whisper, my fingernails digging into the hard rock of the cliff face.

Deaders stumble into our position, waiting underneath us and reaching up with rotten arms. They gurgle louder and hiss, seemingly getting more distressed and pissed off the higher we get.

Can deaders get distressed? I know they get angry and violent, but distressed? That implies feelings, emotions, and that doesn't seem right for deaders.

51

"Nina? Move it."

I look across at Mikey and scowl, but continue to climb nonetheless. Truth be told, I hadn't realized that I'd stopped. I slip my booted foot into a large groove and stretch up higher.

We make it up onto a small ledge, and all four of us shuffle inside a little cave and out of sight. We're not particularly high up, but it's more a case of knowing the simple rule of life: out of sight, out of mind. Stupid zombies.

We rest in the dark, catching our breath and listening to the growls from down below. Nothing stirs tonight other than the deaders and our racing hearts, and somehow, one by one, we quickly fall asleep. Still curled up in our sodden clothes, with our heads resting on our rucksacks, I doubt any of us dream.

I wake to the sound of whispering, slowly peeking one eye open and then the other. My ass is numb and my hipbone feels like someone smashed it with a shovel. I push myself up to a sitting position and look around to see Emily and Alek talking by the entrance. I make my way over to them with a grumble as I stretch, and a series of loud cracks can be heard coming from my back and shoulders. Emily turns to look at me with a wince of sympathy for my aching body.

"You decided to wake up then?"

"It's a Sunday—my day off," I snark and sit down. "Why am I always the last one to wake up?"

"I'm always first to sleep." Emily shrugs. "Is it a Sunday?"

I chuckle. "No idea. Anything happening down there?"

Emily shakes her head. "No deaders this morning and we haven't heard or seen anything from anyone else." She shrugs.

"And Mikey?" I ask, looking back inside the cave and seeing his backpack and him both missing.

"He went to try and find food. We have some stuff with us, but he wanted something more substantial, I guess." She shrugs again. "Or maybe he wanted to scout out further afield for any signs of Fallon."

I sit down next to her and look across at Alek. "I would have thought you would have gone with him."

"I went for firewood, he went for food," he says with a thumb over his shoulder to the firewood lined up to one side. "Besides, I think he wanted some time alone."

And with that we all fall into silence again. I feel a little like a third wheel sitting with the two lovebirds—not that they do anything to make me feel uncomfortable, but it's always awkward when you're the third wheel. I head to my backpack and rummage through it for food, finding a couple of MRE packs and some glucose tablets. I chug down a tablet and wash it down with a ration pack and shudder. These things don't get any better no matter how hungry you are.

Gathering my knife and a rock, I sit and begin trying to sharpen it to a more serious point. If this is my only weapon for now, I'm making damn certain it's as sharp as an arrow.

"Heads up," Emily calls.

I go and stand by her side, looking out onto the sodden plains and seeing Mikey trudging across. His head is low to his chest, as if the world is his burden. In his hand he carries something—rabbit, fowl, I'm not really sure, but I'm more than happy to see food after the bitter taste of gross tasting potatoes and gravy. I shudder at the lingering aftertaste in my mouth.

He looks up as he gets close, offering a small smile that doesn't quite reach his eyes. He's broken, seriously broken, and I want to fix him but I don't know how. How do you fix something when you're broken yourself? Seeing his face lined with worry, pain etched behind his eyes, I know I have to try.

He ties the animal's legs together with some rope or string, I can't tell which, and then ties it onto the waistband of his jeans and begins to climb, finally pulling himself up and over the ledge where we're sitting, his arm muscles straining beneath his too small sweater. He makes that shit look simple, when I distinctly remember that last night my arms were burning and my fingers struggling to find any purchase. Maybe I'm a wimp, maybe it was exhaustion. Right now, as he does it—with a dead animal tied at his waist—it makes me want to see him beat his chest and shout 'me man.' I chuckle and follow up with a small cough to cover it. Now is not the time to start weirding out.

"Hey," he grunts as he clambers up over the edge and sits down.

"How is it out there?" Alek asks, piling the logs together in preparation for a fire.

"It's pretty dead. I don't think we need to worry for a while." Mikey pulls out a knife and begins to skin what I can now see is a rabbit.

I look at Emily, trying to contain another giggle. "Pretty dead out there, huh?" I ask.

Mikey looks up at me. "Yeah, that's what I sa—" He grins as realization dawns on him. "Very funny."

"Mikey made a joke." I push Emily in the shoulder, making her laugh.

"The ice man thaws." Alek joins in with a chuckle of his own.

"It wasn't intentional. It was a slip of the tongue." Mikey shrugs, but his grin remains.

"Slip of the dead tongue, you mean!" Alek laughs loudly.

We all continue to laugh, something between us all finally melting away. My body is still sore and bruised, my mind weary from stress and worry, but with the laughter comes a sense of relief, a possible belief that yes, we might be okay after all.

Alek and Emily are focusing on getting the fire going and I feel like a spare tire, so I turn to Mikey as the laughter dies away. "You want some help with that?" I nod toward the dead rabbit, hoping he'll say no since it looks like an insanely disgusting job.

"Nah, I'm good, thanks." He looks up from his task with a shy smile and then back down to his knife. I internally cheer.

The tip of his knife has made deep scores around the rabbit's back ankles, and as I watch, he drags the knife up the back of each one of its legs. His hand begins to pull on the fur, slipping it away from the meat of the animal. I should feel sick, but truth be told, I'm just damn hungry. My body has no idea what is going on; it's gone from starvation to regular hot wholesome food and back to hungry again in a matter of weeks.

"That's disgusting," Emily says, putting a hand to her nose.

Alek laughs and pulls her to his side. "You're such a girl, Em," he teases with a grin.

The flames from the fire have taken hold and cast an orange glow on their faces. It's both romantic and concerning. What future can they possibly have together? Is companionship enough now? Because surely, in the distant future—the far distant future—they would have wanted children. But who in their right mind would bring children into this hellhole? *Jesus, why am I even thinking about them having children? She's fifteen—or was it sixteen? Shit, she'll be turning seventeen this year. Either way, she's way too young for all of this.* I look at them again. She's a young woman in her head, but in the old world she's still a child—at least in my head—and the time is going to come to have *that* talk with her. I guess I should be grateful that she picked someone similar in age to her; he's a kid himself, though you wouldn't think it to look at him.

The sight makes my heart pang. I look back to Mikey, noticing that he's watching them both also. He notices my stare and continues with his rabbit skinning business by pinching its little ass to find the tailbone jutting out. He cuts through the small bone with his knife and I grimace when it falls to the small plastic bag he's laid out underneath. There's surprisingly little blood, but then I realize that he probably cut its throat and let it drain out on the walk back.

I glance down out of our cave nervously.

"What is it?" Mikey's voice breaks through my panic.

"The blood—won't it attract the deaders?"

He shakes his head, his hand stripping the rabbit of its fur. "No. I drained it where I caught it, and then covered it with mud. I'm hoping that will mask the scent, but let's be extra vigilant just in case." He takes his knife and plunges it into the back of the rabbit's neck, severing the furry little head from its raw, pink body. A little blood leaks out, making my face pinch up in disgust.

"I feel sick," Emily grunts and stands up, going further into the cave. "I can't sit and watch that."

I nod in agreement. "Yeah, I don't think I'll stick around for the gutting part." I stand and go inside with Emily, leaving the two men to chuckle to themselves. My brain wants me to stick around, learn, and become totally self-sufficient, but my stomach is saying *hell no, let the man do the grunt work*. I have to agree with it on this occasion, even if I'm being sexist.

I sit down with Emily and she looks at me cautiously. "So?"

"So?" I start. "How long did you have that little great escape planned?"

"Month or so." She shrugs like it was no big deal, but she can't hide the small raise of her mouth. "The hardest part was not letting you give up hope, and helping you get your strength back—otherwise you would never have made the trek across the plains."

I nod and glance to Mikey. "He seems…broken. I think it was him that needed your help with not giving up hope," I say quietly.

"He never gave up. His only thought was to save you—and me, of course, but you were his hope. The *only* thing that gave him hope. When you said that you hated him, when you called him a murderer, it killed him."

I look at her and know that she's serious, and I feel like shit that… well, I gave him shit for killing those people. Though I can't condone what he did, and I would have gladly died to protect all those innocents, I can't really blame him either. What would I have done to protect Emily? Pretty much anything.

I shake my head sadly. "Don't put that kind of responsibility on my shoulders, Em. That's not fair."

She reaches out a pale hand. "I'm sorry, I don't want you to feel bad. You had no idea what was happening, and I don't blame you for saying those things—for hating him—but know that he was doing everything he could to protect you, me, and as many people as he could. In the end it came to a head and he had no choice but to do it." She swallows. "It was you and me or those people. He chose us."

I take a deep breath, feeling both awful and relieved at the same time. I decided at some point when we were traveling across the land yesterday that my vengeance can suck it. All I want to do is get as far away from this place and those people as possible. "I want to put it all behind us. We can keep moving, keep going until we're far enough away that they won't ever find us again."

"No." Emily looks at me, confused. "We have to stop them," she snaps.

"No, we have to get away from here," I snap back.

Emily stands and I counter her stance with my own, adding an eyebrow lift full of attitude to it for extra effect.

"Mikey!" Emily shouts.

My eyes widen. No way is she playing the 'I'm telling' card!

Mikey looks at us and when he sees our little spat he comes over, wiping his bloodied hands on a rag. "What's up?"

"Nina says we have to run—hide! That we can't go back and kill the Forgotten." Emily keeps her gaze trained on me while she speaks.

"Oh please, I'm the queen of evil glares. Pack that shit in right now, Emily." I look at Mikey, wondering why the hell he would condone this sort of thinking from her. "Yeah, Mikey, I say we run for our lives, what say you?" I snark as bitchily as possible through narrowed eyes, daring him to disagree.

Mikey rubs a hand across his head, the dark brown hair giving a thin layer of cover to his once shiny bald head. "I agree with Nina. If she wants to run, we run. It might be safer for all of us, and for others too."

"But…" Emily interrupts.

"No, Emily. Think about it: if Fallon and the rest of them can't find me, then they can't force me to do anything. We don't have the backup or the firepower to go up against them. So as much as I would like to kill them, let's cut our losses and go. Just get the hell out of here before they find us and take us back."

Emily's eyes tear up. "I want revenge," she hisses out, fury lining her face. It makes me shiver and drop my pissy attitude.

"We all do, Em." Alek reaches a hand out to her but she backs away.

"You have no idea what I went through while they had you, Nina," she sobs angrily, ignoring the comfort Alek is trying to give

58

her while she stares me down. "How much it pained me wondering what was happening to you, the constant worry if you were going to come back alive."

Typical fucking teenager: it's all about them. "What *you* went through? Are you fucking kidding me?" I yell.

"No, I'm not. It was hell, Nina," she shouts.

I grab her by the scruff of her neck and push her up against the wall before she can say or do anything, my face inches from hers. Mikey and Alek shout at me and try to drag me off her, but I'm seriously pissed—and there ain't no stopping a pissed off woman. Just ask your husband.

"Look here, little girl." I point to the scar on my face. "I'm sure as shit that that wasn't pretty to watch happen, but can you imagine what it felt like for me? Just for one minute take your head out of your ass and think about someone other than yourself. It was *me* they beat, tortured and raped. It was *me*—not you. So don't turn my misery into yours." I let go of her and storm away, turning back to add coldly, "This is *my* fucking misery, and I'm keeping it for myself."

EIGHT

I climb down the side of the cliff, anger burning through my muscles. I need to get away from them all, get some space. Once again, I've found myself trapped with a group of people, with no way out. I can't breathe. I drop the last foot to the ground and storm off, praying for a couple of deaders to shamble on by so I can gut them like the evil monsters they are.

I stomp harder, jumping from rock to rock until the plains flatten out again, annoyed at myself for losing my cool but more annoyed for being so aggressive toward her. Jesus. If nothing else, I've learned that violence gets us nowhere.

A bubble of laughter bursts from my throat. Who am I kidding? Violence gets us everywhere. Look at the Forgotten, look at the leaders behind the walls—hell, look at the fucking deaders! Every one of them uses violence to get their own way, and it works: they're all surviving. None of them are being physically beaten, mentally destroyed.

I stop and sit, bringing my knees up to my chest as I cry angry, painful tears until my throat hurts. The rage is still burning, but I'm left tired and weak when Mikey comes to find me.

"Nina?"

"What?" I don't bother to look up, but continue to stare across the soaked landscape. It's started to rain again, and a cold breeze blows, sending shivers through me.

"Come back. Come and get warm."

"I'm fine," I reply tersely.

He sits down next to me, his body closer than I want. I shuffle to the side, away from him.

"Don't do that. Please," he whispers.

I finally turn to look at him. His eyes are so full of hurt and despair, nothing like that man I first met. His hair is getting thicker, giving him a softer, less rugged look. But his body seems bigger, as if he's bulked up in the months that I was gone. Or maybe it's that I'm so small now, having lost so much weight and muscle. I had started to pile some meat back on my bones when Emily was bringing me food every day, but out here food will be scarce again. I'm not nearly as mentally or physically prepared for it as I need to be.

His hand reaches out to touch me and I instinctively start to pull back but stop myself. I take a deep breath, the rain getting heavier, falling over us in sheets of ice. His dark lashes are heavy with rain; it trickles across his cheeks, making small scars visible to me.

I reach out and trace one of them. "What did they do to you?"

He leans into my hand, his eyes never leaving mine. "Nothing I couldn't handle." He closes his eyes, and when he opens them up and looks at me I see the raw pain there again, shining through like a beam of light. "It's what they did to you that killed me."

I throw my arms around him unexpectedly and he welcomes me

with a squeeze, his mouth tracing my neck as he kisses along it. "I'm so sorry, Nina," he whispers into me.

"We've already been through this. You don't need to apologize." I pull out of our hug and look at him. "I'm sorry I lost it back there. I shouldn't have done that. I love that girl, I really do, but sometimes," I make a strangle impression in the air, "I could…you know?"

He chuckles. "Yeah, I know."

"Mikey, I'm scared. I'm scared for us, I'm scared for her. Words like that should never be coming out of her mouth. Kill? What the hell is that all about? Of course I want those bastards dead, too, but she's a child—a young woman."

"Nina, it may be time for you to admit that maybe Emily isn't a kid anymore. She's growing up." He shrugs apologetically.

"Whatever, we're free now, away from them. I don't want to go back there."

He stands and holds a hand down to me, pulling me up to my feet. "So, we won't. We'll keep going, keep hiding. We'll travel further away, somewhere they can't follow. I've done it before, I can do it again. Hell, I'll leave you all and go back to them if you want. You'll all be safe without me with you."

"Don't be stupid. You're not going anywhere," I snap.

We travel back to our cave, finding it much more difficult now that everywhere is slippy. Even my Doc Martens don't seem to be able to find a decent grip on these rocks. On the way back I think of all the friends we've lost to get to this point: good people—and bad, but mostly good. Lives lost because of the selfish greed of others. Lives lost because of the bloodlust for revenge. Poor Josie and Britta. They survived so much, but in the end they died anyway. They were noble deaths, saving the lives of those they cared about. And JD—Jesus, he did everything he could to rescue us, to make his death mean something. Those deaders surrounded him and he still fought with everything that he had, even though he must have known it was pointless.

I look up at the opening to our little cave with a heavy heart.

"Need a boost?" Mikey asks, coming alongside me.

I shake my head. "No, I'll be fine."

He nods and continues to wait for me to climb, but I stay on the ground, trying to think of what to say to Emily.

"I need to apologize to her." I say wearily.

"Probably." He shrugs.

"There's no probably about it. I do. It must have been hard for her, and she's young and still trying to process her emotions. I should know better than to mouth off like that." I roll my eyes, more at myself than anything else. "Why are you being so damn reasonable? This is your opportunity to tell me I was wrong." I frown.

"Because after what you went through, you deserve to be angry at someone. It's not Emily's fault, but she knows you care about her, that you don't mean it, and if lashing out like that heals you a little, then do it. Maybe do it to me next time, though."

I frown deeper, my wet clothes sticking to my sodden body. "After what I went through?"

"Yeah." He nods and then looks sheepish.

"How do you know what I went through?" I snarl.

Mikey pales, which for a Hispanic is impressive. "They made me watch." The sound of the rain nearly washes away his words, he says them that quietly. My eyes go wide. I think of the pain and humiliation they put me through, how I begged and pleaded, and then I think of Mikey having to watch it all—every degrading, brutal attack. My heart stops in my chest, and I know now why he killed those people, why the pain and torture stopped. Hell, I even know why they started it in the first place. It was clear in the car when we talked yesterday, but today every piece of the very twisted jigsaw fits together snugly.

I don't know what to say to him. What can I say? *I'm sorry? You asshole? Don't pity me?* Fuck, I wanted to forget about it all, but I know now that I can't. Because another person knows what they did to me. He slaughtered innocent people to stop the torture of me. No wonder a piece of him has died. No fucking wonder the sparkle has left his eye. Christ, how could I have not seen this before?

My mouth opens to speak but I close it again, still coming up lost for what to say.

Mikey puts a finger to my lips. "I'm sorry, I shouldn't have said anything—I mean, I never meant to." He rubs a hand across the back of his neck.

"Are you guys coming up or what? I'm starving," Emily shouts down to us.

I look up, getting a face full of rainwater for my efforts. "Keep your panties on, we're coming," I snark.

I tug Mikey's hand without saying another word, still trying to process his words, and together we climb up. Once back inside the cave I head over to Emily to apologize.

"Em? I'm sorry." I huff out my apology, embarrassed at having to apologize. I mean, no one likes to admit they were wrong, do they? Not that I was totally to blame—her remarks were insensitive, to say the least. But whatever, we're all tired, stressed, and hungry. More importantly, though, we're free—and that's more important than anything.

I touch her shoulder gently and she turns to me with those big doe eyes of hers, her bottom lip quivering.

"Aah, crap, don't do that. No fucking crying, I don't want to cry anymore. I'm sorry that I shouted." It's times like these that I wished I smoked so I had something to do with my hands.

Emily nods, a clear tear dripping from her eye before she wipes it away and she takes a deep breath to control herself. "I'm sorry too." She glances at Alek and then back to me. "Of course it was harder on you, and I should have thought about that. I want them to pay, but you're right, you're all right, we should run, hide. Mikey didn't run far enough before, but we will this time, all of us—together."

I smile and hug her before whispering in her ear, "Thank you." I look at Alek while I do. He smiles and looks away, heading off to help Mikey. And once again I'm struck by his confidence and maturity. He's only young himself, but mentally he's a full-grown man and he's undeniably strong. It makes me wonder how he got like that.

We sit around the small fire, shaking—well, Mikey and I are shaking, since we're sitting in our underwear with a small blanket wrapped around each of us. The rest of our clothes are drying out.

I pick at the bones of the now consumed rabbit, sucking hungrily on them like they're a lollypop. There wasn't nearly enough for all of us, even mixed in with two ration packs. I take a drink from my water bottle, finishing it off and then going to fill it with rainwater by the cave entrance. The wind is really howling now, a real storm brewing, and I hope it passes over quickly; we can't afford to be stuck out here for too long. There isn't enough food to get us by and it's getting colder by the day. I screw the top back on my bottle and go sit back by the fire, my eyes feeling heavy and ready for sleep.

By the looks on everyone's faces, they're feeling the same way now that we've eaten.

"Let's get some blankets and try and get some rest," Mikey says with a yawn.

We all cover the ground with a thin blanket and then Alek and Emily snuggle under another while Mikey looks to me to do the same.

"Don't be trying anything funny," I quip as I lie down.

He snuggles in behind me, his legs cool against my own as they slip in between. "Wouldn't dream of it," he says, and kisses my cheek and snuggles closer.

I can feel his funny business resting against my backside already, and I push my ass against him. "I'm serious. I need to sleep," I whisper, glancing at Emily and Alek, who are already snoring.

Mikey chuckles quietly and pulls me closer. "Go to sleep, Nina."

"'Night, Mikey." I yawn and chuckle at the same time.

His hand gives a squeeze on my tummy as he holds me close, and for the first time in months—even though I'm cold and hungry—I feel safe. Safe and loved. I want to weep with the realization that these people care about me. That I hadn't been forgotten at all, they had been plotting and working on a way to save me all along. Before I can cry at the thought, I slip into oblivion, the wind howling up a storm outside our snug little cave.

NINE

"We need to get somewhere dry, somewhere warm," Emily chatters, huddling around the dwindling fire.

"It's been three days—do you think it'll be safe to leave here now?" I ask Mikey without looking up. The sight of the orange flames licking at the branches is giving me some semblance of warmth—especially since the fire itself actually isn't doing much of a job.

Mikey scratches his gruff beard, and despite the cold I want to snigger. He hates being hairy—his words, not mine. He prefers a shaved head and a shaved face, but right now he's looking more and more like the caveman he's living like. He sees me watching him with a grin and stops scratching.

"I can't be certain. I don't want any of us walking into a trap." He subconsciously scratches at his face again and I have to look away.

I think the cold is making me delirious. "I think we'll have to chance it, Mikey. Emily is right: we can't stay here much longer. If we do, we'll get stuck for the winter, and we will not survive that."

Winter has struck us hard. One minute it was a rainy autumn day and the next a full-blown winter storm. Mikey looks across at Alek for confirmation. The look makes my blood boil, like he needs another man's approval. I raise an eyebrow at him and huff.

"Fine, we'll go. Pack your shit up and let's roll," he grumbles and storms off.

"Touchy fucker isn't he?" I say and storm off to my corner of the crappy little cave.

I know we're lucky to be alive, lucky to have found this freezing-everyone's-asses-off cave, but the cold and the thought of the imminent winter is making us all grumpy. We've survived summer and the blistering heat, but winter is a new challenge, for me especially. I just about survived winter behind the walls; how I'll manage out here I don't know. I pull out an extra sweater, slipping it over my bony shoulders.

Shit, that didn't take long at all.

"Well, I'm done," I say with a roll of my eyes. Emily still hasn't left the fire, and it looks like Alek is packing her things up for her. I had my reservations about him, but he's more than proved himself. Emily is turning into a young woman, and she's sworn to me they haven't done anything but kiss and cuddle. For some reason I believe her.

I drink another full bottle of rainwater and stand it to fill back up. Sure, it's not the most hygienic thing to do, but it's better than dying of thirst. And anyway, what could be fresher and cleaner than rainwater? There were too many chemicals in our old lives anyway—chemicals in our water, our food, and our hygiene products. Sure, things were easier, but how many of us were actually killing and destroying our bodies with all that crap without even realizing it? Things are simpler now. We wash when we can and nearly all the time with nothing but water. We drink fresh rainwater, we eat food from the land—organically grown, so to speak: rabbits, fowl, weird-tasting plants that taste and look like crap but Alek swears to the almighty heavens that I won't die from eating them. So now our bodies are pure and wholesome. Hell, we should live to be a hundred at this rate. Oh, deep joy.

Can you imagine a couple of old ladies with rusted old walkers being chased by a horde of the undead? Jesus, would the deaders spit out the dried up meat or would they not care? Hell, while I'm thinking about it, what the hell will happen then? At what point will these fuckers die off—again—and we can go about building some normal semblance of a life?

"Earth. To. Nina. I think we're ready to go."

I look over at Mikey with a grim smile.

"Sorry, baby. I know I've been grumpy. I'm just . . . worried." He scratches at his head and then sees my stare and stops. "And I fucking hate being hairy!" He frowns.

I don't know when it happened, when he started calling me by pet names like *baby* and *peaches*. I don't know whether I like it or not, but I haven't stopped him yet, so I guess I'm stuck with it. For now, at least.

We all climb down the cliffside, thankful that it's stopped raining long enough for us to do so without the wind lashing our backs. The chill in the air is heavy with the threat of snow—yet another promise of the oncoming winter. The wind whips loose strands of my dark hair around my face and into my eyes, making them sting and cry fake tears. My booted feet sink into damp earth, mud sucking at them as I try to pull them free. I stumble, nearly falling to my knees, until Alek's arm wraps around my middle and steadies me. He offers me a small smile before letting go and continuing to walk, one of his strong hands covering Emily's. Her eyes are downcast as she carefully dodges the muddy puddle I just stood in, narrowly avoiding being sucked into its depths.

I look up every now and then, scanning around us for signs of life—and death—but thankfully, we're alone. The land has turned, in a matter of days, from a bounty of life to a drab, washed out existence.

We've been walking for a good couple of hours when I look up ahead and see the shadows of buildings and houses. It gives me the extra burst I need to keep me going. My joints are seizing up through cold, and my muscles are aching from the extra strain. I can't wait to get inside one of those buildings. I just hope I have the energy left in me to fight if I need to. Of course I worry that they will be filled to the brim with the living dead, but I'm freezing and nothing is keeping me away out of those four dry walls today. Not undead or alive.

I pass Alek with a newfound determination in my footsteps, eventually finding myself trudging along next to Mikey. He lifts his gaze to mine as we walk.

"How you doing?" he asks.

"Be happier when I'm inside somewhere," I grumble.

"Won't we all," he retorts with a snort.

As the town gets closer, it becomes clear that it's deserted—or from a brief once-over from this distance it certainly looks that way, anyway. My heart does a little leap of joy at the thought. A town with no deaders: wouldn't them be some cool breaks?

Crouching by a burnt-out car with a stack of fleshless bones inside, we each catch our breath, no thoughts but those of getting warm in our minds. Mikey looks from me to Alek and Emily with a nod before heading out from behind the car and into the street.

It's deserted, a dead town. Literally. We slowly walk from building to building, checking in windows and such for any sign of life—or death—but come up empty. The only thing for us to see is destruction. Pretty much everywhere we look things are burnt out, vandalized, or spray-painted upon. It seems odd, eerie even, and I hope to God that we haven't stumbled upon some weird psycho town of hillbilly crazies. My mind can't seem to find any other alternative. I mean, why else would there be no deaders around? As we get closer to the center of town, everything changes and things look cleaner and tidier, which is even more confusing.

"Does anyone else find this shit weird?" I whisper.

Emily raises a hand. "Me. I seriously do—this place is way creepy."

"Well, we're here now," Mikey says. "Let's find somewhere to hold up for the night, then we can figure out what to do and where to go tomorrow. Nightfall is coming, so there isn't time to go anywhere else."

We've somehow made our way back to the edge of town without realizing it, and back into the crummy shithole part.

"We need to pick a building then," I suggest in a whisper as I spin in a circle, trying to pick the easiest-looking building I can. Even whispering, my words carry in the wind and seem louder than they should.

The thing about the apocalypse is that everywhere is silent. You'd be surprised how much noise the world makes until it's all gone. Cars, talking, phones, music—it all adds up. In a world without noise, it doesn't take long to hear something out of place. I guess that's how the deader stumbling toward us found us: our whispers and footsteps in a silent world are a dead giveaway. Pardon the pun.

"I got this." Alek steps forward and raises his gun.

"No guns," Mikey yells. "We don't want to attract every zombie for miles."

Alek puts his gun away, sidestepping out of the deader's way as it reaches for him clumsily. It snaps its jaw, showing blackened, broken teeth, and growls. Alek pulls out a large knife, and as the deader lunges for him again, he rams the knife through its forehead. Black ooze gurgles up around the wound, and when it falls to the ground he leans down and retrieves his knife, wiping it across the deader's back to clean away the gore.

We pick a little cul-de-sac of houses, choosing the one farthest from the main part of town for us to hole up for the night. We head around the back of the house and into the overgrown jungle that used to be a back yard.

"Shit, I was always on my husband's case for not cutting the lawn, but even he wouldn't have let it get this bad!" I snort with a chuckle. Mikey looks at me without saying anything. "What? I resort to tacky humor when I'm nervous." I shrug. Then I realize that I mentioned my husband, and I grimace but don't say anything.

At the back door, Alek uses his elbow to smash in the small window, then reaches inside and unsnags the lock and we all rush inside. The house is eerily quiet, just like the rest of the town, and I have a weird memory of doing this very thing with Emily after we first escaped the walled city. Only this time, there's no banging coming from old man dead guy upstairs, and no thumping at the back door from deaders to let them in. This house is still and quiet; nothing stirs.

I almost jump out of my skin when Emily coughs, and all three of us turn to her and hush her loudly.

"Sorry," she whispers.

Mikey treads quietly along the hallway that leads from the back door to the kitchen. The carpet has long ago grown moldy and mildewed underfoot, but it's as if someone has tried to clean it away, leaving an odd musty lemon smell in the air. The house is the image of perfection. In the kitchen, teacups line shelves perfectly, plates stacked clean and white in their cupboards. The cloth even hangs from the tap over the sink, as if waiting to be used.

I peek into a cupboard, and the one thing that I would want to see is missing—food. I pout and close the door. Into the living room we go, and there upon the table is what was most likely once a beautiful birthday cake but is now a long ago rotted pile of dried up mush. The room is decked out in streamers and birthday signs; unopened presents are piled in the corner, empty glasses upon the table. *This was someone's birthday party at one time,* I think morbidly. Stains dot the carpet where blood must have once soaked through. No bones are here, though; in fact, the room is spookily clean, with only a couple of telltale signs that something isn't right.

"Anyone else finding this all a little weird?" I ask.

"Again, yes, me!" Emily speaks urgently by my side, even raising her hand like she's in school. "I don't like it here, can we go to a different house?"

My eyes look out the window where soft white snowflakes have started to dance down from the skies. "Well, if we're going to a different house, we need to go now, before that gets any heavier." I look around the living room. "In fact, I definitely want to leave." I tug on Mikey's elbow, feeling like a frightened little girl, but something isn't sitting right with this house.

We head back through the house, passing through the clean yet barren-of-food kitchen to the back door, exiting into the back yard and heading over to the next house along the row. We go through the same process of breaking the small window on the door, picking the lock, and sneaking inside, but find the situation is pretty much the same here, too—barring the missing birthday celebration, anyway. Everything is immaculate; the only odd thing out of place is a pinky-brown smudge on the beige walls—which I assume was at one time blood, which someone has tried to clean off—and a pool of browny crusted something-or-other on the floor. Again, I'm going with blood. Bravo, give the lady a prize!

I turn to the others. "It's like someone's tried to clean up the mess. You know, the zombie mess. This is weird."

"I don't like it, I say we keep going," Alek suggests.

"Too late for that," Mikey says.

We follow his gaze out the window to see the sky heavy with snowfall; fat flakes fall endlessly to the ground below, quickly covering it in a light dusting of white.

"Crap," I breathe out.

The tension in the air is thick as we pile to the upstairs of the house. We go from room to room checking out of the windows, seeing nothing but the slowly whitening ground.

"I say one of us keeps watch tonight." Mikey sits on the edge of the bed. "Something isn't sitting right with this place."

I snort. "Really? What, the weird ghost town in the middle of nowhere, freshly cleaned of all zombie remnants and barren of food— is that what doesn't sit right with you?" I shake my head at him. "Can't see why. I mean it's nothing like that crappy old horror movie *House of Wax* or whatever it was called. No, nothing at all like that." I stare out the window with a grumble.

Mikey doesn't say anything, and a tug of guilt lies in my gut.

I turn to look at him, noticing him looking more worried than before. "Jesus, what now?" I snap.

"That movie used to scare the crap out of me," he says with a shudder. "Why would people do that to each other?"

I scowl. "Are you serious? People don't do that to each other, that's why it's a movie."

"But they could." He gestures around us. "Look at this place—it has serial killer town written all over it."

"Shut up, Mikey." A shiver runs down my spine now. Damn it. "It's just a stupid movie that isn't even scary, and this town is nothing like that." I look back out the window. "Nothing at all," I repeat, not believing my own words.

Emily comes in, followed by Alek. "It's freezing."

"I know." I head to a walk-in closet and pull open the pine doors, shuffling through the racks of clothes, finding nothing but summer outfits. "Stupid summer apocalypse."

I reach up to the top shelf of the closet, standing on my tiptoes, and fumble around until my fingers grip a large cardboard box, and I pull it down. I rifle through the contents, finding only old photos, books, and old pottery—mementoes from a life long ago. I step back inside and reach up again, grabbing another box and stepping backwards with it until I can set it down on the bed. I tug open the corners and pull out sweaters and winter coats with a whoop.

"Score."

Emily comes over, sees my find, and smiles the biggest smile I've seen all day. Together we rifle through the belongings until we are decked out in sweaters and thick coats.

"That's so much better," Emily says, snuggling further down into her coat. "You need to see if there's anything in your size, Alek."

"I'm not wearing women's sweaters," he states seriously.

"Dude, it's just a sweater," she says as she roots through some of the drawers in the room. "You'll freeze at this rate. You need dry clothes no matter what color they are. Now stop being a baby."

"I'm not wearing women's clothes," Alek grumbles at Emily's back as she moves on to a second drawer.

"Alek, it's only a sweater," Mikey laughs. "Quit being such a baby."

I look at him with a raised eyebrow. "Well, go on then. Go find something to wear."

"What?" He stops laughing, eyeing the box and then me. "I don't think there'll be anything in my size."

"I bet there will," I reply.

"No, no, I'm a big guy…"

"Not that big," I interject. I shuffle through the box, finding a couple of things that would be around his size, and hold them up. "These'll do."

Mikey's eyes go wide. "No. Hell no, I'm not wearing that!"

Emily turns back around with an armful of clean socks and smiles.

It's my turn to keep watch, but really, only Emily is actually sleeping. That girl can sleep through anything. Alek cuddled her until she fell asleep and then stood up with a stretch and a yawn. He comes into the bedroom where Mikey and I are talking, and sits down.

"You should sleep while you can," I whisper to him.

"I know, but my mind won't turn off. I can't seem to turn it off. I keep coming up with different plans." Alek shuffles on the small sofa bed to get comfy. It groans under his weight. "I keep thinking about Fallon and what he's going to do now."

"I wouldn't worry about that—he'll be getting his soon enough," Mikey says from the window. His dark eyes search the snow-covered streets for signs of movement, but as of yet he's found nothing. It's eerie, the lack of movement—unnerving, even—when we should feel a little more relaxed. He turns to look at us, the brightness of the snow casting shadows across his face. "He'll be staying hidden for the moment. Even he isn't stupid enough to go out in this weather." He plucks at stray fluff on his sweater, inciting a giggle from both me and Alek.

"It really suits you, Mikey," Alek snickers.

Mikey groans. "Like you fared any better than me, man."

It's true—both of them look like complete idiots in matching his and hers Christmas sweaters. Alek got the better of the two with the male counterpart to Mikey's red *All I want for Christmas is you* sweater; but truth be told, his green *You got me babe* sweater is equally hideous. I chuckle, getting dirty looks from both of them.

"They're warm though, right, man?" Mikey tugs his hands into his sleeves.

"Yeah, good fucking thing too," Alek grumbles again. "I'm starving."

"We all are. Hopefully in the morning we can get out of this freak show place. Right now, I'd rather be fighting deaders than waiting around to find out what the hell's going on here," I say.

"Well, this could be a destination for us. I was just showing Nina, I found this downstairs." Mikey hands a little pamphlet to Alek.

"What is it?" He flips through it. "Army barracks?" He looks up to Mikey. "I don't get it."

"I'm thinking this place will be in lockdown, fully secured, and it'll have more ration packs, sleeping bags, equipment—maybe even some weapons." Mikey smiles. "It's a couple of miles from here. If this weather keeps up it'll be a hellish walk, but if we get a break in the storm I reckon we could be there in a couple of hours."

Alek smiles back. "Now that, sounds like a plan."

TEN

I pull another blanket over me, still shivering underneath the giant pile of duvets and fur coats. The temperature has dropped rapidly in the last couple of hours. And from the looks of the snow outside, it ain't going to get better anytime soon.

"I'd do anything for central heating." I shiver.

"I would hug that radiator to death." Emily's muffled voice sounds out from under the covers.

"Oh God, me too. I would turn it up so high I'd be sweating like a pig and only wearing my underwear."

"So hot that I'd be in a bikini!" Emily mumbles.

I close my eyes and picture my once toned body in my favorite electric blue bikini, my feet padding along the beach somewhere with the sea lapping at my feet. Margarita in hand, cool sunglasses on—that would be heaven. "Damn you!" I groan.

"What? Me?"

"Yeah, you. Now all I can think about is being at the beach sipping on a margarita."

"Sorry." She continues, "Sounds like some good thoughts, though. All I can think about is turning into a block of ice right here, right now. Like when you try to wake me in the morning, I'll be a frozen statue."

I squeeze my eyes shut, blocking out Emily's image and keeping the lovely beach image in my mind a little longer. The heat from the sun is beating down on my now golden brown stomach and I'm eating a fresh pineapple. *Jesus, where am I? The Bahamas?* A man walks up, his long dreads swaying by his waist. He's selling juicy ripe melons and I smile and buy one, my mouth instinctively watering as I take a bite and the juice slips down my chin. A thought occurs to me. "Emily?"

"What?" Again, her voice is muffled. I don't know how she can sleep like that—though she's not technically asleep yet, but whatever; I can't have my head under the covers for more than a minute without feeling claustrophobic.

"Do you think there are Rasta deaders?" I ask, giving a small frown as I imagine the Rasta with the melons turning into a deader and invading my harmonious beach scene. His long dreadlocks are now covered in blood, and the watermelons he carries in his straw bag are no longer watermelons but heads. "There must be, right? I mean, the last news I heard was that this thing—whatever it is, was global. So that would mean all kinds of crazy deaders, including Rasta deaders."

"What's a Rasta?" she replies with a yawn.

"What? You don't know...urgh." I frown harder as in my mind the Rasta deader begins to get a little too close for comfort and I have to smash my margarita across the side of his head. Ice cubes and my delicious drink pour down his rotten mangled face. He falls on his back, and then I'm grabbing an umbrella out of the sand and slamming it through his cold, dead brain. Stupid deader, ruining my fantasy.

I open my eyes back up, thinking about how to explain to her what a Rasta is. "Rasta is short for Rastafarian. It was a religious movement that started in Jamaica like way back in the 1930s or something like that. It was only small to start, but ended up getting pretty huge and spreading worldwide."

"How do you know all this?" Emily interrupts.

"There was a Rasta singer I used to listen to all the time called Bob Marley. He used to sing about standing up for yourself and being free, and loving one another." I close my eyes, hearing the music playing in my mind and envisioning dancing around my living room to his songs. "Out of all the religions, this one made the most sense I guess."

Silence encompasses us, and after a minute or two, Emily pipes back up. "I still don't get it."

"You don't have to," I groan. "Forget I said anything."

She shuffles out of her hole. "No, tell me. It sounds important to you. I think I remember my mom talking about some hippies with long hair at one point. Is that the same thing?"

"They're not hippies," I laugh. "They do have long hair, though, or dreads. Their religion says that they can't cut their hair, so they grow it long and twist it into dreads. It could be that they just didn't want to cut their hair and so made that shit up, but either way, that's how they were distinguishable—because of their hair."

In my mind I'm back in my beach chair, soaking up the rays again, with the twice dead Rasta by my feet. I use him as a footstool after stealing a joint out of his pocket. Rasta, priest, monk—he gets the same treatment any deader would get. "I don't even know what my point was anymore. I just had a weird thought about all the different types of deaders that we see."

"It is pretty weird, huh? It makes you wonder, who survived and who didn't. I wonder what celebrities survived. I mean, we've met some people that I wouldn't have thought would survive this sort of existence, yet they do. I never would have thought I would be alive today."

"Bob Marley once said '*You never know how strong you are until being strong is the only choice you have,*'" I reply wistfully.

"Sounds like he was a clever guy," she says and fumbles for my hand under the covers. She finds it and gives it a squeeze.

I snort out a laugh, touched and amused by this whole conversation. "He was a weed smoking Rasta with longer hair than me, but yeah, I guess he was clever. Extremely."

She squeezes my hand again. I know what she's thinking about, but I don't want to go there. I want to put certain things out of my mind, at least for the moment.

"Go to sleep, Emily."

I release her hand and let my breathing even out as if I'm sleeping, and she eventually shuffles back down into her cocoon. But I'm not asleep; really, I'm thinking of another quote from Bob Marley—the one that got me through those scary days and nights trapped in that little dark room of horrors, when all hope seemed lost and I didn't think I could take any more. When all I had to cling onto—to keep me going, to keep me alive—were thoughts of Emily: rescuing her, protecting her, getting her somewhere safe.

The truth is, everyone is going to hurt you. You just got to find the ones worth suffering for.

Snow has blanketed the entire town. From house to house, shop to shop we go, finding nothing but snow. Morning light plays across the snow banks, making them glisten and sparkle as the sun rises higher. Each home we enter is the same: frozen. As if left untouched in all the years that have passed since this began.

"Has anyone noticed that nothing is dusty?" I run a finger along the useless TV and bring away a relatively clean finger. "I mean, there should be dust, right? I liked to keep a clean home, but even I wasn't this good."

Mikey frowns. "Yeah, there should be. A hell of a lot by now."

"So I'm guessing you've come to the conclusion that I have and that someone is living here?" I head into the kitchen and try the cupboards for food. Emily already checked and found nothing, but I have the urge to check again.

"Someone is living here?" Emily looks around us warily.

"Not *here* here, but here." I gesture around us and get frustrated when she doesn't catch my meaning. "Like, the town here."

"Oh, that's less creepy." She sighs.

"Really? It's less creepy having a town with no deaders but a food-hoarding clean freak? Because whoever it is has taken every scrap of food, drink, and medicine from every house we've been in so far. We're in the middle of the apocalypse and their top priority was dusting. That's *less* creepy and weird to you?" I raise an eyebrow.

"Well, when you put it like that . . ." She laughs nervously.

I try not to laugh back, I really try, but a smile graces my lips eventually. It pulls on the scar on my cheek. It's still healing, but getting much better. Of course it will be there forever—not like I can go find a cosmetic surgeon around here. But I'll be glad when I feel comfortable enough to smile again without worrying that my face is going to split open.

"Let's go, get out of this fucking weird town. There's nothing here," Alek grumbles.

"No, let's check a couple more houses, man. Whoever it is, or whatever it is, can't have cleared out all of them. There has to be something…somewhere." Mikey heads to the front door.

We've long ago given up going to the back door and trying to sneak in, since it really makes no difference. No one has confronted us, and we haven't spotted any deaders. It's a ghost town.

"Uh, guys," Mikey yells from the front door. "You might want to come and see this."

We all look between ourselves and then rush to the front door, tripping over each other to get there first. You'd think we'd have more sense than to go barging off into the unknown, but our fear was left in someone's living room about three houses ago, when we all came to the conclusion that there really was nothing to fear around here—or at least nothing we've stumbled upon in the immediate vicinity.

Alek is first to the doorway, closely followed by me and then Emily. I push my way through to the front using elbows and knees, since both men seem to be transfixed by whatever it is out there. I stop when I finally reach the front.

In the middle of the driveway is a basket of food. It's only small, but there's clearly enough in it for us all to get something from it. I take a step out to go and get it, but Mikey grabs my arm and pulls me back.

"Don't."

"Why? I'm hungry," I snap.

"It could be a trap."

"Damn it, I hate it when you're right, Mikey."

I look all around us and up and down the street, from window to window of all the houses surrounding, but don't see anything out of place—just the little basket of food beckoning me to come and get it, and some footsteps in the snow leading away from it.

"There's no one here," I grumble.

"You can't be sure of that. Someone put that basket there. We need to think about this logically. They could have snipers, deader traps, anything," Mikey says in a hushed voice.

I roll my eyes. "Shut up. You do not believe that."

"That's not the point. It *could* happen," he says seriously.

"This is stupid," I whisper.

"Better to be safe than sorry." Mikey turns to Alek. "Go to the bedroom window, see if you can see anyone hiding. Maybe we can attach the curtain poles together, create a long enough stick to pull the basket toward us?"

"Also stupid," I whisper again. I decide to throw caution to the wind when my stomach grumbles loudly, making Emily jump behind me. I take a deep breath and run for the basket.

My feet slip on the fresh snow, my heart beating like a herd of wild buffalo in my chest. I reach the wicker basket, grab it, and head back to the house, all the time waiting for the whizzing of bullets to go zooming past my ears. I hear Mikey shouting—but thankfully no bullets—but I refuse to look up. I just keep placing foot after foot in front of one another until I make it back to the door and charge inside, barging past Mikey and the others and heading straight into the living room.

I hear the door shut and they all storm into the room. I grin, they frown. This is bad.

"What?"

"What do you mean, what?" Mikey shouts. "I just said that it could be a trap, and then you ran out there anyway. You could have been killed." Mikey looks seriously pissed, and it's all I can do to not roll my eyes at him again.

"Well, I couldn't see anything, and we're hungry. This," I point to the food in the basket, "is food. Now stop yelling at me and let's eat." I pull some of the cans out, trying to ignore his angry stare, and begin to distribute everything between us. SpaghettiOs, canned beans, chopped tomatoes, and some tuna. My stomach growls again. Alek and Emily dive straight in, ignoring mine and Mikey's little spat. Sure, he's right and I was being reckless, but hey, aren't I always? Besides, his stupid stick idea was just that: stupid.

Mikey grabs the crook of my elbow. "I want a word with you." He pulls me from the room, and I go with him without argument because let's face it, I kinda knew that he was going to do this. So I'll suck it up and take it like a big girl.

I cross my arms in front of me. "What?"

Mikey places both his hands on my shoulders, looking into my face, his own expression one big giant frown.

"I said what? I'm hungry and I want—"

Mikey cuts me off by placing his lips on mine, gently kissing me as his hands move to the back of my head and he presses his body to mine. He parts my lips with his tongue, and I open up to him, embracing his kiss—almost feeding off it as if he were my life support and the kiss my oxygen. Mikey pulls away, leaving us both a little breathless, and my chin a little itchy from his beard.

"Don't do stupid shit like that anymore, Nina." I can tell he's still angry and trying to control his temper. The kiss seemed to take the edge off it though.

He knows me, he knows how I work, and after what we've been through together, he also knows that losing his temper with me will only cause me to dig my heels in more. I'm not stupid, I know he's playing me, but I'd prefer him to play me than be a nag.

I pout, still reeling from his kiss, still wanting more, feeling dizzy and intoxicated. "I'm not going to break. I'm not as fragile as you might think."

His hand strokes my cheek, a softness in his face now that the frown has gone. "No, but maybe I am." I stare at him, confused, before he continues. "I can't lose you again."

My heart starts beating heavily in my chest: *baboom, baboom, baboom.* Of course it was always beating—I'm not a deader or some shit like that—but up until this point, it was always a low thud. Just your standard run-of-the-mill heartbeat, nothing to see here, move along everyone at your easy steady pace. However, when I look into his face—in his eyes—I see how much I mean to him, and my heart is practically bursting out of my chest with warm glow fuzziness.

"Okay, I'm sorry. Don't lecture me." I smirk. He tries to say something else, but I lean in and kiss him, needing to feel his mouth on mine once more. I thought after what had happened to me that I would be pulling away from contact like this, that I wouldn't be able to stand the thought of his kiss or touch, but the reality is, mentally—and maybe physically—I'm desperate for some kindness, some softness in my life. I survived similar behind the walls, and while they took my body, my mind was my own. I let the kiss come to its natural end, and we stand forehead to forehead and I smile. Finally I grab his hand and begin to pull him back into the other room.

"I'm serious, Nina, stop doing crazy shit all the time."

"Stop nagging now," I chuckle.

I feel guilty. I should have told him how much his words meant to me—how much that kiss meant to me—but I can't, for some reason. There are some walls that won't break, no matter how much I want them to.

ELEVEN

"They could be poisoned or something you know." Emily points out the obvious as we all stare into our open cans of food, each with our own delicacy staring up at us. I have the chopped tomatoes, Alek the tuna, Emily the SpaghettiOs, and Mikey the beans.

I poke my tomatoes with my fork. "It seems such a waste. Surely no one would waste food like this." They look so delicious, all red and juicy. I snag some onto the end of my fork and bring it to my nose to sniff. Everyone watches me with wide eyes. "Smells like tomatoes." I shrug. I dip my tongue onto the end of the fork, barely letting it touch them. My taste buds flare to life with that one small taste, both tangy and juicy. I simply can't resist any longer as pangs of hunger cripple my stomach, and so I tip the contents into my mouth before I can change my mind.

So much for not doing stupid shit anymore.

"Nina!" Mikey yells, but he doesn't do anything to stop me.

Everyone is staring at me, their mouths open in horror, shock, and wide-eyed jealousy. I chew the contents, both enjoying and hating it all at the same time, and swallow.

"It tastes good." I offer another small shrug, accompanied by a large growl from my stomach. Everyone stares at my stomach in horror. "I think it's saying thank you, and it wants more." I smirk.

Emily grins. "To hell with it." She sticks her fork into the SpaghettiOs, the little circles catching on the long fingers of the fork. She brings it to her mouth and copies my earlier action of smelling, tasting, and then stuffing the rest in greedily. She groans and closes her eyes. "So good," she mumbles.

That's all it takes for Alek and Mikey to join in, stuffing their faces with beans and tuna, throwing caution to the wind. It's not until after all the food has gone that we all look around with worry—now that our stomachs have a little something in them and the hunger pangs have died off a little that we think about the possible consequence of our actions.

Emily wipes her mouth with the back of her hand and gives a little burp. "That was amazing." She pauses, scooping more onto her fork. "I remember the last time I had SpaghettiOs, it was a couple of weeks before everything…went bad. It was my dad's turn to cook, since Mom was working late. He was an awful cook, though, so I threw a can of Os into a pan and made some toast and we sat and ate it together at the counter in the kitchen. Dad said they were the best damn SpaghettiOs he'd ever had." She smiles proudly at the memory. "Never thought I'd get to eat those cheery little Os again."

My mouth quirks up in a half smile—how could I not smile at that?

"What if they were poisoned?" she whispers, her happy memory dissipating before my eyes.

"Shit," Mikey whispers. "I'm blaming you." He looks around at all of us. "All of you." He points a finger at us all and then belches loudly.

"Nina, what should we do?" Emily asks, even as her hand dips back inside the can and rubs some of the leftover sauce onto her fingertips, and she begins to suck them clean.

"I don't know. I guess we wait and see what happens." Guilt consumes me. What if I've sentenced these people to death? I watch Alek scraping his fork around to get the last bits of tuna out, and the guilt washes away. They more than likely would have decided to eat this food regardless of me.

"The food wasn't poisoned."

We all look up at the young man—a kid, really—that stands in the doorway. He can't be more than seventeen, with shaggy dark hair and worried brown eyes. A young girl stands close behind him, blonde, short, and paler than snow. She reminds me a little of Emily, actually.

Mikey jumps up, lifting his knife up in front of him. "Who the hell are you?" he growls.

The kid backs up. "Whoa, easy, big fella." He waves a gun in front of him. "Gotta bigger weapon than you, see?" He smiles, even as the young girl clings to his arm and tries to hush him. He must think he's some kind of superhero to be pulling that crap with Mikey.

Alek stands up. "That don't mean shit." He smiles, and gone is the calm and controlled young man that I've gotten to know over the last couple of days; in his place is a vicious thug, a man that would make Fallon proud. I shiver.

I watch the encounter, empty can of chopped tomatoes still firmly in my grip, without moving. The kid in the doorway stops smiling, his eyes flitting between Alek and Mikey. I know Mikey's evil glare and, well, we've already discussed Alek's.

"If I wanted to kill you, I would have done it already," the kid snaps. Neither Alek nor Mikey back down, both continuing to give him the stink eye. "All right, all right, we come in peace!" He backs up, stumbling into the blonde girl, who lets out a little yelp.

"Put down your fucking gun," Mikey shouts.

The kid looks at the weapon and then back to Mikey. "I can't do that!" His voice goes up an octave too high, revealing his youth. "You guys could kill me."

"Says the kid with the gun aimed at us," I quip.

He looks down at his weapon and then back up to me before stuffing it down the back of his pants. He offers a nervous smile as he shows us his empty hands. "Better?"

"Much." I finally stand back up, leaving my can on the little coffee table. I place a hand on Mikey's shoulder. "Down, boys." Mikey glares at me, Alek continues to glare at the young man in the doorway, and I glare at everyone. "And you are?" I point to the young man and his timid girlfriend.

"I'm Dean. This is Anne. We were the ones that left you the food." He smiles hopefully. "And with due respect, I'm not a kid."

The tension in the air still hasn't broken.

I cross my arms in front of me. "We've been here since yesterday and only now you introduce yourselves. Why now—kid?"

"Because you're going around and breaking into everyone's houses." He sounds angry as he continues. "I thought you would get bored after a while and decide to leave like everyone else, but you didn't. You kept going around breaking things and making a mess. Do you know how hard it's been keeping everything clean and tidy?"

I snort out a laugh. "Sweetheart, I think a little dusting should be the least of your worries right now. And while we're asking questions, where the hell are all the deaders?"

Anne shuffles forward, tugging her bangs behind her ears. "You mean the sick people?"

I look from Anne to Mikey and then back again. "Yeah, the really sick people—as in the dead ones! You know, the zombies?" My words make them both flinch. "Sorry, sorry, I didn't mean to sound like such a bitch, but seriously, where are they?"

Anne looks proudly to Dean. "He kept them away." She grips his forearm and keeps on smiling with doe eyes, as if we're not here.

"Um, how?" both Emily and I say at the same time.

"Dean's a whiz with electronics." Anne grins, patting his arm. "He… uh…he should probably explain it. I'm no good with stuff like that."

Dean's cheeks flush red and he smiles. "First, when are you leaving?"

I raise an eyebrow. "What's it to you?"

"This is our town, and you're going around breaking stuff. I don't like it. I've given you some food, but we'd like you to leave." Dean's eyes swing to Mikey, who's practically growling like a goddamned pit bull, almost making me want to laugh as Dean tacks onto the end of his sentence: "As soon as you can, please." He smiles, trying to show his friendliness, like a dog baring its belly at its enemy.

"Your town? This is a free country now, Dean. We were leaving today, since we didn't find anything here worth staying for. Now, however…" I let my words trail off as I look to Alek. "I'm still feeling pretty hungry. How about you?"

Alek rubs a hand over his stomach, still staring Dean down. "Starved."

"Fine, fine, we'll bring you more food if you promise to leave. We don't have much, though." He backs out the doorway, Anne close behind. "Don't go anywhere."

We hear the click of the front door as it closes behind them. Mikey runs up the stairs as soon as he hears it, and Alek runs to the main window. Emily shrugs, looking confused, and I grin. "Watching where they're going, dumbass," I say playfully.

"Oh." She smiles.

Mikey comes back down a couple minutes later. "I watched them go through a gap in the fence of one of the houses across the street, but couldn't see further than that."

"Shouldn't we follow them?" I ask.

"How dangerous can two kids be? Besides, they said they'd come back." Mikey picks up his can and scrapes fingers around the rim, much the same way Emily had.

"What if they don't? What if it's a trap?"

"Then we destroy stuff until they come back," he says matter-of-factly. "And again, how tough can two kids be?"

I yawn and stretch, the little bit of food in my stomach making me feel sleepy despite the tension of the situation. I hardly slept the previous night; constant dreams of Rastas selling me skulls full of margarita cocktails kept waking me up.

I sit back down on the sofa, eager for more food, more answers, and to get a little shuteye at some point today. The sofa isn't particularly nice; it's old fashioned with graying flowers printed on it. The dark stain on the arm of it, though, is more than likely what stops me from resting my head on it and getting in two minutes' worth of a nap.

I'm still eyeing the stain on the arm of the sofa when Dean and Anne return, loaded down with some more canned goods. We hear them stomping their boots on the welcome mat at the front door before coming inside and placing everything on the table in front of us.

"That okay?" Dean asks, his attitude gone now. I'm guessing Anne gave him a grilling when they left here, something along the lines of 'stop trying to intimidate the guests, they're bigger and scarier than you.' Yeah, that would probably do it.

I grab a can from the center—a small can of mushrooms—and start to open it up. "So, Dean, spill it. Where are the deaders? Where is everyone from this town? And do you have an OCD problem? Seriously, this place is way too clean for an apocalypse." I peer inside the can of mushrooms with a grimace. I used to hate these things before everything happened; even starvation can't make me like them. "Anyone want to swap?"

"I will." Alek takes my can and I take his, realizing my misfortune far too late.

"Canned spinach?" I sniff the contents and gag, and look up at Dean. "Well, go on then, don't let me stop you."

"I don't have OCD," he chuckles. "I just want everything to be as normal as possible for everyone when they get back."

I lift out a forkful of the disgusting spinach. "Who . . . gets back?" I say slowly, swallowing the slimy spinach down with a shudder.

"Everyone," Anne replies softly.

"Everyone?" I ask. Anne nods and I continue. "Like, everyone from this town?"

"Yeah." She smiles.

"Where did they go?"

"They all ran away when the sick arrived," Anne says softly, her eyes filling with sadness.

I look around at my friends to see if they are getting the same information as me, and wonder who is going to be the one to tell these poor kids the truth: that they won't be having a family reunion anytime soon.

TWELVE

"**Y**ou know that pretty much everyone is dead, right?" I say slowly, just to make sure they understand everything I'm saying. We didn't draw straws, but somehow I ended up drawing the damn short straw—the grand prize: getting to make these kids well aware of the current state of the world.

Dean shakes his head. "No, they're not. They're just hiding. These sick people, they scared everyone away." His face has paled to match his girlfriend's, and I have the urge to shake the poor sap.

"Dean," I start, but then don't know how to break it to him, so I change my line of questioning. "Have you been here all this time? On your own?"

Dean shakes his head. "No, Anne's been here with me too. We've been securing the place, cleaning, storing food. The mailman stopped coming." He scratches his head, looking lost for a minute. "He was always on time—9:15 a.m., sharp." Anne prods him and he looks down at her startled. "Oh, sorry. Yeah, well, TV went off, and no one seemed

94

to be bringing any more food to the supermarkets, so we decided to gather everything we could, store it, and ration it all until everything went back to normal. The hardest part was getting the sick out of town." He looks away sadly. "There was another one of us, but he got sick, too, so we had to put him outside of town."

"I'm confused. You put the sick outside town?" I ask, pinching the bridge of my nose as I spoon another mouthful of the spinach in. Hungry or not, this stuff tastes like crap. Alek isn't faring too much better with the mushrooms, though, so at least I have that small satisfaction.

"Come on, we'll show you." Anne smiles and gestures for us to follow.

I put down my can, all too eager to quit eating for the minute, and one by one we follow Dean and Anne outside. They head off to the end of the street with us trailing behind them. The sun is shining down on us, the snow glistening up, giving an almost ethereal look to everything. At least it's stopped snowing now. If we set off soon, we could still get to the army barracks before nightfall. I look around us, enjoying the peace and quiet, barring the chirp of small birds in the trees. If there's food here, maybe we could stay—at least until the rest of town gets back. I almost snigger. What are the chances of that happening?

At the end of the street we take a right and head down another snow-covered street lined with white picket fences, and then take a left at the end. We pass tons of cars, covered head to toe—um… wheel—in blankets, and several stores with their shutters down, as if closed for the evening. Dean looks back and sees our stares.

"We closed them all up, to protect everyone's things inside. Insurance premiums will be at an all-time high when everything gets going again, and everyone is going to be rioting. At least our town won't have anything to worry about." He smiles again and I choke back a laugh.

He can't be serious?

"I wasn't sure what to do about the cars." He scratches his head. "I remember watching this program once about cars rusting, and decided to cover them all. Every day we try and get around to start a couple of the cars—the ones we can find the keys for, anyway—you know, to keep the engines turning over." He pouts. "Honestly, I'm not sure it'll do any good, but I tried, right?" He absently brushes snow off the top of a car.

I don't know whether to think that this kid has lost it or is a genius. He's thought of everything and yet doesn't seem to have a clue what the hell's going on. How is that possible? I glance at Mikey with a raised eyebrow and mouth *'Is he for real?'* He shrugs, looking as confused as me before putting a hand on my arm and stopping me. I don't argue with him as I hear what's made him get the heebie-jeebies all of a sudden. In fact, now I have them.

A chorus of moans catches in the wind and blows around us like the putrid breath of the dead. It sounds like there's a lot of them. More than a lot—hundreds, possibly? *Oh God, please not hundreds.*

I grab Emily's arm and we dart across the road, Mikey and Alek closely following, and press our backs to the side of the closed up ice cream parlor, complete with pastel pink shutters with painted-on ice cream cones and everything. Mikey and Alek are beside us too, knives drawn, ready to fight to the death. Another chorus of moans drifts toward us, and I feel the tremble that runs through Emily because it runs through me too.

I look up to the sky as soft snowflakes begin to fall again, and can't help but think what rotten luck we're having today. I close my eyes briefly, trying to calculate the distance the deaders are from us. I open my eyes back up and cast a glance at Dean and Anne, who are still standing in the middle of the road, looking highly amused.

"What are you all doing?" Dean shouts across to us.

"Get out of the road, there's deaders somewhere," Mikey shout-whispers to them.

Anne smirks and elbows Dean. "Come with us," she says. "It's fine, honestly."

The wind picks up, whipping loose strands of hair into my eyes and making them water. I rub at them, confusion and a little bit of fear mixing in with my watery eyes.

"Are you crying?" Emily whispers.

"No, I am not crying," I huff. "I'm getting pissed off with their games, if you want to know."

"You and me both," Mikey says and starts to follow after our unlikely boy scout.

I trail after him, keeping my own knife drawn and ready and feeling Emily close behind me. Alek stays to the rear—I presume to keep lookout behind us. If I'm honest, I don't think it would matter. By the sound of the amount of deaders nearby, if they manage to sneak up behind us, we're goners for sure. There would be no escaping the wrath or teeth of this many deaders trying to eat us.

I'm still working on my pessimism scale, gimme a break.

We turn the final corner and find ourselves in the center of the town. In the middle is a large bandstand, little seats and stands for music sheets still in place. The whole place is creepy, I decide, and I do not want to stay here anymore. Another growl of deader love whistles up into the wind, making me cringe.

"Seriously, where the hell are you taking us?" I snap. A chill is running down my spine, and I can't shake it. Maybe it's a draft from the oncoming storm that's caught the bottom of my jacket. Or maybe it's the fact that the storm means we're going to be stuck here with these freaks and a bunch of deaders, and that's what's really bothering me.

Dean actually looks a little perturbed by my outburst. "Look, lady, it's just at the end of town. It's not something I can explain."

"It really isn't," Anne agrees softly.

"No, it really is. I want answers now." I scowl.

"All will be revealed." He smiles and does a weird hand movement, which I'm guessing is supposed to be an attempt at a magician impersonation. He sees my scowl and drops the act. "Fine. The sick people can't hurt us. Trust me."

"Trust you? Why would I? I don't know you."

He looks down to his shoes sadly. "No, you don't, but we came to you, we brought you food. I don't mean to freak you out, and I'm sorry if that's what I'm doing, I just want you to come and see. Maybe then you can help us."

"Help?" Mikey asks.

"Yes, help. You'll see." With that he smiles widely again, turns tail, and keeps on walking, with my group following behind. As we reach the edge of town, the growling that I'm all too familiar with gets louder until it's an almost deafening roar of white noise. We turn one last corner and there it is—or rather, there they are: deaders. Hundreds of them.

Next to a massive hydro plant they stand, like an army of the undead, being held back by a heavy metal barrier which surrounds the entire place. It's leaning forward in places, and it doesn't look like long before it will collapse. They growl and push and shove each other, not caring when one of their comrades falls to the ground and gets trampled into the soft, ripe earth. Dean and Anne keep walking, but my little happy foursome has stopped dead in its tracks. Emily cowers behind me—why, I have no idea, since she has her big-ass boyfriend now. Mikey is standing slightly ahead of me, looking like a real tough guy brute, though he pulled off the look better when he had a shaved head and no beard. I would snigger but I'm kinda terrified. Dean looks back to us.

"It's okay, they won't come any closer." He smiles, looking proud of himself. "I do need your help, though. There's more today than normal, I'm guessing they smelled or heard you all banging around in town." He frowns with a tut.

"Is he saying I smell?" I look sideways at Mikey. "Did you just say I smell?" I shout to Dean and scowl.

"What? Well, yeah, we all do." He shrugs.

"I do not!" I start to move forward, the eyes of hundreds of hungry undead watching my every movement. The closer I get to them, the more riled up they seem to be. And the stench—sweet Jesus, they stink so bad. I feel even more offended that he had the nerve to say I smelled when standing next to these deaders. That's just fucking rude.

We come within arm's reach of the deaders, most of us gagging and spitting out bile. It's not only the smell, though that's horrendous— kind of like rotten month-old raw toilet sewage mixed in with shitty baby diapers and left in the sun too long. It's the sight of them too. The years have not been good to them, wherever they've come from.

Dried out flesh hangs in ribbons from their puckered faces, rotten eyeballs dangling from graying sockets. Bloated stomachs are stretched far beyond normal limits, and I wonder why they haven't exploded or somehow released the gasses they contain. Then I realize that it more than likely isn't gasses inside them anymore, but flesh, skin, bones, people. Human fucking bodies are inside these walking nightmares. A deader moves, stretching its arms out to us, and as I look, I can see fingers and feet pressing on the stretched skin from the inside of it. It's when I can see the shape of an arm, though; that does it for me. Why an arm out of everything else, I don't know, but it's an arm—particularly the elbow joint that is most visible—and it's that that makes my head spin.

I turn and heave, wanting to purge my stomach of its contents, but my stomach stubbornly refuses to let go. With every new retch I get a new image of each person that these things must have eaten: a mother, a father, a child, a daughter. My knees go weak and I clutch onto Mikey for support.

I should be used to this. I thought I was used to this, but I guess you can never get used to this sort of hell. Every time I think I've seen it all—thought it all—a fresh new horror is shown to me. I'm not scared, I'm horrified. These were people once, and inside them are people. Fuck, why have I never considered what happens once they eat? Why has it never dawned on me that they don't shit and piss, that they hold onto their meals for all eternity—or at least until it rots away inside them.

Holy hell, they're like those little Russian dolls—a body within a body. Or should I say a rotting corpse within a rotting corpse?

THIRTEEN

Dean is still smiling like the cat that got the mouse, the cream, and maybe even a side order of catnip. Even little scaredy cat Anne is smiling, though she doesn't look happy about how close they are to the deaders and backs up a little.

"It's okay, they won't come any closer," Dean says again. Yet even as he says it, and I see it for myself, I have trouble believing it.

"How is this possible?" I whisper, still staring at the bloated corpses. I take a few steps forward, but Mikey's hand clutches my forearm.

"Don't," he says without looking at me.

Dean walks toward us, his head held high and his chest puffed out, obviously feeling pleased with himself for freaking us all out. "I told you, they…won't…come…any…closer." He emphasizes each word, making me want to slap some sense into him.

"But how?" I ask, finally dragging my eyes away from the dead and looking at him. "Why? I don't understand."

"Anne told you, I'm a whiz with electronics. This town was

swarming with the sick people at one point, and Anne and I were hiding out in my grandpa's basement. We had practically run out of food, it was getting colder . . . I didn't know what we were going to do. It seemed like we were going to either starve or freeze. But then one day there was a huge bang—the hydro plant had exploded after a bad storm. You couldn't get near the place without getting electrocuted or burned. Believe me, we tried. We were worried that it would burn down the whole town, but then the fire died out and the strangest thing happened: all the sick started heading for the plant and away from town. I eventually figured out why—well, sort of. I worked out that the frequency of the live current being emitted from the damaged plant was attracting them somehow. So I worked out a better system to keep the frequency going—we didn't want the hydro plant to just stop one day and the town end up flooded with the sick again—and voila."

"Is that possible?" I look at Mikey and then to Alek. "I mean, that can't be possible, can it?"

They swap strange looks before Alek speaks. "Well no, technically it shouldn't be possible, but then there's fucking walking corpses over there and that ain't possible either." He shrugs.

"Of course it's possible," Dean shouts, his face flushing red. "I made it possible—well, sort of—and I've maintained it and made it more efficient. The evidence is right before your eyes." He continues to shout, riling the deaders up as he gestures angrily toward them.

"Listen, with respect, we're not going to take the word of someone who believes that those," I point toward the smelly deaders, "are just sick, and that everyone who ran away from here however long ago it was is going to come back here one day like nothing has happened, all cheery because their insurance premiums aren't going up. Get a grip," I bite out.

"You know, lady, you can be a real bitch," little mousey pants pipes up, her blonde hair blowing around her face. The steam seems to go out of her as fast as it went in and she goes a crimson color after her little outburst.

I laugh. "Please. Tell me something I haven't heard before."

Emily nods, her mouth quirking up as she does.

The deaders are freaking me out with all their gross staring and protruding bellies, exposed bone and rotting flesh. I shudder as a fresh breeze wafts their scent toward us all.

Emily tugs on my elbow. "Can we go now? I don't like the way they're staring at me."

"Yeah, let's go. Mikey, Alek, you coming?" I back up a couple of steps, not wanting to turn my back on the deaders for a second. I don't care what Dean and his little mouse say, I don't trust anything but a bullet to the brain to stop the dead.

"Wait, I thought you said you'd help us?" Dean hurries forward, worry tainting his voice.

"We never said anything, buddy." Mikey turns to walk away. "And the fact that there are over a hundred dead standing at your back gates means that we're going to be getting the hell out of here. Right now."

"But you said..." Dean splutters.

"Again, with the 'you said' business. We didn't say shit, and there's nothing you can do about it." I finally turn my back on the gruesome scene and walk away, but curiosity gets the better of me. "What is it you wanted us to do, anyway?" I say over my shoulder.

"We need you to help us cull the herd."

I frown, still walking. I glance at Mikey, who's looking more and more pissed off by the conversation with every passing second. "Did he say cull the herd?" I turn around. "Did you just say cull the herd?" I look at Dean, seeing a boy in front of me, not a man. And Anne, she's just a kid too, a frightened one. How the hell have they survived this long by themselves? Oh yeah, the whole hydro-plant-attracting-the-deaders-and-keeping-them-out-of-town bullshit.

Dean catches up to us. "Yes." He reaches for Anne's hand as she comes beside him. "We need your help." For the first time since we met him, I see real fear in his eyes.

"You were trying to get us to leave a few minutes ago," Emily says with a raise of her eyebrow. I get the warm fuzzies at my trademark look on her face. My girl's learning.

"And we want you to…just not quite yet." Dean drags a hand down his face. "Look, I'm trying to protect us both and this town. Whatever it takes." He takes a deep breath. "And it takes a lot. We could really use your help. The group of sick is getting bigger and bigger. They're surrounding the hydro plant, crowding it. We've so far managed to keep them to a minimum and only kill them when we really have to—I don't want to get into too much trouble with the police when everything calms down. Most of the time we can attract them and get them to follow us. We lead them away from the town, and they seem pretty stupid, forgetting about us once they don't see us. But it's not been working so well recently, and I need to get them away from there now and build some better defenses for it. Otherwise they're going to crush the power supply and then. . ." His words die off.

He doesn't need to say the next line, we all get it: the deaders will come and the deaders will kill, the deaders will destroy, blah blah blah. That's what always happens.

"But you said that it was dangerous, that the deaders were being electrocuted." I grimace at the thought of deep-fried deader, the smell of their burnt flesh filling my nostrils.

"No, I managed to contain the current."

"Clever," I say.

He shrugs. "I'm good at this stuff. I was graduating early because I was so ahead of my time, but I'm one guy, and I've never done anything on this scale before. My real worry is that if the herd keeps on building like it is, they are going to knock down the fence surrounding the plant and possibly disrupt or destroy whatever it is that created that frequency in the first place." He looks behind him. "And then…" Again, he doesn't need to finish the sentence; it's obvious what will happen.

I glance at the herd of deaders. "Fine. But let's talk more back at the house, I don't want to look at these guys anymore. They're freaking me out."

"So you'll help us?" Dean smiles, the fear vanishing from his face.

Mikey looks at me, a frown etched across his face. He rubs a hand across the back of his neck, looking unhappy—grumpy even. "Well, I want to know more about it before I agree to anything. But I agree with Nina, let's get back to the house and you can talk us through your plan."

We all turn and begin to walk back the way we came. Fresh snow has begun to cover our tracks already, and with it fresh worry about getting the hell out of here anytime soon. Sure, there are worse places to be stuck, but one look at the angry mob behind us tells me this is a horror story waiting to happen.

"How much food do you guys have?" Emily asks between mouthfuls of corn chowder.

"We pretty much got everything and stored it all. It took a long time, but we had nothing better to do, so . . ." Anne shrugs. "I wanted everything to be nice for when my mom came back. She doesn't know that it's safe now. She doesn't even know that I'm still alive." Anne wipes at her eyes.

"How did you both get left behind?" I ask as tactfully as I can. But we all know there's no nice way to ask 'so, you were forgotten, huh?'

Anne looks into her food as she talks. "When the sick attacked, I was at school. The teachers decided to evacuate everyone and get us all to the town hall—that's pretty much standard for an emergency. I got onto one of the school buses. It was crammed way past the point of dangerous. The driver lost control and our bus crashed. When I came to everyone was gone—or dead." Dean pulls her into his arms. "I couldn't believe it—friends, cousins, my teacher, all . . . gone in some way or other. I climbed out of the wreckage and headed for the town hall." She looks up at Dean with a shy smile. "On the way I met Dean. We went to school together. He was in the year above me. He hadn't gotten on a bus—instead he stupidly wanted to go home and find his mom, but he couldn't get near the place. There were sick everywhere. When he found me, I was cornered by some of them. He came in all guns blazing and..."

"He had a gun?" Emily asks.

"Well, no, but I had a baseball bat," Dean chuckles. "I put a couple out of their misery and then dragged Anne to safety. We wanted to get home, but the whole town had gone crazy. I managed to get us to my grandpa's house, but he was gone, there was blood everywhere. I didn't know what else to do, so we went down into the basement, barricaded the doors, and stayed put until it went quiet. My gramps was a real nut-job, always believing in that end of days crap, so we had enough to survive for a while."

"How long were you down there?" I ask.

Dean and Anne look at each other sadly; something crosses between them, but I can't say what. "Couple of weeks, maybe a month...or two."

Emily gasps. Even Alek turns from the window to look at us.

"It was longer than that," Anne says, still looking at Dean.

Silence encompasses the room, a thick and heady tension of what we have all had to do to survive this long.

We slowly continue eating, the sounds of forks in cans and chewing our only accompaniment for a long while. I've learned the hard way that's it's best to keep my opinionated trap shut in situations like this.

"They'll come back soon," Anne whispers.

I look up from my empty food can with a deep sigh. Looking at these two, I know that they are clinging onto hope the best they can, but can they really believe that the people of this town will magically come back? For all they know, the deaders—sorry, the sick—out there are what's left of their town. I decide that it's not my place to break any hearts today. Let them believe, hope, if that's what keeps them going, keeps them fighting. Look how well they are doing. They've fared much better than most of the world. A question is still niggling at me, though, a thought I can't quite grasp onto yet, but I know it will come. Something still doesn't sit right about this place.

Later that day, Dean moves us into a different house—one where we can use the beds, but more importantly the fireplace, while we stay in town. Apparently it was up on the market after the old couple that used to live there moved away. Morally, Dean is okay with us staying in it as long as we don't make too much of a mess, since it wasn't anyone's home anymore. It still seems kinda stupid to me, but since he isn't trying to make us sleep on the streets, I guess it doesn't really matter.

As the night draws in, Dean and Anne make their way back home, leaving my little group to contemplate the next day's events and get some shuteye. Emily heads up to bed pretty much right away, exhausted from the day's antics. Alek stays up with Mikey and me, sipping on a bottle of homemade wine that Dean brought us. It tastes like crap, but it gives my brain a nice fuzzy feeling to it; and that, combined with the crackling coming from the fireplace, is all it takes to send me to sleep.

FOURTEEN

We head over to the hydro plant as soon as the day breaks: no point putting off the inevitable. We promised we'd help; I only hope that we can. As we get closer to the plant, I see the group of undead looking even larger than it did yesterday.

We slide down a small embankment at the back of the hydro plant, the noise from the waterfall louder now. We land one by one in a muddy stream at the bottom with a splash. Mud coats my boots and legs and I grimace. Overnight it rained a little, turning the ice into sludge. I should be grateful that it didn't snow anymore, but these days I tend to disregard being grateful for anything, since you never know what strings come attached to it.

"How is it even possible that you have electricity?" I ask as I climb up the other side of the embankment.

I look up to see Dean shrug and roll his eyes dismissively. "Again, that's the hydro power. The river still runs, and I guess it's keeping everything going. I mean, it's not very efficient—there's nothing to spare, everything is going on the defenses—but we don't use electricity in town, since we didn't want to disrupt anything else after the accident. I mean, whatever caused all this to happen," he gestures to the herd of deaders around the plant, "it was a miracle, and I don't want to mess with it any more than I have and have it turn off or whatever. Plus, we've managed pretty well without electricity so far, and we don't want to attract any attention to ourselves." He shares a look with Anne. "We've both seen those types of movies where people are their own worst enemy. We decided it was best to be on our own until everyone came back."

Again with the 'everyone coming back' crap. I roll my eyes.

As we get close to the main fence of the plant, a loud humming can be heard—oh, and a chorus of deader moans, of course. Can't forget that sweet sound.

"It's there." Dean points up ahead. "You guys sure you're up to this?"

"No," I say wholeheartedly. And I mean it, too, especially after seeing the amount of them. There's definitely a couple hundred more.

Mikey scratches his beard, frowning again. It's becoming an all too familiar look on him. "I'm not happy about this." He looks around at the surrounding fields, stray deaders making their shambly way over to the exact point that we need to get to.

"Look, Lovers' Lookout is just over that hill, the truck's over there. It will be easy—we've done something similar before." He looks around and I don't miss the anxiety that crosses his face. "Of course there weren't nearly as many of the sick then." He shrugs. "I only need them distracted long enough to get this fence secured."

I take a deep breath. "Let's just get this over and done with. Anne, Em, you're both with me then. You know the plan." I start to walk away but Mikey catches my elbow and turns me back around. He reaches down for my chin, tugging my face up to his as he kisses me.

"Be careful." His brown eyes bore into mine like something you see in a movie—intense, full of emotion. I'd swoon if I was the type to.

"Always am." I smirk as I deftly kiss him back and then start walking to the truck.

"I'm serious, don't go doing anything stupid," he shouts after me.

There are several trucks scattered around, but the two we're using are Land Rovers or something similar. I only recognize the shape of the truck as something my own father used to drive when I was younger. He was so proud of that vehicle, always going on about it being a real man's truck.

I smile fondly at the memory and climb into the closest one. Anne climbs in the back and Emily gets in the passenger's seat next to me. The deaders have spotted us and are growling their disgusting asses off, as if afraid that we might be getting away.

Not likely—we're bringing lunch to you.

I start the truck with the key Dean gave me, glad that he had the sense to keep turning some of the vehicles over so the engines didn't all go flat. I have to give the boy some credit; he has some very clever ideas, even if some others are ridiculously stupid.

I swing the truck around, getting a feel for it before stopping and deciding to put on my seatbelt. I tell the girls to do the same—last thing I need is one of us falling out, and this ground is not the easiest to maneuver, I realize.

"Keep your arms inside, guns raised—you know the drill, Em."

We're the bait, intending to lure the deaders away from the area and up to Lovers' Lookout—a.k.a. kids' make-out corner—and then the best part of all: Dean has thoughtfully left a snowplow up there that he's used once or twice to, well, plow the dead over the side, apparently. That part I actually can't wait for.

I pull around the back of the herd and beep my horn several times to get their attention. Slowly they begin to turn, scrambling over one another to get to us. The more unfortunate ones fall right away, the stronger of the dead trampling them into the sodden earth, but mostly they all press forward, intent on reaching us in whatever capacity they can.

When I think enough of them are following, I start to drive away, keeping enough distance between us to keep them following. The men become smaller and smaller as we get further away, and I can't help it, my heart starts pounding heavily in my chest. The truck starts the gentle incline, struggling ever so slightly as we reach the top. The deaders use each other as leverage to make it up the slippery hillside. At the top is a small parking lot, and after that is a beautiful view of the rocky, snow-covered landscape. I can't help but gasp at the magnificence of it, and it seems unfair to ruin it by plowing the dead over the sheer side, but those are the facts.

I pull the truck over to one side of the industrial orange snowplow, feeling it somewhat ironic that with all the snow around, we'll be plowing zombies and not snow. Anne climbs into my seat of the truck as I climb out and hurriedly into the plow. I pull the second set of keys from my pocket and start it up. It's noisier than I expected, and as the deaders come up over the hill and the girls take off, my noisy engine attracts the deaders to me.

I fumble with the controls momentarily, nearly losing my cool as I struggle to steer the damn thing. Eventually I'm heading straight for them, grimacing at the sound of the first bodies to hit the metal scoop on the front. They growl and continue reaching for me even as their legs are torn from their rotten bodies. I press down harder on the accelerator, driving as close to the edge as I feel comfortable with and feeling slightly satisfied when the first group goes tumbling over the edge.

It doesn't last long, as hands begin to hit the back and side of my truck, causing it to rock. I shift it into reverse, imagining the sound of their bones crunching as I roll backwards over any that were stupid enough to get behind me. More come up over the hill as I swing back around, and I continue to shovel them toward the edge and over into the abyss.

The sun is shining down, causing the surrounding snow to twinkle like diamonds, and it would be an almost beautiful sight as the area is more or less cleared of the first group of dead. Unfortunately, the ground is smeared with rotten corpses, blood, entrails, and sludge, and the image is far less wondrous as the sound of the second horde of undead follow behind Anne and Em's truck as they come up and over the hillside.

Em's hand flies to her face, and even from where I sit I can see her pale significantly. Anne's face seems nonchalant about it all, and that's what catches me by surprise. Em doesn't have the strongest stomach, but Anne seemed like such a little mouse—yet here she is acting all tough-girl without a care in the world.

Their truck pulls up beside mine and she rolls down the window.

"They're on their way," Anne says with determination.

"So I hear." I shrug. "Any problems?"

"No, everything is going okay. Mikey and Alek are taking out any that get too close to Dean, and the rest seem to be following us. This next group seems bigger than the last. Want us to hang around and help?" Anne asks, not a hint of humor in her voice.

"Uh, no, I should be good." I frown. If I had a beard I'd scratch it in puzzlement at this girl's new hardcore attitude toward what's going on; she's like a different person from the one we met yesterday.

The first of the dead begin to come up over the hillside. "Better go," I say and let out the breath I had been holding without realizing it.

I rev the engine to get their attention, and once I have it I ease forward, waiting until enough of them are up close before I accelerate and push them toward the edge. A couple grasp onto the steel of the scoop, but as I reverse they lose their grip and fall, or smear against the concrete ground of the parking lot, leaving trails of rotten limbs behind them.

I swing back around and repeat the action, driving away from the initial herd and then spinning full circle to be able to scoop as many as possible in one shot. I've long ago gotten over the sound of their bodies being crushed, but the smell they excrete when they are broken open is worse than I expected.

It's on my third scoop of deader that I panic as a large deader manages to climb the side of the truck. He seems as surprised as me, but not as surprised as the deader that he stood on to get up so high in the first place, when it falls to its knees and goes under the wheel of the plow. The other deader bangs against my window angrily, fingernails snapping as it claws at the glass.

"Don't panic, don't panic," I mutter, speeding up and slamming my brakes on to shake the deader off. He grips onto the side mirror, doggedly determined not to be thrown loose.

I look up and see more deaders spilling over the top of the hillside, but no Emily and Anne preceding them.

"Okay, panicking a little bit now." The deader bangs angrily on my window again, and I can't stop myself from banging back. "Fuck off!"

I decide to dump this next load of deaders over Lovers' Lookout and ignore Angry Pants at my window for now. I can't get him off willingly, and more and more are coming to join the party with every second. I can't say I'm not wishing that Anne and Emily wouldn't have stayed to help out now, though.

I tip my load over the edge and jam it in reverse, but the truck doesn't budge. I try to look around and see why, but Angry Pants is still staring in at me, his growly rotten face snarling. I can only presume there's a bunch of deader bones stuck under my wheel, stopping me from going anywhere. I floor it but only manage to budge the truck an inch or so. All the while, my sideshow companion continues to gnaw at the window.

I stick the truck in park, my hands shaking uncontrollably, and try to catch my breath. I'd be lying if I said I wasn't getting worried, but surely the others would be coming anytime now. I look around, seeing only a wall of dead surrounding me just as Angry Pants hits the window again and a large crack shoots down the glass.

"Sodomize me with a snow shovel, that is not good," I yell, grimacing at both my colorful imagery and Angry Pants at my window.

FIFTEEN

pull the gun from my waistband—a crappy old thing that Dean gave me. Apparently it was his gramps'; the guy had tons of weapons, but they're all old. I spin the barrel, already knowing it's full, since I loaded it fresh before we left.

I need options, good options. Options? Pfft, I can't see any viable ones right now.

I point the gun at the window while simultaneously shoving the truck in reverse again. "Come on, come on!" I yell.

If I'm going out, I'm going out wild and taking as many of these pus bags with me as I can, I decide. Angry fists smash against the metal on all sides of the truck, the noise almost deafening. I try to control my fear instead of letting it control me, taking deep breaths and releasing them as slowly as possible. Fists hit the window next to my head again, and a split second later glass explodes around me and Angry Pants falls through and into my lap, his jaws snapping as I push on his forehead to keep his teeth away from my skin. I reach a hand across and grab the back of his head, my fingers clutching at dirty hair, and I yank his head backwards and away from my thighs as I force my gun into his face.

My eyes squeeze closed as I feel his teeth close around the barrel and his growling becomes muffled by the metal filling its rotten hole. I fire the gun, gray brain matter and skull rain down on me, and I let out a high-pitched scream as I shove the body back out the window. I look out and see another deader attempting to climb up to me.

"Shit!" I bang the steering wheel.

The whole truck is rocking backwards and forwards, and I'd be lying if I said I wasn't totally shitting myself now. The sound of revving in the distance draws my attention to the hillside, and a couple of seconds later Anne and Emily's truck comes over the hill. Neither look surprised by the sight before them, but I don't have time to register the whats or the whys about that. I'm just glad that I stand a fighting chance now.

Anne revs the truck even more, drawing the attention of some of the deaders to her. The front ones move away and give me the leeway to be able to edge forward enough to turn my truck in a small half-circle. Something clunks under my wheel, and when I stick it back into reverse, the trucks obeys and I begin to slowly crush the life—death—out of the deaders behind me. Emily is firing into the herd and—surprisingly—is accurately blowing a ton of dead away. Anne is driving into some of them, snapping their legs like twigs and sending them to the ground, where her tires find their faces and crush them. I'm continuing to back into and crush the ones that are stupid enough to get behind me, and shovel the ones stupid enough to stand in front over the side of Lovers' Lookout—and then my knight in shining armor turns up, all guns blazing, muscles twitching, and manly grimace shining through.

I would be all like, 'bitch please, we have this totally under control' and play my feminist card, but since he has a freaking machine gun and we *don't* have it under control, I merely shrug and yell at him to help us. At least I assume it's some sort of machine gun by the amount of bullets that are spraying out the end of it.

The deaders' bodies bounce around, gunk exploding out of them from all angles—out of the back, front, head. Some drop, some keep moving onward, relentless and ignorant to the amount of bullets that riddle their rotting bodies. Mikey isn't even going for kill shots; he's going for full-on destruction, a crazy gleam in his eye.

I scoop a bunch more deaders over the side, watching as they plummet away from this once beautiful lookout and into oblivion, or whatever is down there—maybe an ex-lover or two. Mikey's gun has finally silenced, Emily's too, and I reverse the truck one last time and park it up as calmly as I can. The blood finally finds its way back into my fingers as I loosen my grip on the wheel and survey the destruction around us.

The ground is littered with body parts and gore. Stringy sinew clings to the fronts of bumpers; the pure white snow has been drowned out with brown and black sludge, rotten intestines, and graying brain matter. Mikey jumps down from the bed of the truck and stalks his way over to me. A stray deader reaches up from the ground, its face partially caved in from the impact of something, its legs laying crushed behind its ravaged body, but Mikey shows it no mercy as he stamps his boot into the back of its head as he passes. In the silence, the sound of crunching bone is loud and echoes around us all.

Mikey climbs up to my door and yanks it open. His eyes wash over me and he frowns when he sees the blacky-brown patch in my lap.

"Were you bitten?" he simply asks. "Are you hurt?"

I wonder if I were to say yes that the deader had bitten me and I was bleeding to death if he would put a bullet straight through my brain, or if he'd look after me until the bitter end. I look down into my lap, feeling glad that I can answer honestly.

"No." My voice comes out quieter than I expected, and it's then that I realize how scared I must have been—still am. "It just kinda gnawed on my pants a little." I look to the edge where I tipped my last load of deaders. The view is still spectacular, but I can almost hear the angry groans from the semi-destroyed deaders down below, growling up to me and promising to find their way to me somehow, someday. Kinda ruins the view, if I'm honest. I shrug it off, clear my throat, and repeat, "No, I'm good." I frown back, harder than him, and raise an eyebrow.

"Okay then. Let's get back." He jumps down, and I let out the breath I'd been holding.

I'm not sure if I expected him to kiss me, dragging me from the vehicle and wrapping me in his arms in a mushy embrace, but his indifference certainly wasn't what I had in mind. I mean, he didn't even shout at me for being reckless. What the hell's that all about?

I climb out of my truck on unsteady legs, keeping my gun aimed at the mass of limbs on the ground and being careful to not stand on any of them. I'm already a mess of nerves; the last thing I need is for one of these ugly fuckers to decide that they aren't completely re-dead and grab hold of me. I climb in behind Emily's seat and offer them a smile.

"Everything okay, girls?" I say nonchalantly.

Anne watches me from her rearview mirror. "Umm, yeah."

Emily has turned in her seat to stare at me.

"What?" I ask with a shrug. "What are you staring at?"

"Nina…" she begins, but then turns around without saying anything else. I have a feeling that she's trying not to cry, but I'm not sure why. I know that was a close call, but I didn't do anything stupid this time. It was just a plan that went to hell. I can't be blamed for that.

I stare out the window, clenching and unclenching my hands and begging for them to stop shaking. Anne swings the truck around, and as we turn to go back down the hill I catch sight of my snowplow. Forgetting the massacre that surrounds it—the bodies, the limbs, the gore—and forgetting that the plow is so close to the cliff edge that I'm not sure how it hasn't fallen over yet, what's so shocking is that the sides of the plow are so dented in that the paint has come away and pure metal is showing through. In some places the metal has been so badly knocked out of shape that it's actually made several small holes *through* and into the inner workings of the plow.

Jesus, how did they have the strength to even do that?

I swallow hard, feeling Anne's eyes on me in the mirror, but I don't look up. I hadn't realized how close—in so many ways—I had just come to death. Is that why no one is saying much to me? Because they know that it's not my fault this time, but they very nearly lost me? Are they all as shocked as me? Are they waiting for me to freak out? If they are, they'll be waiting a long time. I won't freak out. I swallow down the lump in my throat, feeling the blood rush to my head.

The adrenaline leaks from my body in waves and I suddenly feel the very real urge to go to sleep. Or puke. Or puke and then sleep. Instead I continue to stare out the window, feeling a little numb. As we make it back to the hydro plant, I notice that the fence has been put back up and looks much more secure now. It helps that the deaders have gone now, too—well, apart from the odd shambler on the way over, anyway. I guess that's the whole point isn't it? This thing—current, whatever—attracts them. It doesn't matter that we just cleared a couple of hundred of them or that it nearly cost me my life; they'll continue to keep on coming no matter what.

This freak accident at the plant is both a blessing and a curse. They're going to have this problem again in a couple of months, no doubt. I can't help but wonder what the hell they are going to do about it then. Will they find other stragglers to help them, or have they made it safe enough to last this time?

I guess only time will tell.

We stay for another day or so, filling up on food and supplies. Dean and Anne are without a doubt clueless to what's happened in the outside world, but nothing any of us can say can change their minds on things. As we leave the town, they are both still convinced that everyone will come back once the government finds a cure for these sick people. I'm tired of trying to change their minds, and I relent.

"Be careful," I say, squeezing Anne to me.

"We will." She smiles back.

I hug Dean—it's awkward, but I do it anyway. I'm enjoying all sorts of physical contact these days: hugging, hand-holding—I'm a real touchy-feely kinda girl. "Stay safe...and keep dusting," I joke with a smirk.

He doesn't laugh back and I roll my eyes at him. We leave by a small bridge that runs over the top over the river that feeds the hydro plant, and climb into a silver truck that Dean let us take.

"Do you think we're doing the right thing? Leaving them like this?" I ask Mikey.

"I think they know more than they're letting on," he says.

I look back over my shoulder and see them walking away, his arm around her waist.

"You mean they know everything is gone?"

He nods. "Yeah. Yet right now, this is their world, and they want to cling onto the normality while they can. I'm glad we could help them do that for a little longer."

I nod, my mind deep in my thoughts. It feels like we're abandoning them, but maybe we're not after all. Maybe they need to be on their own, and to have their little world back to themselves.

Five miles down the road, the truck breaks down and we're forced to get out and walk. I have a bitter and jaded feeling that Dean and Anne knew that would happen, but despite being pissed off I don't say anything—none of us do. We get out and start to walk. There's a saying, 'no point crying over spilled milk,' and it's true. There's no point in complaining; it is what it is. I'll be sure to give the little shit a piece of my mind if we ever make it back this way.

I look up ahead at Emily and Alek as they walk hand in hand. I'm still not comfortable with their relationship, but what can I say? He's only a year or so older than her, he protects her, cares for her—clearly he has deep feelings for her. How can I tell them that it's wrong? How can it possibly be wrong? If anything happens to me and Mikey, at least she has Alek to look after her.

I reach out and slip my hand into Mikey's. He looks across and offers me a small smile. He's still lost within his own horrors; the memories of what he's done—who he's harmed—are still fresh on his face, like war wounds. I want to tell him that it will be okay—that he'll sleep peacefully soon and won't see the tortured faces of his victims— but I can't. That's more than likely a lie: those faces would haunt me forever, so I'm sure they'll do the same to him. Goddamn Fallon and his backwards thinking.

I push it from my mind as we walk. For the first time in days, the sun is shining. The snow is thick in places, and it's still freezing as hell, but the view is clear: no wind, no rain, and no snow. If we keep at this pace, we could be at the barracks in a couple of hours. This is probably the calm before the storm. Literally. Winter is very clearly here, and things are only going to get worse.

God knows what we'll find when we get there. I can only hope that it hasn't already been raided; otherwise this whole journey is for nothing. We could have stayed in Dean's little town, settled in for the winter. There was food, it was warm, it was a real house—a home that we could have survived in. For as far back as I can remember, all I've wanted was a home again. Unfortunately, my immediate future doesn't have one in it. I'm a roamer, wandering from place to place, town to town, trying to survive. Hell, half the world is doing the same thing now, but no place is safe. And isn't that the point of killing Fallon and the rest of his stupid gang? To make what's left of the world a safer place for other survivors? Or am I just grasping onto vengeance for my own personal means, intent on killing him and destroying his bastard army for no other reason than it might stop some of the burning pain that courses through me, that it might help Mikey sleep better? Fallon is a weed; he's strangling the life and soul out of people because of his own agenda. Maybe I'm as bad as him.

Maybe this is all pointless. Because after all, you kill one weed and two more show up in its place.

SIXTEEN

The landscape passes me by in a blur of white and green. The trees and plants are getting ready for winter—dying back, leaves falling, shriveling under the blanket of snow—but their beauty is still all around us.

Mother Nature did a good job of the world while mankind either died or hid. She adapted and survived, blossomed into something more amazing than anyone would have thought possible. She may be teeming with flesh-hungry rotting corpses and vengeance-riddled humans, but she has things right, she knows what she's doing. She's thriving in this dead world.

Spring used to be my favorite season. It registered as a fresh start—a new beginning. Life bloomed up all around you: lambs, chicks, calves, shoots finally poking their way through the snow, reaching for the sun to help the world awaken into beauty. As I look around, I wonder whether after this winter things will be that way again. Can things ever be that way again? No animals will be born—the deaders will eat them even if they are—but flowers, yes, they continue to thrive and blossom year upon year, each time growing stronger and stronger until maybe there will be nothing left of mankind. We will be a memory, with only the ruins of a society—of a world left behind.

"Can we stop?" Emily says, but I barely register her words.

Mikey pulls on my hand and I look up wearily. "You okay?" I say to her.

"I could do with a five minute break. This bag is really heavy." She slouches to the ground, sliding her backpack off as she does.

Dean let us take some of the town's food and essentials—not that there was much left. It's been two years, getting close to three now, and their supplies are dwindling. They have enough to get them by for a few months, so the fact that they supplied us with things is generous. In our little backpacks we each carry some canned goods, some basic medicine, water, clean socks, and a few other vital things like flashlights and matches. Dean, having never ventured from the town, didn't realize what a lifeline he was handing us by letting us take things like this. Of course we would have taken them by force if we had to, but it was nice not to. It's good knowing that we have another ally somewhere in the world, even if it is just a couple of kids.

I sit down, too, the ground cold beneath my ass. I slide my backpack off and shove my weapon to one side. It's a Mikey favorite: a machete. Apparently Dean and Anne were just as surprised to find out there their principal was a weapons freak. Having been into everyone's homes to gather supplies, they'd seen a lot more than they ever wanted to. Lord help them if the townspeople ever do come back and Dean has to look them in the eye again.

Of course the stories were funny—funnier than he realized when talking about Mrs. Jones, head of the PTA and personal nemesis to

Anne's mother, and informing us that she had the weirdest drawer full of sex toys, but he couldn't quite work out what the beads were for. Dean may be a man in many ways, but in others, he's still a kid.

Anyway, their principal, Mr. Whatever-He-Was-Called, had a thing for weapons—all types of weapons. Old school things like machetes, and a mix of modern blades like katana samurais. Most of them hung proudly on his wall, still sheathed in their protective covers. Others he used for . . . training? Playing? Who the hell knows? Dean looked perplexed that we were going to be taking such valuable things—from his principal, no less—but we promised to return them and explain everything to the principal once everyone came back. Of course we have no intention of coming back, or returning these weapons. Not unless the deaders drop dead—real dead this time—and people like Fallon aren't wandering the earth, anyway.

I pull out my water bottle, taking a long drink from it. I don't realize how thirsty I've gotten until I start to drink. I should ration it, but I never did have much willpower. I look up at Alek and Mikey; they changed from their happy Christmas sweaters into something more manly and less festive. I still think it's a real shame—and hey, Christmas is on the way.

Em and I got clean clothes too—not that they've stayed that way. The new pants that we're wearing are once again covered in mud and are soaked up to the knees. The layers of sweaters I have on are sticky on my back where I've been sweating, but my socks still feel somewhat dry. My Doc Martens to the rescue again.

Fifteen minutes go by before Mikey has us all up on our feet and walking again; he's touchy, and eager to keep moving. Normally we battle for the leadership, but I'm too lost in my thoughts today. Besides, we all know that *I'm* the boss, really.

The wind is picking up again as we stumble along a muddy path, the narrow pathway between two opposing sets of trees creating a wind tunnel of sorts. I splash through another puddle, my chin to my chest to stop the wind from stinging my eyes.

"Heads up," Mikey calls back to us quietly.

It takes me a minute to get his meaning but I finally look up. Deaders are on the pathway in front of us. They're heading the way we're going, so there's no way to avoid them. The five of them are grouped together, moving as one toward some unmarked destination. I guess this is what they do: they start as one and then build upon their group as they walk, until they are too huge a number to *not* overpower someone. These ones look like they have come from all over. Some wear your average Joe clothes, and others are wearing summer dresses and shorts and whatnot.

We don't bother to run or jog or try to get their attention, but continue to walk behind them, standing far enough back and making as little noise as we can for as long as we can. The wind, flowing toward us in the little wind tunnel, seems to mask our sounds and smells. We travel like this for some time, hoping to get off the track from them at some point and avoid any altercation, but the wind eventually changes direction, and one by one the deaders turn to see us with a snarl. Imagine their surprise.

It's like leaving your house to go to McDonald's only to find that they delivered it to your door. Lucky bastards—I'd do anything for a Quarter Pounder.

I swear they look like they smile. But that's impossible, right?

Three females and two males, from what I can tell, shamble toward us with limps, like they're wearing the most uncomfortable shoes ever. It seems they are the same old deaders I've become accustomed to: graying limbs, putrid faces, jaws snapping in hunger and anger. Again, their stomachs are fit to bursting through, and the sight of them as they lurch toward us and their stomachs jostle around makes me feel sick. I don't have the luxury of actually being sick, though—not when it's life or death.

Mikey raises his long-handled samurai, picked for its beautiful and intricate artwork inscribed down one side of the blade. He steps forward and swipes at a deader. The head comes clean off, flying through the air and landing with an unceremonious splat into a puddle, jaw still snapping. He swings again and takes out two of them this time before Alek goes forward and uses his sword against the remainders. The blade of his samurai is as black as the handle once he's finished dispatching of them.

It's over in a matter of moments, before I can even fully register the acts. I take my machete and stab it through the dismembered heads to put an end to the misery of the dead, feeling bone crunching and brain squelching as I pull my weapon back out. I grimace, but refuse to look away from the sad, pathetic being I just sliced and diced. Yeah, I hate them, but the deaders didn't ask for this; they sure as hell wouldn't have chosen to be like this. And everyone, in death, deserves some sort of respect. I look across as Emily stabs her weapon through the head of the last female deader. She doesn't frown, grimace, scowl—nothing. She's like a robot on automatic. As if the dead at her feet mean nothing.

For the first time I really see her as a woman. I just hope this world doesn't destroy her soft nature. Though she's maturing into a strong woman, I'd hate to think of her losing that innocence.

I realize the irony of my thoughts. Losing her innocence? After everything she has managed to survive so far? I shake my head sadly. "Off we go again, I guess," I mutter as I finish off the last of the dead. I put my boot on the side of the head and pull my weapon out. So much for respect. A small amount of gunk oozes out of the hole and sends a vile smell up to me. I scowl and walk away, rubbing the end of my weapon in the snow to clean it.

Mikey has taken out the map that Dean gave him. On it is marked the army base and Dean's town, with a long red trail going from one to the other.

"We'll be there in a couple of hours, still a way to go yet," Mikey announces to us all glumly.

"Urghhh, we've been walking forever," Emily grumbles. "Isn't there a shortcut?" She looks to Alek longingly. "I'm freezing and hot all at the same time."

I know what she means. My toes and fingers feel numb to the bone, yet sweat trickles down my spine. I huff out, and clap my hands together to keep the blood flowing, stamping my feet at the same time.

"Yeah, but it's through the forest. I think we should be sticking to the flats of the path or roadways. It's safer." Mikey folds the map and puts it away.

"But we haven't seen anything other than those rot-bags for hours. I say if we could save some time on the journey, we take a shortcut," she whines relentlessly.

"I say no," Mikey snaps.

"I'm sorry, Emily, I say no, too." I reply.

Emily stamps her foot. "But I'm tired."

I smirk. Here I was thinking that she had really matured over the past year and then she goes all teenage drama queen on me. A laugh bubbles up, and before I know it I'm giggling like an idiot.

Emily has her hands on her hips and a frown on her face that would put any toddler to shame. The image does nothing to stop me and I laugh even louder.

"What are you laughing at?" Emily pouts.

I point at her, struggling to catch my breath. "You." I grip my side to try and steady myself, wiping stray tears from my eyes, which if left any longer would have frozen in their tracks.

"Stop it," she shouts. "Stop laughing at me!" She stamps her foot again, her finger pointing at me.

It only sets me off even louder. I back up a couple of steps as she comes forward, her face in mine.

"Nina, it's not funny!"

I stand up and hug her. She fights me at first and then stops. "I'm sorry, Em," I say between gasps. "I forget that you're just a kid sometimes." The words are meant to appease her, but they only seem to infuriate her more.

"I am not a kid!" She pushes me away and my laughter dries up.

"Fine, whatever. You're not a kid, you're a real grown-up woman who has tantrums. Real mature." I raise an eyebrow at her.

She goes silent, her face going from windswept red to going-to-explode red in a couple of seconds. She looks over at Alek, who only shrugs and then resignedly heads over to comfort her.

"Ladies! Quit it," Mikey shouts. "We're not going through the woods. We're sticking to the route that I chose. Deal with it however you want, but that's what's happening. Now let's get moving before we all freeze our asses off out here." He folds the map, puts it back in his backpack, and starts to walk away.

Alek takes Emily's hand, and as one we all turn to follow Mikey. He doesn't look like he's going to stand for any shit right now, so even Emily doesn't put up any more of a fight.

Our walk is silent for a long time, even when the snow begins to fall again and the sun begins to lower. The knot of worry gnaws at my stomach. We have to make it to the base by nightfall—we have to make it *somewhere* by nightfall. Walking through the woods or along this path is not an option if we want to survive another day.

SEVENTEEN
HILARY & DEACON

"Did you hear that?" I sit up in bed, the movement pulling the covers free from Deacon's chest.

He shivers but sits up, his ears straining to listen for any noise. Minutes go by, but neither of us hears anything.

Deacon climbs out of bed and goes to the window to peer out into the night, and he watches silently. We have worked so hard to make this place safe. So damn hard. He tried to think of everything, but the zombies are persistent and relentless in their pursuit of food. Seconds tick by with the only movement being the heavy snow falling from the clouds and settling on the ground. Deacon used to love the snow; so did I. His favorite season was winter and watching our children playing in it, making fat snowmen and going sledding. Now winter scares him—scares us both.

Winter means that food is harder to come by. Nights are longer, days are shorter. The world is a colder and meaner place. I hear him swallow loudly, narrowing his eyes to see between the flakes and find anything else moving. That was just the way of the world now.

"Well?" I whisper to him.

The sound of my voice makes him jump. I hadn't thought I was being quiet when I got out of bed, but he didn't hear me. I lean into the side of him, my brown eyes looking into the blackness.

"Can't see anything," he replies.

"Do you think we're safe here?"

"For now. I can't think what else we could do to protect ourselves."

"We have weapons." It sounds like more of a reassurance to myself than anything else.

"That we do." Deacon snakes an arm around my waist and hugs me closer, his chest cold against my hot body—hot because of the fever that is building. We have lost so much since this all began, and I don't know what I would do if I lost him. And I know that he feels the same way too.

He kisses the top of my head and I sigh, snuggling myself closer. Some days it feels like I've already lost him. When the zombies came, they took more than just our home and our reassurance of protection. They took even more than just our children. They took away our future. In this world now, there is no future.

"I'm sorry for waking you," I whisper up to him.

I know he hadn't been sleeping anyway. I barely sleep more than an hour or two these days before waking up in cold sweats and crying. This means that he hardly sleeps; Deacon always wants to be there for me whenever I need him, whatever time that may be.

"That's okay, baby. I was awake anyway." He kisses my head again. "Go back to bed. I'll be there in a minute."

I shake my head. "I'm okay. I'm awake now."

Deacon looks up, seeing the moon still heavy in the sky. "There's a lot of night left to go." He guides me back to bed and pushes the covers aside for me to climb into. "Sleep. You can cook me breakfast in the morning." He smirks.

I smile and close my eyes, trying for sleep as Deacon stands watch at the window. My eyes spring open several times as dreams try to intrude, images of our children, of our lives before all this, pushing to the forefront. Our family and friends, all gone. I don't even realize that I'm crying until my pillow grows damp. Not my pillow, but someone else's. The older couple that had lived here. This was their home, and Deacon and I took it from them. I'm not sure how much more my heart can take. I let my eyes open again and I look across at Deacon.

He has taken a seat by the window, a blanket thrown across his shoulders as he watches the dark world outside. I have to keep going, though; he needs me.

I lie in the dark waiting for morning to come. Another day to get through. Another day that they we have to survive.

EIGHTEEN

NINA

"Did you hear something?" I look up at the others.

Night has fallen, but we've had to keep on going regardless. It's too dangerous to stop. Hell, it's too dangerous to keep going, but we don't have much choice.

The path eventually leads into the forest, regardless of Mikey's arguments against going into it. The choice is, however, taken out of his hands since that's the way we have to go now. I can almost see the glee on Emily's face, though she tries to hide it. Almost. As we enter the forest and find it teeming with hungry deaders and have to fight, Mikey gets the upper hand with a roll of his eyes and a very loud *I told you so*. I can't blame him, really, but I wish they'd both stop being assholes. This whole tit-for-tat thing is beginning to drive me nuts.

Now, we all stand silent in the dark forest, looking into the blackness surrounding us. None of us moves; the only thing stirring is the rapidly falling snow. My knees tremble from cold and exertion, my fingers long since numb and useless, yet they still cling onto my weapon for dear life—though what could I could actually do with numb hands, I'm not sure. Dean had managed to find hats for us all, but only one set of gloves for some reason.

Minutes pass before Alek breaks the silence in a hushed whisper. "I can't hear anything."

"I can't see anything either," Emily pipes up.

Mikey shrugs his agreement and I want to snap that they sound like the three monkeys: hear no evil, speak no evil, see no evil.

"I definitely heard something," I whisper instead.

"Let's keep going. Keep your eyes everywhere. It can't be much further." Mikey says this, but he doesn't sound like he believes it himself. Or maybe it's the chattering of his teeth that leads to my lack of belief in his words.

We keep going, watching every angle we can. But as I said, it's cold, dark, and we're exhausted. The snow has been falling for hours, covering the land in a thick layer of cold fluff. The moon reflects back off the white forest, offering us only the reflection of light to go by. It's getting stupid and reckless, but to try and light a torch or use a flashlight to help guide us through the wilderness would be just as careless.

My feet are sore. I know that blisters have formed under both feet, and with each toe-numbing step, I grit my teeth. I regret us leaving Dean and Anne and their deader-free town now—regret it with every cold-numbed bone in my body—even though I understand why we have to do this. I know why we left, and the reasons are moral and just, but I can't help but wonder if that decision could be the death of all of us.

The moon is heavy and swollen above us, glowing down like a beacon of hope, but everywhere we look there is more snow, more trees, and no way out. A couple more miles pass, and our steps are minute. Emily is staggering and clinging onto Alek, and I'm close to giving up too. I literally don't think I'm going to be physically able to walk much further. I can hear things in the dark, things that aren't us, but they sound far away, distant almost.

"We need to stop, Mikey."

"We can't. We're nearly there."

"You don't know that. We've been traipsing through these stupid trees for hours. We need to stop. Even if two of us stay awake to keep watch while the other two sleep." I touch his arm to get him to slow. "We need to rest."

"Nina, we have to keep on moving. Once we get there…"

"What? Once we get there what? Anything could be there— anyone could be there." I pull him gently to a stop. "If there are people there, we might not be welcomed with open arms, looking half dead." I hadn't meant the pun, but I'll take the bad joke on the chin.

Mikey looks away. "I only want to keep you all safe."

"And you will, by letting us rest." I look up into the trees. "Mikey."

"Fine."

"No seriously, Mikey." I point up into the trees.

"Okay, but I'll take first watch. You can all rest."

"Mikey." I grab his chin and tilt his face to the sky. "What the fuck is that?" I point up into the trees again.

He looks up, squinting into the darkness. "It looks like a deader." He puts a hand to his eyes to shield them from the snow that falls. "It's a trap, with a deader in it." He pulls his sword to the front of him, ready to take on this new danger, turning and staring all about him.

I do the same, my heart immediately kicking into gear. I see Alek let go of Emily and do the same thing with his weapon. Emily seems too exhausted to do anything but look frightened, and she cowers behind Alek.

"What is it?" Alek asks, looking up to where Mikey had. "Is that a deader?" he asks incredulously.

"Yes." Mikey points further into the trees. "There's another one."

As we squint into the darkness, more of them become clear. Deaders are strung up in nets, like fish that have been caught. They don't move much, and every once in a while you can hear them growl slightly, but never with much conviction. I wonder if the cold is freezing them. It sure as hell won't kill them—only something through the brain can kill them. But if the cold can freeze them, make them easier to fight, then perhaps the winter could be our ally after all. My heart leaps. Or maybe it doesn't mean shit and they just can't smell us down here and that's why they don't seem too bothered by us.

"Let's keep going. Keep your eyes and ears aware. Those are traps. Fucking deaders have been captured intentionally for whatever reason," Mikey snarls out through gritted teeth, the cold making his breath come out of his nose and mouth like smoke from a dragon.

"Why would someone do that?" Emily asks, her voice quavering. Or maybe it's her jaw trembling through the cold.

"I have no idea," Mikey replies. "It could be protection for them, it could be to warn off intruders."

We keep on walking, the light growls from the deaders more apparent now that we're aware of them. The sound travels through the night, making them sound less like the angry monsters we have come to know and hate and more full of angst and pain. They sound more human than I have ever heard them, and for a moment I wonder if they feel pain, and if that pain is hunger or sorrow, a physical or a mental state. I shake the thoughts away; the last thing I need is to think of them as human. I need to remember what they are now, not what they were.

A creak to my left makes me stop and stare into the blackness again. "Did anyone else hear that?" I whisper out. Another creak sounds to the left of me.

No one has a chance to reply, though, as the ground suddenly gives way beneath us and we tumble downward into a black hole. I try not to scream, really I do, but it's kinda hard when you're falling into blackness with no idea what's below.

We land with a crash, mud, leaves, and things that smell really bad covering us all as we flounder around in the dark and try to make sense of our surroundings. *What the hell just happened?*

"Nina!" Emily sobs.

"Emily!" Alek shouts.

I stumble to my knees, my feet struggling to contend with the slippery ground underneath me. I'm ankle deep in mud and rainwater, making it hard to move. I don't know where my machete is—I've lost it in the fall down. My backpack is still on my back, though; at least I haven't lost that. Mikey is silent—I have no idea where he is in this black void. I'm about to call to Emily to let her know that I'm okay when I hear the worst sound in the world, the sound that pierces my brain and makes me shut the hell up before I make a huge mistake.

In a pitch-black world, with no weapon in hand, I hear the growl of a hungry deader.

NINETEEN

"**N**ina!" Emily yells, her sobs getting louder. I'm not sure if she's crying because she's worried I might not be okay, or in fear because she just heard the same sound that I did.

I listen carefully for it again, finally hearing the growl somewhere in front of me. I shuffle my backpack off and fumble with the zipper for a couple of seconds until my hand lands on a small carving knife and the flashlight Dean gave us. I slide the backpack onto my shoulders again, ready myself with the knife, and point my flashlight straight ahead of me.

I count to three, the sounds of Emily crying, Alek telling her to calm down, and the splash and groan of a hungry deader fading away as I ready myself.

One, two, three…

I switch it on, and the hole that we are in is illuminated into an unreal yellow glow. The rotting deader is momentarily distracted by the light and turns to meet my gaze. It heads toward me without a second zombie thought, not realizing how close it actually was to both Emily and an unconscious Mikey. Most of its mouth has rotted away, revealing a snarling set of black teeth. It comes toward me, snapping its jaws, and I hold my breath and slash forward with my right arm when it gets too close. I skim its face, missing the spot that I wanted—the forehead right through to the brain—yet manage to peel back more of the skin from its face so that it hangs down from its cheek like a flap of moldy cheese.

It reaches for me again, simultaneously grabbing hold of my sleeve and pulling me with its inhuman strength toward its mouth. I cry out, not being able to pull my right arm free from its grip. Its bony fingers dig into my arms as it continues to tug me forward. I thrash around wildly, falling backwards with muddy water splashing up around me as the deader lands on top of me.

I scream and kick out at it, grasping onto the bottom of its jaw with every ounce of strength I have to stop it from biting me while its hands continue to tear at my clothes and skin. My other hand claws back in a mirroring attempt to get it off me. A strangling, gurgling sound comes from the back of its throat as its putrid breath washes over my face. The smell of my blood spurs it on and it growls louder. The flashlight has disappeared somewhere, but residual light shines above us. Mikey comes into view. A large gash covers one side of his face, blood pouring from the open wound and mixing with mud. In his hand is a branch, and with it he begins to smash in the deader's brains.

The deader's skull explodes around me, skull, brains, and gore covering my face and hands. My grip loosens on the deader as I struggle to hold it in place. I cry out, still gripping onto the jaw tightly, still feeling its breath close to my throat, so close to killing me.

"Nina." Mikey's voice is next to me; but I can't let go, I can't release the tension that is coiled up inside of me, the fear trembling along every nerve path that I have.

"Nina." His voice again. I sob louder, still squeezing with my hand. Still holding back the jaws of death.

His hand is suddenly on mine, releasing the rotted piece of bone and flesh from my hand, and then he pulls me into his arms and I tremble and sob.

"Emily." I push away from Mikey, reaching for the glow of my flashlight, half submerged in mud. My fingers touch on spongy sunken flesh and I brush whatever limb it is away and grip on tight to my light. "Emily," I call out again.

"I'm here, I'm here."

I shine the light and see her cowering into Alek's chest. He has his own tree branch to defend them both, and I wonder why I hadn't fared so lucky in the 'finding a weapon as soon as you fall' game.

"Are you okay?" I ask, my light dancing around us.

"I think so," she whispers back. "Where are we?"

"It's another trap," Alek says. I shine the light for him as he feels around in his own backpack for his flashlight, finally finding it and switching it on.

The hole must be around... "Mikey, how big is this thing?" I ask.

"It's roughly six feet by four feet, and maybe," he reaches up, "nine feet high." He claws at the wet sides of the hole, trying to clamber up the sides, but after a couple of small steps up, he loses his grip and slides back down, bringing mud with him. "Alek, give me a lift up."

Alek comes toward Mikey, leading Emily to me. She wraps her arms around my waist and hugs me close. I've never been the huggy type, but I think I need this as much as she does right now. Alek helps push Mikey up the side. He manages to reach the edge of the hole, but again he loses his grip on the loose soil, the sides beginning to crumble away.

I would have thought by now that the ground would have frozen solid and this wouldn't be that hard to do, but clearly, under the cover of the trees and with deaders rotting away, the soil hasn't managed to freeze. We did have a lot of rain the last couple of weeks, and the snow has only really been falling this last week, I guess.

"Maybe if we get Emily out. She's lighter, she'll be easier to push up the last bit. She could find something to help get us out," Mikey suggests.

Emily hugs me tighter, whimpering. Normally I would have told her to stop being such a girl, but we don't know what's out there, and if we're honest, she wouldn't have the strength to pull any of us out of this hole if all she can find is a long branch.

"No, she can't do that," I say firmly.

Mikey doesn't argue, but continues to climb the side, bringing more of the soil away with him.

"This is stupid. I can't get a good grip, there's no roots for me to hold onto," a winded Mikey says.

I shine my light in his direction, seeing the blood still trickling from his wound. "We need to clean that up," I say, handing a shaking Emily over to Alek.

The temperature has dropped even more now, our breath clinging to the air like smoke bombs every time we speak.

Mikey rubs a hand at his face and then looks at the blood on his fingers. "I'll be fine. It's just a scratch."

"Well, scratch or not, it's bleeding, and that means it could attract deaders," I say wearily. I don't have the strength to argue with him now, and hope that he relents quickly.

"Fine," he snaps.

I pull out a pair of the socks from my backpack and dab them on the wound, soaking up the blood. He's right, thankfully: it is just a scratch, but it's deep. Shouldn't need stitches, but it'll take a while to heal. I want to crack a joke about us having matching war wounds, but he doesn't seem in the right frame of mind for jokes. Who am I kidding? Neither am I.

I grab a Band-Aid from the first aid pack and press it along the wound once it's relatively clean. I say relatively because we're in a hole filled with deader gore and mud—there's only so clean I can get it. I just hope it doesn't get infected.

"So what do we do?" I ask quietly, not wanting to worry Emily any more than I have to.

Mikey shrugs. "I don't know. I guess maybe we wait until it starts getting light. We'll have a better chance of seeing what we're up against then. I think I'm doing more harm than good if I keep trying right now. The sides are coming away under my hands. If the temperature keeps dropping, it could freeze and make it easier to get out."

I nod. "Seems like a plan. I don't like it, but it's the only one we have."

"Are you okay?" he asks.

I nod a yes and turn away before he sees my lie, and pack everything away in my backpack. We find our weapons, grateful that none of them broke when we fell, and we huddle up together to keep warm.

"I'll stay awake, you all try to sleep," Mikey says.

I don't think I'll be able to sleep—not here, not like this, not with the fear of whoever set this trap coming back and finding us in it rolling around my head, and certainly not with the thought that another deader might shamble upon our muddy prison and fall in on

144

top of us. No, there's no way I'll be able to sleep, I think. But then exhaustion crushes down on me, my body suddenly bone weary and my muscles throbbing to relax. My stomach rumbles with hunger but sleep wins and I drift off, clutching onto Emily and feeling Mikey next to me.

"Heads up," I whisper, and nudge Mikey and the others.

One by one, they stir and wake. I put a finger to my lips and hush them before they speak. We listen to the stumbling steps of a deader nearby, the gurgle and groan it lets out. The steps falter and stop, the gurgle and hiss from the back of its throat still loud, though. One of us was supposed to stay awake at all times, but somewhere in this horrible night, we have all fallen asleep. Thank God I woke up when I did.

I clutch my machete tightly as the steps pick up again, thankfully moving away from us. Minutes pass before anyone dares to speak, and even then it's with hushed voices. The sun has only just risen, casting weird shadows into our muddy prison.

"I'm freezing." Emily blows on her hands to warm them.

"I know," I whisper back, standing. My ass is numb from cold and probably from sitting in sloppy mud for most of the night. My pants cling to my legs, and I shake them out to work some heat back into them. I turn and look at the others. "Shit."

"What?" Mikey tries to stand abruptly, but his ass is frozen and it takes him a minute to get fully upright.

"You all look like shit," I say. And they do—that's not me trying to be funny or trying to be mean; I'm just saying it as it is.

"Not looking too hot yourself," Emily grumbles, standing up with help from Alek.

She's right, of course. But I don't have to look at me. I can feel the mud in my hair and coating my face. I'm actually grateful that I don't have a mirror. Mikey has already started to try and climb back out, and though the walls of the mud hole we're in have frozen, it's just as impossible to climb out of as it was last night.

"Alek, give me a boost again," Mikey asks.

"Wait. What's that?" Emily freezes in her movements as she says it, her head cocked to one side, listening for the sound she heard. "Is that footsteps?" she whispers.

It sounds like deaders are on their way, lots of them by the sound of it.

"Ready yourself," I whisper, holding my machete tightly again.

One by one we nod to confirm that we are indeed ready, but really, none of us are. We're never ready to look death in the face.

As the footsteps get louder and my heart rate picks up, a low sheen showing on my forehead despite the cold, Alek reaches down and picks up what looks like a large chunk of dirt. The sun is still rising, so it's not quite high enough to allow for much of a visual as shadows group at the top of the hole.

I hear a gun cock a second too late. Lucky for us, Alek was way ahead of me and launches his chunk of dirt at whatever is at the top of the hole. A loud *thump* sounds and then a body comes sprawling into the hole with a splash and an *umph* as the air is knocked out of their lungs.

"Want any more?" Alek shouts up to whoever is there, pulling his samurai out and waving it around menacingly—though there really isn't enough room for that type of weapon down here.

"Holy shit. He just hit James!" a male voice shouts out loudly.

"Oh my god, James, James, is he okay? Do not hurt him," a female voice yells into the hole.

I can see the shadow of people leaning over and looking down at us, but the angle of the sun prevents me from seeing faces. Alek and Mikey already have James on his knees, though I can't tell if he's unconscious or dead…hopefully not dead.

"Throw a rope down and we won't have to," Mikey yells up.

"Okay, okay." The female voice again. "Get the damn rope now!" she whispers to whoever else is up there. "Is he all right? Is he breathing?" she calls down to us.

"Just get us the rope, and we'll worry about him later," Alek shouts up.

I look at him, seeing once again the cruel, hard man that he actually is, despite his young age. A rope is thrown down, with knots at several junctions to make it easier to climb.

"We'll send the women up first. If anything happens to any of them, I'll slit his fucking throat. Do you understand?" Mikey bellows up. "Nina, you good to go first?"

"Yes, of course." I nod and shrug my backpack on, slipping my machete into the top of the bag—ready for me to grab at a moment's notice, but freeing my hands up to climb. "Em, you come up straight after me."

She nods, her eyes wide and frightened, but confident in everyone else's abilities. In my abilities. I just hope I don't let her down.

I begin to climb, my cold fingers struggling on the rough rope. The knots in it are a godsend, though, and make the journey easier. I hear the people up above grunting as they take my weight, and as I near the top of the hole I take one last look down below me.

Emily is there, her backpack and weapon stowed like mine, her muddy face staring up at me. Mikey and Alek stand with their captive on his knees between them, a sword at his throat. I can see from here that Mikey is holding up the guy's weight. Whoever it is has a large gash on his head to compete with Mikey's. The most horrifying thing isn't that I can tell that Mikey and Alek will quite willingly slit this person's throat for me and Emily, or what new hell might await once I reach the top of the hole—it's the realization that we have slept all night in a hole full of rotting deaders.

I'm not talking about the one we killed, but the entire hole, now that I can see properly, has a layer of dead, rotting bodies in it. Bones jut out from weird angles, skulls peering up at me, and the mud that cakes us all is not mud at all—at least not all of it.

It's gore. Deader gore.

TWENTY

I tremble from head to foot, making the rope shake as I realize all these facts in what seems like a matter of minutes but can't be more than a few seconds. Deader in my hair, on my face—deader covering me from head to toe.

"Nina?" Mikey asks quietly.

I look at him, trying to steady my breath, trying to keep my shit together. I look at my arms, seeing not only the mud but blackened blood, rotted flesh, bits of hair and nails clinging to my clothes and skin.

"Nina?" He says my name again.

I beg my body to stop shaking, plead with my heart to get a fucking grip and stop beating so fast. I think I'm going to pass out as my breaths come in and out in rapid succession, making me dizzy. I look at Emily, her pretty features smeared with death. Once she realizes, she's going to freak out—I mean totally lose her shit altogether. This thought grounds me and I grit my teeth and look away, continuing to climb out of this hole of death.

My fingers clutch the top and I peer over it, both anxious and eager. A hand is thrust in front of me, and I take it without question and am helped to my feet, coming face to face with a man. The man seems my roughly my age, with dark hair tied back into a low ponytail. His brown eyes bore into mine in both anger and sympathy.

I snatch my hand away. "We'll kill him if you try anything." I turn and look down at Emily. "Come up."

When I turn back around, the man and woman have picked up the rope to take the slack again. They avoid my gaze as they hold the rope steady for Emily, and I have time to take in the woman. Blonde curly hair pokes out from under a bandana that's tied around her head. She's slim, but clearly strong. Both the man and woman are wearing army camouflage pants and jackets, and I feel the thrill of hope.

I turn back around in time to see Emily's fingers grip the side of the hole, and I reach down and help pull her up and out. She pulls her weapon out as soon as she's standing on her own two feet.

"Did you do this?" She points toward the hole with her machete. "Did you make this?"

"Calm down, Em," I coax, putting an arm around her.

She shrugs me off. "No. We could have died down there, and it would have been all their fault."

"Calm the kid down and get our guy up here," ponytail guy says calmly, his jaw twitching. He's not particularly big, but he doesn't look like someone I want to mess with, either.

"I'm not a kid, asshole!"

I snort out a laugh. "Mikey, you sending that guy up?" I call down, never taking my eyes from the army people.

"I'm sending Alek up first."

"Better pick up the slack," I bite out.

They both flare their nostrils, trying to contain their temper, but pick up the rope regardless. They grunt as they hold Alek's weight. I should help but I don't. I'm too cold, too worried, and too achy too do anything right now. I'm pretty much running on the last of my adrenalin. Within seconds Alek is climbing up over the side, his temper as bad as Emily's, and I worry that it will all start to kick off between our groups before we get Mikey and the unconscious guy out of the deader hole.

"Send our guy up, now," ponytail guy snaps.

"Send him up, Mikey," I call down.

A couple of minutes pass and Mikey calls up that he's ready to go. The two struggle to pull him out, grunting harder than when they had pulled Alek out. As the man's body reaches the top of the hole, the pair look at each other as if struggling to decide how best to get him out.

I go over and grip the back of his jacket, helping to pull him up and out as they give one last pull. He lies on his back, and I deftly untie the rope from around his waist and throw it back down. Alek stands guard as I drag the man's body away from the edge of the hole.

"Pull up our friend now," I say, leaning over the body.

"Is he okay?" the blonde asks.

I check the man's pulse and then the gash on his head. It's deep but I reckon he'll be fine. "Seems fine. Just unconscious." I slap him lightly across his cheek to try and wake him. "Hey, wake up."

I hear them grunting behind me, presumably as they pull out Mikey. The man stirs on the ground but doesn't come around right away; however, after a few more taps on his cheek, he stirs again.

"You could have killed him!"

I turn at the sound of shouting. Mikey is as gore-covered as the rest of us, but more pissed off. I don't think he realizes what he's covered in, or he doesn't give a shit. Me? I want to get cleaned up of this gore before Emily realizes.

The man on the ground murmurs something and I look back and see his eyes flutter open.

"Hey," I say.

"Hey." He smiles up at me. His smile turns into a frown and then quickly changes into a grimace. "Fuck, my head hurts."

I smile. "Getting hit by a brick will do that to you."

He offers a smile back. "A brick? That's a new one. My ex liked to throw pans and the odd frying pan at me, but never bricks."

I choke on a laugh. I don't want to find him funny—I want to be angry at him—but he has a certain kind of charm that I can't ignore.

He blinks once or twice and winces. "The fact that you haven't tried to eat me yet suggests that you're not a rotter," he continues.

I consider it for a moment. "Yeah, I'll let you go with that assumption."

"I'm James." He smiles again; his hand tentatively touches his head. "Is it bad? Will I live, doctor?"

I do laugh this time. "I'm no doctor, but I think you'll be fine. Well, as long as my friends don't go ape shit and kill you all, that is."

His brown eyes look over my shoulder. "Well, let's see if we can calm this situation down, then, shall we?"

I help him up slowly. "Please."

The two groups turn to look at us as James leans on me. "Dizzy," he whispers.

"I gotcha," I reply.

"Rachel, Michael, calm down, please. I'm fine. Nothing a shot of whiskey can't solve anyway." He leans harder on me and closes his eyes.

Everyone has fallen silent. "He's going to be fine," I say, trying to break the tension. I'm not the soft touch kind of girl, but I look at his two friends imploringly, seeing that they have guns trained on us. "He's fine," I repeat.

"You a doctor now?" blondie snaps. She struts toward me, gun raised, and the commotion starts up again. "Let go of him."

Mikey telling her to put down her gun, ponytail guy telling Mikey and Alek to shut the fuck up—even Emily is chiming in with her own F-bombs. It's all very shouty and loud, and I'm so incredibly fucking tired by this point, and wish someone would call a time out on the situation.

"I have no intention of letting James go. For one, I'm almost sure that he couldn't take his own weight right now and would fall over. And two, he's the only leverage we have. So back the fuck away from me," I say as calmly as I can, but with enough edge to my voice for her to know that I'm serious.

Rachel doesn't move, doesn't cock an eyebrow or come back with a snarky remark—nothing at all for me to work with. Her gun stays trained on me, and I'd be lying worse than Bill Clinton if I said I wasn't scared.

"I'm sorry about this," I say to James as I pull out my machete and hold it against his throat. "I really am, but I'm not about to die today. Not like this."

Rachel stops moving forward but keeps her gun trained on me. "I'll put a bullet through your brain if you don't let him go, RIGHT NOW!" she yells, ratcheting up the tension by another ten decibels. At least I have her attention now.

"Rachel, I'm fine. Stop this before someone gets hurt," the man next to me pleads.

Rachel either doesn't hear him or doesn't care much for his opinion, and continues to shout at me. "I said, let go of him."

"I'm not going to do that!" I yell back, joining in with the shouting. If you can't beat 'em, join 'em, as the saying goes.

I press the machete closer to his throat, until the blade is resting against his Adam's apple. "Again, I'm sorry about this," I murmur to him. "Back away, right the fuck now," I yell at her again.

I hear Mikey and Alek shouting over the top of the other guy—Michael, I think he was called—but I can't make out what any of them are saying because everyone is shouting so much. What gets me is that no one seems to be concerned with attracting deaders. I take my eyes off Rachel for a second to check on the others as a scuffle breaks out between Alek and Michael. Both are strong, Alek having pure street fighting skills—skills that he probably honed while with Fallon's crew—but ponytail guy knows his shit without a doubt and has him pinned to the ground in under a minute. Mikey swings his machete wildly and I look away, not wanting to see what will happen next. I've seen this too many times. *All we wanted was to get somewhere safe, somewhere warm,* is all I can think sadly. I squeeze my eyes closed at the sound of a scream.

Rachel takes that opportunity to charge at me, her gun still raised as she squeezes the trigger, even as James shouts next to my ear. It all happens too quickly.

"No, Rachel, don't!" James shouts loudly, too loudly, even though I know it must hurt his head to do so. He pushes me away from him as I hear her gun fire, and I fall to the ground with a heavy thud, the air leaving my lungs and making me gasp.

"Nina!" I hear Emily scream my name but I don't see anything but dirt and snow, and fuck me I can't breathe.

Something hits my back, pushing my face further into the ground, and I cry out and try to push up, but the weight is so heavy and my arms feel so weak. I can still hear Emily screaming, and I can hear shouting coming from both male and female, and then I hear another shot ring out.

TWENTY-ONE

Trees pass by me in a blur, stark of leaves and foliage, their branches crudely piercing the snow-filled sky like rotten fingers dipped in vanilla ice cream.

I think back to simpler times, to days gone by when life revolved around work, not survival. When the worst I had to worry about was paying the mortgage on time, and if I could afford to redecorate or buy that fancy new sofa. I loved that house—all brick and white wooden paneling. A small garden, which I tended to each weekend with my husband Ben. I miss Ben, each and every day; though his face grows distant, his memory is still strong inside me. I am the reason he is dead.

Work was my life. I never had much time for anything else, no matter how much Ben pleaded with me, no matter how many times he asked me to spend more time with him. Work was my priority—meeting deadlines, becoming the company's star employee. That was all I thought about. Well, that and my little garden. *You don't live to work*, Ben used to say, *you work to live*. I never saw the difference—

never understood—even though I knew the saying well.

I understand now.

"He's crashing." A voice interrupts my thoughts, both bleak and enlightening. *"Someone help me, he's bleeding out."*

I drift away on scattered thoughts. I understand now, because these days, I really do work to live. There is no downtime, no time for anything other than survival. Going from one drama to the next struggling for food, for clothes, for stupid, trivial things that I once took for granted.

Struggling, struggling, struggling.

"We're gonna lose her." The voice rings in my ears and I force my eyes to open. I only see blinding white light and burning pain, so I swiftly close them again.

Ben. He would have been good at this, this survival thing. If I wouldn't have killed him. Me, I'm no good at it. I'm surviving, but barely. Or am I? Is this surviving? Living like this? It doesn't seem like much of a life that I've led in the years that have gone by. Maybe it would be easier to give up, to just let go of it all. All the pain, all the sorrow. Say my goodbyes and drift away…

A piercing humming aggravates every last nerve, setting my teeth on edge. It makes my brain hurt. I want it to stop.

"Nina!" A voice. I know that voice. *"Nina!"* I want to tell them to stop crying. It's okay, whoever you are. I'm okay with this. I'm ready to go, ready to say my goodbyes to this world and meet Ben in the next. I'm tired. So fucking tired of it all. I can't do this anymore.

I can feel Ben's hand gliding over my body. I'm lying in bed, turned on my side, and his hand is stroking up the gentle curve of my hip, across the dip of my waist and up to my shoulder. I open my eyes and smile, turning to look over my shoulder at him. *I know what you want*. I smile. Only…it's not Ben. It's Mikey. I smile at him and he smiles back. A simple gesture, but it offers so much comfort.

"I've stopped the bleeding, I've got a weak pulse." Voices, lots of voices. *All talking in riddles.*

"And the woman?"

"We're doing everything we can."

Mikey smiles at me, leaning over to kiss me. He presses my back into the bed and I wrap my arms around his neck, and I wonder, *is this goodbye?*

TWENTY-TWO

My eyes flutter open.

The room is dark and warm, and my thoughts swim and mush together as I try to pick up on something familiar. Dark shapes surround me—taunting me, almost—and making my heart pound in my chest. The moon shining on the opposite wall is my only light source, from what I can tell. I try to move, but every muscle burns in pain. Well maybe not *every* muscle; I've always been a drama queen.

I close my eyes and take deep breaths as I ground myself in the room. A soft beeping to my left, a soft beeping to my right, a tick of a clock. My breath, in and out, in and out, in and out.

A pretty woman with light green eyes, which in the darkness remind me of cat eyes, the dim lighting reflecting from them and making them almost glow. She has brown hair tied back into a low ponytail, which falls onto her shoulder as she leans over me and smiles. Even in the dark, her face is soothing and I know I have nothing to fear from her. She pulls out a needle and injects it into an IV line, and within a few moments I feel the world growing hazy and I go numb and slip back to sleep.

I open my eyes and look across at the man called James. He's still sleeping. He sleeps a lot; his wound was much worse than mine. The bitch called Rachel comes to see him often. She doesn't talk and she doesn't look my way. It's almost like she blames me for her being so trigger-happy. Go figure that shit out.

Lucky me, guess I made a new friend, as usual. Thank God she's not here today, but Becky—my sort-of nurse—is. She smiles at me and heads back out of the room carrying various things.

"Nina."

I look up as Emily comes in, Alek following closely behind her. She rushes to my bedside, smiling, and leans over and kisses my forehead. I roll my eyes at her with a smile. She knows I can't fight her off right now, and she's taking full advantage of that fact.

"Get off me and help me with my pillows," I say through dry lips.

I sit up slowly and she comes around and plumps them. I shuffle backwards as she passes me some water, and I take huge, greedy gulps of it. I can reach it for myself, but I keep forgetting to. Time seems to have stopped for the last couple of days, and I've finally had the time I wanted to sit and think and process everything that's happened without worrying that someone is going to come in and torture me, or deaders are going to burst in. It feels like I'm in some sort of limbo. Though my gunshot was a straight through and through, and it was only my shoulder so nothing vital was hit, I lost a lot of blood on the way here.

We made it to the army base, but this isn't quite how I expected to make it. I mean, I at least expected to make it here on my own two feet and not flung over Mikey's shoulder like an animal carcass. I shiver and pull the covers tighter around me.

"How are you feeling?" Emily asks, perching herself on the edge of my bed and looking at me with concern.

"Better," I croak out. I touch my shoulder tentatively. "It's definitely getting better."

"Couldn't have gotten much worse." She shrugs. "Could it, Alek?"

He nods, looking uncomfortable. He always does whenever he visits me—I'm guessing he was one of those types that hates hospitals and doctors—but he seems to follow Emily wherever she goes.

"Maybe." I look across at James. "How's he doing?"

"They think he'll be fine. The bullet hit some important stuff, but he's pulled through the worst of it," Alek says seriously, frowning at the prone body of James.

I sigh. "He seemed really nice. I feel like a real bitch, like this was all my fault."

"It was that blonde chick's fault, not yours. She shouldn't be so eager to shoot innocent people," Emily grumbles.

"Whatever, it's done now, and that Becky woman says it was just a graze. Nothing too serious." I bite down on my lip. My shoulder hurts like a bitch, and sure as hell doesn't feel like nothing serious, but I don't want Emily knowing that. "What's this place like?"

"This place is great." She waves a hand around, but she's still pouting. "Isn't it?" she looks up to Alek who nods and takes a steadying breath, looking like he wants to run far from this room. "You can go," she laughs. "I'll be fine. I know you have other things to do and I'll be here for a while."

"You sure?" he asks, already kissing her on the forehead. She nods and he waves goodbye and practically jogs out of the room.

I can't help but smirk and turn my attention back to Emily. "Mikey definitely had the right idea by coming here, smartass."

"Definitely," she agrees.

It looks like this place was set up as a safe spot at one point and equipped with all sorts of luxuries that we haven't been used to in a long time: showers with hot water, food—and not just MRE packs but real luxuries like chocolate cookies, and more importantly, safety. I haven't had the chance to experience most things yet, thanks to the stupid gunshot in the shoulder, but I'm definitely attempting a shower today, and perhaps a chocolate cookie or two. Okay, definitely two.

Of course the medical equipment is what saved both me and James— well, and Becky, of course. Emily told me how she helped Becky stitch me up, not even thinking about all the blood. She seems happy, and eager to learn, and Becky seems happy to have someone to help her— someone who wants to be here. They make a great little team.

"Well, I'm hoping that you're here to help me get out of bed. I want a shower and some food, and then I want to see this place for myself. I might need some help, though."

Emily smiles happily. "Sure."

She helps me up and out of bed, and carefully we make our way to some shower cubicles in another room, while she holds the back of my hospital gown together to hide my modesty. She helps me undress right down to my shabby, graying underwear, and I hear her gasp as she steps back, examining my body with a pained expression.

I look down and see the scars and bruises across my body, marks from the fall, from fighting deaders, from fighting the Forgotten. Scars from surviving, I guess. I reach out, take her chin gently in my hand,

and tilt her face up to mine.

"It's okay," I whisper.

She looks at me with tears in her eyes. "But, Nina…" Her hand reaches out and touches one of the deeper scars across my stomach, her finger tracing the jagged red line.

I smile at her. "I remember reading a quote once. It was something like *'your body is not ruined, you're a goddamn tiger who earned her stripes.'* These marks," I take her hand in mine, "these are my stripes, Emily, and these are my proof that I survived." I turn around, tears in my eyes. "They're the proof that no matter what or who tried to kill me, tried to take away who I am, I survived it." I turn back to her. "I'm not going anywhere."

She smiles back, her eyes warily gazing over the burn marks on my thighs and the rings around my wrists. She looks back at me somewhat more satisfied, nods her head firmly, and steps back.

"The water doesn't stay hot for long. Do you need me to help wash your hair?" she asks.

"Help me untie it. I should be able to do the rest."

She does as I ask and then she helps me to wrap Saran Wrap tightly over the top of the bandage on my shoulder. I wince—it stings like a bitch—but she does a good job of it.

"I'll be outside." She turns to leave. "There's some things for you near the sink."

I take a minute to examine the array of bottles—shampoos and body washes of all different scents—before picking the ones I want. I strip out of my dirty underwear and turn on the shower. I stare mesmerized for a second or two. It all seems so surreal: showers, shampoos. I stand underneath the water as it pounds my body, the heat barely noticeable, yet it's the most delicious and delectable feeling I've had for as far back as I can remember. I even sigh loudly.

The dirt pours away from me in rivers of black and brown; lumps of things that I don't even want to think about drain away. I try to keep my shoulder out of the water as much as possible, even though it's wrapped in the Saran Wrap. I grab a bottle of shampoo with my good hand, squeeze a good amount on my head, and begin to scrub it into my scalp. I rub until my fingers feel sore, and then I tip my head back and rinse the dirty suds away, taking a second to delight in the feel of warm...*ish* water running over my body. I grab a second bottle and squeeze the creamy orange liquid onto my hand, and gently rub it over my bruised and battered body. I rub every curve, crack, and part of myself that I can find, and as the water turns an icy cold, I quickly wash away the dirty bubbles.

I still find it therapeutic, even with the cold water, as if washing away the past couple of years will somehow make it easier. With every body part cleansed I feel better, stronger, and more like myself. Less a victim and more a warrior—perhaps truly believing the words I said to Emily.

When I can't take the cold any longer, I turn the shower off and wrap a towel around myself clumsily, making sure to dry my shoulder as I carefully unwrap the Saran Wrap from my bandage. It's a little damp, and I'm sure Becky will flip out about it, but it's not so bad. I step toward a mirror on the opposite side of the room and stare at my reflection. I'm almost unrecognizable from the woman I was before the apocalypse. I squeeze toothpaste onto a toothbrush that was left for me, and I scrub until all I can taste is blood mixed with mint. I struggle to brush my hair; the knots—even with the help of shampoo and conditioner—are huge, and I shout Emily in.

"What's up?" she asks as she comes in. I turn to her and she smiles.

"Wow, you look so much better."

"It's been a while since I've been clean," I chuckle.

"It makes such a difference," she says in amazement.

"All right," I grumble and frown. "I want some scissors: I need to cut this stupid hair," I say firmly.

"I can help get the knots out."

"No." I turn back to the mirror. "I want to cut it. It's too long for an apocalypse," I say. "Never thought I'd say those words." I lean over the sink, feeling tired and ready for some sleep, my body betraying me again. "Please, Em, get me some scissors."

I sit on a stool to rest and close my eyes as she goes to find some scissors. I feel myself ready to nod off, but she's back before I'm fully gone. I yawn and stand, taking the scissors from her as I try and decide how much hair I want to cut away.

Right now it's waist length, though I haven't worn it down for over a year, and so it's a mass of dark knots. I hadn't realized how long it had gotten, actually. I take a large handful of it, holding it shoulder height, and then realize that I can't cut it and hold it at the same time because of the restricted movements in my shoulder. Emily comes over without saying anything and takes the scissors from me. She looks me in the eye and I nod once before she begins to cut away my hair. She grimaces with each snip of the metal, but me? I feel like I have a new lease on life. As if cutting away the matted dark hair allows me to breathe again.

A part of my past falls away with each snip of the scissors, and again I feel stronger, less who I was, less a bitch with an attitude because of what I've been through and more a bitch because I want to survive in this new world.

And then it hits me: I *do* want to survive. I want to build a home and a community and not live day to day. I want to build the world back up from what it was, because this, right now, this isn't living, this is existing. And the two things are very different.

And damn it, I want to live.

I struggle back from the bathroom with Emily's help, still wrapped in my towel, feeling more like myself than I have in days—hell, longer in fact. I feel stronger and ready to take on the world. When I get back to my room, James is snoring soundly and Mikey is sitting on the edge of my bed. He looks up as I come in, and smiles. His face looks handsome and more like the carefree man I met so many months ago.

"Hey you," I say as I sit down next to him, letting my feet trail to the floor. Emily smiles at me and heads out, whispering a goodbye.

"Hey." He leans over and tentatively kisses me on the cheek. "I like this." He tugs on my hair gently and I smile. "How are you feeling?"

"Better. I'd like to get dressed today, see this place a bit." I stifle a yawn.

"If you think that you're up to it." He smiles again. His face is clean and clear of his scratchy beard, but a five o'clock shadow starting to grow back. His hair is still long or long for him. It suits him, but I miss his shaved head too. The shaved head seems more the man he was, not this pretense of a man.

I run my fingers through his dark waves. "Thought you were cutting this."

He presses his head into my hand, obviously enjoying my touch. "I'm gonna, just not had the time."

"Hmm." I watch him. "Is it busy out there?"

"Yeah, there's plenty to do. They have it pretty secure, though." He nods his head across to James. "How's he doing?"

"Better, I think." I look at the sleeping man that I've become fond of in the last couple of days. He's pale, but gaining some color every day. "We even got to talk last night."

"Oh yeah?" Mikey looks up at me, pulling my hand from his hair. "He have anything interesting to say?"

"We talked about life, I guess. Not really anything in particular." I shrug. "He's a nice guy, I like him."

"Oh?" Mikey smirks.

I smack his shoulder. "Oh shush, you know what I mean. Help me find some clothes. I need to start helping out and earning my keep around here." I swing my feet to the floor.

"Your other clothes were ruined..."

"My boots?" I interrupt.

"They're fine. I cleaned them up, gave them a polish, even put some new laces in them. The soles are beginning to go, though. You may need to accept the fact that they're not gonna last much longer." He looks at me, guilt evident on his face.

"They're fine," I snap, suddenly feeling my feisty self rising back up to the surface. I swallow the bitch back down; it's not his fault my boots have been to hell and back with me. "I appreciate you rescuing them." I offer a small smile.

Mikey hands me some army wear: green T-shirt, camouflage pants, and matching jacket—and best of all, thick socks. He passes me some underwear that I don't recognize; it's certainly not new, though. Graying bra and panties, not real sexy, but he handles them as if they are delicate silks all the way from Europe. I grin and he blushes. I don't bother to ask where they came from. They may look old, but at least they're clean.

"Little privacy." I raise an eyebrow and smirk.

"Oh shit, yeah, sorry." He stands and pulls a dull flowery curtain around my bed, and I slide on the ancient panties and pull on my bra. I can't fasten it so I shrug into my pants and poke my head through the curtain.

"Can I get some help?"

"Sure." He joins me behind the curtain, blushing even more when he sees my predicament.

I turn around, showing him my back as I cover my breasts with my hands. "Never figured you for a blusher." I chuckle.

"It's hot in here is all," he mutters as his fingers graze the skin on my back, sending goose pimples dancing across my flesh. I can almost feel his fingers trembling as he tries to hook the clasp on my bra. He curses under his breath as he struggles to fasten it and I let out another chuckle.

"Funny shit, huh?" he mutters grumpily.

"Uh huh." I grin "What is it that men find so hard about bras? I mean really, it's not that difficult—you just stick the hook through the little eyelet. Women do this every day without even being able to see what they're doing."

"They're just so…fiddly. Wait, I've nearly got it." I feel the bra become more secure around me. "Done." I can hear the smile in his voice.

I turn around to face Mikey. "Ta-da," I say with a grin. "Well done. Good boy, aren't you clever?" I laugh again.

Mikey's eyes travel to my now secured breasts, his cheeks reddening further. We stand there staring at one another for a moment, thoughts colliding, both unsure and yet certain of what we want all at the same time. Am I ready for this? I think of Fallon's men and I think of being behind the walls, and then I look into Mikey's face and see adoration and not anger or greed. Lust? Yes, very much so, but not the dirty lust of wanting to take something that isn't being freely given. Because I do so freely give myself to him.

I lean in to kiss him and he meets me halfway, pressing his lips against mine. It's sweet and soft; he's being gentle with me, and while I appreciate the sentiment, I know I have nothing to fear from him. I coax him on, kissing him more passionately until he pulls me roughly against him. I gasp in pleasure and pain, as the stitches in my shoulder tug from the movement, but the rest of my body swells with eagerness to be closer to him.

I continue to kiss him. My hands trail up and down his back as his tongue dances against mine, both eager and hesitant, yet this isn't something either of us can stop. Every movement of my shoulder sends a sharp pang of pain through it, but it doesn't stop me from grabbing at him. I moan into his mouth as his hands move to my hair and grip it gently, keeping me pressed against him.

His hands make their way down my back and to my ass cheeks and he pulls me closer, my chest heaving against his. His mouth moves to my neck, and he trails hot kisses from one side of my throat to the other.

"Mikey." His name slips out of my mouth for no reason other than to say it, to secure myself in the moment, that this is him—Mikey—and it's okay. This—us—is okay. My heart beats wildly in my chest, ready to explode, my temperature rising as the heat between us grows.

Mikey's hands move back to my hair, his fingers clasping the side of my head as he tips my face up to his. He looks into my eyes, the warmth radiating from him in waves of deep lust. His breath comes in pants as he presses his mouth to mine and kisses me again, gently pushing me until the backs of my knees hit the edge of the bed and I fall on to it, with Mikey following.

He looks at me and smiles, and then his mouth moves between my breasts and down to my navel, leaving wet kisses in his wake. His hands find my hips, and between gasping breaths he looks up to me with hooded, lust-filled eyes. I give him a tentative smile and a nod, letting him know that it's okay to keep going. Hell, it's more than okay, I realize. This man doesn't want to hurt me, would never hurt me. No matter what type of bitch-fest I throw at him, or how reckless I get, he continues to care about me.

His fingers work the button on my pants, popping it out of the hole, and then he begins to slide my pants down my legs, his hot breath on the inside of my thigh.

"Hello?"

Mikey jumps, and I giggle.

I swallow to catch my runaway breath before speaking. "You okay, James?" I call to him, feeling guilty that we were about to do the dirty while he lay in his sick bed next to me.

"I've been better," he replies.

I hold back another laugh as we both stand back up. Mikey looks decidedly frustrated as he hands me my T-shirt and helps me slip it over my head. I hiss in pain as I shrug it down over my shoulder.

"You okay in there?" James calls out.

Mikey sticks his head around the curtain. "She's fine, man, she's getting dressed."

"Oh, oh right, sorry."

I smirk and pull the curtain back. "He was just helping me, since I can't lift my arm yet. Damn shoulder makes it hard to do on my own." I push Mikey and grin. "Stupid ass."

James smiles. "Any chance one of you could hand me the water?

Feeling mighty thirsty over here."

"Sure." I help him sit up and hand him the water. "You want me to get Rachel for you?"

He takes a big drink, finishing the entire glass in only a couple of gulps, and hands it back to me. "Told you I was thirsty."

"You can say that again."

"And yes, if you would, that would be great. She's still feeling guilty about the whole nearly killing me thing." He shrugs but I see the amusement in his face.

"And she should. She damn near killed us both." I hold up a hand when he tries to protest. "It's fine, I'll play nice, don't worry so much."

I sit in the chair and Mikey helps me put on my socks and boots, and I'll be damned if they don't look as good as new. I check the underside and see what he means about the soles of them, though: the tread is nearly worn away. I'm definitely not going to get much longer out of them—maybe a couple of months, tops. They've served me well in this hellish world, I guess.

I put the thought to one side and together Mikey and I head out. "Be right back, James."

"I'll be here." He laughs. "Oh, and Nina?"

I look back in. "Yeah?"

"See if you can find me a chocolate cookie." He grins.

I roll my eyes and laugh. "Sure thing."

The hallway is gloomy; small lights have been set up on strings all along the top, but they don't do much to light the way. Several doors lead off from here, but most are closed. As we pass them, Becky looks out of one.

"Look after my patient," she says to Mikey.

"Will do," he replies, and we continue toward the main exit.

Mikey slips behind me with my jacket and I shrug it on. As we near the door at the end of the short hallway, my breath becomes more evident in the air, and a small sliver of light shines from under the door.

Mikey reaches for the handle, pressing down on it. It screeches, metal against metal, and then there is blinding light as my eyes adjust to the white world outside.

"Jesus, snowed a bit while I was out, huh?" I say without any humor.

"Just a bit, yeah," he replies.

Everywhere I look is white. The entire world drowned out by snow, the earth is still and quiet for now. Around us are various brick buildings of all sizes. I look at Mikey.

"I'm hoping one of those is a mess hall." I nod to one of the other structures.

"Always hungry." He laughs. "That's my girl."

TWENTY-THREE

T he mess hall is a mixture of heat and the smell of cooked food. It's a delicious sensory overload as the scent of potatoes, meat, vegetables and gravy invades my nose and makes my head swim.

"Have I died and gone to heaven?" I ask in seriousness.

"Nope, this is just what happens when people work together." Mikey shrugs. "Come on—let's get you something to eat. You're all skin and bones."

I raise an eyebrow at him, but he only chuckles and puts a warm hand on my lower back to guide me toward the food. He grabs a tray as we get close and places two plates on it, loading all sorts of different things on each of them. It's a self-serve community, which I find surprising since I would have expected everything to be rationed out to everyone individually. He pours me a glass of fresh water and then leads us to a table, placing the tray on it and then pulling out my chair for me.

I smirk. "Turning into a real gentleman, Mikey. What's that all about?"

"Gentleman? Me? No way." He smiles. "Aah, shit, I forgot the forks, I'll just be a sec." He strides off to a small stand and grabs what he needs.

I can't help but pick at the delicious food on my plate with my free hand, delighting at the feeling of warm food traveling down my throat. I lick my fingers with a sigh.

"You're an animal—and here I was thinking that you were a lady." He chuckles as he comes back and sits down.

I grin. "Me, a lady? Well, that's as ridiculous as me calling you a gentleman." I take the fork and start to eat. "This...is...so...good," I mumble between mouthfuls.

The food barely touches the hunger inside me as I scoop, chew, swallow, and repeat until my plate is empty. I pick up my glass and down the water, and then struggle to contain a burp.

Mikey is still eating. He's not going easy on his food, either, which just goes to show how hungry I must have been for me to finish before him. "That was so good," I say, more to myself than him.

I take a proper look around us, taking in everyone else in here. There's maybe ten or so people, all sitting at different tables, eating greedily. The sounds of silverware upon plates and low mutterings fill the space. Occasionally eyes glance my way, the odd smile even gets thrown, but everyone seems to be so focused on eating right now that I'm generally ignored. It's fine by me; I'm not in the mood to chit-chat right now.

"You okay?" Mikey places his fork on his plate and gulps his water down.

I nod. "Yeah, this place seems great. Weird, but great."

"Weird?"

"Yeah. Civilized, I guess," I chuckle.

"I try to take my girl to all the nice places," he laughs back. "You want coffee, or more food?"

"Coffee? Fuck yeah."

He laughs again and wanders off to get the infamous coffee for me. My mouth waters in expectation.

"Hey."

I look up at the sound of someone's voice. It's the trigger-happy blonde, Rachel. *Awesome. Just as my day was getting good.*

I roll my eyes. "Hey."

She sits down in Mikey's chair. "Can I sit for a minute?"

"Seems like a dumb question, given that you already did," I snap.

"I wanted to apologize, you know, for—"

"Shooting me? Nearly killing me? Which one?" I raise an eyebrow. God, it feels good to speak my mind.

She doesn't flinch at my harsh tone, though. Instead, she huffs. "It's a graze."

"Well, hand me a gun and let me shoot you then," I snap.

She looks away, her face statuesque, not showing any emotions. Her hair is tied back with a bandana and she fiddles with it nervously while she contemplates what she wants to say, but I don't have the time or the patience for her.

"Great, well, thanks for the dandy apology," I huff out, scraping my fork along my plate to get some leftover gravy on it.

"It's Nina, right?" she asks, looking back to me. I notice then that her eyes are different colors: one is a mixture of green and brown, and the other blue and brown. It's subtle, but gives her an almost hypnotic stare.

I continue to stare. "Yeah. What of it?"

She huffs and stands, her chair scraping back as she does. "Forget it. I'm sorry is all I wanted to say. I know now that you're all okay—not

175

assholes or whatever. I did what I did to try and protect us. I'm not sorry about that." She starts to walk away without looking back.

"Rachel?"

She looks over her shoulder at me, and I bite down on my lip.

"James wanted to see you." I look back down at my plate before she can say anything else.

I feel guilty for a minute, but then the burning in my shoulder returns and the anger glows deeper again. Closing my eyes, I take a couple of deep breaths—some to calm my frayed temper and some to control the pain in my shoulder.

"Everything okay?" Mikey comes back and sits down, placing two mugs of steaming coffee in front of us. "I gave you cream and sugar—figured you could do with the glucose even if you don't normally take it."

I take the mug, my hands wrapping around the heat, and I stare into the milky brown, the smell wafting up to my nose and taking me back to another time. I think back to Steve, and the coffee he made for us when we were running from the Forgotten. I remember his chickens and his vegetable patch and his missing wife Jane.

"Hey." Mikey's hand touches my chin, wiping away the tears I hadn't realized I was crying. "What happened?"

I look back up to him, his handsome face full of concern and worry. "I'm fine. The smell," I nod toward the coffee, "brought back some memories." I bite my lip, not wanting to cry anymore—certainly not in front of a room full of strangers. I wipe away the tears and pick up my coffee and take a sip, savoring the taste of it.

Mikey returns his hand to his own mug and mimics my action. "Yeah, I get that. I've had a few of those types of moments recently too."

"Do you think...do you think Steve is dead?" I ask quietly.

Mikey frowns hard. "What do you mean? Of course he is. I mean, you saw him . . ." His words trail off. I know what he's thinking, of course. I was there and I saw the same as he did. The image of Steve being eaten alive, deaders dining on his innards as he swigged the last of his Jack is still very vivid.

"That's not what I mean." I look away guiltily. "I mean, do you think he's dead-dead or did he come back? He'd hate that, to come back as a deader." The last part of my sentence is almost whispered. "I can't help but think that we should have finished him off at least."

I look back at Mikey and his face is frozen in horror, possibly mimicking my own, but he doesn't say anything. It's something I've wondered for a long time now. I hope that Steve is truly gone.

We finish the rest of our coffee in silence, our thoughts consumed with the past and the present but never venturing to the uncertain future. Emily finds us as we're clearing our things away, and she wraps me in a hug.

"All right, all right, enough with the mushy crap." I scowl.

Emily laughs. "Whatever. There's a meeting in the recon center. I think everyone is supposed to go to it. I've gotta let everyone else know and I'll meet you there." She smiles and wanders off to the other people in the mess hall. She moves around the room and talks to them one by one, and they begin to clear away their things.

"Recon center?" I ask Mikey.

"Yeah, it's actually the old education center or something like that. They hold meetings there frequently, mainly to distribute jobs to everyone." He holds the door open and we head out, making our way across the frozen courtyard to another large brick building.

Inside are lots of chairs and benches distributed around a dimly lit room. There are windows on each side, but all the lower ones have been boarded up, and there are same lights are strung up around the room as everywhere else. Mikey leads me to a seat near the back, and we sit and watch everyone else come in and take their seats. Some are dressed in army camouflage, some in civilian clothing. I don't think it's an intentional thing to separate people—more like people are wearing what they feel comfortable wearing, I guess. I look down at my own clothes. I'd never considered joining the army, and still wouldn't, but these clothes are way better than my old threadbare ones. Even better than the zombie-gore-soaked ones I was wearing previously.

Fifteen or so minutes pass by before a man with light brown skin and jet black hair comes in and stands at the front of the room. He's wearing army wear, with several badges pinned to the front of his jacket. His face is stern, yet behind his steely façade is a warmth that shines through.

"That's Zee. He's been helping to run the place while James has been down for the count." Mikey whispers to me.

"James was running this place?" I ask. James had never mentioned that to me.

"Yeah, he was one of the founders," Mikey says.

"Founders?" This place is starting to sound like a damn cult.

Mikey nods a little impatiently and I drop the subject, instead looking around the room to get a better read on everyone. Most seem to be pretty rapt to Zee, watching with attention. There's a good mix of people from the looks of it, though I wonder how many wearing camouflage are actually army issued or are just normal people that lost everything like me.

Zee clears his throat. "Okay, so today's jobs have been listed on the board, but I'll give a brief rundown as usual." He coughs and unfolds a piece of paper. "So, we have Melanie and Mathew on latrine duties."

He looks up. "Sorry. Nova, Michael, and I will be on trap duty. Rachel and Julie, you're on weapons and ammo check. Susan and Jessica, you two need to be checking on food rations and the consignment shop, please. Becky, you and one of our newest members, Emily, are doing great over at the medical center, so keep that up." He turns the paper over and continues to read out everyone's jobs.

I look at Mikey. "This place seems pretty damn organized."

"It is," he replies earnestly.

"Seems too good to be true."

"Chill out. It's all good, Nina. Stop being so suspicious."

"Did you tell me to chill out?" I scowl.

"I'd also like to extend a warm welcome to our latest comrade and ally." Zee continues to talk.

I look up, knowing it's me that he's referring too. I feel the heat in my cheeks before I even glance around me and see everyone staring with hesitant smiles. I'm damn glad the room is dark.

"Hi," I say quickly and then lower my head, hoping to be absorbed into the darkness.

"Would you like to come and introduce yourself?" Zee offers.

"No!" I bark out a laugh. Zee's face remains unamused. "Umm, sorry. Yeah, sure." I stand, making sure to dig Mikey in the ribs for the grin that covers his face, and make my way to the front.

"It's Nina, right?" Zee offers his hand to me and I take it, giving it a small shake.

"Sorry, I'm not good at public speaking." I grimace.

He smiles, which immediately puts me at ease. "That's okay, this isn't a test. I'm glad to see you're up on your feet again. As soon as you feel ready and able, I'll add you to our list so you can help out. This is a big facility and it works by everyone contributing."

"Yeah, sure. I'm happy to help in any way."

"I'm sorry that you had such a bad introduction to our community," he continues. "We're not always gun-toting maniacs." He smiles again, glancing in the direction of the crowd, I'm sure looking at Rachel. "Well, not unless there are zombies or peace-hating criminals involved, anyway."

The crowd laughs. I laugh too, but my laugh is less manic and more nervous.

He's either talking about the Forgotten or some other crazy maniacs, and I don't like the sound of either one of them.

TWENTY-FOUR

After the meeting, Mikey takes me back to the medical center to pack up my things. Becky gives me a quick once-over, with Emily assisting her. They check my various cuts and bruises, and she re-bandages my shoulder—even takes a look at the scar on my cheek. Not much she can do for that, though. Fallon completely fucked me over with that one.

In her previous life she was a nurse, working in a hospital, which I find lucky. Upon further probing, I find that she was actually still in training. Apparently it puts people at ease to think she was fully qualified. Me? I'm just glad that she had at least some idea what she was doing when she patched me and James back up. Fully qualified or not, it's a hell of a lot better than leaving us both to bleed out.

"Keep that dry." She pins the bandage back in place and helps lower my T-shirt back down. "You'll need to come back every day to get your antibiotics and pain relief." Becky smiles. "I know it's a total pain, but we don't hand out full courses of antibiotics since it's all on rations and basically, if you lose it, we can't really afford to spare anymore."

"It's not a problem. I'll be coming to check on Emily and James every day anyway. I know how boring it can be lying there all day." I roll my eyes at Emily, who laughs. She's been intently watching everything Becky does.

"Are you saying my company wasn't riveting?" Becky says with a playful nudge.

"No," I laugh. "Not at all. I mean, yes it was, um . . ."

"It's fine, my bedside manner isn't what it used to be." She grins. "And I think he'll be fine. I hope in a couple of weeks he can go back to his home, too, but he'll need some help for a while."

I hop down from the bed. "So do I get the all-clear, then?"

"Perhaps not the all-clear, but more the *don't get shot again* orders, please." She packs her things up and looks up at me through her lashes and smiles.

"Like that's the sort of thing I get up to on my downtime," I snark.

Becky heads over to check on James's IV and Emily follows. Emily continues to watch over Becky, asking questions and learning, I guess. I'm happy to see that she may have found her little place in this new world, maybe becoming a future doctor or nurse in the medical center under Becky's guidance. It could be a great thing for her. I mean, we all have our parts to play, and I would be happier knowing that she was working here fixing people up instead of fighting deaders and gunning people down.

As we're leaving, Jessica is arriving, holding onto Rachel. Jessica offers me a smile even as she clutches her stomach and leans heavily on Rachel.

"Everything okay?" Mikey asks, following my stare.

"Fine," Rachel snaps and barges past us. "We just drank too much last night."

Mikey carries my backpack—thankfully gore-free—across the frozen encampment as we head over to the housing units. Previously, each home was decked out for various families, but a lot of the facility has been closed off to save with electricity and such. There aren't that many homes left in the open sections, and people are starting to bunk up and share. It's at this point that Mikey looks at me uncertainly.

He runs a hand across the back of his neck, his nerves showing as a warm blush rises in his cheeks, even in the cold air.

"Umm, I wasn't sure where you'd be wanting to sleep."

I grin, nerves fluttering in my stomach. "Sleep?" I ask with a cock of my eyebrow.

He looks at me, puzzled. "Umm, yeah. Like where do you want to sleep? The women's housing is over there," he points over to the left, "but there's family housing, and couples' housing. I wasn't sure if, you know . . ." He trails off.

"What?" I shake my head trying not to grin. "You weren't sure, what?" I furrow my brow in mock confusion.

"You know?"

"No. What?" I tease, trying to contain my grin.

"I wasn't sure if you . . ." He takes a deep breath. "Jesus, what is it with you? You always make me nervous," he says in a fluster.

I crack up laughing. "What? No other woman ever made you nervous, Mikey? Or you've just never met a strong woman before?"

He looks at me in all seriousness. "No, not like this. Not like you." He drags a hand down his face. "I sound like a fucking idiot. Damn you, woman." He laughs, but I can still hear the nerves in his laughter. "Do you want to share a unit with me? Like a couples' unit? "

"Like our first house?"

He looks horrified and then relaxes. "Well, yeah, I guess that's what it is." He shrugs, trying to appear casual.

I reach over on tiptoes and give him a quick kiss on the lips. "I would love to share a house with you," I laugh. "But don't ask me to marry you—I mean, I hardly know you!" I laugh again as he flushes bright red.

He smiles, all trace of nervousness vanishing. "Good. I mean, that's what I thought you'd say. Why wouldn't you want to?" He smirks, his demeanor all arrogant masculinity once again.

I roll my eyes. "Don't make me change my mind."

Our small house is just that: small. It has a brown front door with a boarded up window in it, brown brickwork, and a tiled roof. Inside there's a small kitchen with wood paneled cabinets and a small steel sink, a living room, bathroom, and a small double bedroom. The paintwork is dated and the furniture is old, but I love it.

"Homey," I state, keeping my poker face.

Mikey laughs and drops my bag on the floor by the bed.

I turn in a circle as I look around me. "I'm serious. You've really made this place your own." I grip the bottom of the dowdy-looking curtains.

Mikey sits on the edge of the bed, a smirk playing on his mouth. "You can see that, huh?"

"Oh yeah, totally."

He reaches out to me, his hands gripping the backs of my thighs, and pulls me closer to him. He looks up to me through dark lashes, and my heart skips a beat when he runs his tongue across his bottom lip as his eyes search my face for something.

Woot, there it is. Now it's my turn to smirk. I raise an eyebrow at him.

"I think this place could use a feminine touch," he says, slowly lying back and pulling me with him.

I look around mockingly. "Feminine touch? I don't see any feminine females around here." I place my hands on his chest and push up so we're not so up close and personal, though I can see that's his plan.

"You're all the feminine I need, baby." I start to eye roll at him, but he reaches up, placing his hand on the back of my head, and pulls my mouth to his. "Shut up now, Nina." I feel him grin as he kisses me, and I let him get away with having a smart mouth, for now at least.

I kiss him back fervently, gasping as he pulls at my clothes, sliding both himself and me out of our jackets and T-shirts. He runs cool fingers over my lean stomach, small white scars puckering the flesh. He frowns and trails his hands up to my breasts where he lowers the straps on my bra and leans in to kiss at my neck.

My head lolls to the side and I moan at the feel of his hot mouth on my cool skin. Memories surface of the last time we were together; the fear and death that came afterwards was life-changing, yet this is so much different. My heart races as I struggle to push the memories away, memories of death and violence, of greedy fingers and whips. I swallow, my breath catching in my throat.

"We don't have to do this if you're not ready. I can wait," he says.

I open my eyes and look at him. In his face is so much desire, but behind that is pain—pain in what he had to do, pain in what he had to witness.

"I want to." I shiver. The heat suddenly leaves me and cold drenches my soul.

Mikey lifts me and slides the covers from underneath us. He lays me back down and lowers the covers on top of us. "Let me make it right." His eyes wash over my face, his fingers stroking the long scar from my mouth to my cheek. "Let me give you a good memory and take away the bad."

I stare at him, rapt for his words.

"I want you to forget…" His words trail off. I know what he's trying to say, though. He doesn't need to say it. "I don't want you to think of them again, not like that. I want you to think of me now. Okay?"

I shake my head in amazement, finding it utterly bizarre and yet perfect that he should know exactly how I'm feeling. I frown, a deep furrow between my eyebrows, and he reaches up and strokes the frown, kissing my forehead until I stop.

"Let me try, at least," he pleads.

I nod, feeling ridiculously nervous, as if I'm doing this for the first time. I'd make a joke out of that thought, but the only thing I can focus on right now is him kissing my breast and taking my nipple into his deliciously warm mouth, and his hand shuffling my pants down.

I swallow again, trying not to choke on the golf ball in my throat as I let my hands go to his back, feeling the raised scars dancing across the surface of his flesh. With each scar I touch, I lose myself more, yet find myself in a new way. We're both broken and damaged, but we've found something in each other that makes the nightmares go away, at least for a little while.

I feel hungry for him, for his body and his touch, and I grip him, trailing nails down his back to add to his patterns of crisscross already there. I moan loudly as his fingers find my warmth, my head falling sideways on the pillow as I beg myself to relax and not panic—to enjoy this, enjoy him, loving my body and making it mine again.

I stare up into his face, his hooded eyes looking into mine as his tongue flicks across his lower lip. I tilt my mouth up to his and let his tongue invade me. Tasting his desire, his heat, as our mouths work together like a well rehearsed orchestra and his hands and fingers make my body supple under him. I moan against his mouth as his hand is swapped for something more and I gasp, breathing through it and relishing in the pleasure as he presses into me, finally feeling no fear or pain, finally letting go and letting myself belong to him.

Because I don't need to fear anymore. This is Mikey.

I wake to kisses pattering across my shoulder, and I grin before my eyes even open.

"Go away, I'm sleeping," I murmur, burying myself beneath the covers.

"I'm on duty. I have to leave in twenty." He lands more soft kisses on me and I giggle. *Jesus fuck, when did I become a giggler?*

I open my eyes. "Duty?"

He nods, his hand moving across my stomach and over my hips.

"What kind of duty?" I ask, slapping his hand away.

He shrugs. "You know, guard duty. We all have to do it at some point."

That makes sense; I guess I hadn't really thought about it before. "So there's always someone on guard?"

He nods. "Yeah, two actually." He leans over to kiss my mouth, and I briefly kiss him back before I dive out of bed, leaving Mikey pouting.

"You didn't really show me everywhere before. If you're going off on guard duty, I need to know what I'm going to do. I can't just sit here like the good little wife and do nothing." I pull my clothes on, struggling with my top until Mikey comes and helps.

"I would never expect you to be a good little wife, Nina. You're far too naughty for that." He wiggles his eyebrows at me.

"Urghhh, did you just wiggle your eyebrows at me suggestively?" I scowl.

"Yeah, sorry," he laughs.

I hold up a hand. "I'm serious, you ever do that again and I'll kick your ass. That was," I swallow down pretend bile, "disgusting." I shake my head at him and walk out of the room, eager to inspect our new home, and I guess new community too.

I look out the downstairs window, seeing the snow falling again, and huff. I never did like winter; making snowmen and having snowballs fights did nothing for me. Give me glaring sunshine and a light breeze any day.

"I'll take you over to the consignment shop first, get you loaded up with some clothes, coats, and shit. You know," Mikey shrugs, "I'm sure they'll have some girly crap there too." He smiles like he's hit the nail on the head.

"Girly crap?" I repeat, slipping into the jacket he hands me.

"Yeah."

I shake my head at him. "Do you know anything about women? Anything at all?"

He goes to answer but I cut him off by walking out the front door, checking the number posted on it as I go. He locks the door on his way out, and jogs to catch up to me, handing me a key.

"Sorry." He scratches at his chin, his five o'clock shadow, now more like a ten o'clock one.

"It's like you got laid and turned into a hormonal teenager," I snap. "Girly shit."

He pulls a hat out of his pocket and pulls it down over my head. "Sorry, it's been a while since I've done this." He smiles, and I'll be damned if all isn't forgiven.

"So what's the consignment shop?" I ask, moving on from his relationship fails.

"That's where you trade shit for shit." He rolls his eyes. "Sorry, where you trade something for something else. Since currency is basically worthless these days, people trade items or skills or whatever."

"Oh, okay," I say without much conviction. I don't have anything to trade, and I'm not quite up to working yet, either.

We walk the rest of the way in silence, the snow falling all around us. Occasionally we see someone run from one building to another, but it's beginning to get dark now so I can't make out who they are. I worry for a second about deaders, but then remember that Mikey said there was always someone on duty and the place is secure all the way around. I can't help but wonder, though, how secure everything is.

People become lax and lazy when they think everything is safe; look at every situation I've been in since I left the walled city. No good can come from laziness. For now, at least, I'll have to let my trust be in Mikey. I couldn't fight even if I wanted to. To be fair, he's earned my trust. But these other people? I'm not completely sure. I certainly don't want to be putting my life in their hands just yet.

TWENTY-FIVE

We make it into the consignment shop just as my fingers are starting to go numb. It's still early, though it's already getting dark. We both stamp our feet as we enter the little shop to get rid of excess snow.

I look around me in surprise. I don't know what I expected—a bustling supermarket-style store? A thrift shop full of racks of clothing and bric-a-brac? Perhaps, but though the shop is large, virtually every shelf is empty. I look at Mikey with a raised eyebrow, but he barely acknowledges it.

A small woman with coppery red hair is talking to a slim blonde. They're laughing about something—something X-rated, by the dirty laugh the blonde has. They stop when we come in, and the blonde waves bye to the redhead.

She passes us, giving Mikey a once over.

"Yes?" I snap.

She smirks and keeps on going, not in the least bit intimidated by me.

"That's Melanie—you don't want to mess with her." Mikey chuckles. "She's got an attitude worse than yours."

"Sounds like we could be related," I huff.

The woman from behind the counter comes over to us; her smile is wide and her eyes are friendly, and I automatically warm to her.

"Hey, Susan." Mikey wraps her in a big bear hug and she laughs and hugs him back. "This is Nina." He gestures to me. "She needs some stuff—anything, really. We kinda lost everything." He shrugs.

Susan smiles again and holds out a hand for me to take. I do, too—no idea why, but she has that motherly quality about her that says *I'll look after you,* but with an equal edge of *don't fuck with me.*

"We got a couple of things in today—nothing big, though. There wasn't much on the scavenge, since they had to come back early." She leads me over to the front of the shop, where a till once sat. It's been moved now, however, and along the top are neatly folded piles of clothes and various baskets, each with an array of different things like creams, brushes, and makeup.

"They came back early?" Mikey asks.

"Have a look through, my love, see if there's anything you like." She turns to Mikey. "Yes, there was an accident. No one got hurt, but they ran into trouble on the road. Some assholes spoiling for a fight." She tuts and gives me a smile like I'm some blonde bimbo that doesn't know what's going on.

"What kind of assholes?" I bite out.

I feel Mikey's hand on my shoulder, and with that small gesture I realize he hasn't told them that trouble is chasing us down.

Susan flips her red hair off her thin shoulders. "Oh, you know the type—opportunists looking for a fight." She purses her lips. "There's always someone wanting to destroy the peace, isn't there?" Her eyes are downcast, her fingers probing some of the items in the baskets without thought.

"Mikey." I look at him and he nods. I don't even need to say anything else; he gets it. He knows what's running through my mind, what's worrying me.

"What is it, my loves?"

We both look at Susan, and guilt pours from me. Mikey gives my shoulder a little squeeze again. I don't know if he's trying to get me to shut up or trying to comfort me—either way, I'm stumped by what to say. On the one hand, I want to warn everyone here of the trouble we might have brought to their door; but on the other, we won't survive if they ask us to leave. It's winter and we have nowhere to go. That and we're in the middle of nowhere, meaning we'd be completely fucked.

"Nothing," I say, biting down on my lip. "It's always worrisome when you hear of trouble." I shrug.

I don't think she's entirely convinced, but she drops the subject either way.

"Well, no one was hurt—well, no one in *our* team—but they decided to call it a day anyway. The roads are getting worse out there and I think it just about wore them out getting as far as they did. So anyway, we got a few things, but nothing fancy."

"How do I pay for this?" I ask, checking through the clothes. I unfold a baggy gray sweatshirt. It reminds me of something my father used to wear, and I decide I want it.

"We trade," she says with a smile, her eyes flitting from me to Mikey. "We all take turns in the shop, and whoever is here when a shipment comes in gets the goods. If you want anything, you have to trade either something you have or something that you can do for me." She smiles widely again. Her brown eyes have a little sparkle to them that I haven't seen in a long while. "It's like recycling."

"So, if I want this," I hold up my sweatshirt and then grab a toothbrush and some socks, "and these. What do you want?" I look at Mikey, who's smiling too. Jesus, I feel like I'm in the Twilight Zone or some shit. "Stop smiling you two, you're weirding me out." I scowl.

"Mikey already covered whatever you needed." Susan pats his hand. "He's a good man, this one. You keep hold of him. Good ones are hard to come by these days."

I choke on a laugh. "No seriously, I want to buy my own crap."

"It's already done," Mikey states nonchalantly.

"I don't need you looking after me, Mikey," I snap.

"Whatever, Nina, it's done. So get what you need."

I glare at him but he doesn't budge, his jaw working slightly as we have a stare-off in the middle of the shop. I'd be embarrassed if I wasn't so pissed off with him.

I turn to Susan when I realize that he isn't going to buckle. "What did he trade?"

She looks from me to Mikey nervously. "I don't want to get in the middle of anything."

"Just pick your crap and let's go—I'm on duty tonight."

I ignore him. "Susan, what did he trade you?"

"A week's worth of reading," she says rather coyly.

"Pardon me?" I look between them both.

"I like to be read to. My daughter used to do it for me before…well, before everything. It was my favorite thing to be curled up in front of a roaring fireplace, her soft voice reading to me," she says wistfully.

"Oh." I look at Mikey, who shrugs. "Well, I can read to you, I guess. I mean, I like to read. It's been a while since I sat down to read anything, though. Like years." I force out a laugh.

Susan reaches under the counter and pulls out a tattered-looking book. My eyes nearly bug out of my head when I see what it is.

"Are you serious?" I ask in horror. I don't even want to touch the damn cover, never mind *read* it.

"Oh yes, my love." She nods and smiles that pretty, wide smile of hers again. "I love reading zombie horror books. It's not quite the same as living it, so it's nice to be able to close the book when I've had enough of it. Not like this world, where it's day in, day out."

I give the scruffy book a cold, hard look, the torn up zombie on the cover snarling up at me almost mockingly. "Fine, when do we start?" I ask with a grimace.

The inside of Susan's house is cluttered with two other people's belongings. Her home is a little larger than ours, with three bedrooms instead of the two in ours. I realize how lucky Mikey and I are to have a place to ourselves and wonder for how long it'll be like that.

"Have a seat, my love, I'll fetch us a drink and get everything set up." She wanders off to the kitchen and I sit down on the crowded sofa.

I fidget, unable to get comfy, and stand back up, moving the cushion I had been sitting on and subsequently finding a high-heeled shoe underneath.

"What the fuck?" I mutter to myself, and put it on the floor as I sit back down.

"Don't mind the mess, it's all Max's." Susan hands me a cup of creamy coffee.

In my old life I wouldn't have drunk coffee after six p.m., in case the caffeine kept me awake, but these days it's such a rare commodity that I couldn't give a shit if it was midnight, I'd still be drinking it. And without a doubt, I'll still be sleeping tonight. It's only when I get it to within distance of my mouth that I realize it is something so much better.

"Holy shit, are you some kind of crazy witch?" I take a sip, letting the smooth, watered-down powdered chocolate melt down my throat.

Susan giggles. "I've heard that before—mainly from my ex-husband, Ken. He was a total shit to me, but it's okay, he got his." She taps the side of her nose and I snort.

"He did, huh?" I take another mouthful. "Dear God, this is heavenly."

"Oh yes, watched that selfish bastard getting eaten by a zombie or two. Oh, it brought me such joy to see him so miserable." Susan gets a faraway look in her eyes, a smile playing on her lips, and I know—I just fucking know—that this woman is a hundred percent serious and possibly a little crazy. But hey, as long as I stay on her good side, I guess it's okay. Plus, who am I to judge?

She throws some logs into the small fireplace and lights them. The fire take hold and begin to dance and flicker; orange flames lick the wood and spark and pop. I stare, transfixed by the fire as the hot chocolate warms both my stomach and the palm of my hand that holds it.

"Are you ready?" Susan's voice interrupts my blankness.

I shake myself out of the weird starey thing I'm doing and take a last drink of the hot chocolate before putting it down on the wooden table next to me.

"Sorry, yeah, let's do this." I open the book, carefully handling the torn cover and trying to make sure my fingers don't touch the zombie in blue overalls. It's childish, but it looks like it's banging on a brown front door much like the one to my own house, which kinda creeps me out even more. "I don't get why you like this stuff." I scowl, trying to read the author's name on the front—T.W. something-or-other.

"Just read it or I'll take the sweatshirt back," she snaps, but there's playfulness in her eyes—at least I sure hope that's what it is. She could have slipped a bit of vodka in her drink, for all I know about her.

With a shrug I begin, somewhat reluctantly, reading what is literally my worst nightmare. As the pages turn, and the characters dwindle from either being eaten or turned into one of the living dead themselves, I begin to see what she means: when things get real bad for the characters in the book, we can take breaks, and we do. Some are for drinks and snacks, some are to top up the fire with fresh logs, and some are for bathroom breaks. Each time it becomes clearer to me not only how much I've missed reading, but that she's right: reading about the zombie apocalypse is so much better than actually living it.

I thought it would be traumatic, but it's not. In some ways, reading about it feels like we're mocking it, having a pissing contest to see what's worse—real life or this fucked up little book. Of course when the shit really hits the fan we can close the book, but in real life we have to keep on going. Keep on fighting, slaying, and surviving. Doing whatever it takes to survive.

I stretch out my back, feeling a couple of the bones pop and crack as I do, and take a good long drink of my water. My eyes are getting sore from all the reading, and my throat feels dry even after I drink, but I need to finish this last chapter; I need to find out what happens with the woman in the book—otherwise I won't sleep tonight. Does she succumb to death like her husband did? Or does she make it to the safe haven?

However, at the end of the chapter it's another cliffhanger, and I groan, knowing I won't be able to read the next chapter tonight. I've been reading for two hours straight and I need to sleep. I look over at

Susan, who's curled up in a brown armchair by the fireplace, her head resting against a cushion, and realize that she's sleeping. I curse myself for not realizing sooner.

I fold the corner of the page over and place it on the table, ready for tomorrow and I wonder where her other roomies are: Max and whatever the other one is called—she never actually told me, and of course I didn't ask.

I slip on my boots and coat, grab my new backpack with all my new gear in it, and head out the door. I have no idea what time it is. It could be nine p.m. or it could be midnight—all I know is it's dark and cold and incredibly quiet out here. I stand in the road and strain my ears for any sound, but after a couple minutes of the wind biting at my earlobes, I head home, the snow crunching under my boots and my chin tucked low to my chest.

After a couple of wrong turns, I make it back to our little house, go inside, and head straight up to bed. I climb the stairs, only slipping my boots and coat off as I enter the bedroom. I put them next to the bed, ready to grab at a moment's notice; I guess old habits die hard—hell, better than dying...hard. I snicker at my own joke and then look at the empty bed, reaching my hand across the cold covers.

Mikey isn't home and the bed looks kinda big and cold without him in it. My chest aches with discomfort, an oddness creeping over me. This is home. Mikey and I are...a couple. It all suddenly seems too surreal, too weird to be true.

Home.

Mikey.

I burst into tears, unable to hold it in any longer. I cry for hours. I cry until my throat burns and my eyes feel like they are full of sawdust. I cry and wail for no reason and for everything. I cry to get it out of my system once and for all and then I cry until I fall asleep from the exhaustion.

And then I dream of struggling to survive in an apocalyptic world, only I can't close the book on this life, this story. I'm the main character in it, and my life is forever trapped within the pages of this torment. I'm running, forever running to and from things, forever fighting and struggling and only just surviving.

I wake myself several times in the night, feeling the side of the bed for Mikey, but each time finding it empty. The last time I wake, the sun is beginning to rise and a faint glow shines through the curtains. I reach an arm out to Mikey's side of the bed, my hand touching warm flesh. I shuffle over to him, draping an arm across his middle, and snuggle myself into his warm back.

Finally I'm able to sleep without feeling tormented.

TWENTY-SIX

"**S**o then this little fat teenage kid turns around and tries to take my gun from me." Nova laughs as she spoons some more porridge into her mouth and quickly swallows. "So I turn around and give the little shit a good beating. The entire time he's still trying to get at my gun. I'm like give it the fuck up! The little shit is clinging onto the barrel of my gun, and doesn't let go until I break his nose, and then guess what he says?" She spoons more into her mouth, tossing her long red hair from back from her shoulder.

"What?" asks Max, the tall, blonde, Barbie wannabe, her pink lips pouting. She's a little made up for my tastes, but that's not such a bad thing, I guess; it's just unusual in this world to actually give a shit about appearances.

Whenever we're in the same room, she makes me question myself. It's not her fault, it's mine—and the world's, I guess. Yeah, let's blame the world, that's a better pill to swallow. And to be fair, she's really nice. Not too bright, but she tries hard. I mean, I wouldn't want her on my team—girl can't fight for shit, but she tries. Actually the more I think about it, the more I wonder how she isn't dead. Then I see Constance staring doe-eyed at Max and know she's the reason Max is still alive.

"He shakes his pudgy little fist at me," Nova mimics, "and says, 'lady, you're just lucky that my crew ain't here.'" Nova laughs loudly. In fact, the noise could probably be considered a guffaw. She stands up, placing a black-booted foot on her chair, and pulls out a twelve-inch hunting knife before slamming it down into the table. It wobbles but stays stuck up like a little flagpole. "I said, 'little boy, you better run before I gut you and your motherfucking crew like pigs.'" She laughs again. "Kid ran off faster than his legs could carry him, went flying face first into the ground." She pulls out a pack of cigarettes and shakes one out, lights it, and takes a long pull.

The entire table of women bursts out laughing—even Rachel cracks a grin, and that's pretty much unheard of for her. Emily comes in holding hands with Alek, and she shoots me a smile before heading over to get some food. I smile back and yawn into my oatmeal.

"Oh, I'm sorry, am I keeping you awake, darlin'?" Nova pulls her knife from the table and checks the tip of it.

"No, sorry, I'm just not sleeping too good. Mikey has been tossing and turning all night. It's driving me mad." I finish my oatmeal and down my water. "I'll be glad when he's on duty tomorrow night so I can get a full night's sleep." I yawn again.

I feel like a selfish bitch saying that, but it's true. He's had me up all night—and not for the right reasons—for the past couple of weeks. I don't think I'll get much sympathy from this table of women, though. How I came to sit with them, I'll never know. They seem to be attracted to me like flies to shit—wait, that makes me sound like I'm shit, and that's not what I meant at all. It's just that I seem to be attracting more and more…what do you call those people that like to talk to you and have fun with you? Oh, yeah: friends. I seem to be making more and more friends recently, and that kinda goes against everything I believe in.

I have to admit, though, I do get the warm fuzzies that people seem to want to talk to me and not avoid me these days. There's a lot of people here, and most of them I haven't had the chance to really get to meet yet, but Nova is awesome and always makes me smile. Then there's Jessica: she's shy but friendly enough and seems to be good friends with Rachel, who has nearly as bad an attitude as me. Rachel hardly talks—she's more of the silent brooding type—but wherever Nova goes, she seems to be. Then there's Melanie: slim and cocky and likes to fight; if anyone around here is likely to cause trouble, I'm guessing it would be her. Then there's Max and Constance. I don't know if their relationship is a new thing or an old thing, but they seem happy and make it work. They're both real pretty women, and Mikey has said a couple of the guys are upset by the fact they're off the shelf as far as men are concerned.

"Hey! Eyes front: sexy pants at twelve o'clock." Nova snaps her fingers in front of my face.

I come back to the present. "What?"

"Mikey." She nods as Mikey heads over to our table.

Mikey comes to stand behind me, placing his hands on my shoulders. I reach up automatically and touch his hand. "Nina, can I grab a word with you?"

"Sure." I stand and nudge Nova's leg as I walk away, making her stumble.

"Bitch!" she calls after me with a laugh, but she could be directing that at Mikey.

I really like Nova. She's bad-ass, with long red hair that she always wears in a long ponytail. She kinda reminds me of an old *Street Fighter* character. She's funny and really smart—like brain surgeon smart. Well, maybe not brain surgeon smart, but she knows a lot. We've become quite close, what with us both having the same sarcastic humor. Unfortunately, she's very good friends with Rachel, and we still don't see eye to eye on pretty much anything. There's no bitchiness there; Rachel just keeps to herself, since she's not much of a talker.

Mikey and I turn into the hallway outside the mess hall, the sound of overly loud women dulling as the door swings shut behind us. I turn to Mikey with a *what's up?* expression.

"Zee wants you out on a scavenge today."

I nod. "Okay." I process the information and nod again. "Yeah, okay, I can do this."

Mikey shakes his head and huffs at me. "No, you need to say that your shoulder isn't right yet." He frowns hard at me, as if I'm not getting the big picture.

"But it *is* okay. I mean, not totally, but I can shoot a gun, or drive. I just can't get into any hand-to-hand trouble, and make sure that I do the exercises Becky gave me." I frown back and grit my teeth. "Stop it right now. We're not doing this again. You know I have to help out—hell, I *want* to help out—and I don't need anyone babying me." I cross my arms in front of my chest and lean against the wall with a roll of my eyes, feeling more like a teenager than a grown woman.

Emily peeks her head around the door. "Everything okay?" She scowls at Mikey, but smiles at me.

"It's fine, go back inside," I say with a nod. She scowls again and goes back to Alek.

"Nina, I'm not babying you, I just don't want you to get hurt. It's bad out there," Mikey continues. He stands in front of me, so close that I have to look into his face. "Really bad."

I roll my eyes again. "You've got to stop this," I mutter. "I can't keep doing this with you." I sigh, long and hard. "If Zee says it's my time to go, I'm going. You need to deal with that." I push past him and head for Zee's office.

Once outside I pull my hood up and scrunch my shoulders against the icy rain, and run across the frozen grounds to Wing HQ. We all know that supplies, while still looking okay for now, need to be constantly restocked. In the spring they're hoping to plant crops in some of the unused parts of the base, like the outdoor rec center, but for now we need to grin and bear it and get through this winter.

It's hit us hard and fast, and we had several weeks of not being able to leave the base other than to kill the deaders in the direct vicinity. Thankfully, the snow has backed off and allowed us to get back out there. Unfortunately, everyone out there is as desperate as we are—or perhaps more desperate—and people are turning even more vicious than normal.

Several times we've had people try and take gear directly from the truck. One particularly small but vicious group even tried to take the entire truck. Unfortunately, they didn't count on Nova being there. Of course she showed them no mercy because of the savage beating they tried to give her.

I push open the heavy door to Wing HQ and head for Zee's office. He's normally there, going over maps and ration figures and ammo numbers. I don't think I've ever seen him *not* working. I knock on the door and after a second the door opens. As predicted, he's trawling over a large map that is spread across an unused desk.

"Nina, come in. How are you?" He heads straight back to his map and continues doing whatever it was he was doing previously.

"Good, thanks." I follow him over. "Mikey said that I'm going out today?" I pose it as a question, though it's not really one.

"Yes, that okay with you? Mikey wasn't sure that you were ready." He crosses a red X through a building and turns to me. "If you're not, that's okay. There's no rush."

"No, I'm fine about it. It's Mikey who's not." I roll my eyes, though if I want to be really truthful, I should say that I'm obviously not okay with going out there. I mean, who would want to? Other than Nova, of course. And Michael. And possibly Rachel. Those three are all ex-army, or what little is left of the army here, give or take. They literally live for this shit, and would much rather be out killing deaders and stuff than counting MRE packs and ammo.

Zee places his pen down and rubs a hand across his face, looking wearily at us. "Well, if you're sure you're okay to. You'll be out with Nova and Michael, but maybe for your first I should send Rachel as well?" He thinks about it for a second. "Yes, all three can go. I'm sure all of you together will go far." He smiles a tired smile.

I nod. "That's great. I'm sure Mikey will be fine once he sees I can handle myself again."

"I'm going too." I turn as Mikey comes into the office, and I scowl when I realize that he's more than likely been eavesdropping on the conversation.

"Mikey!" I snap, but have nothing else to add other than *fuck you* and *get the fuck out of here*. I don't think Zee would appreciate either of those things, so I bite my tongue and scowl instead.

"I don't think that's a good idea, actually," Zee says. His tone, as usual, is calm.

"That wasn't a request," Mikey bites out, his jaw grinding as he stares down Zee like he's a playground bully.

"No, but this *is* an order: you are not going. You're going to put my entire team and the mission into more danger with your over-protectiveness of Nina, and that I simply won't allow." Zee goes to sit at his desk, pulling out paperwork from one of his many overflowing trays. "Nina has stated that she feels well enough to go, I'm sending my three best soldiers, and we need you here, Mikey." He looks up at us both, his expression softening. "I understand, Mikey. I do, but . . ." He seems to flounder for his words, so I decide to cut in.

"Stop being such an uptight asshole. I'm tough and I'm going," I snap.

"Before we got here, we were being chased," Mikey says hurriedly. "You heard of the Forgotten?" Zee nods and frowns. "We were their prisoners for a while, and now we're on the run from them. They'll do anything to get us back."

"And you didn't think to tell me this until now?" Zee snaps. "Where was this?"

"You are such an asshole, Mikey!" I yell. "Really, this is how low you would stoop to stop me from going?" I kick a chair, sending it skidding across the floor until it bangs into the tables.

"It's about seventy miles east of here, I think. I'm sorry." Mikey runs a hand across the back of his neck. "We should have told you, but I'll do anything to protect these women, and I didn't want you asking us to leave. Especially not with the condition Nina was in."

Zee rubs a hand down his face. "Do you think they followed you here?" he asks carefully.

Mikey shakes his head. "No. If they did, we'd know about it by now. In fact, I don't think they have any idea where we are."

Silence descends on the room, with only the odd mumble of annoyance from me. Zee stands and walks back around his desk, coming to stand in front of us both. "Well, I think we should be fine then."

"What? No, she should stay here. They could capture her if they see her out there, or follow her back here." Mikey starts to yell but Zee holds up a hand.

"I have the utmost confidence in my team, and I trust that they will keep her safe. Besides, there's a lot of mountain and forest between us and them. You really need to take a step back from this, Mikey."

I grin at Zee. "Thanks."

I push past Mikey for the second time in less than ten minutes, making sure to really dig him so he stumbles a little. It's bitchy, I know, but he's being a dick and making me feel like a feeble woman, and I do not want that label. I stop at the doorway and turn back to Zee. "Where do I need to go?" I ask, feeling like a jackass for needing to ask and potentially ruining my little storm-out scene.

"Rec center." Zee nods to me and then turns back to his paperwork without another word to Mikey.

I feel Mikey following me down the hall, his eyes boring holes into my back, but he doesn't say anything else. Maybe he realizes that he's fighting a losing battle; maybe he's going to spring a trap on me and hide me away somewhere so I can't go. I doubt it. And I know I should be grateful that he gives a shit, but I'm not. It's just irritating. I push open the door and don't bother to hold it open for him. In fact, as I head outside and the rain lashes down on me, I'm pretty sure I hear a *thump* and a muttered "fuck." I'm so pissed off that I can't even afford a snigger at his expense. Well, maybe I give a small one.

The rain drenches me through, and by the time I reach the rec center I'm about ready to go back home before I catch the flu, but then Nova is there all geared up to the teeth and still smiling despite the crappy weather, so I suck it up and pretend it doesn't bother me.

"Lock and load, bitches!" she hollers from the top of a large military truck.

"Nova, get the fuck in here," Rachel yells from the doorway of the rec center.

I look up at her as I pass. The truck is huge, with dual tires on either end of the twin rear axles; it looks like that thing could drive just about anywhere. It's about twenty feet long and Nova seems to be having the time of her life trying to tie down the green canvas that covers the entirety of the back. No, seriously, she's grinning from ear to ear.

I laugh as I run to the door. Rachel opens it wider for me and I slip past her and mutter a "thanks." Inside, Michael is one, weirdly topless and showing off a colorful array of tattoo designs across every inch of bare skin that I can see, and two, going through a weapons check of some sort. I head to him to find out what he needs from me, squeezing out my sopping wet hair as I walk.

"Nina reporting for duty!" I salute sarcastically.

"I want you to drive. Can you do that?" he snaps without looking up.

"Well, do I at least get a gun?" I mutter, feeling kinda fucking stupid now. And shy, since he's semi-naked.

"No, you don't need one. You just need to drive." Again he doesn't bother to look up and I huff out my annoyance.

I'm about ready to rip him a new asshole when Nova comes in with Rachel by her side. She's still grinning from ear to ear, a big-assed gun in her hand, and her long, red, wet ponytail dangling halfway down her back.

"I fucking love the rain." Nova twirls in a circle, sending raindrops flying around her. "It makes me feel so free!" She laughs.

"Nova, did you get your fucking gun wet again?" Michael storms over from his mass collection of weapons and snatches the gun from her hand.

"It's just a little of God's tears, darlin'," she cackles and then snatches some smokes from Rachel's pocket. "Thanks for watching my babies." She lights one up and exhales, and I have a sense of déjà vu from twenty minutes earlier.

Rachel rolls her eyes and heads over to a long table. "Nina, come with me so I can show you the route," she calls back over her shoulder.

I wander over, leaving Michael and Nova bitching at each other. Well, Michael bitching at Nova, anyway. She seems completely unfazed by the entire thing, a big shit-eating grin on her face while he lectures her. I can't help but smile at her nonchalance.

Rachel spreads a map across a long table and grabs a thick black marker. She circles where we are, and then much further out, she makes another circle. She grabs some fancy piece of plastic and slaps it on the map before drawing circles and Xs and lines and such. I'm getting a headache just from watching her, but after a minute she pulls everything away and looks up to me.

"So this is where we are, and this is where we're heading." She points out both places and looks at me as I nod. "The places with red Xs on them are places we've encountered big trouble. The places with black Xs on them are or were safe zones—the last time we were there, anyway."

I nod again and then frown. "Wait—big trouble? Isn't everywhere kinda big trouble, or do you have a specific way to term big trouble? I mean on a scale of one to ten, where does big trouble lie? Because I've been in big trouble before and I'd class those as tens, but is your ten as big as mine?" *What can I say? I talk a lot when I'm nervous.* "Zee talked about peace-hating crackheads or something—are they the big trouble, or are we talking about something else?"

Nova struts over to us and slaps me on the back. "What the fuck are you talking about?" She grins. "Big trouble is mass hordes of zombies, road collisions that we couldn't clear because they were so damn big. Big trouble is groups of assholes we got to meet on these lovely excursions. All of those things are big trouble, and they're all on the scale of ten." She smiles at me again. "But it'll be fun, you'll see." She nods happily and then pauses, lost in thought before she looks me in the eye seriously. "Oh, piss break before we leave." She strides off without saying anything else, leaving me and Rachel to stare at one another.

Rachel grins. "Love that girl."

"Are you two...you know...together? Like Max and Constance?"

"No, she's..." Rachel chuckles and then pauses, a weird look crossing her face before she continues. "She's like a sister to me is all. She makes everything seem...like it's worth all the heartache, I guess. She makes it all bearable." Her eyes meet mine, and I notice again the color difference of her eyes. In those eyes I also see her pain, and I know that she's seen way more than one woman should have to see. I wonder if that's what people see when they look into my eyes.

"Aah, okay. Sorry, I shouldn't have assumed." I roll my eyes and smile.

Rachel laughs again. "It's fine. If I dug chicks, I'm sure she would be at the top of my list."

We both laugh, but stop when Michael comes over, a scowl planted firmly on his face. He looks us both over and readies himself to say something, but must think better of it as he huffs and storms away without a word.

"So, when do we leave?" I ask, looking at the map again.

"Twenty minutes or so. Nova's finished refitting the canvas over the truck. We haven't taken this one out in a couple of months, but the roads are a mess out there. The snow is pretty thick in places and," she shakes her head, "you'll see soon enough. It's nothing to worry about, though—not while we're up high in Betty."

"Betty?" I quirk an eyebrow.

"That's what Nova called the truck. Said she had a big ass like her friend Betty."

We both laugh, receiving filthy looks from Michael for the trouble, but I've already decided that he's an asshole and I'm going to make it my mission to piss him off several times a day on this trip, or at least try to make him smile—the latter being more of a challenge, of course. I'm sure underneath his gruff exterior there's a warm, cuddly teddy bear dying to get out. I'm warming to Rachel, despite the fact that she nearly killed me, though I can't say we'll ever be good friends. And there it is again. That fucking cursed word: friends.

A shiver runs down my spine, like someone walked over my grave—or my new friends' graves. God, I hope not. I shake off my morbidity, excited and nervous to be leaving the base.

TWENTY-SEVEN

T he truck tumbles along at a slow speed. I could drive quicker, but this thing is bigger than anything I've driven before, and while I'm learning to handle it, I don't want to risk anything. Plus I'm still trying to flex out my shoulder, testing its strength. It's been a month or so since I was shot; the wound itself actually wasn't really the problem, but the amount of blood loss I suffered on the way back to base. A gunshot wound is a gunshot wound. I'll grin and bear it like a trooper, of course. Rachel is in the seat next to me, while Michael is in the back with Nova. Rachel doesn't talk much, and that's fine, really. I need to concentrate on the road and the vehicle, and the fact that it's still raining hard and I can't see jack shit.

"Damn it," I curse as I roll the truck over something.

Rachel continues to look out the window, her legs stretched out in front of her with her feet resting on the dashboard. She barely flinches at the sound of something crunching under the tire or my cursing. I'm hoping that's a positive sign that I'm not doing too bad, but I'm pretty sure Michael is going bat-shit crazy in the back right about now. Unsurprisingly, that puts a smile on my face.

Mikey had come to see me off; he'd packed an overnight bag and brought me his samurai sword. Lucky for me, he's been giving me lessons on how to handle such a deadly knife. It's nothing like using a machete, where you just aim and hack; it's more graceful and precise, and a shitload deadlier in some ways. I have to admire the fact that he can use one of these with the finesse of an old samurai master—or at least be jealous as hell that he can use it better than me. More than likely the latter option. I'm pretty good at learning new things—always have been. I guess I have one of those minds that sort of learns and remembers right away. It in no way makes me an expert at anything, but it means I know lots of weird little facts and have some great little skills. I still prefer my machete, but he wouldn't take no for an answer when I tried to refuse his sword. I guess in some ways, he was trying to send a little piece of him with me for protection.

Emily didn't say goodbye to me, mainly because we didn't tell her I was going. Okay, so that was the only reason she didn't come to say goodbye. She'd only worry, and with any luck we'll be back in two days, maybe three, and she'll only know I'm missing for one of them. She's been so busy working with Becky in the hospital that we've hardly seen each other recently. It's a good and a bad thing, I guess.

Rachel suddenly drops her heavy-booted feet down and grabs the map. She scours it for a minute before looking up at the road again. "Whatever happens, do not stop." She thumps twice on the partition between the cab and the bed of the truck, and only seems satisfied when we hear a steady two-thump beat returned.

"What's going on?" I ask, my throat suddenly dry.

"Big trouble spot," she says without missing a beat and points to the first red *X* on the map.

I swallow. "What kind of big trouble?"

"Zombie hordes have been seen around these parts every time we travel through here. Don't know where the fuckers keep coming from. It's like they're breeding." She shivers comically and sticks her tongue out with a grin.

I don't know whether to laugh or be amazed that she said all that in one go *and* cracked a fucking joke at the same time. I smirk and shake my head, keeping a more vigilant eye on the road. Sure enough, up ahead I see gray masses moving through the storm.

"Shit, is that what I think it is?"

Rachel makes an *uh huh* sound and rolls down her window, pushing her gun out of the gap. Freezing cold rain lashes in at her, but she aims and doesn't wince or move in any way. Up ahead, deaders slowly move out of the tree line as if they have been waiting to hijack us. They begin moving toward us slowly, the moaning reaching over the sound of the wind and rain and this monster of a truck.

"Don't stop," Rachel murmurs.

I snort out a laugh. I have no fucking intention of stopping this truck for anything. I will happily run those fuckers down. Hell, I've wanted to do it for the past couple of years but never had the right vehicle to do it in. But now here I am sitting in Betty's throne. I grin and accelerate. Rachel moves under the abrupt momentum though she quickly rights her position, I don't bother to apologize as she begins to fire into the trees and I start to roll over the deaders. The feeling of bones crushing under my tires gets lost because of the heavy suspension of the truck as it bounces and thumps along. I grip the wheel tighter, my knuckles going white as I struggle to control it. The road is slippy with gore and sleet, and I'm not used to driving in these conditions. Jesus, before all this end-of-the-world crap, I wouldn't have left the house until winter was over, never mind going out zombie slaying and scavenging for food and supplies. *Lucky me, I'm a changed fucking woman.*

Shooting starts up and I glance in my mirrors, watching as the road behind us closes up with starving deaders. Michael and Nova are not wasting ammo, though, and aren't shooting all that much. Rachel seems to be doing most of that at the side of me. She slips fresh ammo into the bottom of her gun and continues to fire for another minute or so before pulling her gun back inside and closing up the window.

The truck seems especially quiet after all that commotion, and when I turn to say so to Rachel, I can't help the laugh that explodes from me. Rachel is drenched through, her blonde hair sticking to her face, water dripping from her nose and chin. Her cheeks are bright red against the stark paleness of the rest of her face.

"Are you okay?" I say between laughs.

"Yeah, totally fine." She chuckles and blows some of the sopping hair from her face.

I laugh even harder, wiping tears away as she shakes her head like a dog, spraying water around the cab. She smirks and grabs a towel from her bag, wrapping it around her shoulders and pulling it over the top of her head. She scrubs her head to towel dry it and wipes down her face, and I turn up the heaters.

A couple minutes later she looks a little more like herself and she finally decides to talk a little more than her usual yes and no answers.

"So, how long have you been at the base?" I ask, trying to sound casual. Christ, look at me: I'm a real chatty Cathy these days. I sigh. I mean to do it inwardly, but it comes out.

"I haven't even answered you yet and here you are bored already,"

Rachel says, still looking out the window.

"Sorry, it's not you. Well, it is, but, never mind." I shrug. Silence encompasses the vehicle again, but after a couple of miles alone with my thoughts and only the ravaged landscape and driving rain for company, I realize that she didn't reply to me.

I glance at her. "Talk to me please."

"I'm not really one for talking," she replies.

"I can see that."

"Now Nova, that woman can talk. She's funny, too, though I don't think she realizes it. But she doesn't give a shit, and says it how it is."

I glance at her again and see her watching me.

"I can see why she likes you. You two are the same."

"I'm not chatty!" I laugh, only a little offended. "Sure, I have a tendency to express my opinion and do what I like, but that's what survival does to you. I wasn't always like this—well, maybe a little like this."

Rachel holds her hands up. "It's okay, you don't have to explain. I think it's admirable. You don't try and pacify anyone with bullshit— there's nothing wrong with that. In some ways I'm the same. What you see is what you get." A thoughtful look crosses her eyes, but before I can work it out, it's gone again.

She's right and wrong: there's been times that I should have most definitely kept my big trap shut, or at least softened the blow for the other person. Too many times I dive straight in and don't think how my words could affect another person. It's not a purposeful thing to be an asshole, it just sort of comes natural to me. I really should try to censor my mouth sometimes. I'm also not buying her *what you see is what you get* line. She definitely seems to have hidden depths that I don't know about. She has those eyes—you know, the ones that are old before their time, that look like they have seen a thousand things they shouldn't have.

"I've only been at the base for six or seven months, I think," Rachel says quietly. "Maybe a little less than that."

I watch her from the corner of my eye and guess that was hard for her to say. I decide to try out my whole 'keeping my mouth shut' theory. So we ride along for another mile in silence while I let her ponder her thoughts and I go crazy with wanting to ask questions but refusing to ask them. I realize that I must give at least a little bit of a shit about these people if I'm asking questions. Or maybe I'm moving forward. I never asked anything of JD or Josie; I never gave a shit—or maybe I was fooling myself into not wanting to give a shit. Either way, they're gone now and I'll never get to ask them those questions.

"I was in a city before the base," she mumbles. I nearly miss it I'm so wrapped up in my own inner monologue.

"A city?" I ask, before shutting my mouth and waiting for her again.

"Yeah, one of *those* cities."

The way she says *those* makes me think that we may have more in common than we realized. It takes me a moment to decide on how to broach the subject. She seems pretty closed off about it all, as if just saying that one sentence was enough speaking about it to last her a lifetime. Me, I'm only just beginning.

"You were behind a walled city?" I say with horror. Well, that explains a lot then—her quiet demeanor, her closed off personality.

She nods and makes her little *uh huh* noise again. The blood rushes to my ears, anxiety beginning to eat away at my gut. The last time I mentioned that I had been behind one of those walls, I got the pretty facial scarring that I carry around with me now. But she brought it to me first, and these people don't seem like crazy fucking lunatics like the Forgotten were. Then again, I'm not the best judge of character.

"Before you start, it wasn't all roses and chocolates back there." She holds up a hand to stop me from arguing with her. Clearly, she's been through this before.

"I know, I know…I was behind one too," I whisper.

I don't mean to whisper, but it comes out that way all the same, as if my own throat is closing up and trying to stop me from getting the words out. *No, no, don't do it, you crazy bitch. Do you really want the other side of your face cut to pieces?* my brain cries out loudly, but I've said it. Or at least I think I did. I turn to look at her. She's still staring out the window blankly, her shoulders hunched.

"Did you hear me? I said I was behind one of them too." I swallow the golf ball in my throat, feeling a mixture of both sadness and anger. Anger at me for saying anything, and anger at her for *not* saying anything.

"I heard you. I was just hoping that I imagined it is all." She turns to look at me, her different colored eyes taking me in with uncertainty. "I'm sorry you had to go through that. They're not nice places."

She looks back out the window and I'm close to slamming my brakes on and shaking the living shit out of her. *Not a nice place? What the fuck is that all about? A horror story, more like. Not a nice place does not cover it, not even close.* My vision blurs. *Am I crying? Hell no, stop those damn tears.* I'm furious, but I don't know why.

"You need to slow down, Nina."

Her words trickle into my thoughts and I look down at my speedometer and see that I've crept up to eighty miles an hour—a fucking stupid idea in weather like this, and certainly not in the emotional state I'm getting myself into. Jesus, what is wrong with me lately?

I ground myself on thoughts of revenge, seeing my knife piercing Fallon's gut from groin to throat. I feel the smile on my face before I even realize I'm doing it. Surprisingly, the image works and I feel my heartbeat slowing back down and I loosen my grip on the wheel and ease off the gas, so at least I'm not white-knuckle driving.

"Sorry. I never met anyone else other than Em that had been behind the walls before." I bite down hard on my lip before speaking again. "So how did you get out? I mean, why aren't you still there?" I rub a clammy hand down my thigh quickly before putting it back on the wheel so as not to lose control of the truck. "I'm sorry, you don't have to tell me if you don't want to." I wait a beat before continuing. "Please tell me. I'm sorry. God, I'm sorry."

Rachel reaches out and places a hand on top of my leg. "It's okay. I get it. I'd be lying if I said I wasn't curious too. It's just hard, I don't really talk about it much. I can live with what happened to me, but I miss Sasha so much . . ." Her words trail off, and when I look, she's wiping her eyes. "I miss her so much. She gave her life for me."

My hand flies to my mouth. "Your daughter?" I mumble between my fingers.

She coughs out a small laugh. "Sort of. She was my dog. She was a beautiful black and white Huskita with the most sincere eyes you could ever imagine. She went everywhere with me. After the zombies came, she..." Her words trail off, and she seems to gather her thoughts together before she continues. "She wouldn't leave my side for even a minute. We were out traveling, going from town to town, living off what we could find. It was no way to live, but it was living all the same, which is more than can be said for others. We came across a convoy one day. They had this stupid white flag raised over the lead truck, so I made myself known to them. Sasha and me stepped out into the road and they pulled over. This asshole got out, said he could take us to a safe haven. Of course I jumped at the chance. Since everything had happened, all I had wanted was for me and Sasha to be safe. I wanted everything to go back to normal again, for us all to get on with our lives. I just wanted to protect everyone!" Rachel grabs strands of her hair, pulling at it nervously and twisting it into tangles. "But when we got to the walled city, they wouldn't let Sasha in." Her chin trembles. "I told them I wouldn't leave her, and this," she moves her hair out of the way and points to a small, jagged scar at the top of her head close to the hairline, "this is what happened. When I woke, I was behind the walls and Sasha was gone."

The truck lapses into silence; apart from the truck's rumbling engine and the rain splashing the windshield, there's nothing else. I fumble around for the right words. People have lost friends, mothers have lost children, children have lost fathers, and this woman lost her dog. Yet her dog was her family; she was her child, her everything, and to have that stripped away must be equally devastating for her.

"So how did you get out of there? And why did they take you in the first place?" I ask gently. Most people didn't want to leave the cities; sure, it was bad—hell, even—but better the devil you know, right?

She snorts out a laugh. "I snuck out on one of their convoys a couple of months later. Stupid assholes never even noticed me among all the bodies." She chuckles to herself.

"Bodies? What do you mean bodies?" I frown hard, my blood pressure spiking again.

"The dead bodies—the zombies. They have to get rid of them somehow. Every couple of weeks they take them out to a landfill and dump them." She looks across at me nervously, as if deciding on whether to share something with me. She comes to a conclusion and continues. "They were testing on them—zombies—trying to work out why they were what they were, you know, and how they were up and walking when they should be dead, I guess. Once they stopped walking and they were truly dead, there was no use for them, and of course then they started to really rot and stink."

We both grimace at that. Deaders stink to high hell, so I can understand the logic of wanting to get rid of the bodies, but something else dawns on me as we're talking.

"They left the cities? I thought there was no way out once you were in."

"That's what I thought, that's why I'd never tried to get to one before." She watches me for a second. I can feel her stare at the side of my face without looking, and when I do chance a glance at her, I find I was right. "This one was special—this city. This wasn't just a place to live, it was a testing plant. That's why they wanted me…and any other people they could get their hands on. So they could test on us." She frowns hard and then pinches the bridge of her nose.

I slam my foot down on the brake pedal and the truck comes to a screeching halt. "Are you fucking serious?" She nods rapidly, her eyes wide. "They are testing on us? On humans? Turning us into those, those…things?"

She nods again. "I, I don't think that they wanted to, I think that they were trying to cure it…the disease."

I frown at her, my lips pulled into a tight line as I try to hold back all the vicious, vile words I want to throw at someone. But there's no point in saying them to Rachel; this wasn't her fault, wasn't her idea.

"We need to keep moving," she states quietly.

I nod and start the truck moving again, my thoughts whirling at a million miles an hour, realizing that the game just changed in the most dramatic fashion. Every time I think I've met the worst of the worst, human beings manage to sink to a whole new level.

"I'm sorry," I say quietly, still deep in thought and wanting to get back and talk to Mikey. "I just can't believe they would do that—test on people."

She shrugs nervously.

"Did it work? Did they find out how to stop it?" I ask.

Rachel shakes her head, looking depressed as hell. "Nope, not even close." Her chin trembles. "I miss my dog. I miss Sasha," she says, and I want to whoop the silly out of her. What she's talking about and what she's thinking about seem to be on very different scales: testing on people and turning them into zombies and her missing dog are two very fucking different scales of conversation. I try to ignore my inner temper tantrum and be nice.

I frown at her. "You know she could still be alive." I don't know why I say it—maybe to calm my own temper down. It seems so random to be talking about her dog, given what she just told me about that walled city and the experiments, but I don't know what else to say.

"In some ways that would be worse, knowing that she was still looking for me. I mean, I couldn't even find that place again if I tried. I could never go back there, not now."

It's my turn to reach over and give her leg a squeeze. It's a lame move, and not something I would normally do, but she seems to appreciate the gesture all the same, and I'm glad.

Two more days, I realize, two more days before I can tell Mikey all this information. That's if I make it back alive, anyway. Another thought creeps up on me: what if she's wrong? What if each city was a cover for something else? Maybe they weren't built for safety. It stands to reason that if one of them was built for testing, then surely others were built for other things too.

"Big trouble spot coming up," she says without looking at me.

TWENTY-EIGHT

Rachel reaches over and gives three sharp knocks on the cab wall instead of two like the previous time. We wait and listen for the knocks to be returned, and I turn to stare at her with an eyebrow lift.

"What trouble is it this time?"

"It might be nothing, but the last two out of three times we came down this road there was an ambush—at least an attempt at one. So again, no matter what, you don't stop the truck for anything, you got it?"

I nod. "Okay."

"You keep us at forty miles an hour, no less. These assholes will take us for everything we have and then some," she says grimly. She reaches down to the floor and grabs another gun. I wonder why she doesn't open the window this time, but when a bullet hits the side of the truck, I understand why. Rachel looks over and sees I'm only at thirty-five. "Speed up," she yells, as more bullets hit the metal.

I do as she says, pressing down harder on the accelerator and making the truck lurch forward. I try to keep my eyes on the road in front, but every now and then movement catches my eye and I look left and right, seeing faces in the tree line. I look to the front again as a woman steps out into the middle of the road up ahead.

"Rachel!" I yell. "There's no way I can avoid hitting her." I look at her nervously, but she doesn't return my stare, merely bows her head.

"Keep going," she says without hesitation.

I watch the woman getting closer and closer and realize that she's crying; she doesn't want to be standing there—she's being forced to.

"Rachel, I can't fucking hit her, I'll kill her!" I ease off the accelerator.

"Don't stop!"

"But, Rachel . . ."

"Don't fucking stop, Nina!" She leans over as the truck hits twenty-five miles an hour and presses down on my thigh, making me speed back up again.

"Get off me! I can't kill her, Rachel, don't make me fucking kill her!" I try to bat her hands off me, making the truck swerve violently to the left. The woman in the road covers her head with both hands, and through the rain and the swishing of the windshield wipers I see her tortured and starved figure as she gets closer to me. "Fuck, Rachel!" I scream as the truck hits the woman's frail body at forty-five miles an hour. The truck lurches over her body, finding it harder than the deaders' rotting corpses but still easier than it would be with any other type of vehicle.

Maybe I imagine the feel of her bones crunching under my tires. Maybe I imagine her screams and the pop of her skull. All I know is that I murdered an innocent woman. I gag on the bile that flies up my throat, but swallow it back down. Rachel keeps herself pressed against my thigh for another mile or so, and I don't bother to fight her. There's no point now; I killed that poor woman.

We don't talk for a long time; there seems nothing left to say to one another. That and I fear that if I speak to her now, I'm more than likely going to pull my samurai sword out and hack her into tiny pieces. So I say nothing, I keep quiet and follow the road. She only talks to me when she needs to tell me which direction to turn. The rain even begins to calm down a little, which is a nice reprieve.

As night begins to fall, Rachel looks at the map again and bangs four times on the cab wall. When it's returned, she points at a small circle on the map.

"Take the next left and at the end of that road we'll be going right."

I nod but still don't say anything.

"Don't hate me," she whispers. It's funny, I know she's not a weak woman—she's very far from it—but right now she seems it.

"I don't hate you," I reply. "I just don't like you very much right now." I fight back the tears that are threatening to fall. *She had her reasons, I know she had her reasons,* is all I can think.

"Okay, I can handle that."

At the end of the road I turn right like she said, and now that the rain has all but stopped, I can see a lot clearer. This road is wider, though we're still on back roads and not main highways. I know we're getting back to real civilization, and with that could be more trouble. I grit my teeth and keep on driving. Whatever happens, there's no going back now.

We enter a run-down town. Most of it seems like someone has tried to burn it down to the ground at one point: houses with roofs caved in, melted playground equipment in what was once a front yard, cars nothing more than burnt-out rusted shells. Bones litter the roadway—either from residents that got caught by the deaders or by deaders that got caught by someone's rampage, I'm not sure. I try not to pay too close attention to those.

We keep going straight through the town, passing vandalized storefronts. One after another they have succumbed to the years, through fire or ruin. Time has not been good to this town. I get a bad feeling about this place, and Rachel seems to be back on high alert, her window rolled all the way down, gun in place; but her finger is free from the trigger, so I guess it must be just precautionary.

We come to a small intersection and Rachel tells me to go left. Trees have overturned here after getting too large for their spots, and I have to drive up and over the sidewalk to get past. I know it's okay to do this now, but human nature still wants me to adhere to the rules of the road. Sometimes it's harder to ignore those feelings, and I can't help but be glad when I can get back on the road.

"Keep going all the way to the bottom of the road and take another left," she says, keeping her eyes firmly out the window.

I nod, and then realize she can't see me. "Okay," I say quietly. It seems like a time to keep quiet, even though this truck is the noisiest damn thing around here.

A deader steps out into the road, turning toward us with jerky, slow movements. It raises one arm, the other lying dormant at its side, and opens its mouth to groan at us. It takes one or two steps forward, finding it difficult with what looks like a snapped anklebone, and then stumbles to its knees. I feel a little sorry for it: how long must it have taken to get up to walking? It reminds me of a tortoise trying to roll over. As we pass it, it continues to reach and I slow down, taking a cautionary look at it. Both eyes have been gouged out, and the arm that was still by its side was only still because it wasn't actually there at all. The arm seems to be missing completely; a single shirt sleeve hangs down, blowing in the breeze. I look away, not wanting to see any more, but wonder how long that image is going to stay in my head.

"That was pretty gross," I mumble to myself.

"They're all pretty gross."

I look across at her and shrug. "Yeah, they are, but some are just so…" I struggle for the right word.

"Over the top?" Rachel suggests.

"Yeah, exactly. They're so over the top dead. I mean, I don't even want to think about how they got into such a shitty state. They're rotting, I get that, but that guy only had one arm, and where the fuck were his eyes?" I wrinkle up my nose. "God help me, if I die out here, please put a bullet in my head and don't let me come back as one of these things." I roll my shoulders, feeling all kinds of gross.

"You're not going to die out here. For one, Mikey would kill us for letting that happen, and two, you're as bad-ass as they come," she chuckles.

I snort out a laugh. "I'll take that compliment and raise you a 'you're pretty bad-ass yourself,'" I joke.

"I'm sorry I made you kill that woman. Please believe me when I say it's for the best."

I clench my teeth hard. "Okay," I say. "I'm taking it you have experience with stopping to help and getting fucked over?"

I see her nod from my peripheral vision. "It didn't end well. We lost a couple of crew members and more innocents on their side than I would like to remember. It wasn't pretty."

"If they're innocent, then why are they with them?"

"They have nowhere else to go. Better the devil you know…" She trails off and I leave the rest of my questions unanswered.

We pass a supermarket and I see movement inside. Rachel sees it, too, and gestures for me to slow the truck. I don't stop, but roll at an easy five miles an hour. A deader shambles out of the store, a filthy flowery skirt flapping around its ankles for its trouble. It growls and heads toward us, almost tripping over a decaying corpse on the sidewalk to get to us.

Another follows close behind it, a once obese balding man whose guts look like they may have been rotting from the inside out, the way his stomach looks so overly bloated with toxic gasses. I wipe my hand across my lips, feeling my mouth water at the thought of his churning rotten guts. As another deader pulls itself along the ground in an army SAS fashion, I see Nova come from around the back of the truck. She and Michael must have jumped down, and together they head for the trio of dead. I stop the truck and watch as Nova grips hold of the flowery deader by the throat and it returns the favor and grasps to her jacket. She's careful to keep her fingers away from its snapping jaws as her other hand swings around and rams her knife into its forehead. It begins to slump to the ground, its hands still gripping her clothing as she steps back and shrugs out of its grip. Michael, meanwhile, has tackled the obese deader to the ground by grabbing it from behind. He sits astride it, his entire weight resting on top of the bloated stomach as he tries to keep a grip on it and keep it in place. Nova jogs over and happily slams her knife through its forehead. At the same time, the guy's stomach decides to give way and a weird suck and pop sound can be heard as Michael collapses into the insides of the now very dead zombie.

He jumps up and out of the rot, swearing, while Nova bursts out laughing. She stops when she gets wind of the smell coming from the rotting insides, though, and covers her mouth. Both Rachel and I are laughing too: Michael looks so pissed off, and I think we're both more than glad that we don't have to sit in the back of the truck with him.

"Jesus, that's gotta be worse than skunk stink, right?" I say. "Urghh, roll the fucking window up, Rachel." I gag on the toxic fumes that have made their way over to the truck.

Rachel happily obliges and looks at me with a half grin and a smirk. I roll my eyes and smile back before glancing over her shoulder.

Nova and Mikey are arguing again, and for once Nova doesn't look too happy. Who can blame her, really, though? I realize we're missing a deader and I frown.

"There's a deader missing," I mumble.

"What?"

"A deader. There's a deader missing," I say again, louder this time. I lean right over in my seat to try and scan the ground, but there's no sign of it anywhere. The creepy little SAS deader has disappeared.

Rachel opens her door and jumps down. "I'll look for it," she says, looking back in at me before screaming in pain. Her face contorts as she stamps her foot down, over and over, and I realize where the missing deader is hiding.

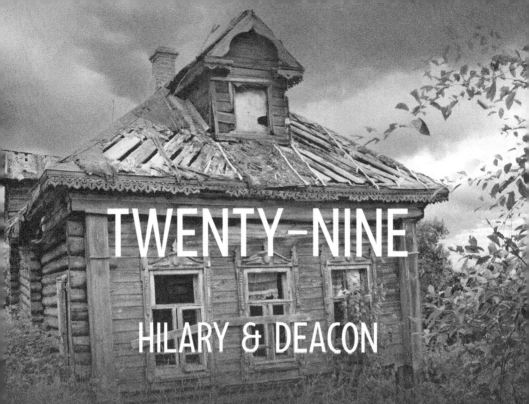

TWENTY-NINE

HILARY & DEACON

"I 'm cold." I shiver, trying to stop my teeth from chattering.

Deacon hugs me closer, squashing any cold air away from me and wrapping his warmth around me. "I know, baby," is all he says.

There's not much more to say. It's freezing. Even now after the worst of the winter is over, it's still freezing, and it will be for the foreseeable future. I can handle the cold, though—most days, anyway—but today has been a bad day. Today we ran out of ramen noodles and Deacon has been grumpy all day, and I'm so hungry because he didn't go hunting for any meat. I've hardly felt the baby move all day, either, and that's a worry too.

Deacon's beard is rough against my head. I can feel it through the woolen hat I'm wearing to keep my ears warm. I can't expect him to shave it off, though. For one he doesn't have a decent razor, and for two he says it keeps his face warm.

"Shhh, baby. Try to get some sleep," Deacon whispers onto my hat, placing a soft kiss after it to seal in his words.

I hadn't even realized I was mumbling out loud. Okay, go to sleep now, Hil.

Deacon's heavy breathing gets heavier, and I try to concentrate on his steady heartbeat, hoping it will lull me to sleep. *Boom, boom, boom, boom…*

The sound of barking wakes me up, and I flinch as Deacon reacts quicker than I, flinging the covers back and diving out of bed. I lie there for a minute trying to work out what's happening, until I hear the dog barking again and realize that I'm not dreaming.

I push myself up to sitting. "D? What is it?"

He's standing by the window with the curtain pulled back as he peeps outside. He doesn't answer right away, but I'm not sure if it's because he didn't hear me or because he's concentrating. I wait a few minutes and then ask again.

"There's a damn dog somewhere out there." He continues to stare out the window.

"Should we do something?" I ask, though I'm not sure what I expect him to do.

"Maybe. Stupid mutt is going to attract those things to us if I don't shut it up."

"It could be scared. Maybe it's fighting one. It could need our help." I panic. Even though it could be rabid, I hate the thought of something being in trouble—in danger with no one to help it. My thoughts cast back to the old couple that Deacon killed—this is their house that we've been living in, and here I am concerned with a dog.

I'm a sick individual.

"It could be lunch," is all he says as he picks up his boots and shoves them on. He grabs his jacket and buttons it up, and then finally his gun. "Stay here," he says darkly, and then he leaves.

I listen in the dark to his heavy footsteps down the stairs and through the living room. I listen to the front door open and close, and then I hear the creaky *clank* of the metal ladders as he places them over the moat-type hole he dug in front of the house. I hear him climb over the steps, grunting into the dark as he does, and all the while the damn dog continues to bark.

THIRTY

NINA

"Rachel!" I dive over the cab to grab her, help her—fuck, I don't know, it's just a stupid instinctual thing that people do. Like, 'Oh someone's in trouble, here I come to save the day! Oh wait, shit, I can't do anything!'

Nova takes out the gun from her waist, aims, and fires. Rachel stops stamping and I look down at her. There's blood everywhere; some is hers, but thankfully most of it is the sneaky fucking deader's.

"Are you okay?" I ask, jumping down next to her.

I kick the deader out of the way and crouch down to look at the damage. The damn thing chewed up her ankle and blood is still pumping from it, but if this was a battle, then Rachel clearly won. The deader's head is fifty shades of crushed-to-a-pulp; rotten brain matter has exploded out of its ears and is slowly oozing out of the large crack in the back of its skull.

Michael pushes me out of the way and lifts Rachel back up into the cab. He rolls her pant leg up so he can better see exactly what he's dealing with. I mean, obviously that's what I was going to do next. Nova comes to stand beside him, opening up a small black bag and pulling out bandages and liquids and shit. She hands a stick to Rachel, who puts it in her mouth and reaches down for my hand.

I stare at it in confusion, unsure what's going on, and then like the fucking clever girl I am, I decide to ask. "What's going on?"

"We haven't got time for this," Michael growls at me.

I grab Rachel's hand and look up at her, seeing tears streaming from her eyes. "Seriously, what are you doing?" I ask again.

I watch Michael pull on some heavy black rubber gloves and then carefully begin to open a bottle of liquid. "We need to clean the bite out before it infects her and turns her into one of them."

I nod. "Right, okay." I look at Rachel again with the wooden stick in her mouth, tears still running freely. "What the fuck is that?" I gesture to the bottle in his hand, realizing that something isn't right with this situation at all.

"Acid. I need to burn the infection out of her." He goes to pour the acid over her leg and I scream and knock it from his hand. "What the fuck?" He reaches back with a heavy fist and I flinch and back away from him.

"It's not an infection. You could kill her with that shit," I yell. My hand goes to my waist to grab my knife and I realize that I'm stupidly unarmed after taking it off in the truck and leaving it on the dashboard. I have no qualms about killing him if it saves my own skin, though it doesn't look like I'll get the chance. Nova pushes in front of him.

"Calm the fuck down, let her talk."

"We don't have time. We have to burn it out now, before it takes hold!" he yells into Nova's face, but continues to cast glances in my direction.

"Stop fucking yelling at me, asshole." She shoves him in the chest, making him back up a step. "Speak," she says to me.

"Flush out the wound with a cleaning solution, stitch her up, and get her some meds to stop any infection from starting. That's the best bet on saving her, but really," I look at the bite marks again, "I don't think it's even all that bad if you clean away all the blood." I look at Rachel. "Sorry, that sounds shitty, but it's really not that bad. Suck it up." I smile, trying to calm her down. "And take that stick out of your mouth, you're not a dog."

Nova puts a hand on my shoulder and frowns. "Are you sure?" She says the words carefully, as if to make sure I understand exactly what she's saying to me.

"Yes, Jesus, you people don't know shit about these things." I roll my eyes. "Death is what turns you, not a bite mark, or saliva. I mean I'm sure it's not good for you and could possibly lead to an infection and then maybe death, but a good bottle of meds should sort that out." My words come out in a jumble. Michael is making me antsy with his googly-eyed stare. I take a deep breath. "Please, trust me. You don't need to do this to her."

Nova and Michael exchange nervous glances before both looking at Rachel. Neither of them say anything to her, and I'm all out of comforting words to convince them to not butcher this poor woman. That and I don't have shit to protect myself or her with if they decide to take matters into their own hands.

"How certain are you?" Nova says to me, her normal happy-go-lucky self still missing.

"Pretty damn certain. Like ninety-five percent," I huff. "Look, I've seen this shit happen before—the turning. It was an infection that got him, not a virus, so let me do my thing. You get your meds and we'll both ignore Mr. Grumpy Pants over there." I jerk a thumb in Michael's direction.

Nova looks up to Rachel. "It's your choice. It's your leg, life and shit." I can tell she's trying to appear easy about everything, but the tightness in her shoulders is hard to deny.

"I want to try what Nina says. It's my leg—my life—and I'm willing to take the risk." Rachel looks at us all one by one. "She seems to know a lot about it—about the turning." She eyes me curiously.

"After everything—everything we've been through and seen, you're going to take her word on this? Really?" Michael yells and storms off without another word and I turn around and look at Rachel, offering up a smile to her before turning back around.

"You heard the woman, Nova. We need meds, stat. I always wanted to say that." I chuckle darkly and reach for the fancy first aid kit that Nova has. She willingly opens it up but doesn't surrender the precious kit.

"What else do you need?" she asks.

"I need a cleaning solution to wash out the wound. We still need to clean it, just not with something that will melt her flesh away," I huff. "There's nothing broken thanks to thick socks and bad-ass boots—oh, and our gummy deader." I'm more talking to myself now than anyone else, nerves getting the better of me.

Nova reaches in and grabs a small bottle. "This should do it."

I take it with a nod of thanks and then turn back to Rachel. "This will still hurt. You may want your stick thingy back if you don't think you can contain a scream."

I unscrew the lid and when I look back at her, she's got the stick back in her mouth. I roll my eyes again and grab the bottom of her foot. "On four." I nod. "One, two."

"Wait, who goes on four?" Nova asks in confusion. "It's always three, right?" She tilts her head to the side and frowns.

"Really, Nova, that's your biggest question in all of this?" Michael snaps as he comes back around the truck with a large rifle in hand.

"Fuck off!" Nova shouts and flips him the finger. "You always go on three. It's not a ridiculous fucking question. You always think you're so smart, little Michael who always thinks he knows better than everyone else, but you're not. You're an asshole with PMT!"

"PMT?" he snorts.

"Perfect Michael Tension." She laughs in his face—a nasty, meant-to-piss-someone-off laugh. "You always think you're so damn perfect."

"Four," I whisper, deciding to ignore the argument and squirt the liquid into the bites. Rachel tenses up and groans behind the wood, but doesn't scream. "Well done, just a little more." I can see a tooth embedded in one of the deeper bites, but I figure that she'll freak out if she knows that. "Don't look," I say, and watch as she closes her eyes, putting her total trust in me.

I want to feel grateful that she trusts me so much, but instead I feel scared. Seriously, it's a dumb move to trust me under normal circumstances—I don't exactly have a good track record. With a finger, I dig inside the deep bite and pull out the tooth before throwing it to the ground. I shudder as fresh blood oozes from her and I quickly squeeze more liquid into the wound.

"I need a bandage," I mutter. The bites aren't nearly as bad as they could have been. It looks like our sneaky deader had bad teeth in its previous life, so thankfully there wasn't much in its jaw to actually chew with. A bandage comes into my line of sight and I point toward the deepest bite. "Right here, wrap it tight."

I hold up Rachel's leg as Nova winds the bandage tightly around the wound. Rachel hisses every once in a while, but she's a tough cookie, she can hack it. "Stop being a baby," I joke.

The entire time Michael stands guard, watching for any other deader sneaking up on us. Five minutes later and we're done, and Rachel hops down from the truck. She puts some weight on her ankle, testing it out.

"Aah," she grumbles.

Nova pushes her shoulder. "Nina's right, you're being a baby. I've seen you bleed worse on your period." She laughs loudly and pulls out her smokes. She lights two and hands one to Rachel. "Fuck, that was intense."

I grab my canteen, unscrew the lid with my clean hand, and tip some of the contents over my bloodied hand. It's not perfect, but it'll have to do for now, since I used all the cleaning solution on Rachel's ankle.

"You're sure that this will work?" Rachel says.

I nod. "Pretty much, yeah."

"How do you know so much about it?" she asks, inhaling deeply on her cigarette. "Were you a scientist previously?"

I burst out laughing. "A scientist? Really?" Nova and Rachel look at each other in annoyance. "I thought it was common fucking knowledge, if you want to know the truth. Death always brings you back. You only turn from a bite if it kills you. Your bite didn't look bad enough to kill." I shrug, feeling uncomfortable under everyone's stares. I wish I smoked so I'd have something to do. "And no, I was no doctor or scientist or anything, but I've seen this happen before."

Rachel looks away in thought, and Michael seems like he has the weight of the world on his shoulders and keeps glancing at Rachel with worry. Nova seems like the only person unperturbed by it all.

"So what's the plan now?" I ask anyone and everyone listening.

"Well, we know there's nothing in the store, but we like to keep a clean house and make sure we kill any strays as we travel through here. Our objective is," Nova starts, but stops as she hands Rachel some meds and water to wash them down with, "a small warehouse south of here. We think it will more than likely be ransacked, but it's on the far edge of town, and was a holding-before-shipment warehouse. From the outside, it looks like a boring old metal building—or that's how we were told it looked." Nova shrugs and takes a final hit on her cigarette before crushing it underfoot. "We could get lucky."

It turns out we are lucky after all. We drive past the turnoff for the warehouse three times before we realize that the small bridge going over a stream is the turnoff. Most of the road up to it is unmanageable even in this truck, mainly from falling debris and other vehicles that have either broken down in the road or the owners have abandoned. Michael and Nova have to keep getting out to clear the way for me, since none of us want to risk going off road and wrecking the truck. Michael seems to be getting more and more pissed off while Nova grins and bears it. I have a feeling she's winding Michael up in the back of the truck, which is hilarious, but counterproductive to the mission. Night is falling and the rain is starting up again, and this does nothing to keep up everyone's spirits. Yet the fact that the turnoff and the road leading up to it is a total mess is a positive thing: it means there's a chance no one else has found it yet.

We pull up to the gates of the building, finding them unlocked and swinging on rusty hinges in the wind. Nova jumps down from the back to make sure it stays open as I pull the truck through, and then she closes it after us. It creaks and groans as she clanks it shut, suggesting that it hasn't been moved in a long time. Even more positive stuff, I decide.

A couple of deaders are shambling around the courtyard of the warehouse—old employees, by the looks of the tattered blue overalls they're wearing. One even still has his little yellow hat on to protect him from falling boxes…or bullets, whatever. *Bet he never knew safety was going to be so important in his afterlife,* I muse.

Nova walks alongside the truck instead of climbing back aboard, and she heads straight over to helmet dude. She swings the handle end of her knife against the deader's head and the deader falls over. Before it can even get back up, she's stamping down on its skull without mercy.

I pull the truck to a stop, and Michael jumps down and heads for another of the dead. A couple more seem to have been attracted to the noise we've made getting here and are coming toward us, with more joining them by the minute. There's at least ten of them, which is more than I like—hell, *one* is more than I like, so I guess ten just makes this whole day a write-off. Yeah, let's scratch this day and start again in the morning, shall we?

I grab my sword and climb out. "Keep your ass in here unless we really need your help," I say to Rachel and slam the door shut, making my way over to help. The stench of the dead in the air makes my nose crinkle in disgust. "Why the fuck am I doing this?" I can't help but mutter.

I get close enough to a once bottle-blonde deader to see that it had once had a terrific rack—not its own, of course; all surgically modified. I'm sure they looked real good when this chick was alive and kicking, but now, as she stumbles toward me with her blouse ripped open down the middle and that dried-up, emaciated body sporting perfectly round breasts, it just looks a little fucking gross.

I take my stance like Mikey has been teaching me, take a breath, and swing. Her head comes clean off, making her body drop to the ground instantly. Her mouth continues to snap away and I head over—*snigger*—and stab the samurai through her brain, putting an end to her torment.

I look up in time to see another deader shambling my way—a male, for all intents and purposes. Maybe he's not chasing me, but chasing blondie? I jog around it until it's at a comfortable distance and then I do the same maneuver I just did on Miss Perfect Tits and slice his head straight off. His head rolls away much the way Perfect Tits' did, but his snapping head lands in a dirty puddle, and every time he opens his jaw, water flushes into it. It's like he's drowning, but not. I shake my head in disgust and stab through his brain, giving it a little twist as I do.

Nova woops like only she can and I look up at her with a smile. Michael's still scowling like a jackass, but I can see the hint of approval in his eyes. I didn't give a shit about his approval, but I like the fact that he and the others will know I can take care of myself.

We regroup with Rachel now that the area is secure, and head to the main doors. We're all pretty tired now, and really need to crash for the night, but we still have this place to clear before we get any respite. Life only ever hands me damn lemons.

Michael turns to look at us as a crack of lightning flashes through the sky. "Everyone ready?"

"As ready as I'll ever be," I say.

"If you're not up to this…" he starts.

"Shut the fuck up and open the damn door," I bite out.

He huffs and turns away, and I swear I hear him mutter '*women*' under his breath.

THIRTY-ONE

The warehouse is made up of huge sheets of corrugated metal that form a rectangular shape, with two small windows by the main double door entryway; both have long been boarded over. I'm guessing this wasn't made to be pretty.

Inside it's dark, and creepy as hell if I'm being honest. The sound of water dripping is coming from somewhere deep within the building, but it's too dark to see anything properly. Nova pulls out a flashlight and shines it ahead of us, illuminating the path for us.

It doesn't matter how many times you see an abandoned building—chairs toppled over, blood smeared along the walls, and decomposing corpses by your feet—it's still depressing. It's not the sort of thing you get used to in any way. You don't suddenly wake up and decide it doesn't bother you anymore. The death, the destruction—it's still a bitter pill to swallow, no matter how long goes by.

A *bang* of something falling over makes us all jump. That's another thing that you don't get used to: shit making you jump. It's not like in the movies where you suddenly turn into this bad-ass woman warrior who has no fear of the boogeyman anymore. You still get scared and you still get worried, but you learn to get on with it and live with it.

A moan comes from the left and Nova quickly shines her flashlight toward the noise. It takes a second before we see it: a lone deader glares at us—yeah, it fucking glares, *don't judge me*—and heads in our direction. It bumps into tables and chairs in its eagerness to get to us. I guess starving for a couple of years will do that to you.

"I got it," Rachel says and limps towards it. She grabs the military knife from her belt, and after a small tussle with the deader over the top of a table she slams its head down on the tabletop and pushes her blade through its skull, effectively pinning it in place until she removes her knife.

The room falls silent again, barring the dripping of water and the sound of cracking thunder coming from outside.

"It's going to be a long night," Rachel says and limps back over. "I didn't realize that it would be so dark inside. I need to get my flashlight too."

Michael huffs and I can almost hear him roll his eyes. I roll mine right back at him. Not that he can see me do that, but you know, a woman likes to get the last word in and I feel like I won that battle, so fuck you Michael.

"Fine, let's go back and get some shit together before we go any further." He turns and heads back to the door. "A little light, please," he says and snaps his fingers like he's Michael fucking Soprano.

Nova giggles. "Let's go get some shit. Whose shit exactly?" she chuckles again. "I don't need a shit right now. Rachel? How about you?"

"That's disgusting," Rachel laughs back.

"Knock it off, Nova. I need you to have your game face on right now. Anything could be in here, and anything could happen. And I'm still waiting for the fucking light!" Michael yells as he finally reaches the door.

He grabs the handle and begins to pull it open, but it suddenly flies back and smacks him in the face. He cries out as blood explodes from his nose and a deader topples in and lands on top of him. It's completely unfazed by its abrupt entrance and leans straight over to take a chunk out of his shoulder as a souvenir.

"Michael!" Nova shouts and runs over to him. She jumps up on one of the tables and down the other side for a quick shortcut. Her foot flies into the side of the deader with a bone-crunching *crack* and it tumbles off him, still snapping angrily.

Another deader makes its way through the open doorway as Nova rams her knife into the side of the first deader's head. She yanks it back out, sending a gush of dark brown congealed deader blood spraying around her—mainly over Michael—then turns and rams her knife into the second deader. As it falls to the floor, she kicks it back outside.

"Disgusting fuckbag, did I invite you in? No, I fucking didn't." Its arm is still inside the doorway and she slams it repeatedly against the rotten ligament until it makes a loud cracking sound and the door shuts, too, leaving half the arm inside the warehouse and the rest of the body out.

Michael is back up on his feet and dusting himself off. I say dusting—he's covered in deader gore from face to foot. He looks like he just escaped from an old school slasher movie.

Nova turns back around to him. "Well?" she says with a lift of her eyebrow and a flick of her long red ponytail.

"Well?" he retorts, pulling out a scrap of material from his pocket and wiping it across his face.

"Don't worry about it." She pushes past him. "I forgot, douchebags never say thank you." She walks back to where Rachel stands and takes her flashlight from her. "Sisters before misters, right, babes?"

I laugh at Michael's pinched expression. I don't think he means to be such a dick; he's just a little uptight. Dude really needs to let go a little.

"Come on, let's get this over and done with." I stand beside Michael, my samurai in hand. He looks at me skeptically. "Flashlight," I state blankly to remind him of what we were doing before he got the shit scared out of him—whether he admits that last part or not is not a mystery to anyone.

Together we head back outside, with no more surprises, thankfully—just the rain and the flash of lightning in the distance. I'm glad that the worst of the storm has passed over quickly, since we're basically locking ourselves in a metal box. We retrieve a couple of flashlights from our supply bags in the back of the truck and meet up with Nova and Rachel back inside. They're sitting on a table smoking again, legs swinging down like twelve-year-old girls without a care in the world. You sure as hell wouldn't think we just nearly got eaten—again. With the light coming in from the open doorway, we get a full look at the foyer of the warehouse.

"It looks like a fucking bomb went off in here," I say, my eyes gazing around us at the destruction.

Nova shrugs and jumps down from the table, and then lifts Rachel down too. "Same as everywhere else in this world. It's all either broken, empty, or someone else's." She drops her cigarette butt to the floor and stamps it out. "Same old, same old, darlin', now let's get moving. I'm feeling hungry." She pats her stomach, licks her lips, and gives a rotting limb by the table leg a hard kick. "Shame we can't roast these things. I used to grill a mean steak."

She pulls out her sword with one hand, holds her flashlight in the other, and leads the way, further into the building. I grimace at the thought of barbequed deader. The smell of rancid flesh burning is one I've experienced, and it was not a good smell by any standard.

Michael shuts the door behind him, and it takes a minute for my eyes to adjust to the gloom. Even with three groups of fake daylight streaming, this place still seems to suck the very life out of everything. I give myself a mental kick for my shitty choice of thoughts. I do not want the life sucked, chewed, or in any other way taken out of me.

Double doors with a broom handle threaded through them seal off the rest of the building. Nova stands on one side of the door and nods as she readies herself to withdraw the makeshift lock. She pulls it free and we all wait with bated breath for the sudden surge of dead to shamble out, ravenous with hunger; but instead there's nothing—no sounds, no stumbling footsteps.

Nova shrugs and grips the handle of the door, and still keeping to one side, she swings it wide open. Michael flashes his light inside and then gestures for us to follow him. We do and Nova wedges something under the door to keep it open. Michael has taken lead with me second, Rachel behind, and Nova last. I've somehow managed to grab myself the lucky spot right in the middle, and while I wouldn't admit it to anyone else, there's no place I'd rather be in this kind of situation than being the baloney-and-cheese filling to the Nova and Michael sandwich I've found myself in. Seems like the safest damn place to be, for sure.

We look around, shining lights into all areas, but everything seems relatively quiet on the whole deader-in-the-dark front. Unfortunately, the finding food, drink, and equipment situation seems less lucky. This place was offices, by the looks of it. Who the hell would want to work in this type of office, I don't know, and what the hell they could have been typing up is anyone's guess. There's row after row of small desks, each one with its own laptop on it. Well, I'm guessing the general gist of it, anyway, since a lot of the desks are toppled over, laptops smashed, power cords dangling. But the real kicker is the dried blood that's everywhere. Even in the dim lighting, it's evident that it was a massacre in here at one point. The floor looks like it was literally swimming in blood. My heart plummets to the floor as my eyes fall on bones—lots and lots of bones.

"Hey, did anyone ever read those *Funny Bones* books when you were a kid?" Nova whispers.

"What?" I ask automatically, my eyes still taking in the death around us.

"You know, 'in a dark dark town, on a dark dark street,' blah blah."

I turn to stare at her after dragging my eyes away from the carnage. "Are you cracking a joke?" I ask, though I'm ninety-nine percent sure she is. "Because that's not funny."

"If we can't laugh about it, we're already dead," she says flatly.

Michael steps next to me. "This is the sort of shit I have to put up with on a daily basis," he says confidentially to me.

"Oh shut up, you're just a grumpy asshole. But seriously, Nova, that's not funny, that's cruel. These people died. I mean, not just died, but they were fucking devoured, limb from limb. They were doing their job, and," I gesture around us, "this happened. They never expected to not get to go home ever again, they just came to work."

"She doesn't mean anything by it," Rachel says from the other side of me.

"Yeah I do, actually," Nova bites back out. "After what I've seen, nothing can faze me anymore. So if I want to crack a joke about it, I fucking will. You don't find it funny? That's too damn bad."

"Be bothered!" I yell at her, losing my cool, though I'm not sure I ever actually had any cool to lose. But still, shouting in an enclosed dark area with unknown X amount of deaders close by is seriously very uncool. So if I had any cool to lose—I just fucking lost it.

Nova laughs. It's not humorous, it's not funny; it's dark and nasty. "No. Looks like you got that covered for both of us, darlin'."

I grind my teeth, and yeah, I want to stamp my foot, too, but then I think about what she said, the 'after what I've seen,' and I think, *shit, if it's that much worse than this, who the hell am I to judge?* I turn away from her and decide to keep my trap shut.

We move as a unit, weaving through the desks. I grit my teeth and try to not think about the piles of bones, the half-eaten limbs, and the occasional headless corpse. It's not true what the movies say: zombies never seem to give a shit about brains. They will gladly eat any part of you—brains, legs, arms, face. They really don't care which part of you they get to sink their teeth into. If anything, the brain's one of the toughest places for them to get to.

At the other side of the weird office room is another set of doors. These ones are sealed, too, but from the other side, and it takes a lot of noise and a lot of effort for us all to crash through them. We wait again, listening intently into the dark for any sign of movement. And there is some: faintly, in the distance, there's movement. We take a cursory look at our close vicinity, seeing box after box stacked high on shelving, all labeled with little white cardboard signs.

The shuffling gets closer, and we all shine our flashlights down the center path between the rows of shelving, and gasp.

Hundreds of the dead are lurching toward us, cold, dead eyes going wide in excitement at the sight of us—fresh meat. Or maybe not hundreds; that's just stupid. But there's certainly enough to make us all take a deep, panicked breath, and in the darkness there seems to be even more.

Michael, Rachel, and Nova pull out their guns—I guess it seems pointless trying to be cautionary and quiet now that we've been spotted by the living-dead army. I grab for the gun at my waist and pull it out, but it's a pointless task. The deaders are at around ninety yards away, and there's not a chance in hell I can shoot anything at that range. I make a mental note to brush up on my shooting skills when we get back to base—*if* we get back to base.

Michael fires his pistol and I shine my flashlight as best I can to help him aim into the approaching horde. Nova copies my idea and does the same for Rachel. One after another, the dead go down. Some are dead-dead, others are pulled to the ground by their dead companions and continue to slink toward us with the grace of a cat with no legs as their dead friends continue to clamber over their backs to get to us.

Michael and Rachel are excellent shots; I'd be impressed and applaud if there wasn't the whole issue of imminent death. Their shots get more accurate the closer the dead get, yet the closer the dead get, the more worried I get. Maybe it's because I'm going to have to start shooting at some point and I know I'm useless at that, or maybe it's because the closer the deaders get, the more there appears to be—despite the fact that Rachel and Michael have already taken down so many.

"Fifty feet, reloading," Michael yells. He grabs more ammo from his waist and slams it in as quick as he can, and takes back up his position in less than a minute. "Forty-five feet and closing," he shouts. He doesn't sound panicked in any way, but incredibly calm, which is unnerving to me.

The sound of the gunfire echoes loudly around us, reverberating against the steel walls and high ceilings, with a nice backdrop of deader moans just for shits and giggles. It's at times like these that I wonder why I don't learn to keep my big fucking mouth shut. I wouldn't be in this situation if it weren't for trying to prove a point to Mikey that I'm some bad-ass woman who can take care of herself. Well done, Nina, real fucking splendid job.

"Forty feet, reloading." Rachel shouts next to me.

My heart beats against my breastplate so hard I think that it's going to explode out of my chest any minute. And really, what's the fucking point in shooting these things? Shouldn't we hightail it out of here? After all, it doesn't seem like this place has food or any other useful supplies. Aren't we wasting ammo? Or is that the coward in me talking?

Rachel's gunfire starts back up again, and I think my brain is about ready to melt from the noise. Her gun seems louder now than it did before, and I take a quick glance and see that Nova has started to fire into the horde now too. I panic. *Shit, should I be shooting now too?* I look at the approaching dead, the mob somewhat thinned out by my bad-ass zombie killing team, but there's still a lot of them and it only takes one to chew your face off and kill you, and I don't have the skillset to hit them, even from this distance. I'm not stupid—one thing I learned early on in the apocalypse is that you have to know your skillset, and I know mine isn't with a gun.

"We need to go!" I shout out, hoping that someone will hear me. I don't care who, anyone will do.

None of them listen, though; they all continue to shoot, the bullets popping as they are expelled from their guns, and making a *thwack*ing sound as they hit their targets. Some are headshots, and of course those deaders fall to the ground only to be trampled on by another set of feet.

Others are chest shots, which have no effect on them.

"Thirty feet, re-loading," Michael shouts, and pulls out more ammo. He slams it in place and takes his position back up before glancing at me. "You can do this. Shoot them, Nina."

"Let's just go!" I retort back, trying not to sound desperate and pathetic.

"We have to take them down, now shoot." He aims and fires with total ease. The bullet lands in the forehead of one of the dead, and then he looks at me again. "Now!" he barks, and turns back and continues shooting.

I grab my gun from my waist again and take aim. I think about things that I had overheard: don't be tense, loosen your shoulders, don't grip it too hard, and aim directly above your target. I do all those things and squeeze the trigger, but the bullet goes off somewhere else instead of into the forehead of the deader I was aiming for.

"Twenty feet," Nova says loudly.

I roll my shoulders, frustration burning through me, and take aim again. I take a breath, slowly releasing it as I squeeze the trigger again. This time the shot hits the deader's shoulder—or I presume that was my shot. There's so many bullets going flying that I could be wrong and mine just slammed into the ground, but I'll take the shoulder shot for my own because I need this small victory. I'm so focused on taking the next shot that I don't realize how close the fucking thing gets to us, so when I do fire, the bullet hits its target and blows part of the deader's face away, the soft tissue sliding away to reveal shattered bone beneath. It isn't enough to kill it, though, and it continues toward us, its face a crumpled mess of bone and gore. I fire again. This time I must hit something important, because the thing collapses to the ground.

"Yeah! Take that, fucker!" I hoot loudly and then stop abruptly, realizing that they are still gaining distance on us and there are still plenty more to go.

However, with the distance between them and us so close, Michael, Nova, and Rachel hit pretty much all headshots, even on a moving target. Occasionally one must go astray and is a body shot, but in less than five minutes the deaders are no more—again—and we all stop, reload, and take deep, panting breaths of stale, rotten, gore-filled air.

My ears are ringing loudly, my shoulders burning from the effort of shooting, and my eyes are a little twitchy from seeing constant muzzle flashes in the dark, but as I look around and survey the damage—seeing body after rotten body of the dead   I feel a small victory.

It's strange how seeing the bones of humans in the other room filled me with such despair and dread, yet seeing the corpses of the dead in here fills me with such animalistic joy. I want to whoop at our victory, rejoice in the fact that we just kicked ass, but I don't, because that would be kinda fucked up. Instead I look to my other team members. Michael is—as usual—frowning and counting up his ammo, Rachel is staring blankly at the bodies, her face possibly mimicking my earlier expression, and Nova is grinning from ear to ear.

Wait, what?

"That was awesome! High-five!" She laughs and holds up a hand.

THIRTY-TWO

"L et's go," Michael simply says. "Keep a lookout and be careful." He sets off at a brisk pace and we all follow like little sheep.

We pass rack after rack of boxes. Michael occasionally grabs one down and roots inside, but it's all plastic parts for something or paperwork. No food, no ammo, nothing of actual use to us, which makes the whole journey and waste of ammo all the more pointless. We come to the back of the warehouse where there's another set of doors that look to be barricaded from the inside, given the image through the small glass windows in the doors. I hear Michael huff out an annoyance before turning to us.

"All right, we need to decide what to do. There doesn't appear to be anything useful here. The info we had was wrong. So, do we clear the building and keep it as a possible safe spot or leave? Personally, I think we're wasting time and we should leave." He sounds seriously pissed off.

"I think it's too late to head somewhere else today," I reply. "I say we secure the rest of this place, or at least a good portion of it. That way we can spend the night here and head back out tomorrow." I offer up my suggestion, fully expecting him to come back with some smartass remark, but lo and behold, he doesn't.

He nods in approval. "Okay, that sounds like a good plan, actually. Everyone else agree?"

"Aye aye, captain," Nova snarks and salutes him, still grinning.

Rachel shrugs, seemingly not bothered either way. Or maybe she is, I don't know. My adrenalin rush is wearing down and I really want to sit down and feel somewhat safe for five or ten minutes; I'm sure she feels the same way. After all, she's been traveling on an injury, and that shit has got to be hurting.

Michael looks toward the door in front of us, I presume assessing what kind of noise it would make to force our way through. There's no way he can have enough ammo on him to take on another horde like the last one we encountered. He bangs on the door, the sound echoing inside the darkened room. I scan behind us, gun in one hand and flashlight in the other, my samurai safely stored in its sheath on my back. Nothing comes, and it's not a pretty sight looking at the destruction we left in our wake.

The tap-tapping of the rain on the metal roof is somewhat calming in such a terrifying situation. My heart continues to beat heavily, and when Michael knocks on the doors again, I jump. Nothing comes from inside the room and we take it as a unanimous decision to push our way in. It takes a shitload of effort on everyone's part. These doors were barricaded real strong, and I can't help but wonder what the hell happened to the people that did it.

It doesn't take long to find out: two bodies sit prone against the wall, the splatter behind them indicating that they chose the quickest route out of this hell. Looking at their emaciated bodies, I wonder if it *was* the quickest way out; perhaps they starved for months in here before choosing this option. I shake my head sadly. I guess it doesn't really matter anymore. They are out of this world, away from the hell and slaughter, and safely kicking it up in heaven—or that's what I hope for them. Because of all the places to go out, this seems like a darker hell than most.

We find more deaders trapped in a small bathroom; one is so rotted away, it's barely clinging to its false life that it can hardly move. It still does, though, squirming its way across the cold tiles floor to us, partially eaten by another one that we find in a stall still sitting on the toilet with its head smashed in and its pants around its ankles. Sadness washes over me in waves. Such a sad end for these people.

The windows in this room are once again covered by cardboard, and we peel it back to look outside. The storm is back in full force, but no thunder and lightning this time. However, the rain pounds down on the ground, making swamp-like puddles in the fields behind the warehouse. The back is locked up tight with no deaders, but beyond that, I catch stray ones shambling back and forth through the mud. I watch them hypnotically succumbing to the mud and being sucked down to their knees, not having the strength to stand back up.

"Nina." Rachel's voice interrupts my thoughts and I turn to look at her. "Everything okay out there?" she asks, even though she knows it's not. It's like one of those things you used to do out of politeness: *Hey, everything okay? Good, good, blah, blah.* Fucking niceties and politeness don't mean anything, really, but we get on with it, we nod our heads like everything actually is okay, like we're holding up fine and none of this affects us. I decide to admit my weakness, my dark thoughts.

I shake my head lightly. "I don't know, is it? Will it ever be?" I purse my lips, realizing that it isn't helping in any way and finally understanding why everyone always says yes that they're fine. "God, that was fucking morbid." I give a small, soft laugh, but there's no real humor in it. "Yeah, everything is locked up. We're good from this end."

Without another word, we both head back over to the makeshift camp we've set up. This was again offices of some sort. But the two bodies that we found with their brains blown out must have been living here for some time, because it is already arranged into a small bed made up from layers of paperwork with a sheet thrown over it all, probably to avoid any paper cuts—you know how much those hurt. A small table and chairs is set up, too, with more paper on top.

We found a note left—again—presumably by the dead couple. It's like a last will and testament, I suppose. Not that that shit matters anymore, but I guess they wrote in the hopes that the world would be fixed by now. It was depressing to think that nothing has changed in the time that had passed since they wrote it, but the letter itself was short, sweet, and to the point:

To my sweet Julie…my lost princess,
Momma loves you. I hope that you're safe. We'll meet again one day.
Momma. X

The other message states simply:

Jack was here, and it sucked so I moved on to better and brighter places.
Rock on Motherfuckers!

I don't know which note started the waterworks, but I looked away before anyone saw them.

I bite into my granola bar, feeling the crunchy oats getting stuck between my teeth. I pick them out with the tip of my finger. With the next bite I suffer the same thing and I have an urge to launch the stupid thing across the room, but beggars can't be choosers when it comes to food. Still, it's a pain in the ass and bland as crap.

I rummage around in my mouth again and grumble out my frustration. Nova snickers and keeps smoking her cigarettes.

"I used to love this stuff," I say to her—shit, to anyone who's listening. I need to speak, and stop getting frustrated with oats for a second. "Always on a damn diet, watching what I was eating, calorie counting." I laugh. "I still am, I guess, just the other way around. Now I actually want the calories."

"Never thought I'd hear a woman say that," Michael pipes up. He's slumped down in one of the chairs, his head hanging back and his eyes closed. His gun, of course, is right by his side.

"Never dieted in my life." Nova makes smoke rings in the air, her feet up on the table we're sitting around. "I actually used to be a real fussy eater. I guess that was my diet in a way." She chuckles to herself, reaches into her bag, and pulls out a bottle of white rum. She unscrews the lid and takes a long swig, and then offers it to me.

"Probably not the best idea, but what the hell." I grab the bottle and take a gulp. It burns all the way down, and damn, it feels good. I cough and hand it to Rachel. "I was always more of a wine girl before—well, before."

"Snap. That was my poison," Nova says with a grin.

"What about you, Rachel? What was your drink?" I ask.

"I used to love to drink a good rosé wine. I can't handle it very well, though, anymore, so I'll pass." She takes the bottle from me and hands it back around to Nova.

"Hey, big man, you having some of this?" She holds out the bottle to Michael.

He doesn't open his eyes to reply. "No, Nova, you know I'm good," he grumbles.

He doesn't say it with any sort of malice—more like he's used to being the sober one around these two. It's funny, until this moment, I hadn't realized that these three were more like siblings than anything else: the way that they argue and bicker with one another, yet have each other's backs no matter what. I would hate to piss any of them off for fear that the other two would turn on me. It's a good thing, I think, to have other people so willing to have your back for you that others will be afraid. I know I have that with Mikey, but that feels different from this.

I frown, and Nova sees it and smirks. "Michael doesn't drink. Hasn't touched a drop in eighteen years…so he says."

"That's because it's true," he says, his eyes still closed. "I'm teetotal."

Nova hands the bottle back to me but I shake my head. "No, it's been too long since I had a drink. I don't want to get drunk."

She shrugs and swigs some more back. "Jesus, it's fucking catching."

"Can I ask a question?" I ask.

"You're a chatty one tonight," she laughs.

I roll my eyes. "I know, I'm not usually. I'm more of a 'my thoughts aren't actually appropriate for human consumption so it's best to keep my trap shut' kind of girl, but go figure." I smile. "Why didn't we run earlier? Why did you waste all that ammo killing those deaders? It seems such a waste."

Michael opens his eyes and looks at me. "What if there *were* people in here?" His eyes stray to the two bodies, which we've covered up. "Alive people. Would it have been a waste then? How many bullets would you want us to waste saving Emily or Mikey?" Again, he doesn't say it with anger; more like he's used to being asked this question.

"Okay, I see your point." I drink from my water canteen, but Michael isn't finished.

"At some point, if mankind is going to come back from near extinction, these things—these fucking deaders, as you call them—they're all going to need to be killed." He yawns and stretches his arms above his head. "If we're gonna be the hero in this story, might as well do it right." He smiles—actually fucking smiles—and I feel my eyes widen in shock. He wipes the smile from his face quickly and closes his eyes, going back to sleeping off the day's dramas.

Nova leans her head back against the wall, takes one more swig of the white rum, and closes her eyes like Michael. She keeps the bottle in her hand, though.

I pick up my stupid granola bar and continue to nibble on it. I'm starved, but this tastes like crap. Maybe I've been spoiled the last couple of weeks with all the food at the base. There was a time that I wouldn't have turned my nose up at any type of food—food was food, and if it stopped the aching in my stomach, I'd eat it. But things are different now. Sure, things are still shitty, but I finally feel like all the pieces of my life are clicking back into place after years of misplacement.

My arms and back and especially my shoulder are still aching from all the driving I've done today, but it felt good to be out on the road, it felt good knowing that I had three people that could take care of themselves—and hopefully me, if I got into trouble. And somehow I always get myself into trouble. I love Emily, but the constant worrying about her is endless and exhausting. I think back to the woman that

I ran over—the one they stood in front of the truck and Rachel had forced me to run down. *Will they do that on the way back? Surely not.* I look across at Rachel. She's busy staring into the flame of one of the candles we've lit.

"Why did you make me kill that woman? Surely there must be another way?" I ask her.

Her eyes look up and meet mine, and they're filled with such dark sorrow that my heart aches for her. "There isn't," she says simply.

"But why would they keep killing their own?" I ask, taking a quick glance at Nova's drink. God, I could do with that now. The feel of the woman's bones crunching beneath my wheels is as realistic as if it were happening right now.

"If you stop, you're done for. They'll take your equipment, they'll take…whatever they can and whatever they want, and they'll kill you if they don't get their own way."

"Hence the woman in the road," I say quietly.

Rachel nods. "It's not like I wanted you to have to kill her, but if it's her or me, there's no question of who is coming out of this alive." Rachel looks up at me quizzically. "What did you do before all this? You know a lot about the infection—the zombies. How they're made. Do you know how to stop it?" She looks almost angry when she says the last part.

"What? Stop it? Don't be stupid. There's no way to stop it. You just have to live and survive." I shake my head, annoyed. "What kind of question is that, anyway?"

Rachel looks away. "I've heard that there are people trying to find a cure, is all. If you know anything, then you should tell someone."

I shake my head again, rolling my eyes just for the sake of rolling them. "I don't know anything about a cure, or anyone who is trying to make a cure, so I sure as hell wouldn't know who to go fucking talk to about it. As far as I know, there is no cure. Death is the trigger and death is the only cure in that same respect."

I look away, my teeth grinding in frustration and anger. I know what she's saying, and I get it; and maybe it's the naïve part of me, but I still find it hard to believe that people would turn on each other so much. It makes no sense: in a world where we all need to stand proud and help one another, we're going around slaughtering.

Is any of this really worth saving? Maybe the zombies were God's way of wiping us out. What other excuse could he have for letting things get like this? I've never been what you might call a believer, but this is definitely hell, and the deaders are hell's minions unleashed upon the earth, which means there must be a counterpart to it. A heaven of sorts.

After everything I've seen and experienced, humans have been far worse than the deaders. At least the deaders have no choice. They can't help themselves: feeding and killing is their only thought process.

What excuse do we humans have?

THIRTY-THREE

The next day seems to have cleared away a lot of the storm clouds, and we finally get to see a hint of blue sky for the first time in many months. Of course it literally is just a hint, but a hint is all we need to give us the small boost that maybe winter is coming to an end. Well, at least at some point in the future.

We load back up, taking the very meager supplies we find—stupid things like pens and paper for the kids back at the base, some cleaning supplies from the janitor's closet, toilet paper. Like I said, stupid things really—though you can never have enough toilet paper. Yes, it's the small things that please me. Don't judge until you've had to wipe your ass on leaves. We still haven't found any food or weapons, which is the important stuff. We talk about where to head to next, the map stretched over the front of an old car.

"It just makes no sense. The warehouse is right here on the map." Rachel points again.

"Well, this *is* a warehouse," I offer, to which I receive a glare from

Rachel. "What? I'm only saying that . . . well, why the fuck did you think food was in there, anyway?"

"We bumped into a trucker a couple of months back," Michael says as he sharpens his knife on a rock. "He told us about this place he was heading to, somewhere that he used to deliver to. He gave us the address, circled it on a map, said if we ever get to the area to look him up,"

The act reminds me of Mikey and I feel a little homesick, which is stupid and weird because I haven't had a home in a long time, and we don't intend on staying at the base, so what the fuck am I getting all weirded out for? Or maybe I do want to stay at the base now, bury my head in the sand and pretend that the Forgotten and the walled cities don't exist. And I'm still talking to myself, so I better stop before everyone thinks I'm weirder than they already do. I shake my head to clear the fog.

"So maybe he gave you a false address. I mean, why would he share his stash with you anyway?" I ask, frowning at the sight of an approaching deader.

"Because we saved his life and then we helped him rescue his wife, and he owed us big time," Nova says between plumes of cigarette smoke. She has it between her lips as she also sharpens her knife on a rock.

I think about the samurai sword and worry that it might need sharpening, but it's not really seen any action yet. I continue to watch the approaching deader; it's close enough to be annoyingly loud now, its smell wafting over to us on the tail of a small breeze. I pull out the sword and head over to it. It's on the other side of the fence, its hands gripping the thin metal, its fingers clawing to get through.

It gnaws at the fence to get to me. Putrid, rotten gums squash on the metal, leaving liquid dripping from its mouth. Its teeth are broken and black, and its tongue is flapping around as if it were trying to lick an ice cream that was melting. This thing—this woman with her long brown matted hair—deserves a burial, but I can't do that for her. The least I can do is put her out of her misery.

I raise my sword and ram it through a hole in the fence, straight through into her skull and into her brain. I pull the sword back out and she falls to the ground without another noise. When I look up I can see more of them coming.

With a heavy sigh, I head back to my three partners feeling depressed.

Nova wraps an arm around my shoulders. "Cheer up, chica. It's not all bad." She scrubs the top of my head with her knuckles, making me yelp and jump away from her. "Just think, you could look like Mr. Miserable over there." She chuckles and lets me get away.

Michael doesn't say anything, but instead climbs into the back of the truck, his lips pressed together in irritation.

I smirk. "So we've decided where we're heading next, then?"

Rachel points to another X a couple of miles from where we are. "Supermarket."

"Are you serious? That's like an Apocalypse 101 no-no. There's no point going to supermarkets, as they are either overrun and or ransacked to shit." I look from Nova to Rachel and then to Michael. They all seem pretty calm and unfazed by it all. "Fine." I throw my hands up in defeat and head to the front of the truck and climb in.

A couple of minutes pass, and the passenger door opens and Rachel climbs up. She's been taking antibiotics since the attack yesterday; we need to get some more for her before we head back. The bite doesn't seem infected, and she's not in as much pain as yesterday, but we all think it will be best to keep her on meds for a couple of days at least.

I think back to Duncan and how quickly his infection had set in after being bitten. Had it been a worse bite? I can't be sure now, but I think so. It seems like a lifetime ago. And those people—JD, Duncan, Crunch—they all seem like storybook characters to me. And just like in a favorite book, I still miss some of those characters. Some days the ache in my chest is hard to contend with.

I start up the engine. It's noisy and we're going to need gas soon, but it feels good to be driving again. I turn the wheel and we head out through the gates. I hadn't noticed Nova standing by them, and I stop when I drive through. From my mirrors, I watch her close the gates and climb back inside.

Heading back down the remnants of the road is much easier today than yesterday since we did most of the hard work by clearing debris from the path. But the storms haven't been kind to the road, either, and the truck rocks from side to side as we drive through giant potholes. It's nothing the truck can't handle; if anything, the road probably seems worse because of the heavy suspension of the truck.

Back on a fairly normal stretch of road, we travel east, the trees lining either side making me nervous. I look across at Rachel, who's staring out the window, her gun poised in her lap.

"So, yesterday, you said that they were testing on humans in your city." I try for casual, but she catches on pretty quick.

"Yep." She looks across at me, curiosity behind her eyes. "Why?"

"They didn't do that in mine," I say with a swallow. It's funny how it doesn't fill me with dread anymore—only anger, and worry for the people still living there.

She looks at me with curiosity. "How long were you there?"

"Pretty much from off the bat of this whole end-of-the-fucking-world-as-we-know-it thing." I wave a hand around.

"What was it like—where you were?" she asks.

"Pretty shitty, to be honest, though there were no experiments. But it wasn't the fucking Ritz, that's for sure." I laugh, and it's genuine, too. It feels good to talk to someone about this, someone who knows in some small way how horrible it was. I can't speak to Emily about it, because she refuses to discuss that time in her life. Though they didn't do half the things to her that they did to me, I have a feeling she witnessed more than any child should have to. She's growing into a woman now; I'm just glad she wasn't a woman back then.

Rachel watches me for a minute without speaking. Perhaps she's thinking what to say, or maybe she's thinking up a witty fucking reply—who knows?—but it's me who speaks up first.

"Are there more of these cities? Ones that do things to people?" I ask carefully.

She nods. "From what we've heard, there are plenty of them. The story goes that the government knew the apocalypse was coming, and they were initially trying to stop it. Of course we know how well that worked out," she says with a pinched expression.

"So this wasn't their fault then?" I add for clarification.

She shrugs. "No idea. All we know is that they knew it was coming, and when they realized they couldn't stop it, they tried to put precautions in place to protect themselves and fuck everyone else." She shakes her head and looks out the window. "The testing plants or cities—whatever you want to call them—they started as a place to try and find a cure, but when I was there, they weren't trying to find a cure, they were trying to mutate whatever causes the death virus to reanimate people. They wanted to have an army of these monsters to control." She frowns, and I can see her jaw twitching away in anger as she grinds her teeth.

"I don't know what to say," I say. "I mean, I'm completely shocked, that's the story of horror movies. I never thought in a million years that they knew, never mind that they would be trying to put these things to work like blue-collar fucking workers! Jesus Christ, could things get any fucking worse for this world?" My body feels like snake coiled and ready to strike, I'm so pissed off with it all.

"It is what it is, Nina."

"How can you be so nonchalant about it? That is seriously messed up. I know I'm new to this little horror story, but fuck me if that isn't crazy bad!" I say, getting angrier by the second.

"I'm not nonchalant, there's just nothing I can do about it other than survive and protect those I care about." She looks at me in confusion. "It does piss me off, but it's a big world and who knows what other people are doing out there. Maybe one of them can be a hero of this sad little story and put an end to it."

"Don't you think we should try and protect people, help them somehow?"

Rachel laughs. "What, like a rag-tag A-team? Come on, Nina, get real. Most of the people back at the base barely made it there alive, most of them wouldn't be able to last in this world without us. I'm happy that I'm helping *these* people. Because I can do something about that—I can protect them where they are."

I bite down on my lip, frustration in my veins. "I know you're right, but it seems so…" I shake my head, not wanting to finish the sentence.

"Unfair?" she offers.

"Yeah." I quirk an eyebrow. "Really fucking unfair. People are dying out there because of these deaders, and some asshole is rounding up the small amount of survivors and turning them for the sole purpose of trying to control them. That's fucked up."

She shrugs. "Like I said, it is what it is."

We travel in silence for a good while, and for the first time since this all began I realize how lucky I am that I've made it this far, and that I was behind the walls of a city that didn't turn people into flesh-hungry zombies.

We're only driving for twenty minutes or so when we come to another town. The town looks like what you'd expect any town that has been abandoned for a while would to look like: barren, dusty, some buildings partially destroyed, burnt-out cars, yada yada, same old, same old.

A couple of zombies come out to say hello as our noisy ass truck passes through, but they can't keep up with us and Michael and Nova take them out from the back of the truck. They're scary accurate at shooting. I see the sign for the shopping mall before Rachel and begin to head to it. We pass a small supermarket on the way. The windows are smashed in and it looks as barren as the rest of the town. I suggest stopping but we agree that it's best to head to the shopping mall and see how it looks.

I pull the truck around a bend and over a small rise in the road, and from here I can see the large shopping mall. There's deaders for sure, but it doesn't look like some *Dawn of the Dead*-type movie, which always gets bonus points in my book. Then again, if the world were overrun with those types of zombies, we'd all be royally fucked in the ass anyway, which kinda makes my point moot.

"Pull over. I need to let Michael and Nova know what's going on," Rachel says.

I stop the truck in the middle of the road—no need for rules of the road these days. Plus I've learned the hard way to always stop in the middle of the road so you can see all around your vehicle before getting out. I still check my mirrors thoroughly before climbing out, already seeing Nova's happy face looking back at me.

I laugh as I walk around to the side of the truck. Nova has pulled some of the tarp away so she can stand up while I drive, and has clearly been like that for a while.

"What are you doing, you crazy bitch?" I laugh. It's dangerous, but she doesn't seem to give a damn.

"It's boring back here with only miserable Michael for company." She lights a cigarette. "So, I take it we decided the supermarket was a no-go," she states as she surveys the landscape.

I nod. "Place looked more looted than a whore's panties. I'm thinking we head to the shopping mall. I think there's less chance that everything will be gone, and more chance that we get some serious bounty. I know it's more dangerous, but the rewards outweigh the risk—in my opinion, anyway."

"And that is why I suggested you come along on this trip, darlin'. I knew you had the smarts for this job," she hoots and points at me. "And don't worry your pretty head about getting in there. Rachel will get us in there no problem." She grins.

Michael stands next to her. "No explosives this time," he says, looking between Rachel and Nova. "Well, only if they're really needed, anyway," he adds with a sly grin.

"Explosives?" I smile.

"Rachel here is a clever girl," Nova says mysteriously.

We all go to the front of the truck to scope out the area for a couple of minutes before we head over to it, but barring the deaders stumbling around in the front parking lot, there are no other signs of life or death, which is a good thing.

"Head for the main entrance?" I suggest with a grimace. I don't really like that idea, but I can't think of any other way in. I mean, that was always the way I went into a mall—what other way is there?

"There's always the loading bay, but those things are usually closed off to the general public, so unless everything went to shit here when a load came in, that's a no-go. We can check it out, though—you never know when you could get lucky," Michael says.

I frown at him, confused by his optimistic and—let's be honest—slightly cheery nature. It's out of character for him. Nova laughs and pushes his shoulder as she flicks her cigarette butt away.

"Don't worry about Michael, Nina. He's just excited to see if he can get some clean pants. He's been wearing the same underwear for months now." Nova laughs loudly.

We all turn and groan in unison when we hear the low moan of a deader. Stupid deaders, always ruining the moment.

"Better get a move on then if we're going to get you those pants, huh?" I laugh and head to the driver's side of the truck. "You on that?" I say to Michael and nod toward the deader making its way up the road to us.

He looks back at it. "Nah, leave it to its shambling," he says, sounding out of character for him, and heads for the back of the truck.

We set off again, at a slower pace so I can see the best route. The deaders turn toward the sound of our truck and begin to make their way over to us right away. Damn things always know where a meal is, like sniffing out pizza in the dark.

I head around the back to see if there's a way in. There's a small barrier over the road. It's metal and I check to see if I'll be able to drive through it, but it doesn't seem possible. I try to lift it but the stupid thing is locked down tight. I climb back into the truck and sigh.

"Defeated by a length of metal," I grumble dramatically, and begin to back up the truck.

I hear a small pop of a pistol and watch in the mirror as a deader falls to the ground. I hadn't even seen that one getting so close. I roll my eyes at myself like a five-year-old. I need to get my game hat on and stop being so relaxed about this shit. I keep on reversing, turning the wheel as the road forks out. I hit the curb, riding it up a little; the truck's so damn big it's only by pure luck that I haven't crushed something more substantial with it—yet, anyway.

I continue to swing round to the left until I'm facing the right way again. By now a lot of the deaders have made their way over to see what all the commotion is about, and I take the opportunity to drive the truck into them. Sure, I could swing past them, but the creepy fuckers would only follow us. Might as well kill them—or at least maim them—while I can.

Rotten hands slam onto the hood shortly before being dragged under the truck, which bumps and jostles as bones crush beneath the wheels. I'm beginning to wonder if this was such a good idea. Rachel rolls down her window and the sound of the dead fills the cab. You know that sound—the weird, gargling phlegm-type growl noise they make at the backs of their throats. Well, multiply that by thirty, throw in a couple of bags of rotting meat and shit, and you're living in my world. Fucking joyous, isn't it?

Rachel's gun begins to pop next to me. We're high up, so I don't worry too much about them getting at her, and she can easily take them out. I check the mirrors and see that Michael and Nova are taking out their fair share too. I press down on the gas and ease the truck forward over the heaving mass of bodies, the crunching from them sounding uncomfortably loud with the windows down, making my skin crawl.

Rachel continues to shoot from next to me, and I can hear that

Michael and Nova are still firing away. Unfortunately, though the mass is shrinking in size, as I come back around the corner to the front of the mall, all our noise has been attracting even more attention.

"Holy shit," I shout.

Deaders are coming from all different directions, across the parking lot, dodging around cars, dragging themselves from under bushes. I try to think of the best plan of action while still keeping the truck inching forward, but not going too fast as to let the next group of dead catch up to us.

"What do I do?" I ask Rachel, since my good idea bag is running on empty.

"Figure something out, and quick," is her tense reply.

Fucking helpful, is all I can think in return.

THIRTY-FOUR

I continue to drive across the parking lot, dodging deaders as I go. With the windows open I can hear Nova and Michael shouting to each other, and I'm pretty sure Nova is laughing at something—but that would be all kinds of fucked up given our current situation, so I shrug that off.

I head out of the parking lot and around the east side of the mall, with twenty or so deaders following in our wake. There's only one or two around this side—for the moment at least—so I floor it to the opposite end of the building. At this end is another gigantic parking lot and yet more deaders. The front doors here have all been boarded up from the inside, as have the arched windows that go along the entire front wall. It's worrying but also relieving. If it's been boarded up that means people are—or were—inside, meaning that hopefully the place is pretty secure with no deaders inside. That's my thought process anyway. I just need to get us inside the damn place now.

As I pull across the front and down the side, looking everywhere and nowhere for a great idea, I see a fire escape at the end, between a part of the wall that juts out and a security door. The door is flush against the wall, and seems only accessible with a key card, but across from that is the fire escape. I drive down to it and look up; it seems pretty doable. The fire escape leads all the way to the top of the mall and up to the roof, where there'll definitely be doors to get inside. Effectively we'd be going in from the top—if we could get in through the doors, of course. I'm more than sure they will be heavily locked. After all, that would have been in the mall's utmost interest—to protect everything inside. In fact, it's more than likely only accessible with a key card, also, but it's a helluva lot safer to work out a way to get through it when we don't have deaders on our tails. Plus, Nova said not to worry about getting in, so I guess this is our best shot.

I pull up as close to the stairs as possible.

"This is the only thing I can think of," I say, biting down on my lower lip.

Rachel looks up and then back to me. "Let's do it." She climbs out, leaving me trailing behind her.

By the time I make it to the back of the truck, Nova and Michael are shrugging on backpacks and holstering weapons as Rachel talks quickly and tells them the plan.

Michael slides a backpack to me. "Do you think you can carry that one?"

I nod yes, but when I try to put it on, it's much heavier than I expected and pulls on my gunshot. It's healing nicely, and much quicker than I anticipated, but I still don't want to put too much weight on it. I shake my head. "It's too heavy," I mumble, feeling like a baby for not being able to carry it.

He takes it back and opens it up, pulling out some of the heavier items and distributing them between everyone else's bags while nervously looking over his shoulder as the smell of rotten meat gets closer. He hands the backpack back to me and I'm glad that it feels a shitload lighter. I try it on, and while it's uncomfortable, it's manageable.

"That's better, I can do that," I say, and shift the position of the backpack so I can still get to my sword with ease. I have my gun at my waist in a holster, but I'm a terrible shot.

"We've got company," Nova whoops with a smile and jumps down from the truck, pointing to the deaders that are rounding the corner and heading our way.

We head around to the front of the truck and climb up onto the hood one after another. I reach across to the fire exit ladders and start to climb, with Nova going first since she seems like a great shot and we don't know what to expect once we get to the roof. The deaders reach us quicker than expected and the smell of them wafts up to me, making me want to rain barf down on top of them in retaliation. I won't, though—that would be a waste of barf, and these creeps wouldn't give a shit anyway.

It's only a three-story mall, more wide than tall, so it doesn't take too long to climb all the way up. Even so, the higher I get, the more of a death grip I get on the metal rungs of the ladder. I'm not afraid of heights—living in the treetop houses put that fear to bed—but a large horde of the dead are underneath us now, and we have no idea what's up at the top. I'm trapped between a rock and a hard place.

Nova reaches the top and peers over. She's quiet for a few seconds as she scans the area, but finally looks down at us with a smile.

"All good," she says with a wiggle of her eyebrows, and climbs over the top wall.

One by one we follow her over the side, glad to be away from the reaching deaders. She's right that everything is clear, but it's not a pretty sight by any means. There are blood smears all over the ground, with several piles of bones. There's a small gray door, which must lead back inside the mall, covered in smears of dried blood. There's no way that whatever was up here could get back in, so it's either still up here or it went over the side. I look at the piles of emaciated bodies and brittle bones, realizing that it could very well be one of those.

Michael stands guard with his gun as Rachel applies a charge down the hinge side of the door. I wander off to the edge of the building to check on our truck. There's a shit-ton of the damn things down there now, all scrambling around the truck. I frown and tut as I see their smears of gore over the hood.

"'Sup?" Nova says from next to me. She peers over the side and then looks at me questioningly.

"They're fucking up the truck," I pout.

She looks back over and then back to me. "It'll wash." She shrugs and reaches into her pocket. With a grin, she pulls out a stick of gum. "You want?"

"Yes!" I grin back and reach for it.

She pulls it out of my reach just before I grab it, and I frown again. "What the fuck?" I snap.

"Nearly ready," Rachel yells to us, stretching out a long fuse.

"I need you to get something for me when we're in there," Nova says, all traces of humor gone. In fact, this is the most serious I've ever seen her.

"Well, I'm curious enough to ask what it is, but that doesn't mean I'll do it," I retort, trying my damndest not to look at the stick of gum and give away how desperate I am for it.

Nova runs her tongue across her lips before replying, quickly checking that the other two are far enough away from us. "I need you to find me…" She looks away shiftily, her face flushing a little.

"What?" I whisper, fearing the worst.

"I want you to find me a motherfucking Baby Ruth bar."

I gasp, and then realize that it isn't dramatic in any way. "What? That's it? Why can't you find it yourself?" I frown and reach for the gum again. She's clearly playing a joke of some sort.

"Because I always look, but I never find one," she pouts.

My hand grasps the gum and she looks me in the eye and lets it go. My mouth is already watering for it, and I quickly unwrap it and fold the little stick into my mouth, groaning as flavors explode on my tongue.

"I need you to look for one more thing," she says, while I'm mid-chew. I nod and gesture for her to keep going, not wanting to stop chewing for a second. "I need you to find me a pregnancy test."

I cough on all the extra saliva that's built up in my mouth and nearly swallow my gum. "A what?" I gasp. *Yep, totally appropriate time for gasping now.*

"You heard me." She watches me for a second, and I see the hint of vulnerability there. I nod an *okay* and she smiles. "Thank you."

I stand there struck numb for a minute; I didn't even know she was with anyone, never mind pregnant. Jesus, what will she do if she is? What kind of world is this to bring a child into? I can't imagine anything worse.

"Fire in the hole," Rachel yells.

I look across at her as she clambers up from her knees and jogs some distance away, and I look for a suitable place to take cover.

"Get down, in five, four, three…" Rachel shouts over to us and coves her ears. I mimic her but don't look away. "…two, one."

There's a loud explosion, and a ball of orange and yellow blows from the bottom of the door where the charge was, and gray smoke quickly follows.

"Stand clear," Rachel's voice carries over the ringing in my ears.

A minute or so passes before I see anyone getting up and moving toward the door. I do the same, and am surprised to see that the door is still perfectly intact, but the lock has been blown clean off, leaving the door swinging in the breeze.

Nova laughs, raises her gun, and heads into the gloom without another word. Michael follows her with a wide grin. *Jesus, these people are bat-shit crazy.* I pull out my sword, excited and nervous to get inside. I glance at Rachel over my shoulder as she throws everything back into her backpack and slings it over her shoulders quickly. She follows me down, and I feel the security of the gun in her hand behind me.

As we reach the first landing, we head into a long gray corridor and I realize that this must be an employee area. It's ridiculously dark, but one by one we grab our flashlights and light the way. I scan the walls and floor with my limited amount of light, trying to see if there is any sign of blood and gore; I guess I'm looking for any sign of deaders. It's only a short corridor, with one small door leading off from it on the left and one door at the end. We stop by the door on the left and count to three, and Nova yanks the handle and pushes it open wide. It swings with a creak and I hold my breath, waiting for the usual groan, but nothing happens.

Michael swings his flashlight around the dingy-looking staff room, but other than a couple of overturned chairs, nothing seems out of place. Michael closes it back up and we head toward the end of the corridor, reaching the end sooner than I'd like. Sure, this dark hallway is creepy as shit, but I'm comfortable in the knowledge that there's nothing in here with us—unlike out there.

Nova and I stand either side of the door while Michael and Rachel stand in front. On a whispered count of three, Rachel opens the door and we rush out, weapons drawn and hearts beating so hard they might just pop right out of our chests.

I crouch down low and swivel left and right, waiting for the surge of dead, but other than a distant smell of dirty laundry and bad breath, things seem pretty normal for a shopping mall. I straighten my spine and shoot a questioning look to Rachel. She shrugs, points left without saying anything, and moves off. I keep my ears keen as we move along the top balcony of the once busy mall, but I can't stop my eyes from straying to the mannequins in the window, all dressed in their best Spring/Summer collection.

The place is silent apart from our booted feet making their way from storefront to storefront. I edge over to the side to look down on the lower level, but don't see anything down there—no humans, no deaders. I frown; this doesn't seem right at all.

I move closer to Nova, giving her a poke in the back. She turns her head a fraction and raises an eyebrow.

"This is weird, right?" I whisper as quietly as possible, but even as quiet as I am, it seems incredibly loud.

Michael puts a finger to his lips but doesn't actually make a shushing sound at me. We all stop, heads craned to one side as we listen intently. Nothing. Could it be we've stumbled upon an untapped resource? Surely we're not that lucky. Surely *I'm* not that lucky.

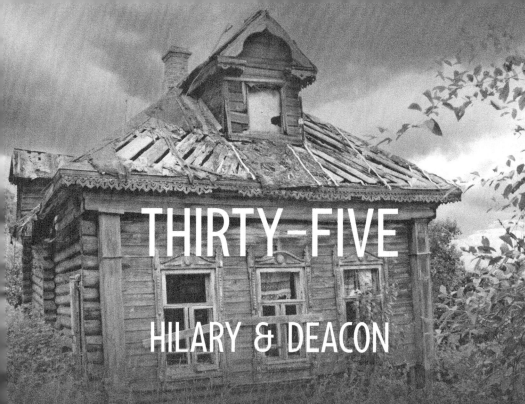

THIRTY-FIVE

HILARY & DEACON

"I can't, Deacon, I can't go any further," I sob, tears burning hot streaks down my dirty face.

Deacon grips my hand tighter, his eyes looking from me to my ever-growing bump. "You have to, baby," he says cringing at his own bad choice of words, and continues pulling me through the forest. His words hold more meaning than just telling me to suck it up and get a move on.

His words mean that I have to hurry up, that I have to dig deep, that this responsibility—this life growing inside of me—is ours, but it's me that must not give up, because against all odds, this baby is coming.

The trees are still stripped bare of foliage, stark against the cold gray sky with only the hint of blue underneath. I swallow down my rising panic as the groans of the dead echo behind us. I'm used to the call of zombies; they scare me of course, but they scare me more now that I have something to lose. My hand clutches around my bump protectively.

I stumble over a tree trunk, my shoes sliding on the damp wood. Deacon is there to catch me, though, as always.

"Need to get you some new shoes." He smiles affectionately.

I know he's saying it to make me feel better, to put me at ease and stop me from panicking. I used to love shopping for shoes, and previously would never have been seen dead in these ugly, worn-down things; but beggars can't be choosers, and if you make it to the end of the world, fancy footwear is not a priority.

"Tell me something I don't know," I try to joke back, nearly choking on a mixture of tears and fake laughter.

"We'll get you some real pretty ones soon," he says between panting breaths. His hands circle my waist and he lifts me over a small dip in the ground. "Promise."

The baby kicks hard, making me gasp, and I have to pant through the pain. Deacon steps over the gap and stares at me, his brow furrowing with worry. I put a hand up and bend over to catch my breath. I feel his strong hand lightly touching the base of my back. When the pain subsides I look back up at him and force out a smile, letting him know I'm okay.

"Promise?" I ask.

Deacon looks confused for a minute and then remembers what we were talking about and nods. "Promise."

"What's the occasion?" I ask as we keep moving. "For the new shoes," I add on. "Gotta be a reason for shoes—we don't have the money to squander on luxury items these days." I chuckle to hide my anxiety.

We have to get somewhere safe before nightfall. The house was overrun, there was no food left, and we were freezing to death in there. Literally freezing to death. This isn't any better an option for us—being on the run while being pregnant—but we had no other choice but to leave.

"Your birthday is coming up. I'll take you shopping for some new birthday shoes." He smiles, but it falls from his face as quickly as it came.

My birthday. I haven't celebrated a birthday since the day this all started. I don't even know when it is anymore, I just know that I blame all this on me—the apocalypse. And that's stupid, I know, because it had nothing to do with me. But I can't help but feel like I'm the one to blame because it all started on my happy occasion.

I lost everything that day: my son, my daughter, all of my family and friends. Nothing will ever be the same again.

"I'm sorry," he says, trapped in his own grief, and I fight back the guilty tears once again.

They were *our* children, and they were *our* friends, and now they're all gone and I'll never stop blaming myself. My birthday seems like the focal point for when everything went wrong, even though I know that's stupid. It wasn't my fault, no matter how much I blame myself for it.

"It's okay, D," I say through a tight throat.

He nods, but doesn't believe me. We've come to a small brown wooden fence, which opens up onto an old farming field. I can see a town in the distance, which could be either a blessing or a curse; but whatever it means, it's better than being chased through the forest by zombies.

Deacon lifts me up and over the fence with ease; even with his diminished weight, he's still my big strong firefighter—he just doesn't have any fires to put out anymore. That's one less thing I have to worry about, I guess. I always used to fret when I knew he was on the job, working a fire and saving lives. I dread to think what would have happened if he hadn't taken the day off to celebrate my birthday with me.

He climbs up and over the fence, and takes my hand again as his feet splash in the mud. "Come on."

We crouch at the tree line, scouting the field for the zombies. Behind us, I can hear the other ones still looking for us. As long as they don't see or smell us, we'll be fine. I reach down and grab a handful of the sloppy mud and rub it over my face—maybe it'll mask my scent, maybe it won't. Deacon watches me and then does the same.

There are one or two zombies in the field, but not many, and we might even be able to keep out of sight from them long enough to get across and to safety. Safety. Now that's laughable. I don't think I'll ever feel safe again. And this child growing in me definitely won't ever be safe, not in this world.

The government is looking for a cure, but there is no cure. Dead is dead, and there is no end to that, no stopping it. I should know: I helped start all of this.

THIRTY-SIX

NINA

Sometimes being a total smartass is a bad thing—to know all the answers and get to say *I told you so*. Today is one of those days.

"I think we're good here," Nova whispers, a little less whispery than I would prefer.

I shake my head. "No, something's not right."

Nova nudges me with the tip of her gun and tuts. Rachel chuckles, seemingly feeling as relaxed about all of this as Nova.

"Dude, don't poke me with that thing," I snap, and move out of her way, bumping Rachel.

"This is my weirdo-poking gun. I poke weirdos with it." Nova pokes me again and grins.

"Seriously, fuck off with that," I snap, a little louder this time.

She shrugs. "Can't. It's my gun's job. Poking weirdos is its dream, I won't sabotage its dream." She pokes me again, and I yelp and move far away, practically hiding next to Michael.

"Help me out here. You can't think that this is all okay," I plead with Michael as Nova stretches her gun over to me again. "That's really dangerous!" I half laugh at her as she makes a weird face at me.

"It's fine, there's fuck-all in here. We totally have the run of the show." Nova laughs and makes the same weird face again. "Now cheer up and don't make me poke you again."

I hold my hands up in defense. "Okay, okay." I hold my hands up again. I still don't feel comfortable. I know something isn't right here, but I don't want to get poked by Nova's gun again, so it's easier to just agree with her.

Nova pulls out her cigarettes and lights one up. "Time to go shopping, ladies." She barges past us all, purposefully pushing Michael more than me and Rachel, and flashes him a teasing look, and I can't help it, I have to laugh. She has the biggest balls I've ever known on a person. Michael scowls and we all follow her. Our guns are still ready to fire, but it's a lazy hold at best.

As we trail the mall, passing shop after shop filled with luxury things that I haven't seen in too long to remember, even my nerves decide to give me a little reprieve and I can't help but grin and feel excited at the prospect of getting new things. Like a kid in a candy store, my fingers are eager to grab and stuff items into my pockets before running home to look at my spoils. I can't help but go through a mental checklist of items I want, compared to things that I need, and yeah, of course we need to get shit for everyone else—supplies and whatnot—but I'm allowing myself a little selfishness in all of this. I fucking deserve it.

I stop, gazing in a window at a pretty, white summer dress with yellow daisies on it, and a ridiculously high price tag that I wouldn't have thought twice about paying previously. Of course I don't think anything of the price tag now, either, but for wholly different reasons. I mean, there's jack-all point in me wearing something like that. Even when summer swings around again, what would be the point? To look pretty while killing deaders? Hmmm, I think not.

Today's fashion trend focuses more on the practical side rather than which celebrity is wearing what label—especially since the celebrity world blends into the undead world these days. No one gives a shit what they wear, not unless they're wearing practically nothing. You'd be surprised how often that's actually the case, for whatever reason.

"Pretty," Rachel says next to me.

I snort a laugh. "You didn't take me for a floral kind of girl."

"I'm not—wasn't, whatever—but that would look really pretty on you, though. You should get it." She smiles sweetly.

"What for? It's not practical, and it looks like it would need ironing. I didn't like to iron pre-apocalypse—that shit ain't happening now." I shrug. "It is pretty, though. My husband would have liked it."

"Mikey?" Rachel smiles, her eyes leaving the dress, and I feel her gazing at the side of my face.

I shake my head but don't say anything else, and neither does Rachel. Instead we move on to the next window: a health food shop. I used to shop in these all the time—pills for this and pills for that. And what for? Never did me any good. So what if my skin was acne free and I had an inner glow? That's not helpful at the end of the world.

"We should get vitamins to take back," Rachel says, and goes to catch up with Michael and Nova.

I didn't even think of that. "Yeah," I mumble, putting a hand to the glass to get a closer look at the inside. "Good idea."

Actually now that I think about it, there's lots of useful stuff in there—really useful, in fact: vitamins and supplements, nutrition shakes, creams, natural pain relief. I make it a point to stock up on everything I can from this shop.

I walk faster to catch up with the others, passing some children's clothing stores and a jewelry shop with smashed out windows. Some people are total idiots. Who thinks that way? *End of the world—oh, I know, let's go rob a jewelry store.* Because that shit is going to be really useful to someone? Assholes.

I step over the crunching glass, the sound especially loud in the quiet. Everyone else walks around, but not me: I've just traipsed my pretty self right on through the center of it. I'll be picking this crap out of the bottoms of my boots for days. Awesome.

We round a corner, and up front I can see a wide staircase that leads to the lower floor. I watch my feet as I walk, my mood a typical mixture of my Gemini star sign: one minute upbeat at the prospect of gaining new, clean clothes, and the next wanting to cry because of a stupid flowery dress. *I'm pathetic.*

Nova puts a hand up in the air, halting us all in our hurried steps. She juts her chin out and I hear her taking a deep breath. I take a breath, too, smelling the problem way before we see it. My nerves jangle and tiny invisible ants crawl up my arms and back, a warning that yes, I was right, something is definitely very wrong here. I take small, quiet steps to the edge of the balcony ledge and take another look down. There's nothing at first, and then I see them: deaders. Snarling, rotten fucking deaders. Wait, not *fucking* deaders—that would be all kinds of fucked up—but aggressive, mood-spoiling, life-destroying, rotten deaders.

I look back at the others, who are all still frozen in place and looking at me in eagerness. I nod and point down to the lower level, and I see their shoulders visibly slump in disappointment. Disappointment that no, we didn't catch a break, this place is infested with the dead too. I look back down. The deaders are completely oblivious to our presence. Where normally they are quite vocal, there is only the low slap of rotten bare feet on the cold granite flooring from one of them, the weird shuffling sound of clothing, and the occasional gargle of something in the back of one of their dried-out throats. I count ten, but even as I count, more come from underneath the balcony where I can't see.

I look back at the others and show a hand, flashing it twice to gesture ten, and then I flash my hand again with a shrug, to give them a rough idea of ten plus however many more I can't see. Michael cricks his neck to one side, fixing a grim look on his face, and pulls out a second gun from the holster on his hip. Rachel does something similar, a snarl on her face and two long-barreled silver guns, one in each hand. Nova is grinning, and I raise my eyes in a *what the fuck* gesture, to which she smiles some more, like it's her birthday and I've presented her with a giant cake. I shake my head and grip my sword, edging away from the ledge so I'm not spotted just yet.

We all back up against a storefront—a music store at one time. "Plan?" I ask quietly.

"Rip these fuckers a new asshole," Nova suggests helpfully with a nod of her head.

Michael looks toward the wide staircase that we were just approaching. "I don't think they can climb up, so I guess we go down to them, and," he looks at Nova, "we do more than just rip them a new asshole. Let's take their heads."

Rachel nods in agreement, ever the quiet one of our group. Me? I'm not a coward, but I'd prefer to hide up here than go down there and risk possible death. But I'm outnumbered and I'm hardly going to wait up here while my friends do all the hard work, am I? As much as I'd like to. *Jesus, did I just consider them friends?*

"Fine," I agree, with as big of a pissed off look as I can muster. It's not a pretty sight, I'm sure, but it does nothing to change everyone's minds. They walk forward, continuing to be as quiet as possible and I presume not ruin the element of surprise, and I roll my eyes and follow them.

My heart feels like it's in my throat, choking me and stopping me from taking a fulfilling breath. My muscles twitch in eagerness to swing my blade and take rotten heads from rotten bodies. Stupid fucking muscles, don't they know what's coming? It's going to be a bloodbath, one way or another.

We all reach the stairs and begin to descend, crouching as low as possible as we do. The staircase swings around in an arc, and as we find ourselves on the large step that provides a view over the length of the lower floor, we see what we're up against.

Not ten or twenty deaders, but somewhere close to fifty. And lucky fucking us, as we see them, they see us, their eyes igniting with cold, hard fury and an eagerness for a feast. They groan, moan, and hiss, gargling on their dried-up, torn-out throats, and increase their shamble toward us.

"Holy shit," I yelp. Yeah, I yelp, like a little puppy about to piss itself.

THIRTY-SEVEN

"Michael!" I yell. Not sure why his name out of these three is the one I choose, or what the fuck I expect him to do, but it seems like a moment to shout someone's name.

Rachel kneels down on the floor and begins opening her bag and taking things out. "Distract them," she says without looking up.

Nova and Michael set up shop, dropping their pistols and pulling their rifles from their backs. Michael leans against the long brass railing and fires a shot. I jump, not expecting him to just shoot into the horde right away.

"A foot over, low and left," Nova says loudly.

Michael adjusts what seems only a fraction and fires again, and when I look into the horde, one of them is on the floor with its head exploded.

"Shit," I say quietly.

Rachel glances up at me and smirks. "That's their thing." She looks back down and continues doing whatever it is she's doing. "Michael used to be special forces and Nova is—well, she's just Nova:

289

bad-ass and proud."

I take my gun out, but really, I know I can't shoot them from here, and I'm not heading down into the horde on my own. So I stand here feeling awkward with a gut full of dread, with Michael's rifle blasting every couple of seconds.

"Fifteen inches out of center," Nova says mechanically and Michael fires and puts another down. "Okay, close enough," she says and raises her own rifle and begins to shoot into the horde too.

I raise my own pistol, but I know it's still pointless. "Can I do anything, Rachel?" I ask, wanting to feel less like a useless piece of shit and do something to helpful.

"Not right now," she replies distractedly as she twists some different colored wiring together and inserts it into a small black box.

I look around us, irritation building in me. As soon as we get back, someone needs to teach me how to shoot a fucking gun. I look into the horde, seeing the same rotten, disgusting faces of the dead I see everywhere else. I feel useless—less than useless. If these deaders got a chance, they would rip out our throats, and I can't do anything about it from the safety of my position. And for some messed up reason, my flight-or-fight response isn't working and I'm not happy sitting up here in the safety of the stairs watching everyone else save our sorry asses. I want to help, damn it.

"Fuck it," I say, and run down the stairs, taking them two at a time. I vaguely hear Michael shout at me, but then he's drowned out by his own gunfire and the close proximity growls of the dead.

I aim for the small pocket of deaders that have reached the base of the stairs. They came from a different angle and are separate from the larger herd, which now have their eyes on a new prize: me.

I swing back hard and then let the blade drift forward under its own momentum, keeping my stance light and my grip firm as I aim to hit the deader's neck roughly a quarter way up the sword, like Mikey had shown me. The sword cuts through the flesh of the first and second deaders with ease. I feel every stringy sinew being cut through, and then the subtle crunch of bone breaking ricochet up the sword and through my arm, before the blade reaches the other side of their necks and their heads fly off somewhere to the left. I swing back as another one comes at me from behind, and I only just manage to jump out of its way and chop its head off before it grabs me. I back up a couple of steps as three more come forward, their hands reaching for me like they want to give me the world's best hug. The great thing about this sword compared to my machete is that it puts a little more distance between me and the dead.

I'm petrified, beyond fucking frightened out of my mind, but somewhere deep down inside of me, I feel alive: putting an end to these monsters' misery feels right and just. I continue to swing and sever heads from bodies until the bigger horde gets too close, and I head back up the stairs and out of their reach.

I'm panting and sweating as I head back up to my friends. I don't make eye contact with any of them, not wanting to get a lecture about being an asshole and heading into danger, yada yada—you know, typical Mikey style. Instead I put my sword away and take out my pistol. From here I can hit the deaders; that's how close they are now. Well, I can shoot at them and hope for the best, which is better odds than a couple of minutes ago.

We've made an impressive dent in their numbers in a matter of five minutes: between my kills and Nova and Michael's, we've at least halved them.

"Ready, stand back," Rachel yells calmly.

Nova and Michael lower their weapons, grab their stuff, and head back up to the top balcony. I don't need asking twice and do the same, crouching down next to them behind the low railing. "Clear," Rachel's voice sounds out.

I count eight before an explosion goes off and the world goes silent for a split second. Then it rains gore and marble flooring, and my ears ring loudly. I dodge large slabs of the marble, which clank next to my head, and then Michael is pulling me up by the back of my shirt. I grab my sword from my back and dizzily stand. A cloud of dust is still in the air, making it hard to see clearly.

I cough and waft a hand in front of my face. "Rachel?" I yell and look around. Nova and Michael have headed into the dust cloud and down the stairs, but I can't see Rachel anywhere.

I stand still for a moment and try to get my bearings. I rub at my eyes, trying to get rid of the dust that's landed in them, but the action only seems to make it worse as they stream tears down my dirty cheeks and I continue to cough on dust.

A cry for help comes from somewhere ahead of me and I run forward, letting the cloud of dust descend around me. A minute or so later and I can finally see a little more clearly. Nova and Michael have headed down the stairs and into the bloodbath—see? I told you it would be—and are dismembering the last of the dead that still stand, or crawl. They never fucking give up, no matter how many limbs they lose; deaders are like the most persistent thing on the planet.

I still can't see Rachel, though, and am about to go down the steps and help out with the last of the deaders when I hear her voice.

"Nina."

I look down at my feet, my eyes traveling the ground quickly. Between rubble and dust and chunks of rotten flesh, I can't see anything, and I again head to go down the stairs, hitting the first one before I hear Rachel again.

"Nina!"

I glance back up. "Rachel? Where are you?" I look around me in confusion and go back to stand where I had last seen her crouched down over her little bomb, but I still can't see her. I lean over the barrier and there she is, hanging onto the railings as she dangles the twenty-foot drop to the lower level. "Aah crap, how'd you get there?"

"Long story," she says grimly.

"Really?" I ask as I look for a way to help her.

"Not really," she replies tensely. "Little help please?"

She's dangling from the opposite side of the balcony, and I can't see a way to help her get back up. My shoulder isn't strong enough to take her weight.

"Michael!" I yell, coughing again as more dust flies into my mouth.

Michael looks up, his eyes going wide, and nods as he runs over to us.

"Well, this is new," he says with a low chuckle as he leans down, grips Rachel's wrist through the bars, and begins to pull her up. "Fancy seeing you here."

"Yeah, real fucking hilarious, Michael," she grunts as he pulls her to standing, still on the opposite side of the balcony.

"You think you can climb over?" he asks, still trying not to grin now that the immediate danger is over.

Rachel nods and climbs, though Michael keeps a hand through the bars and on her waist in case she slips. When she's back on the right side of the railing, we finally survey the damage. There's still one or two deaders, but Nova is quietly hacking away at them—almost nonchalantly, a cigarette between her lips. There's a crater-sized hole in what was once the perfect marble flooring, and dead—or should I say *re*-dead—bodies lie scattered both in and out of it. Body parts are everywhere, and when I take a closer look at Michael, I see that he's no exception.

"Gross," I say with a grimace and point to a flap of something on his shoulder, not sure exactly what the something is—or *was,* to be more precise.

"You, too," he says and picks what looks like an ear off my back.

"Oh God, that's disgusting." I jump up and down and shake my head to remove any debris. I feel something dislodge from my hair, but don't look to see what. I don't want to know. Michael snickers, enjoying my discomfort. Asshole.

"I think we're good," Nova calls up to us. Her cigarette is gone and in its place is a lollypop.

I head down to meet her. "Where did you get that?" I ask almost aggressively and look around us, trying to find the source. And then I spot it: a candy store. It's like the holy grail beckoning me to it.

I jog over to it and walk inside, all thoughts of the undead army we just destroyed gone. I step over broken glass and rotten corpses, and stare in awe at the beautiful displays of colorful candy. Racks of Nerds and gumballs line dusty shelves like I'm trapped inside a rainbow. If this is heaven, kill me now.

I lift a hesitant hand to grab some Nerds off a shelf. The little boxes have toppled over, but they are still amazing, a full shelf of various flavors and various vibrant colors. I loved these tiny candies. My hand hovers over the boxes as I choose my victim, eventually picking a super sour apple variety. I tear the top open, not bothering with niceties, and tip the contents into my waiting mouth.

Flavors burst onto my tongue, making my toes curl and my eyes water as the sourness explodes in my mouth. I suck the flavor off them and then crunch down, more than enjoying every second of this moment before swallowing and repeating the action several times until the box is empty. I drop the box to the floor and grin like it's prom night and I've scored with the school quarterback *and* he just gave me my first multiple orgasm. Yeah, it's *that* good.

Rachel comes to stand next to me, bumping me with her shoulder.

"You okay?" I ask, still staring at the shelves of goodies and deciding what I'm going to eat next.

"Of course," she says simply, as if I just asked her the dumbest question ever.

"What happened up there?"

She shrugs. "A dead body hit me as I was standing back up and it blasted me over the fucking railing." She chuckles low in her throat, obviously pissed off and embarrassed.

"I had an ear on my back," I laugh back. "So, thanks for that." I roll my eyes comically.

We both start laughing as Nova comes in and grabs another lollypop from the stand. "Come on, you two, we've still got to clear this place." She heads back out, and we follow.

"So, you're like the bomb expert or something," I state to Rachel by my side.

"Sort of." She smiles.

Nova throws an arm over Rachel's shoulder. "This one here was a juvenile delinquent back in the day, wasn't you, girl? Back before she signed up, anyway." She scuffs Rachel's head with her knuckles, only stopping when Rachel pushes her away.

"Something like that." She walks on ahead, kicking through body parts as she goes.

I step over them, not wanting to mess up my boots any more than they already are. I glance at a head on the ground, its eyes following as we pass it. I shudder as it snaps its jaws at me, and I take out my hand knife, crouch down, and jam it into the side of its head. It stops its snapping instantly, and I pull out my knife slowly to avoid any backsplash of brain matter and rancid blood.

I stand back up and follow everyone else. Barring the odd random shambler here and there, the place is pretty secure. For some reason deaders always prefer the company of their own kind, and you always find groups of them together, as if they know they are more of a force to be reckoned with when there are more of them. Clever zombies.

We regroup after scouting from one end to the other, up and down both levels. And although my nerves are always on high alert, I let them go down a notch, knowing that we're in relative safety for the moment.

The ceiling of the mall is mostly glass, giving us a good view of the weather outside. It's raining—again—though not as heavily at the moment. It's actually very noisy in here with the rain hammering on the glass overhead. I suppose the sound would previously have been masked by the comforting sounds of backing tracks repeatedly played over the sound system, but now with nothing but our incessant chatter and our footsteps, the sound is loud. Loud but comforting.

We head to the food court first, to check on possible supplies. I'm not expecting much, since most of the food here was fast food and generally the type that would rot pretty quickly, but you never know. Hunting through the large McDonald's, we find mainly rotten meat and bread, vegetables long since disintegrated into a mush. But there are barrels of cooking oil, ketchup, and salt, which are all pretty damn useful. We drag them out to the front of the store for easy retrieval later on, and head to the next greasy food stand: a Chinese noodle shop.

There's the same in here as in the McDonald's—oil, salt, other sauces. But there are also large cans of vegetables—corn and canned mushrooms and such—which, again, is all really useful stuff. We grab the mass of napkins too: you never know when shit like this will come in handy.

After several stops, we have gotten a pretty big collection together and realize that we're going to need to pack up everything we can and head back tomorrow, perhaps bringing back a couple of trucks next time to get as much as we can.

The base is growing in its populace, and that's a good thing— for both safety and humanity—but it also means that we need more supplies: more food, more clothing, more everything. There's a couple of young children there now, and Zee has been talking about turning one of the buildings into a school for them and giving them something to do—perhaps even opening up the training classroom, and some of us with better skillsets helping to train some of the civilians in how to handle themselves and more practical things to do with survival. He thinks we have a real chance at living past this whole bullshit apocalypse.

It all seems so dreamy, as if he's living in a la-la land: school, training, survival. I don't want to believe him, but it's hard not to when everyone around you is so damn positive. However, I know what it's like to lose home after home after home, to watch your friends die, and have everyone turn on each other. Most of the people at the base have only lost everything once; I've lost it all several times over. I don't want to lose it again. For the second time in recent days, I realize that vengeance isn't the first thing on my mind. The Forgotten, the walled cities, it all seems so far away out here, as if none of that ever happened.

Of course my face begs to differ, but I think I can learn to live with that if it means being safe, keeping Emily and Mikey safe. Surely I'd be stupid to chase vengeance? To risk my life, their lives, for what? I don't owe the people behind the walls anything.

My guard is always up, and the walls around my heart always strong, but despite myself, despite everything I've learned to keep myself safe and protected, I can feel myself beginning to thaw.

Beginning to hope.

THIRTY-EIGHT

Rachel makes a weird noise from the back of her throat and grimaces. "This stuff makes me sick." She fishes out the last of the vegetables and throws the can across the home department, sending liquid flying through the air. "I'd do anything for some fresh fruit and vegetables right now," she says sulkily, and pokes the fire in the metal bin with a broken chair leg. "I miss real, fresh food."

"Me too," I reply, continuing to munch on diced tomatoes. "Though these, I won't deny, are fucking delicious."

"You better not have gotten food on my bed," Nova growls. That's the only time she seems to get cranky: when she's tired. Everything else she takes in her stride. She finishes up her rice and beans and heads over to check out her bed. She throws a backward glance at Rachel, grunts, and climbs under the soft duvet with a loud groan of satisfaction.

Michael comes back from the camping store just then, a smile on his face. "Tons of shit that we can take," he says, rubbing his hands together by the fire as he takes a seat. "I mean tons. I thought this place would have been cleared out, but shit, this is one of the biggest hauls we've ever had." He grins from ear to ear and it's hard not to smile back.

He's right to be pleased: this place is amazing. I always loved going to the mall. It didn't even matter if I was just window shopping, I just loved being around so many shops, so many things. It meant that there were choices, and I liked choices. Shit, yeah, I'll admit I was a materialistic kind of girl, but I thought I'd outgrown it. Looking around at all the things I've picked just for me, I clearly haven't. I refuse to feel guilty about it, though. I mean I did wear the same dirty underwear for years, the same shitty socks, the same roughed-up T-shirt. The only change of clothes I've managed are some army camo from the base, which is itchy, and a borrowed sweater from that weird town with the zombie repellent. Oh, and my sweatshirt from the consignment shop.

To go shopping and pick clothes just for me is a great fucking feeling, and even my conscience won't spoil it for me. The only shame is that it was summer when the deaders rose from their wormy graves, or wherever the fuck they came from. Winter would have been far better—at least then it would have been easier to find jumpers and thick coats.

We raided the health food shop for pretty much everything we could get, and then headed to a pharmacy and grabbed all the meds and toiletry stuff we could physically carry. I grabbed some makeup for Max, knowing how pleased she would be, and of course how big a favor she would owe me. I grabbed new boots for Emily from a fancy department store, along with several sets of underwear, and I grabbed Mikey a couple of packs of shaving cream and razors. I even managed to find some Baby Ruths for Nova, which she stuffed in her mouth eagerly.

After I grabbed things for me, I set about going through the list of things I knew the group needed. Zee had given one to each of us, so we all separated and trawled the mall for as much of it as we could get.

Medicines, bandages, weapons, camping equipment, maps, radios, batteries (though they were mostly all no good anymore)—the list was endless for things that the base needed to run efficiently. The main thing we struggled to get to take back was weapons: other than some large knives, there was nothing else.

The base was stocked with guns and ammo, but we had blown through a large load of it on this trip, and every subsequent trip was going to be the same; the ammo that was reserved wouldn't last too long. And weapons were just as important as food in this world.

I finish my tomatoes and grab my tub of cooked rice. After starting the fire, we boiled some rice and pasta. Trying to fill the hole inside of us with something relatively healthy and filling was always a difficult task, and that was something that wouldn't change until spring and summer, when the base could grow some of its own food.

"Pass me some more of that," Rachel says, still sulking. "I hate this food, it makes me sick," she pouts.

"It makes us all sick," Michael says, still grinning as he spoons some of his own canned vegetables into his mouth. It seems nothing is going to put an end to his good mood.

"No, I mean, it really makes me sick. I've had a headache for the entire damn apocalypse because of this disgusting food. I need something fresh and crunchy." I hand her a bowl of the rice and she stuffs it in her mouth, still frowning hard.

"This is better than the stuff I was used to eating," I say around a mouthful of sticky rice.

"Better than what most of us are used to," Michael says, raising an eyebrow at Rachel's sulking.

"I'm going to bed," she says, standing and taking her rice with her, clearly not liking being judged by Michael.

We made our base in the home department store, the ones where they have the stupid beds made up to showcase their best duvet covers. I always thought it was stupid, but I'm grateful for it now—or I will be as soon as I've eaten and head to my bed.

Michael shakes his head and dismisses her tantrum. "She's spoiled."

"It sounds like she's had it pretty rough," I say, thinking he sounds like a total dick. So what if she wants fresh food—don't we all? The only difference is that most people don't bother to say it out loud. But we've all been there and we all understand.

"Spoiled!" Michael repeats.

The room dims as both Rachel and Nova turn off their camping lanterns. His disregard of what she's been through pisses me off, and I can feel my temper beginning to grow.

"No seriously, she's been through a lot," I say, trying to swallow the rice that seems to be forming into a solid lump in my throat.

Michael looks up from his food, his jaw working. "She's had it easier than most," he says darkly and slams down his food. "I'm going to do a perimeter check."

He stands and storms off, and I rack my brain trying to work out what's up his ass. I remember her story about what happened to her— the whole dog and getting behind the walls only to find that it was a testing facility. That sounds pretty fucking horrendous. The more I think about it the angrier I become, and even when I climb into my deliciously comfy bed with the floral bedding that reminds me of a life before all this, I can't sleep; I'm that angry.

I can hear Rachel and Nova lightly snoring and I turn over, tugging the covers around my neck, feeling warmer than I have in weeks. The pillow is so damn soft and cozy, my face sinking into it and smooshing my cheeks. It's amazing, the feel of the clean bedspread on my skin, the smell of newness. But I still can't sleep. Michael's words have struck a chord, hit a nerve, and all the other stupid fucking cliché things you say to describe it when someone royally pisses you off.

I throw back the covers, plant my feet in my Doc Martens, and head off to find him. I need to know what he was talking about. I swear to God, though, if he is talking about her cozy life behind the walls, I will go psycho on his ass.

I traipse the rows of shops in search of him, eventually finding him in an old music store, rifling through the CDs and humming to himself as if imagining the music on each CD. He doesn't see me when I come in, and under other circumstances I would have tried to jump out and scare the crap out of him. But not today.

"What did you mean, she's spoiled?" I say, making him jump anyway. I don't take any satisfaction from it, though.

He breathes heavily. "It doesn't matter." He continues shuffling through the CDs but doesn't hum anymore.

I walk to him, standing on the opposite side of the rack he's looking through. "It does matter. You said she was spoiled. From what she told me, she had it as bad as the rest of us, maybe worse. So now I'm thinking you either judge us all that harshly—maybe me for living behind those fucking torturous walls—or you know something I don't. Something it sounds like I should damn well know."

His shoulders slump and he continues to avoid eye contact. "It doesn't matter now. It makes no difference to you."

I narrow my eyes. "Well now you definitely have me all kinds of interested. I need to know what kind of people I'm working with—what kind of people I'm living with."

We don't say anything for a minute, the silence becoming thick between us; I continue to stare at him and he continues to avoid my gaze. I watch his Adam's apple bob up and down as he swallows.

"I shouldn't have fucking said anything. I love that woman like a sister," he says and shakes his head.

I tilt my head to the side. "Well, you did—now fucking spill it before I go and ask her myself."

I let the silence swallow the rest of my unspoken words. I was beginning to trust these people, beginning to think of them as my little substitute family, but it seems that this little family has a dirty secret.

"She didn't just live there and then escape," he says darkly, his face finally looking up to meet my gaze. "She was helping them."

He says the words, but I don't understand them. Now I'm not a dumbass, but trying to piece together what he's trying to say to me is like completing a jigsaw with some of the pieces missing. I scratch at my scalp, puzzling everything together.

"She was one of the scientists. One of the original scientists," he says quietly, looking toward the doorway with a nervousness I've never seen on him before.

"Rachel?" I laugh, but there's no humor in it. "She's a scientist?" My head's still cocked to the side like a dog looking for a lost ball. "Don't be stupid." I laugh again.

Michael doesn't laugh, though; he continues to stare at me, and one by one the missing pieces clink together. "She's not a scientist as such, but she's damn clever . . . or they thought they were."

"She was working with them? Testing on people?" I ask, my stomach feeling queasy.

Michael nods, shame washing his features. Shame that he told me—told her secret—or because of something else, I don't know.

"But she had no choice, right? I mean, she wouldn't really test on innocent people," I add on, my voice barely a whisper.

Now Michael laughs. "Of course she had a choice, and she chose to test on people. She's not a bad person. She was trying to stop it, stop the reanimation." He looks away, dragging a hand down his face as if to wipe away the words he's telling me.

I grip the CD rack. "Jesus, she's really a scientist," I say, more to myself than to Michael.

"Yeah. I mean, she was always an army brat, but her specialty was always chemicals, hence the bomb-making skills." He looks away. "I really shouldn't have said anything, I don't know why I did, she'll never forgive me, I've just carried all this around with me for so long." He taps his chest. "It hurts sometimes, when I think of the things she did, and then having no one to talk to about it."

It all makes a bit more sense now in some ways, though I still can't picture Rachel in a lab coat and working with test tubes and chemicals. But we were all different people before this happened.

"You can't tell her you know. She's not right in the fucking head. All she wanted was to be the hero in this story, but..." His words trail off.

"The hero?" I shake my head. "This isn't a story, Michael, this is real life. There are no heroes here, only survivors."

"I know, I know, but she's messed up. All those chemicals messed her up. It's not really her fault—everyone just went along with her, thinking she knew what she was doing." He throws the CDs across the floor angrily. "They used her. They made her worse."

"So why did she leave?" I ask, dumbfounded. "She said she left. I mean, if everything was going so wonderfully with testing on humans, why the fuck did she leave?"

"Because they took it too far," Rachel says quietly.

I look up to the doorway. She's standing there with a gun in her hands, and fear flashes through me. She's going to shoot me for a second time—only this time, no one's going to save me.

THIRTY-NINE

NINA

"So, what? Now you're going to kill me? You didn't manage it the first time, so what makes you think you can this time?" I bite out, anger burning through my words. Probably not a good time to let my inner bitch out of her cave, but fuck it and fuck her if she thinks I'm going down without a fight—or at least without a couple of shitty remarks.

"Because there's no one here to save you this time." Rachel looks at the gun and then at Michael. I glance at him, seeing his gaze fixed solely on Rachel.

He holds up his hands. "I want no part in this." He backs up a couple of steps.

Rachel looks unsure of what she wants to do, and I play on that. "You don't have to do this, Rachel," I say. God, I sound so cliché I want to vomit on my own words.

She shakes her head, and even from this distance I can see her eyes are glassy with unshed tears. "I know, but I can't have you telling everyone about me. They'll all hate me." She chokes on her words and clears her throat. "I'm not a bad person. None of us were, we just wanted to find a cure, to stop this thing." She gestures around us.

"Of course not," I say as calmly as possible, even as my temper is begging me to go take a running jump at her face. "It's just one of those things that happens: one day you're thinking up a cure, the next you're sentencing innocent people to death." I shrug with a bitter snarl.

"It is!" she snaps back loudly.

"Bet it would have felt pretty damn good if you would have been able to cure everyone, huh?" I glare. "Wiped your dirty conscience clean."

Rachel's gaze seems far away. "Yeah," she mumbles. "We didn't seem to be getting anywhere. I mean, there seemed to be no cure at all. But then someone came up with a great plan, and it really was a great idea and it seemed doable, it just meant...." She looks to her feet. "It just meant infecting an embryo."

"A what?" My eyes bug out, I know they do. I can feel them wanting to pop right out of my head. "A fucking baby!"

Rachel shakes her head quickly. "No, just an embryo. Not a real baby." She looks up at me. "The cure didn't work on babies. We tried."

I gasp, loudly enough for her to flush red in shame. "You infected children? Babies! You mean you killed children? Turned them into deaders?" I sob, a weird, strangled sound coming from the back of my throat, which I have no control over.

"I know that sounds bad, but if we could have found a cure, or at least found out why people turn into these things, it would be worth it. Every death would be worth it to end it." She speaks quickly, the words spilling out of her mouth. "But when that didn't work, we thought maybe if we grow a baby already infected with the virus, that maybe, maybe that baby could hold the cure in its DNA."

A hand flies to my mouth to hold in my gasp of hatred and repulsion for this woman and her horrible team of wacko scientists. "You grew a zombie baby?" My heart thuds in my chest, reminding me of my mortality and of the ease with which she could kill me any second now. But I can't stop the words from leaving my mouth. I can't stop the anger and hatred for her; they pour from me in waves of disgust. "How could you do that? Why would you think that that would work?"

She looks at Michael. "Why did you have to tell her? I really liked Nina."

Oh shit, she's talking about me in past tense already. I am fucked. This is fucked and Mikey is going to go ape shit when I don't return home. Tears spring to my eyes—not sad tears, angry tears. I don't want to die, not like this. What about Emily? I love that girl. I wouldn't get to see her grow up—and then I remember she's pretty much grown up anyway, because childhood is pretty nonexistent in this piece of shit world. And then I want to cry even more, because it's my piece of shit life and Rachel is going to ruin it.

"She knew something was wrong. It's not my fault, Rachel." Michael looks exhausted. Did he know all along? I bet he was sick of hiding the truth, but how did he know?

"I'm a little lost, and I think if I'm going to die that I should get the full story, last rites and all that bullshit," I say. I've seen that in every damn Bond movie—the hero buying time by getting the villain to tell them their evil plan. It seemed stupid in the movies, but I'll do anything right now to put off the whole *impending death* thing.

"That's fair." Rachel leans against the doorframe. "What do you want to know?"

"You told me they were testing on people—that you escaped

because of that," I say carefully, trying to lean against the CDs so she won't notice as I grab my knife.

"Oh, that part was true, it was just the part where I told you I got picked up that I lied about. I was already living behind the walls. My city was one of the very first built, long before the stupid apocalypse thing, actually. It was a testing facility for the army. Modern warfare ain't got nothing on the shit that was happening back then." She rubs her face, her gun hanging limply in her hand. "I never meant for any of this to happen—honestly, I didn't. I didn't want anyone to get hurt. I wanted to help, but we needed to test the stupid cure on someone—how else could we see if it worked?" She stands and looks at me, waiting for me to reply.

I shrug, not wanting to actually say what's on my mind because that shit would send Rachel over the edge. My thoughts right now are not of the comforting variety, they're more of the 'wait till I get my hands on you and wring your scrawny fucking neck you mental case' variety.

"But then the first test subject reanimated, and the second, and the third, and then the volunteers dried up. No one wanted to help the cause, so we had to *make* people!" she says and looks from Michael to me. I glance at him, seeing his worried but somewhat bored expression—like he's heard this story a thousand times, and the only thing he gives a shit about is making it out of this with his pride intact. "It was for the good of mankind."

"Of course," I reply dryly. "I'm sure that's how those poor people saw it when you kidnapped and murdered them." I lift an eyebrow, my fingers wrapping around the handle of my knife.

Rachel shakes her head. "Don't say it like that, like I'm some evil villain."

I laugh sharply. "You *are* an evil fucking villain, asshole!"

"I am not," she whines back.

I grit my teeth, trying to contain some of the anger that's building inside me. Anger won't do me any good right now, but trying to keep a lid on what I want to say is a losing battle. "Yes, you are. You didn't save anyone. There was no super-cure in the end, was there?"

Rachel shakes her head. "No. We hadn't made a cure for the reanimation, we'd just made it an extremely painful death for the test subject, and they still reanimated." Her different-colored eyes widen. "It was really gross, to tell you the truth. Their skin rejected their bodies, sliding off their bones, but the brain," she points to her head as if I don't know where a brain is, "the brain kept ticking no matter what we pumped those bodies with. It really is fascinating."

I finally had my knife in my hand. If I could dodge a bullet and get to her, I could slit her throat if need be. It was a big *if,* and if I did manage to do all of that, there was still the begging question on what Michael and Nova would do to me afterwards. Shit, Nova was still sleeping, completely oblivious. Would she question where I was? Would she give a shit? She and Rachel are really close; if I slit the bitch's throat, Nova will more than likely slit mine. It's a lose-lose situation whichever way I look at it.

I turn to look at Michael, trying to stall for more time. "So what's your deal in all this? Why keep quiet on it all?"

He gives me a shifty sideways look. "I love her. She's my sister."

"You mean, *like* a sister?"

He shakes his head. "No, she's actually my sister."

"And Nova?" I ask warily.

"Yep, my other sister." He smiles with pride at that fact. "We were all together when she was testing on those people. Nova had no idea what was really going on—still doesn't. She can't stomach that sort of thing. She thought they were trying to find a cure. And that was all I cared about for a while, but when I found out about the embryo experiment, I told Rachel enough was enough, but the team didn't want to let it go—let her go—so we snuck out of there."

The final pieces fall into place: their closeness, their bickering—they really do fight like brothers and sisters.

My head is pounding, and I want nothing more than to have a long shot of something really fucking strong to sort it out. Maybe a quick nap, too, but there's not much chance of that. I try to give a casual glance around me for an escape route, but Rachel is blocking the one and only. My odds aren't looking very good.

"So what about the embryo? The baby?" I ask, still stalling for time.

"The last I saw of the woman they were going to infect, she and her man were running across country to escape just as much as we were," Michael says, his eyes flashing to Rachel.

"Well you helped them escape, that's a good thing. You did a good thing. Maybe it isn't all that bad after all." I try for lighthearted happiness, but it comes out more desperate than anything else.

"She was already pregnant," Rachel says quietly.

My heart freezes in my chest. "You impregnated her?" I ask, just to make sure I'm hearing things right.

Rachel nods, tears streaming down her face. "She'll be seven months now, I think."

Vomit and bile curdle in my stomach. "She's pregnant with demon spawn? With fucking deader DNA?" I clutch a hand to my own stomach. "What will happen to her?"

"The cure will either work or it won't," Rachel says coldly, wiping away her tears and snot. She lifts her gun back up and aims it at me.

"And if it doesn't work?" I ask, sort of knowing the answer

anyway. It's an inevitable answer, really. We all know what happens when deaders feed, when they get hungry. I shouldn't ask; I should be more concerned with me, with my life that's dangling loosely in front of me by some crazy madwoman. "What will happen to the baby? To the mother?"

"It will eat her." She looks at her gun and then at me. "It will eat her from the inside out when it's strong enough." She laughs cruelly, her laugh ending in a small sob.

I have no idea why she is crying, but it makes me angry, makes me want to hurt her and make her pay; I want her to die with my hands around her throat, my angry face the last thing she ever sees. Rachel begins to sob, her laughing dissolving further away into a wail.

"Rachel?" Michael says and takes a step forward.

She stops crying, the tears still pouring silently down her cheeks. "I really am sorry, Nina. I'll tell Mikey and Emily that you went out fighting. I'll give you a great death." She smiles, a little spark shining in her eyes.

"Are you fucking serious? You think that will make up for it?" I yell, my hand gripping my knife so hard that the palm of my hand hurts.

"Well, no, obviously not. But it's either you or me, and it will always be me. I'd rather you be dead than everyone hate me. But I am sorry. I mean that sincerely." She bites her lip and holds the gun steady, pointing it square at my chest.

"Fuck you," I whisper, and duck down below the CDs as a shot rings out.

I scream as a bullet ricochets against the CDs and they smash, exploding into a thousand pieces that rain down on me. I hear Michael shouting and running, and I know that I'm alive, but my heart is about to burst out of my chest and I think I might have a heart attack at any point. The acrid smell of bullets and melted plastic surrounds me, and I stifle a cough as I shuffle backwards. I have no idea where I'm going, but I can't stay here. I get to the end of the aisle and take a peek toward the door, and see not Rachel with a gun, but Nova.

I realize something isn't right, that somehow I've yet again misjudged these people and this situation. Nova looks over to me, sadness engulfing her features. I stand slowly, cautiously, staying as much behind the racks as possible.

"Nova?" I say quietly.

Michael stands up, his face mimicking Nova's sadness. But he doesn't cry. Not Michael. He never cries.

I walk slowly toward the front of the shop. Rachel's body lies prone on the floor, her brain splattered across the granite flooring. Her eyes stare at me accusingly, and I gulp down a cry. Of course this was the better outcome: her, not me. Like Mikey said, it can't ever be me, but Rachel was my friend—or at least I thought she was. And now she's dead. By her sister's hand.

"Nova?" I say again, just as quietly as the first time.

She looks at me, pulls her cigarettes out of her pocket, and lights one up with a sad shrug. "Bitches be crazy," she says sadly and walks away.

FORTY

I look at Michael, wondering what he's going to do now, but before I can ask him he walks away. I stand there, alone—well, apart from the dead Rachel on the floor—wondering what the fuck just happened and how things got screwed up so quickly. I walk toward Rachel's body, wanting to cover her up, wanting to give her a little dignity, but then I think of that poor woman out there somewhere in this world full of death and destruction, carrying a monster around with her, oblivious to the fact that it's going to kill her soon. If it hasn't already.

I step over Rachel's body, leaving her there all alone like she would have done to me. I don't feel good about it, and I know it's not the right thing to do, but I can't stand the thought of helping her in any way, giving her any pride—pride that she doesn't deserve—because she stripped that away from those poor people, those children, and that mother. No, Rachel deserves everything she got.

I head back to the department store, feeling exhausted both physically and mentally. Nova is back in bed, but Michael is nowhere to be seen. When I climb beneath the soft duvet that smells of newness and cleanliness, when my head sinks into the soft pillows filled with duck feathers, I don't feel contented, but tortured.

In the darkness I hear Nova crying, but it's not my place to comfort her. In truth, Rachel brought this on herself, but I still feel responsible for her death—as if I pulled the trigger, not Nova. If I hadn't been so damn nosy, if I hadn't gone snooping and sticking my nose in where it wasn't needed, then…then what? Nova wouldn't know the truth, that her sister was a head case. That she infected and killed innocent people. That she bred a zombie baby inside an innocent woman and then sent her off into the world without telling her.

I'm a piece of shit for opening Nova's eyes to the truth, and for that I feel terrible, but Rachel brought her death upon herself—not Nova, and not me.

The darkness surrounds me. The silence in this place would be eerie if it wasn't for the noisy thoughts rattling about in my head and stopping me from sleeping. At some point I do sleep, though. At some point in that eternal guilty darkness I sleep fitfully, and when I wake I don't remember my dreams. I only know that my pillow is wet from my tears, and my heart heavy with guilt at the burden that Nova is carrying.

We pack up our things, dragging everything close to the fire exit where the truck is parked before opening the door. The deaders have moved on—don't get me wrong, they're still around somewhere close by: I can smell them and I can hear their groans—but at least we can safely load up the truck with all of our supplies.

None of us speak this morning. Through our breakfast of canned soup and a shopping spree for luxury items for everyone, not a word is spoken, not a smile displayed or a joke cracked. Nova avoids Michael but not me, I guess feeling bitter and resentful that he knew what their sister was up to, what she had been doing all along.

I check the map of the mall, which is on a stand in the middle of the food court, seeing what other shops there are and trying to decide if there is anything else that might be useful for us. There's not much room left in the truck after packing everything else, but we can always squeeze a little more in—hell, we could get another truck, if need be. We haven't been down to the underground parking garage, but there's bound to be some good vehicles down there if we get desperate.

I point at the map, mentally marking off the health food shop, the pharmacy, the candy store, the home department store, and camping and outdoor activity store—all the places that we've raided. We ransacked the place for new underwear and socks and grabbed plenty of boots and sweaters for people, making sure to also grab children's clothing for the small group of children we have. We took the little food we could find, feeling lucky that we found cans of cooking oil, salt, and condiments, but even happier that we found the tons of dried noodles and pastas at the Italian and Chinese restaurants. We had hoped for more food, but what we lacked in food, we gained in other unexpected provisions. I truly wish we could take more with us, or even that the base was closer to the damn mall so we could get back here easier, but it's not and we don't, and that's the way it is.

My finger lands on the pharmacy again, and I realize that I didn't get Nova's item—the pregnancy test she asked me to get her. I head over there to grab it, passing the music store on the way, and see that Rachel's body is gone. Long red smears of blood show that the body was dragged, and I know that Nova or Michael have moved her body. Secretly I'm glad. Even though I hate what she did, she was doing it for the right reasons and I can't hate her for that. Well, maybe a little bit.

I walk the rows of products—nail polish, lipsticks, hair products. I grab a couple of boxes of the red hair dye and stuff them in my bag, remembering seeing Nova's dark roots showing yesterday. We grabbed all the sanitary products last night; you don't realize how much you miss those things until they're gone, so we made sure to clear every shelf out.

I pass the perfumes, each bottle glistening with unused scents. Each one will smell stale and rank now, their beauty gone, like everything else in this world. And then I see the baby aisle—the baby formula and diapers, the wipes and cotton balls, creams and bubble baths. Sadness creeps up on me. What kind of world is this for a baby or a child to grow up in? What do they have to look forward to? Safety? Sanctuary? That's all gone. No matter how many times we try to rebuild it, those simple luxuries are gone. All we're doing is working to establish some sort of environment that makes it bearable.

My hand glides across the top of a baby blanket. It's soft beneath my palm, and I can imagine a little bundle of joy nestled into it. Soft chubby cheeks, pink lips opening on a gurgle, and wide eyes so innocent and lost. My heart aches for what can never be, because I can never—will never—bring a baby into this world.

I grab the blanket. If Nova is pregnant she'll need this—among other things, of course. Or maybe it's me that doesn't want to let go of the blanket, this symbol of what will never be.

I grab a pregnancy test and stuff it in my backpack. It's a twin pack, so we'll have a spare, too, which is good. While I'm there I grab condoms as well. Hell, if she isn't pregnant, maybe she'll be more careful next time. I never thought protection would be important— hell, I never thought sex would be important, but it is. For some people it's a coping mechanism, for some people it's the only way to express themselves now. In this world, every day you have to be on guard and on top of your game, aware of everything and everyone, so if you manage to find that one person you can physically connect with, that's the best feeling in the world.

As I leave the store, my backpack bursting with the last of my essential items, I realize that as a community we're going to have to talk about protection and prevention of babies. We definitely need something more long-term.

I meet Nova and Michael by the emergency exit, both still quiet from what happened in here, and I wonder if they will ever be able to stand to come back for more supplies. I couldn't blame them if they didn't want to. They lost their sister here, Nova found out some dark secrets and that part of her life was actually a lie, and as a community we lost an important member of the team.

As we drive away, I can't help but worry how everyone is going to take the news, if I will be accepted anymore. After all, this is partly my fault for sticking my nose in and asking questions.

The funny thing is, though, with all the questions that it did answer, it also brought up many more.

Nova rides with up front with me. I'm pretty sure it was her choice, and I'm glad. I don't know how polite I could be to Michael right now. He knew what was going on, he knew that they were killing people—children—and then making some sort of freaky zombie baby. He knew this and he did nothing. And he was going to let her kill me. That really pisses me off. His love for his sister isn't a good enough reason in my books.

We drive in silence for a while, Nova eventually breaking it with some humming, and then finally she grabs a CD out of her bag and pops it in the player. These trucks didn't normally come with one of those, but Nova has upgraded it many times to make it more comfortable, from what I can see.

She looks at the back of the case, picking a track before hitting *play*, and as *Highway to Hell* by AC/DC blares through the speakers, I see the cellophane from the CD and realize it's a new CD that she picked up from the music store, and that she must be the one who moved Rachel's body.

She grabs out her bottle of rum, unscrews the lid, and chugs some back before singing along loudly to the song. It seems fitting somehow—this song, right now—and I sing along too.

I nudge Nova in the shoulder. Her snores have been ringing in my ears for the past hour and it's driving me crazy now.

"Wake up." I push her again and her head slides to the other side and thumps against the window lightly. She snuffles but doesn't wake up. "Wake up!" I yell, louder this time.

She opens her eyes, takes a deep breath and stretches, and then looks across at me. "'Sup?" she asks, retrieving her cigarettes and lighting one up.

"You were snoring loudly," I grumble. Sure, I'm tired and cranky, and I'm ready to pull over somewhere for the night, but I haven't found anywhere that seems safe yet.

Nova frowns at me. "I don't snore," she says with confusion.

"Sure you do."

She shakes her head. "No, I don't snore. That was, like, the truck or something."

I roll my eyes and ignore her, giving an overly exaggerated yawn as I sit up and attempt to stretch out my back.

"You tired? Do you want me to take over for a little while?" she asks.

"Is that okay? I'm no good with a gun, so if something happens I won't be very useful."

"Not like I'm much use when I'm sleeping." Nova grins.

She has a point but I still feel nervous, even as I stop the truck and we swap places. Nova stares ahead through the windshield. Nighttime is creeping up on us and we should probably pull in somewhere, but we all want to get home. It's been a pretty shitty trip, and one that hasn't exactly ended well.

"Nova?" I say quietly.

She turns to look at me, her eyes sad even though her mouth quirks up into an awkward smile. "I never fucking knew," she says. "I want you to know that. I didn't know any of that shit was happening. I thought we were helping that woman and her husband escape, I didn't know that they had knocked her up or whatever."

I look down at my feet, the guilt weighing heavily on me. "I know," I say, but I don't, not really. How would I?

"I knew about the zombie tests, that was it. I didn't know about the people—the children, I didn't know about those tests." I look back up and see her staring back out the window again. "I didn't know about that poor woman." She looks back to me again. "What do you think happened to her? Do you think she died?"

Even in the darkness of the cab I can see how pale and worried she looks. But I haven't got any comforting words for her. Hell, I'm not the comforting type, but I wish I could be for her—for Nova. She deserves that much to be free from her conscience.

"I don't know," I say simply, because I don't know what else to say and I really don't know.

"I hope she's okay, and the baby…do you think the baby is okay?" She picks at her fingernails, cleaning the grime from underneath them.

"I don't know," I say again.

Nova breathes heavily. "I need to let dumbass back there know that we're switching. If you can't shoot for shit, he needs to be aware that he's covering us all." And with that she climbs out of the truck and heads toward the rear.

The engine is noisy and so I can't hear her talking, but a couple minutes later she climbs back in and pulls the truck back out onto the road and we continue to head home. I see the trails down her face, the smears of dirt washed away by fresh tears, and I call bullshit on her telling Michael that we swapped places. But I don't say anything; she needed those couple of minutes.

FORTY-ONE

"**W**e're coming up to a bad patch," Nova says, checking that all her weapons are within reach.

Nova had driven through most of the night without complaint, and I had slept fitfully. When I woke for the second time, a scream caught in my throat, I decided to not bother trying to get any more rest, and we had swapped places again. Nova hadn't slept, though; she'd sat staring out into the darkness, occasionally swigging on her rum, and smoking. I knew she was hurting, but couldn't think of any way to ease that pain. She had shot Rachel, her own sister—chosen me over her kin, and for that I'm eternally grateful, but of course her sacrifice comes with restrictions.

I know she feels more betrayed by Michael than anything else; that much she did say, and I can't blame her. They were all supposed to have each other's backs, but they were keeping dark secrets from her. She helped them all escape, helped that other woman escape, and she thought she was helping but really she was making the problem worse.

In hindsight, though, we'd all do things differently.

"No matter what," Nova begins.

"I don't stop," I finish for her quickly. "I know."

She nods, understanding that Rachel told me that on the way out. My mind is on what will happen, what happened last time, and the fact that it's not raining and hasn't rained for at least twenty-four hours, so I can afford to go a little faster. I'm debating all this when I see a dark smear along the middle of the road, and I know that's where I hit the woman on our way out. I floor it, not thinking anymore, just hoping not to experience the same thing again.

Nova opens up her window, levels the barrel of her gun out of it, and starts shooting. I don't know if she's aiming for anyone in particular or just shooting to scare the crap out of whoever is there. I know she's a good shot, but she can't seriously be hitting anyone at these speeds.

I hit sixty miles an hour, feeling every bump in this old damaged road. I see shapes in the trees, movements of people, but I try to keep my eyes on the goal and keep driving forward, increasing my speed a little more. The sound of bullets ricocheting against the metal of the truck is unmistakable, but unlike last time I'm not frightened by it. I feel different from the woman that came out on this trip. I can't say how—I mean, I can't harden any more than I have these past few months—but something has definitely changed in me.

Nova crouches down in her seat, a snarl on her face as she reloads her gun. I slouch down as low as I can while keeping a decent amount of control on the wheel—not an easy job at this speed, I'll tell you.

I hear Michael's return gunfire from the back, and even over all the shooting I can hear him cursing something fierce, but we're over the worst of it and thankfully nobody seems to have gotten hurt this time.

At least I didn't have to run anyone over. It's all a little underwhelming, if I'm honest. That sounds stupid—I know, I know, I'm evil and insensitive, but I was all geared up for something really bad.

The truck hits seventy and I look in my rearview mirror as we speed away, watching as several people come running from either side of the road. I can see them still shooting at us, but we're too far away now and going way too fast for them to do any real harm, and all I can think is that they should probably save their ammo, fucking assholes.

"They're not real clever, these guys, are they?"

Nova laughs loudly. "I wouldn't think so. If they were, they would be laying better traps than these ones."

"Other than the throwing a random person in the middle of the road ones you mean?" I say with only a hint of humor because, you know, that's not really funny. But sometimes you have to laugh or your brain gets fried from all the bad shit that keeps happening.

She takes a deep breath. "Yeah, other than that."

"Desperate people do desperate things. Let's be glad that they don't have any real ammo." I roll my eyes at the thought. These guys with big-assed guns would be a bad combination.

"They're like those really irritating little flies that hang around no matter how many times you swat them away." She laughs.

I laugh back because I couldn't agree more. I ease off the gas, slowing to fifty miles an hour. Stopping for gas is never one of my favorite things, and I'd like to make it back without having to fill up again; leadfooting it isn't going to help. I keep checking the rearview mirror to make sure we're not being followed. Not that I really need to—Michael will be on high alert or whatever now, and he'll take care of anyone that tries to follow us. He's totally silent now, which is a good sign.

We drive in silence for a while, both our thoughts wandering in their own directions. The only sound is the noisy-ass truck, which probably signals everyone and everything to our location. My ass is numb from the vibrations and my back and shoulders are getting stiff. I know we're nearly back now, and I can't wait. I want a long, hot shower, some decent food, and to see Mikey and Emily.

My stomach sinks when I realize how much I've come to depend on them—not on their skillset or how they can help me, but on them being there, their affection and love.

"Fuck me," I whisper to myself.

"Say what now?"

I look at Nova, my face white. "I just realized that I give a shit. Like, really give a shit."

She stares at me for a minute before lighting a cigarette. "Happens to the best of us, darlin'." She shrugs and looks sad again, even with the smile she flashes to me. "You've got to think—what would be the point in surviving if you didn't give a damn."

I think about what she said, and know she's right. If you don't care, then you're just surviving. And I don't want to just survive, I want to live. I've done the whole surviving thing and it sucked: it wasn't a life worth living. But now I have purpose again. With that purpose comes responsibility for other people, but I know I would be willing to do anything to help them survive—to live.

The rain pitter-patters on the roof; it's therapeutic but also makes me tired. I know we'll be home any time now: we passed the zombie attack hot-spot—as Nova calls it—a while back. The road is still littered with bones and dead zombies. I'm not sure if they're the same ones I ran over on the way out or if these are some others that someone else ran over. Either way, I'm glad we pass it with no trouble.

We finally pull into the circular entrance of the base, and we're let in through the security gates. Mathew and Jessica are on duty today and both of them look extremely happy to see us. Nova rolls her window down and leans out. I don't know either of them much, but they seem nice enough. I've chatted with Jessica a couple of times; she's sweet but keeps to herself. Mathew is boyishly good-looking and I'm sure all the girls go crazy for him, especially when he carries around his bad-ass bow and arrow.

"You get anything good?" Jessica asks, leaning out of the small security box doorway.

Nova smiles. "Of course, darlin'. I got you some of that fancy bubble bath you asked for, and I picked up some rub-in hair product thingy—it sounded like the one you asked for." Nova shrugs. "I'll get it to you later today."

Mathew is staring at us both eagerly.

"Yes, we got you your books," Nova says. "Michael even got you some new arrows for your bow."

"Are you serious? That's awesome." Mathew cheers and fist pumps the air, and I can't help but laugh, even though a dread has taken me over. "Did you get the comics I asked for?" He chews on his bottom lip, worry crossing his face.

Nova shakes her head and rolls her eyes. "Yes, I got your damn Punisher comics. Didn't know which ones I was getting, but I grabbed a bunch of them. Now let us through and stop hassling me."

"Sorry, sorry, yep, no problem. Straight through." He smiles, looking genuinely pleased for himself.

Nova starts to roll up the window as I begin to pull away, but I hear Jessica shout to me and I slam on the brakes again.

She jogs up to the side of the truck. "Emily is pissed at you," she says with regret. "Thought I'd give you a heads up."

"Figured as much." I nod a *thanks* and set off again.

A deep and unsettling feeling sits in my gut. Not for the fact that Emily is pissed at me—she'll get over it and I have bigger problems—but because of Rachel. She lived here before me. She was their bomb-maker, a great fighter, and a friend to most. Not to mention that she was clearly insanely up on her science, and lord knows if she used that skill around here for anything useful. I can't help but wonder if everyone will turn against me now. I didn't kill her, Nova did, but will everyone be as disgusted as I was to hear what she had been doing previously? Or will they think that I overreacted?

I pull the truck up to the warehouse bunker and Nova jumps out and opens the doors. I watch from my rearview as Michael jumps out and wanders off without saying anything—I'm guessing to go and speak to Zee about everything that happened. He still hasn't spoken a word to me and I'm unsure on how to take that. Is he processing it all or is he plotting on his revenge? I mean, none of this would have come to light if I hadn't hassled him so much.

I back up the truck and, once inside, climb down from it and close the heavy steel doors. Nova and I set about unloading everything. Others will be along shortly to do this for us, but we both want to pick out the couple of things we got just for us before anyone else arrives and it gets taken to the consignment shop. It's no big secret—I don't think anyway—and I'm sure everyone does this when they get back. Call it first dibs or whatever you will.

We're about halfway done when Zee and Michael come in. Zee looks grave and heads straight for me. Michael joins Nova in unpacking the truck, and I hear them whispering angrily as Zee takes the crook of my arm and attempts to lead me away.

I shrug out of his grip. "What the fuck?" I manage to say it somewhat discreetly and surprise myself.

"We need to talk, now. Not here," he says and stalks off, leaving me to follow. He reaches the small door that leads to office space further inside the bunker and turns back to look at me. "Well?"

I roll my eyes. "Fine, let me get my bag." I stomp over and grab it along with Mikey's samurai and then stomp all the way back over to him. He holds the door for me as I walk through, and then barges back in front to lead the way. Seems stupid to me, to be polite and then an asshole all at the same time. It also seems uncharacteristic for him.

He leads us into a dusty office with chairs still up on the desks ready for cleaners to come in. Of course cleaners aren't going to be coming in anytime soon—that would be weird, given the whole-end-of-the-world thing going on, and completely pointless. I grab a chair down and sit on it, hands folded in front of me like I'm in high school detention.

Zee gets a chair and sits in front of me, a lot more calmly than I did, making me look like a bigger asshole. I roll my eyes at him and huff.

"What?" I snap. "I'm tired and have shit to be doing. I don't need your weird starey thing right now." I huff again.

Zee clasps his hands in front of him, trying to compose himself. "I'm sorry for the way I grabbed you back there. That was rude of me, and you didn't deserve that."

"You can say that again." I look out the window. The rain is coming down heavy again, I note.

"The thing is, I didn't want you leaving and speaking to anyone before I had chance to speak to you," Zee continues.

I look back at him, a frown crossing my face. "You mean about Rachel? I'm sure that's what Michael went tittle-tattling to you about." I stand up, my temper getting the better of me again.

"Please sit down, Nina. Everything will be okay." He sits up straighter, yet looks concerned.

"Then why am I being pulled in here and not those two?" I arch an eyebrow. "If everything is going to be okay, then why the hell am I the one being singled out?" I stomp over to the window and stare out into the rain. I can see a couple of shadows moving through it toward us—people coming to help unload, no doubt.

Zcc stands next to me. "Look, we don't have much time. Please listen to me."

I can feel him staring at me but I refuse to look at him. I'm being pissy and unreasonable, I know, but I can't stop myself. "What do you want?"

"I want you not to say anything about Rachel. If anyone asks, she got killed in the line of duty," he says calmly.

I turn to look at him now, an even bigger frown on my face than previously. "What? Why? Do you know what she did?"

He nods, his eyes looking away before meeting mine again. "Michael just told me, and I understand that she threatened you, but I believe it is in your best interest if we don't tell people that part. It's the best for everyone. Michael has specifically requested that nobody find out what she did previous to being here. He doesn't want her memory tarnished."

"What about my face? She would have blown that clean off. Does no one give a shit about that? And that poor woman that she's impregnated is out there somewhere, dying with the spawn of evil inside her. Does no one care about her?" I'd spit at him if I could gather enough moisture in my mouth, and I *hate* spitting. I'm so angry, the room feels like it is throbbing around me.

Zee walks away, looking at the old dusty chalkboard fixed to the wall. "Of course we care about you. Every member of this community— of this team—is important, but Michael has said that if it gets out about Rachel, he'll leave. He says Nova will leave with him. The thing is, Nina, I need their skillset. I need them to help keep everyone safe, and while I agree that what she did was disgusting and inhumane, telling everyone won't help anyone. It won't change things." He turns to look at me. "Do you understand?"

I roll my eyes again. "I'm not fucking stupid, of course I understand." I take a deep breath and grumble loudly. "Fine. I won't say anything. Keep him the hell away from me, though. I don't want to be on duty with him or work near him. I don't even want to eat near him. You got that?" I point a finger at his chest, and while he isn't intimidated in the slightest, he does back away. "Do *you* understand that, Zee?"

He nods. "I do, Nina. That's perfectly acceptable. Go rest, you deserve it."

I pick up my backpack and head out of the office without another word, and come crashing into Mikey.

"Fuck, Mikey!" I yell.

He holds his hands up and frowns. "Sorry." He frowns as Zee comes out behind me.

"You should go get some rest, Nina. It's been a long couple of days, I'm sure," Zee says as he passes us and heads off to meet the others.

I snarl at his retreating back. "Thanks."

Mikey looks at me. "What's going on?" He still has his hands on my arms, as if trying to stop me from falling. I shrug out of his grip, not missing this hurt look on his face that he quickly replaces with indifference.

"I'm sorry." I reach out to touch his arm but he pulls away from me. *Jesus, this is stupid.*

"Don't be, it's fine. It's been a hard couple of days. Let's go get you cleaned up. You stink." He laughs dryly and walks off, following in Zee's footsteps, and I'm left standing like an idiot all on my own.

I wring my hands, feeling a headache coming on. *How did I become the asshole in all of this?*

FORTY-TWO

I shower in our little home, the water turned up as hot as I can stand it in an attempt to wash away the grime, guilt, and worry of the past couple days. My jumbled thoughts mix with my shampoo suds that swirl away down the drain. But unlike my dirty suds, my thoughts don't wash away. The heat does nothing to clear my head, only making my weird sense of sisterhood to the unnamed pregnant woman increase.

I step out and wrap a towel around myself before clearing the fog on the mirror and staring at my reflection. I roll my eyes. This isn't one of those moments that you get in the movies, where the woman stands and makes some life-changing decision while staring at her reflection. Hell, no. I'm not *that* woman.

I do notice that the scar on my face, from my mouth to midway up my cheekbone, is now just a thin, jagged, red line. It will always be there, a constant reminder of Fallon and the Forgotten, and I think I can live with that. Revenge is one thing, but my family's safety is another.

I think of Michael and Rachel, and how it must have hurt him to go through with everything she suggested; but he did it, because like her, he thought they could save the world, save everyone. And poor Nova: she killed her sister for me. Or did she? I wonder if it was more of knee-jerk reaction to kill her. She was angry—though she's not shown any anger, per se. But she had to be: she was kept out of the loop for so long by both of them—how could that not hurt? And she hasn't spoken to Michael since she got back.

So maybe she didn't pick me, and maybe now she's suffering, thinking of how her quick temper killed her sister. I shouldn't feel guilty for that but I do, and that pisses me off more than anything else.

A knock comes on the door, and Mikey's voice sounds from outside. "You okay in there?"

"I'm fine, I'll be right out," I say.

I listen to his footsteps retreat as he goes back downstairs. He knows that something is wrong, but I promised Zee I wouldn't say anything, that I would keep Rachel's secret, and I intend on keeping it. If it keeps the people I love safe, then what's a little secret?

I brush my teeth and dress before heading downstairs, still drying my hair with a towel. Mikey is sitting in the kitchen, nursing a bottle of bourbon. The curtains are drawn and a small lamp is lit. Shadows dance around the room, creating a weird atmosphere—or maybe I'm imagining the atmosphere.

"This is all very spooky and cliché," I joke with a cocked eyebrow.

He looks up to me and offers me a soft smile. "Just glad that you're back."

"Yeah, you seem it." I turn on the tap and fill a glass with water before downing it.

"I am," he says, and pours another shot. "You want?" He offers me the bottle.

I hand my glass to him. "Yeah, why not?" He fills it and hands it back and I take a large swallow. It's warm as it goes down, but does nothing to improve the chill that I'm feeling deep inside. "Gotta enjoy the little things in life, right?" I lean against the kitchen counter, watching as he stares at me with a look that's hard to distinguish, and then looks down with a deep exaggerated, sigh. "So?" I say.

"So," he replies, and looks back up from the heavy brooding he's doing into his bourbon to stare at me again. He clears his throat before speaking. "So, what happened out there?"

I shrug and drink some more of the fiery liquid, looking away. "Just what you heard: there were bad guys and deaders in equal measure, they both tried to kill us, we won—mostly. Rachel lost her life," I pause, hating to lie, "saving us all."

"You sure about that story, Nina?" He continues to stare into his glass and I take the opportunity to drink the rest of my drink.

"Uh huh," I say and clear my throat.

"Thirsty?" Mikey says with a quirk of his eyebrow as he looks back up at me.

I hand him my glass for a refill. "Guess so."

Mikey wraps his hand around the glass and stands, keeping my own hand pinned to it. He steps closer to me, so close that even in the tragic lighting I can see his jaw muscles twitching, the dark shadows from a two-day beard bristling.

"Nina," he says hoarsely.

"Mikey," I mimic with my own brooding voice and smile at him.

We stare at each other for what seems like an age before he finally lets go of my hand.

"Stop with this weird bullshit, Mikey. I don't need this right now."

He continues to stare at me, making me feel more uncomfortable. "Jesus, what is wrong with you and this Mr. Tough Guy routine?"

Mikey looks down before walking away. He knows I'm lying, and I don't know what to do about it. I suck at this girlfriend shit. I'm trying to do the right thing by everyone, but clearly failing. I sit down in Mikey's chair and reach for the bottle before realizing that he's taken it with him.

I roll my eyes and pout into the darkness, listening as he shuts the bedroom door behind him. I want to go upstairs and tell him everything he deserves to know, but if truth be told, I don't trust what he might do. The last thing we all need is another hothead on the base. I head over to the sofa and climb onto it, snuggling down into the cushions and trying to drift off to sleep. Knowing that I can't tell anyone what happened out there, about that woman, it hurts, but Mikey's rejection of me hurts more. Still, I'm too proud to go upstairs and tell him now.

I close my eyes with a yawn. It's been a long couple of days, and I have a lot of sleeping to catch up on. The sofa, a bed—it doesn't really matter to me. I've slept in worse places. The important thing is that I feel safe here.

The front door shuts with a soft click, stirring me from my dreams—dreams of a woman with a bulging stomach and hands clawing at her from the inside out, little teeth gnawing on her flesh and tearing away at her stomach lining.

I jump and fall off the sofa, landing in a jumbled heap on the floor. I scramble up to my knees and then back onto the sofa, pushing knotty hair back from my face.

"Mikey?" I look around but don't see him.

I head up the stairs. He'll have to put up with me sleeping next to him; I'm not falling on the floor again. I sit down on the edge of the bed, realizing he isn't there. The bottle of bourbon stands empty and proud on the bedside table and I sigh out a frustrated breath.

I head back downstairs and grab a jacket as I leave the house, looking in both directions before setting off. It's still dark out, meaning it must be the middle of the night. I still find that frustrating, not knowing the time. I used to be a slave to the time—I guess everyone did—and some people have found a great freedom in the fact that there is no time for things now. Me, I find the whole thing irritating.

I can see Mikey's kerosene lamp bobbing in the distance as he walks, and I jog to catch up to him, finding him in the old park, sitting on a swing and swigging on another bottle of something.

"You should be sleeping," I say, making him jump and turn around. *Ha! Serves you right,* is all I can think.

"So should you," he retorts and keeps on drinking.

It's cold out, an icy chill wailing through the trees. I look up to the sky, seeing not a cloud there, every star shining down brightly, their beauty an oxymoron in this once beautiful world. In some ways it is beautiful still. Mother Nature has flourished under man's passing. Trees have grown tall, flowers have sprung up everywhere, but the ugliness is in what is left behind: the deaders and the people that have survived, the ones that still think they can control others. It makes my heart grow heavy thinking about all the deaths at the hands of these stupid people.

"I was. I fell off the sofa." I sit down on a swing next to him, pulling my jacket tighter around me. "That's your fault, just so you know."

"Always with the loose tongue, huh?" he says.

"You know me," I reply with a small laugh.

"Do I?" he replies, and looks at me as he swings his legs out from under him.

"Don't be like that." I look away, guilt flaming my face. "Don't be an asshole."

Mikey stops swinging and looks at me. "Me? An asshole?" He stands up with a bitter laugh and starts to walk away.

I roll my eyes, refusing to go after him. Yes, this is my fault. Yes, I know what's pissing him off. But fuck this and fuck him. I stand up and begin walking back to the house. A couple of seconds pass with only the howling wind for company before I hear him jogging up behind me.

"You've got some fucking nerve, Nina. You lie to me, straight to my damn face, and expect me to roll over and be okay with it. How fucking dare you, after everything that I've done for you!" He stands in front of me and I push past him and keep on walking.

I feel him tug on my arm a second later, and I stop as he again stands in front of me. I bite down on my lip, seeing the hurt and anger on his face. I know I'm about to lose my shit and shout at him, but I'm trying not to. He has every right to be angry at me. It doesn't mean I have to like it.

"Tell me what the fuck happened out there," he says with a shaking voice and cold eyes.

I look down and try to push past him. I can't tell him; I promised Zee, and Zee promised Michael. Like Zee said, we need Michael, and it will be my fault if he leaves—if he finds out I told anyone. And if he leaves, Nova will leave, and this camp—these people—need soldiers; they need protecting. I've caused enough damage as it is. I can't cause any more.

337

"Nothing happened, Mikey. Jesus, just drop it. It was shitty—as usual. Now let's just get on with this whole surviving thing and stop being an asshole with me," I snap. I swallow down the rest of the sentence and try to compose myself. I reach out to touch him but he pulls away, and I feel my cheeks flame with embarrassment.

"Nina, I know that you're lying," he yells, his nostrils flaring. "Damn well tell me now!"

"Will you calm the hell down? You're being unreasonable," I yell back.

"We're together—you should be able to tell me anything." He points his finger at me. "I put up with a lot of your shit, Nina, but I won't put up with you keeping things from me. I'll ask you again: what happened out there? Did you get it on with Michael? Is that it? I'm not good enough for you?" he sneers.

I slap him hard. "How fucking dare you? No, I didn't. But you know what? You're not my damn husband, Mikey, you're my boyfriend. And if I wanted to screw somebody else, I would." My hand burns from slapping him and I regret it instantly, nearly as much as I regret my vicious words. I don't know why I hit him, why I said that to him. I'm just so hurt that he would even think that of me.

Mikey rubs a hand across his cheek; even in this light I can see a handprint appearing. "Why won't you tell me the truth then?"

"I'm—I'm sorry." I take a deep breath, feeling an ache in my gut. "Can't you just trust me?" I say quietly.

He looks confused for a moment, his features softening before quickly hardening back up. He looks away, his arms dropping away from me. "No."

We stand there together, inches apart but separated by so much. I refuse to cry, refuse to get upset by his pigheadedness. He should trust me and he doesn't, and that hurts me more than anything.

"Then there's nothing left to say to each other," I say to him stubbornly.

He looks at me, his face full of hurt and anger. "Fine. I guess this is it, then."

He doesn't look back at me as he turns and walks away, leaving me in the darkness of the park by myself. I don't chase after him, don't shout him back like I want to. And it's only when he's gone that I sit down on the swing he occupied only moments ago and I cry, letting the tears give way to my anger at him and everything else in this shitty, unfair world.

I realize that I have to tell him. I'll have to make him understand—force him to, if I have to—that he can't tell anyone, that he can't be different with Michael. Because I can't lose Mikey, not after everything we've been through. Hell, maybe we'll leave here together. Either way I have to tell him everything. Even as angry at him as I am, I know it's the right thing to do.

It takes half an hour or so for everything to subside—my sadness, my anger—and I head back home. I open the door, finding it still dark. Mikey isn't down here and though I don't want another argument, I head upstairs to him.

In the dark of the room, I can see the unmade bed and the closet doors open with all his things gone. And I know that he's left me.

FORTY-THREE

Mikey and I avoid each other at all costs. There seems little point in telling him that I came back and was going to tell him the truth the whole truth and nothing but the truth…so help me God. Because, really, if I was so easy to dismiss, then basically fuck him. Or rather not.

I settle into a semi comfortable routine, with Emily moving in with me. She had previously been living with Becky in a wing of the hospital, but since James had been released from there, Becky was ready to go back to her own house share. Emily made the choice to live with me instead of Alek, no matter how much I protested, and while I won't ever admit it to her, I'm really very grateful.

Alek comes over most nights, anyway, when he's not on duty. Turns out the boy can cook a mean chili con carne from practically anything.

"What's that?" I stir the pot while Alek tears up some green plant and drops it in the pan. "That's not what you used last time."

"No, that was sage—this is basil. The last batch of sage hasn't finished growing, so this will have to do."

He wanders off again, leaving me feeling stupid for not knowing my sage from my basil. I was never one to cook: that was always my husband's job—Ben, he loved cooking and never let me near the kitchen. In fact, that was the only thing he actually did around the house—cook. Alek comes back in and looks over my shoulder.

"How do you even know all of this?" I ask.

"Dad was away a lot, and Mom worked most nights, so I was alone a lot. She taught me basic stuff so I didn't burn the place down." He shrugs.

"Wow, multi-talented," I mock jokingly.

"Multi?" he asks.

"There's also the way you handle yourself. You're not a street fighter, but you can handle yourself for sure," I say offhandedly, not wanting to inflate his ego too much.

"Yeah, that was down to my dad as well," he says. "Another ten minutes and it'll be ready. You okay to handle that? I want to go sit with Em."

He's gone before I can reply, though, so I guess he wasn't really asking. Anyway, how hard can it be to stir a pot and not let food burn? I let my thoughts drift to Nova while I watch the food bubbling away. I've noticed that she's been avoiding both me and Michael at all costs. I feel sad for her: not only has she lost her sister, but in a way she's lost her brother, too, now; because no matter what, things will never be the same again.

Michael, on the other hand, doesn't seem too bothered by anything that has happened. If anything, I've actually seen him crack a smile one or two times. I wonder whether the burden of carrying Rachel's secret had been eating away at him. Maybe that's why he was always so damn grumpy? Either way I've tried to ignore him as much as possible and, true to his word, Zee has made sure that we haven't been put together for any of the duties.

I know it's made Mikey all the more suspicious, but I guess it doesn't matter anymore—not now that we're not together. I look into the pan, realizing that I've stopped stirring and when I scrape the wooden spoon along the bottom of the pan I can feel some of the beans have stuck to the bottom.

"Shit," I mutter, and begin scooping it into bowls for us all, hoping to conceal my failure before they come in.

"Nina!" Emily grumbles as she sees me scraping the burnt beans into the garbage.

"Shush, don't tell Alek," I grimace.

Emily helps me carry the bowls of food to the table and we sit and start eating, not talking until we've consumed everything. Alek belches loudly and Emily scolds him for not using his manners. He doesn't argue with her, but rolls his eyes and picks at his teeth, which only riles her up more.

"You know, I was brought up to be respectful." She quirks an eyebrow at him. "That we use our manners at *all* times and in *any* company."

"I was brought up to show my appreciation for the food I just ate, but I didn't hear you saying thank you." He forces out another burp, and it takes everything I have to contain a laugh.

The old me would have agreed with her; the old me would have been disgusted about burping at the table. But then the old me was an uptight, selfish asshole most of the time. The new me thinks it's hilarious that she's complaining about something so stupid.

Emily looks at me. "I did say thank you, didn't I, Nina?"

I shrug and smirk but don't say anything as Alek says it for me. "No, you didn't. Now don't be spoiled." He reaches a hand out to her, but she merely scowls at it. "Babes, I'm serious, stop being a brat."

Emily shoves away from the table and I roll my eyes and smirk even more. "I can't believe you just called me a brat!" She stomps away from the table and Alek trails after her with a sigh.

She's not my problem anymore, she's Alek's. They're each other's problem. As they storm off into the kitchen, having their nightly argument about something stupid, I realize how bizarre all this is. I mean this is it, this is the end of days, and yet I'm sitting here with Emily and Alek eating chili con carne and listening to Emily scold Alek like they're husband and wife. As far as the end of the world goes, this isn't too bad. I think I finally get why Zee and James want to protect it so much.

It's not just the safety of this place, though of course that's a huge thing—I'm not stupid enough to not realize that—but it's the life people are building for themselves. The fact that everyone is actually living instead of just surviving.

I never thought that would happen, and yet here I am. I'd like to think all the pain and torment I've been through was worth all of this, but I refuse to think about the past anymore. The future is what I have to look toward—what we all have to look toward now. There's no going back anymore.

Being on guard duty with Mathew is always fun. After leaving Alek and Emily to kiss and make up—literally—I head over to my station. I hate guard duty, but it's what helps keep this place secure and running. There's always four people on duty, since the base is so huge. Most of it has been closed off and made secure, but there are constant checks on the fencing surrounding the place—even the places that aren't used anymore. We begin our walk around the base, starting at medical and working our way around past the gym and toward the old library. Next to the library is an old cinema that used to play movies for the kids, but it's not been used in so long that it's hard to even imagine ever watching a movie again.

"I used to love these old Jackie Chan movies when I was a kid. My dad used to let me stay up late and watch them with him all the time. Mom never liked it, always worried I'd end up getting into fights and things like that. Always thought I'd end up in prison or something. She'd hit the roof if she saw me now with this thing." Mathew raises his crossbow to the air and laughs quietly to himself. "Walking around like a regular bad-ass."

"I'm sure she'd be real proud of you. You're helping people, protecting them," I say, kicking a stone. It scoots across the ground and bounces off the side of the old cinema.

"Do you ever wonder what happened to your family?" he asks and kicks a stone against the building too.

I shrug. "Nope. My mother and father died a long time ago." I think back to Ben's parents and their cabin that we were heading to so many years ago.

"I think about mine a lot. My dad was a cop, real tough bastard," Mathew laughs. "But he turned to butter around my mom." Even in the moonlight I can see him smile.

"I'm sure that they're holed up somewhere safe. Your dad wouldn't have let anything happen to her," I reply.

Mathew looks at me and sees my comments for what they are, but he doesn't say anything. He smiles and we keep on walking. In the distance I can hear the sound of deaders at the fence and we follow the sound around the back of the one of the old office buildings. There's three there, though one is so emaciated it looks more like a skeleton. They can't get in and seem to be stuck in a particularly bad patch of mud. It clings to their ankles and legs and stops them from moving on.

I look up and along the fence, seeing a little too much sway for my liking in the metal. The winter has been bad and has soaked the ground right through, and with the recent storms we've had, it's growing too soft to support the fence posts. This area is secure for now, but I'm guessing it won't be long before it's going to need fortifying with something. I make a mental note to tell Zee or James about it tomorrow. For tonight, the best we can do is kill the deaders.

I grab my machete from the holder at my waist and walk toward the fence. One of the deaders leans forward in its eagerness to get to me. It stands at near enough a right angle, since it's legs are still stuck in the mud, and claws at the fence. Of course, all of their growls and weird gargly throat noises increase once they see us.

Mathew takes a knife from his pocket and as I dispense of the first deader, he coaxes one of the others to get closer to the fence so he can finish it off. Neither of us can reach the third, meaning tomorrow we're going to have to head out of the base and find it. Deaders attract deaders, and it's a battle to clear the area of them as much as we do. The only thing that gives me any hope is that with each season that passes they decay more and more until, like this last one here, they are nothing but a pile of walking bones. Sure, they can still kill you, but they're also easier to kill.

"I don't like leaving one out there," Mathew says. He puts his knife away and raises his crossbow, but even as good a shot as he is, at this angle, in this lighting, I can't see how he can make the kill.

"You'll never make that," I say matter-of-factly.

Mathew grins at me and stares down the length of his bow. He breathes steadily for a couple of seconds and then fires. The arrow slices through the air, through the small gap in the fence, and jams itself home in the deader's skull.

"Damn," I laugh. "Glad I didn't make a bet on that."

"Lost my arrow, though." He laughs lightly. Things are always easy with Mathew: he never takes anything too seriously, which is why I like being on duty with him. And since I requested to not be with Michael and I can't be with Mikey, it's meant us spending a lot of time together. He's a good guy, and as I said, doesn't take things too seriously.

"You can get it tomorrow." I sheath my machete after wiping it clean of the deader gore and we keep on walking.

"I'm going to be teaching lessons on how to shoot when the weather gets better. I can teach you too."

"I'd like that," I reply with a smile.

When we get back to the medic building, we begin our tour again. As the rain patters down on us, Mathew talks to me about his comic books. Yet again it was another thing that his dad used to love and his mom hated, and he reminisces about his dad sneaking him comic books when his mom wasn't looking.

I can't help but smile at his stories, getting lost in the animated way he talks about his family. Yet I also can't help but be glad I never had any other family—other than Ben—because I don't know how I'd cope with not knowing what happened to them. Not knowing if they were alive or dead, or if they were the walking dead. Part of the pain these people are going through is not knowing, and I can sympathize with that.

My thoughts return, as they have every day since I got back from our nightmare scouting trip, to Rachel and her siblings—the bond that they shared to have survived together through the apocalypse, to have come so far and been through so much, and all together. In some respects, I guess I can actually understand Michael and why he went along with Rachel—why he protected her even though he knew what she was doing was wrong. And if I really dig deep and see past my own bitterness, I can understand why he wants to protect her memory.

But as always when I think like this, I think about the unnamed woman—the one possibly carrying deader spawn—and all thoughts of sympathy and understanding fly away.

FORTY-FOUR

"**E**arth to Nina." Max flutters her lashes at me and Emily laughs. "She does this a lot," Emily says with a grin. "Goes off in her own head. Can't say I blame her, though."

I offer them both a smile. Max is still beaming from ear to ear about her false lashes. It's amusing, really: at the end of the world and the thing that she wanted more than anything else was some false lashes. In fact, it's funny what most people view as their essential item. You'd think it would be something survivalist—a weapon or water purification tablets or some shit—but more often than not it's false eyelashes, comic books, or photographs—utterly useless items, but each help you to feel grounded and more like the person you used to be than the person you are now. And let's face it, most of us are a shittier version of the person we used to be.

"Sorry, I'm in my own world today." I spoon some more of the porridge into my mouth. The ration is noticeably smaller than yesterday's, and less than the day previous to that.

348

"It's okay." She smiles again. She's always smiling; we're like apples and oranges in this place. "I was just saying that they're heading back to that mall you found tomorrow. I put in an order for some more lashes. Did you notice if they had any NYX ones? They were my favorite . . ." Max continues to ramble, but again my thoughts have drifted on to something else—or someone else.

"Is Mikey going?" I ask, interrupting Max's ramblings.

"Um, yeah." Her eyes slip to Emily and then back to me.

"Shit," I mutter, more to myself than anyone else. "Is Alek going?" I ask, because I like Alek, I trust him.

Emily shakes her head. "No, Zee wants him here to help do the maintenance on the fencing, but Michael is going and he's seriously tough. Mikey will be totally fine!" she says with too much zeal.

Her words are meant to put my mind at ease, but instead they fill me with dread. I don't trust Michael, and Mikey thinks something happened between me and him so he isn't going to be Mr. Friendly or cooperative. That trip is going to be all kinds of fucked up.

Damn it and damn me for giving a shit. I stand up abruptly, my chair falling down behind me; Max stops talking automatically and Emily eyes me warily.

"You K?" Max says, as if she's texting me. I hate it when she uses abbreviations.

"Yeah, ummm . . ." I look around uncertainly.

"Nina...I love you," Emily stands up, her eyes finding mine. "You know this, so I'm saying this for your own good: don't go and see him. You're only just starting to be like you again."

"But..." I start. "What if something happens out there?"

"He'll be fine, you know he will. I have to get back to Becky in the medic building—she's showing me how to suture today—,but I'll come by later and we can talk." She hugs me and picks up her tray, casting nervous glances behind her as she leaves.

I look down at Max who seems sweetly oblivious. Emily doesn't realize that half of the reason I haven't seemed like myself is because of everything that happened with Rachel. Emily is just another person that I've had to lie to.

"I gotta go," I say to Max and walk off, leaving my tray on the table.

"KK, I'll clear this away for you," she says cheerily, but I'm out the door and not listening anymore. As I exit, Constance is coming in and she offers me a smile, but I charge past her without even an 'excuse me.'

I head straight over to the fitness center, where I know Mikey will be. I have no idea what I'm going to say to him—he probably won't listen to a damn word I say, anyway—but the urge to see him is something I can't ignore.

The fitness center is one of the only luxury areas still open on the base—the movie theater and bowling center and the golf course have all been decommissioned since the apocalypse. The fitness center still has a major use and a lot of us have taken refuge there, seeking a place to vent our frustrations without worrying about looking like a total headcase. A lot of the equipment was electrical and we don't use that, but weights are for free, and there are other things everyone uses.

The days are getting longer, and I'm glad that spring is now well underway. Winter was long and hard on all of us, and I hope that things will get a little easier in the coming months.

I push open the metal door to the fitness center, already hearing the grunts from people working out inside. The smell of sweat clings to the walls like old lady smell in a nursing home. It's rank and stale, but I've spent many an hour in here myself, so I get to take credit for some of that smell.

I head past the changing rooms and into the main gym, where large, intimidating equipment stands proud at every turn. James has spent quite a bit of time in here building up his strength after being shot by Rachel, so I'm surprised to not see him in here today. Instead I find Alek, who offers me a weird grimace smile as he does some sit-ups while strapped to a piece of machinery.

I wave back and look around for Mikey. My eyes land on Michael; he's topless as normal, his array of beautiful artwork tattooed across his upper torso. He's lifting weights, working on his upper body strength, and I'd be lying if I said that I wasn't impressed by how much he could bench press. I'd also be lying if I said I knew how much it was he was lifting—I just know that there is a lot of metal on each side of the bar.

I spy Mikey doing push-ups on some gym mats, unfortunately not topless. *What? I never said I stopped liking the look of him, just that he was being a douchebag. I mean, the man's got mad abs and a six-pack to die for. I'm pissed off, not blind.* I march over, get halfway there, and realize that I'm being a typical female cliché, so I stop and turn my bratty march into a casual walk.

He doesn't look at me when I stand in front of him so I lift an eyebrow, which he still ignores. I wave a hand at him but he continues to keep his eyes on the floor in front of him as he lowers himself down and then pushes himself back up.

"Mikey." I say his name both loud and trying to keep it as hushed as possible so as not to draw attention to us. "Please don't ignore me."

He stops his workout and stands up, coming face to face with me. Sweat glistens down the sides of his face, dark patches in the middle of his chest making his T-shirt cling to him in all the right ways. His head is shaved and shiny, his beard the right length for being both equally hot and scratchy.

"What?" He grabs a towel and rubs it over his face, and I take the moment to compose myself.

"You're going on a run tomorrow?" I ask, stumbling over my words, because I have no idea what to say to him now.

"Yeah," he says and grabs his water bottle. "So?"

I bite down on my lower lip, feeling like a total asshole for coming over to see him now. "Be careful." I shrug, feeling heat rise to my cheeks.

What the ever-loving fuck is happening to me?

Mikey stares at me for a long moment, his deep chocolate eyes boring into mine. He reaches over and pulls my lip free from my teeth and my heart skips a beat. "I will be." He looks at me again and then takes off toward the showers with a frown.

I don't follow because honestly I still don't know what else to say, and I feel completely unnerved by him. I hadn't expected the indifference from him, but equally I hadn't expected his touch to ignite something in me.

I turn to head back home. I pass Michael still bench-pressing, but he stops as I pass him.

"Nina," he calls.

I turn and look at him, all thoughts of Mikey leaving me as I raise an eyebrow. "What?" I look away, uninterested in anything he has to say.

He comes toward me when I make no move to go to him. "No need to be such a bitch with me," he grumbles.

"Fuck off," I return and spin on my heel.

His hand grabs the crook of my elbow. "Wait, I wanted to say something."

I shrug out of his hold but don't turn to face him. His face makes me want to punch him in the nose.

"I'm sorry. I heard you two broke up. I feel responsible for that."

352

"Because you are," I yell as I storm off, thinking it's best to leave before I turn around and kick him in the shins.

As evening falls I head over to Susan's place. I've come to love our evenings reading. My debt has long since been paid off, but I keep doing it because I enjoy it. Even reading about zombies and a post-apocalyptic world isn't a turn-off anymore. In fact it's like she said, and when it get too hard or a scene hits too close to home, we call it a night and close the book, as if that can erase the horrors from our minds. We've long since finished the other book; turns out it was the first in a series and we don't have the rest of them. It's a shame—I really wanted to know what happened to the characters in it. We're on to something else now, though. Not zombies this time, but still a post-apocalyptic world. It's a book about a mother and her daughters traveling across the country and trying to find somewhere safe from the monsters or beasties or whatever they're called.

It makes me happy that I've never had children and I don't have to experience what this poor woman goes through. Several times Susan and I have discussed what might have become of the author. Susan thinks she is most likely dead, much like the rest of the world. I don't, though. Anyone who is smart enough to write the way she does knows how to survive. This woman—this Elizabeth—she's alive somewhere, I just know it.

I turn the book over in my hands, seeing the tortured expression of the little girl on the front cover. For some reason this image haunts me more than the one with the zombie on the front. Susan hands me my cocoa and I take a sip as she finds her spot by the fire and I begin tonight's reading. It's therapeutic, and after a clunky start I find my tongue sliding over the words as they spill from the pages.

I lose myself in the story for the next hour, not thinking of Mikey and our breakup, or Michael and Rachel. It's only when the story progresses to a part about a pregnancy that I begin to stumble as thoughts intrude on the story.

"You finished for the night, love?"

I look up from the book. "Sorry, I'm feeling a bit distracted." I close the book after marking our place. "I'll read some more tomorrow if that's okay?"

Susan smiles and runs her hands through her hair. "That's fine. I could do with an early night anyway. I was on duty last night—it was a busy one. A group of the things found their way up to the fence."

I raise an eyebrow at her. Dense woods surround this place and only the central units are used, so mostly you only get one or two stray deaders at the fencing every now and then. A group of them is disquieting.

"Don't worry so much—me and Mathew took care of them." She laughs and throws another log on the fire. "He's a great shot with that bow. He's going to be giving lessons soon."

"So I've heard," I say and yawn.

"I think when summer rolls around, we'll see a lot more action around the base. People aren't content with hiding and letting people protect them anymore. We want to fight and protect ourselves. Even Max wants to learn to use a bow, though Constance isn't too keen on the idea."

I shrug. "If she loves her, she should want her to be able to protect herself."

Susan picks up our mugs and I follow her into the kitchen where she deposits them into the sink. "Yes, she should, but don't dismiss so easily how much she loves Max. People will do anything to protect the ones they love."

I bite down on my lower lip, knowing that she's right, of course. Much more than she even realizes. "I'm going to get going, I'll see you tomorrow."

Susan leans over and hugs me, catching me by surprise. I loosely hug her back and try not to feel uncomfortable.

"You be careful," she says as her way of dismissing me.

I roll my eyes and head out the door and back over to my house, the air as cold as ice and biting at my ears. Once again there are no clouds in the sky and all the stars are out. I look up and find Venus— the brightest star in the sky. My dad always used to say to look up and make a wish on Venus. I try to think up a good wish, but nothing seems right. I could wish for the world to go back to normal, or for the dead to fall where they stand; I could wish for all the assholes in the world to stop being their assholey selves and start being good—but none of those things are going to come true. So I tuck my chin down and keep walking.

At my front door is Nova. She's sitting on the steps smoking, not looking the slightest bit cold, weirdly. She looks up as I approach, and even in the dark I can see her eyes are glistening from tears not yet shed.

"'Sup?" she says, and stands to move out of my way so I can open the door.

"You coming in?" I say and head inside.

We haven't spoken since we came back from our little road trip from hell, but I can see that she hasn't been faring too well. I head to the kitchen and grab two glasses and a small bottle of vodka that I traded for a months' worth of vegetable peeling duties. I pour us both a glass, hand her one, and sit down at the stool in the kitchen.

She takes it and downs it in one. "I can't stop thinking about Rachel. Michael says I shouldn't have killed her, that I'm a bad sister, but—"

"You are not a bad sister. Your brother's a dick," I interrupt her.

She lights up another cigarette after finishing off her vodka, and I swallow mine down and pour us both another.

"I can't sleep, I keep thinking of things…things that didn't make sense at the time but do now, you know what I mean?" she says, smoke coming out of her nose as she exhales it but continues to talk. "Like everything is so obvious to me now."

"It's called hindsight," I say. I'm tired and don't need this shit—I have enough of my own going on—but the woman is falling apart in front of me. "None of this was your fault, Nova."

"Michael says it is, Michael says—"

"Again, Michael is a dick!" I interrupt with a shout. "Look, pull your shit together. Your sister was a nutcase. Granted, her heart was—at the start—in the right place. She wanted to help save the world, but she tested on humans, on children. She impregnated a woman with zombie crap to see what the fuck would happen. Who does that? That's like some sci-fi fucking mental shit going on." I stand up, feeling agitated to hell and back. "Look, I don't want to upset you any more than you clearly are, but I can't say I'm not grateful that you killed her. I'd be dead if you hadn't, and I did nothing other than stick my nose in where it wasn't wanted." I down my vodka and start to pour another one but think better of it: it's hard to come by and damn expensive when we do get it.

"I know, I know," Nova sobs.

I groan. "I'm sorry. I didn't mean to make you feel worse. It's just my big mouth has no filter for the crap it spews. I'm sorry." I take a deep breath. "Look, think about it this way: somewhere out there is a woman with something growing inside her—something human, not human, who the hell knows, right? Every time you feel like shit about killing Rachel, think about that woman, her fear of bringing a child into this world. A child that may very well kill her."

As I say it, guilt burns my conscience. I have no idea why guilt—*I* didn't do it to her—but it's guilt, one hundred percent. I remember something with a frown, something I hadn't given much thought about until now.

"Nova, you asked me to get you a pregnancy test. Why was that?" I ask cautiously.

Nova sobs again. "I'm so sorry, fuck, I'm so sorry." She heads for the door and I run to catch up to her.

"Nova!" I grab her shoulder and spin her around. "What do you know?" I watch her face: anger, fear, sorrow, every emotion possible swims across her features. "Nova, what did she do?" I ask cautiously, my eyes slipping down her to her stomach.

She cries again. "Not me, it's Jessica. She said she wanted a baby. We were all drinking one night and we were talking about the future, and Jessica said the thing that she would miss most was that she would never have a family, because she would never bring a child into this world knowing that one day it would turn into one of those things. We were drunk and Rachel was blabbing about how she could create a baby that was immune to the zombie virus. One thing led to another and . . ." Her words trail off.

"And what?" I ask, unable to close my mouth, which hangs open like that of a fish.

"And she said that she'd done it before, that the only way to become immune to the virus was to use zombie DNA. I didn't believe her at first, but she kept going on and on about it until I believed her. I never stopped to think about any of the whys or whatever. It made sense when I was wasted. So we rounded one up—a zombie—and," she shrugs, "you know?"

"Holy fuck! Are you serious?" I step away from Nova, feeling dirty just by being this close to her—as if by touching her I could catch her assholeness.

She nods frantically, her eyes fixing me to the spot.

"Does Michael know?" I hiss at her, anger at her—at their stupidity— growing. Everything is ten times worse than what I first thought. "I can't even wrap my mind around this. It's not a fucking virus, it's death that turns us. How many times do I have to tell you people this?" I back up further, running hands across my face.

"I know, and that's why we completely lost it when Rachel was bitten. Because it was the most obvious fucking thing, and Rachel in all her clever wisdom didn't even realize it. She was—they were looking for the disease pattern, a way to kill it, but—"

"There isn't a way to kill it," I finish for her. "Death starts it and only death can end it."

Nova nods her head again, fresh tears spilling down her cheeks. "The answer was right there under her nose the whole time."

"Does Jessica know?" I ask.

Nova shakes her head.

"Shit, you bitch. How far along is she?"

Nova shrugs. "I don't know, maybe six weeks, eight weeks, something like that."

"And you're certain?" I ask.

Nova nods. "Got me the pregnancy test, didn't you?" She shrugs.

I walk back to the kitchen and unscrew the vodka bottle, downing half its contents. Nova follows me.

"I thought we were helping, I thought Rachel was the fucking savior of mankind. She said we had to leave because the other scientists wanted to take her ideas and use them for bad. That they wanted to use her research to take control of the world or some crazy shit. I thought it sounded stupid, to be honest, but then she brought that other woman and her husband to me, and they confirmed that they had been tested on. So I helped get us all out of there."

"And then what?" I ask, feeling numb to everything she's saying.

"I didn't know it was Rachel that had tested on her—shit, that *woman* didn't realize it was Rachel that had tested on her," Nova says frantically.

"So, what happened?"

"When we got out, we separated. The woman thanked us and left with her husband, and that's the last I saw of her—I swear!" Nova holds her hands up.

Neither of us says anything for a while. I'm struck dumb by all this new information. I don't know how to process it, what to do with any of it. A dark thought occurs to me, and I turn to Nova with a dread in my gut.

"Did she know?" I say.

Nova looks at me in confusion. "Who? What?"

"The woman? Did she know she had demon spawn inside her?"

Nova shrugs. "I honestly don't know. I don't think so, though."

"We have to go find her." I turn to Nova, expecting an argument, expecting some sort of disagreement from her, but all she says is…

"Okay."

I nod and continue drinking. "We have to know what we're dealing with, see if there is any hope for Jessica. We'll go tomorrow, after the team sets off on their scavenging mission. We'll take a truck, just you and me, some weapons, and we'll go and find her we'll bring her back here and hope that Becky can help her." I mumble it out loud, more to confirm it with myself than her, but she agrees all the same.

"I can get us weapons, big weapons, and I can get keys to a truck and some gas for it." Nova continues with my mumbling monologue, and I take up her place with the nodding.

"Where did you last see her? Do we know her name? Or the husband's? Shit, we don't know anything." It's the world's stupidest rescue plan, but I don't think I could live with myself if I didn't do something.

The thing that keeps coming back to me, though, is what happens after we find her, after we bring her back? If we can't help her, she'll die. And then what?

"It was north of here." She shrugs. "I can get us there, though. That won't be a problem." I can almost hear the cogs turning in her head as she thinks. "She was going east the last time I saw her. She said she had family back there."

"And her name?" I prompt.

"Hilary. Her name was Hilary."

FORTY-FIVE

N ova and I watch as Mikey, Michael, and Melanie head out in Betty. I feel a strange longing seeing Mikey in the passenger's seat of Betty. I want to go and say goodbye, to tell him yet again to be safe and not to do anything stupid and rash—basically anything that I would do. Instead I turn to Nova and say . . .

"They're like M&M's." I chuckle, despite my grim mood.

"How so?" she asks, smoking a cigarette.

"Michael, Mikey, and Melanie." I point, emphasizing the *M*s in their names.

"Ohhh, but that's three *M*s."

I roll my eyes. "There's more than two M&M's in a bag."

"Ha, yeah." She looks thoughtful for a moment. "I could do with some of those right now."

I roll my eyes again. "Come on, let's get our shit together."

I walk back inside the truck depot. Nova has loaded up enough weapons to blow up a small army. I'm hoping we won't need to use them, but you never know. In fact, I'm hoping that we find this woman and get back here before Mikey and the rest return. Not that he'll say anything—he doesn't seem to give much of a shit about me anymore, and I've made peace with that. Who am I kidding? Of course I haven't. But there's nothing I can do about it now.

We head over to talk to Zee and James before we leave. We want them to know what we're doing, though we don't expect any help. It's more of an *'it would be fucking moronic to go out there without telling at least one person.'* We're living in a horror story—doesn't mean we have to make stupid mistakes like they do in movies.

I knock on Zee's door, thankfully finding James is inside with him. At least it will save us from having to go hunt him down and tell this sick story twice. Nova does surprisingly well telling both men what happened previously—filling Zee in on the parts that Michael left out, and saving on the waterworks. Michael is a bigger dick than I first thought, having only told Zee that they were testing on humans and missing out the important part of impregnating innocent women with demon spawn, including our very own Jessica.

"So she doesn't know?" Zee asks gravely.

"No, she has no idea. She thinks the baby will be immune to the zombie virus. But again, it's not a fucking virus," I say angrily. "Look, maybe the baby will be fine, maybe it will be deformed, maybe there's nothing even growing in her. It's all a lot of maybes and not a lot of answers. But we need to find out."

James is standing at the window, looking out. He turns around and casts a judgmental eye on Nova. "And you went along with this?"

She shakes her head. "No, I didn't know what she was doing, what any of them were doing to people." She swallows hard. "Please don't judge her too harshly. She wanted to help, in her own way."

"I don't see how it's even feasibly possible. The zombies are dead—everything about them is dead and rotting." Zee huffs out an angry sigh. "You can't grow something from a dead seed."

Nova shrugs. "I was never the brains of the operation so I can't tell you more than I know, but Rachel used to say that they weren't totally dead—parts of them were still alive." She points to her head. "Like the brain, there's a spark or whatever. That's why they are still up and moving. They wanted to try and cure the zombies at first, but they realized that wouldn't be possible and so they thought that maybe they could…"

"Grow a cure," I say with a shake of my head.

"So, the sperm is alive?" James grimaces.

"Well, I don't actually know," Nova says. "Rachel seemed to think there was something special with it—enough so that others believed her—but something scared her away from the experiments. Something was obviously wrong for her to drag us all out of there." She reaches for her cigarettes.

"Please don't," Zee says to her. "So am I correct in thinking we don't really know very much about this? And you want to track down this woman to see what became of her? To maybe bring her back here and…and we'll see if Jessica will be okay . . . ?" His words trail off.

I nod. "Yeah, that's about it. We don't really have more of a plan than that. I mean, she could be fine, we could all be worrying for nothing."

Nova nods. "But we need to find out if it's…it's," she looks at us all, "human or not."

"We should just get Jessica to abort whatever it is," James says matter-of-factly.

"Tried that. She said no way, that it could be her only chance to have a child without the zombie virus." She holds up a hand. "And before you say it, I told her it's not a virus and that she could have a child naturally without all the zombie sperm." She grimaces and squirms in her seat. "But again, she said she doesn't care, that this is her baby, yada yada, you get the idea." She taps her cigarette pack again. "I really need to smoke," she mumbles to Zee.

"We could force her," I say coldly.

"We could. It would seem that would be the most sensible plan of action for all involved." Zee stands and clears his throat. "In fact, I think that's exactly what must be done." He rubs his hands together.

"What about the other woman? She's still carrying…something inside her," I say, not feeling wholly comfortable with my own suggestion of forcing someone to have an abortion.

"That's not our problem, Nina," Zee says.

"Like hell it's not," I snap. "That woman—Hilary—could need our help. You housed Rachel, she was a citizen of your little community here, and she did that to her. We need to find and help her."

"Nina, I think you're letting your own emotions cloud your judgment," James says with a frown.

I fish-mouth for a second. "I'm sorry, my emotions? What the hell are you talking about?" I scowl.

"I know that your breakup with Mikey has hit you hard, but it's time to move on," James says as delicately as he can, but every word is a dagger in my stomach.

My face flushes in embarrassment. "Are you fucking serious? My relationship or lack of has nothing to do with this. I want to help this woman because it's the right thing to do." I stand up. "I'm going to try and find her, and I'll be bringing her back here no matter what. Do not, I repeat, do *not* fucking touch Jessica until I get back," I yell as I storm out of the room, needing to get away from all the sympathetic stares before I throat-punch someone.

I storm down the hall and out the door, heading across the yard and toward the depot again.

"Nina, wait up, darlin'," Nova shouts behind me.

I don't stop but I slow down and allow her to catch up to me. "Jesus, have I been a total flake lately? I mean, honestly, give it to me straight, is everyone looking at me liking I'm a total loser because Mikey and I broke up?" I pull open one of the heavy metal doors while Nova grabs the other one.

She shrugs. "No, not really." She waves a hand in front of her face. "Pfft, I mean, hardly anyone is talking about it—not now, anyway."

"Not now? Wait, what?" I climb into the truck and start the engine, waiting as Nova climbs into the passenger's side. "Fuck it, I don't care." I drive the truck out of the depot.

We drive through the base, passing my home and the consignment shop. The place is busy today, and people look up as I drive past. I drive by the medical center and think about going in to say goodbye to Emily, but don't.

It's a shitty thing to do, really—she nearly didn't forgive me for going on that scavenger mission and not telling her, so this might seal our fate as far as friendship goes—but I know she'll want to come with me if I tell her, and that is not going to happen.

She's safer here, with these people. These are better friends to her than I ever was. At least they've never put her in harm's way—unlike me. I continue driving, and when we get to the main gates, we stop and wait for them to open. Susan and Eric—a man that I've seen around but haven't had time to get to know much—are on guard today. They smile but don't ask any questions as we leave.

"You sure that you want to do this?" Nova asks, lighting up a cigarette.

I look at her. "Yeah." I swallow. "Zee told you about the Forgotten, I'm guessing?"

She nods. "He did. I'm part of security, it's my job to know the dangers. I think that's what pisses me off about the whole Michael thing: he knows how important safety is, and yet there was a threat under our noses and he didn't tell me. Now I might have sentenced Jessica to death because of it."

I purse my lips, deciding it's best for me to keep my mouth shut right now.

"You know," she continues, "she could be dead already, right?" She pulls out a bottle of vodka, unscrews the lid, and takes a swig. "This could be for nothing."

I shrug. "We have to try."

"And you know that Emily and Mikey are going to go bat-shit crazy when they realize that you're gone, right?"

I raise an eyebrow. "Dude, do you want to do this with me or not?"

Nova smiles. "Fuck yeah."

"Then shut the hell up." I rev the engine and we pull away.

I watch in my rearview mirror as the base fades into the distance, and a dark feeling settles in the pit of my stomach. Mentally I say goodbye to Mikey and Emily, but in my heart I know that we'll meet again. In this life or the next.

I reach a fork in the road. "Nova?"

"Yep?" She stops making smoke circles and looks at me.

"Umm, which way is north?" I scratch my head and laugh: some things never change.

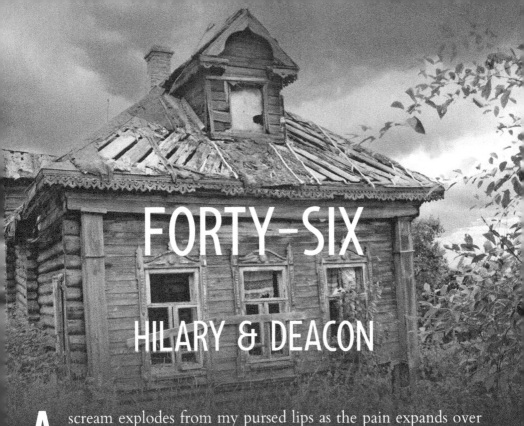

FORTY-SIX

HILARY & DEACON

A scream explodes from my pursed lips as the pain expands over my stomach and spreads through my back and legs.

"Just pant, baby." Deacon checks between my legs for the tenth time and then comes back up to my face. "It's okay, don't panic. Remember from when you had the others. Don't panic, breathe, visualize." He mimics panting for me. "It's too early for the baby, it can't come yet. These are just Braxton Hicks—practice contractions. It's not real, it can't be real, not yet." He closes his eyes for a second and focuses himself.

I want to reach up and kiss him and tell him that it will be okay, that I'll be fine, that the baby will be fine, but I can't—because I don't believe that. The baby is coming too early, and this pain is nothing like the pain from birthing my other two children. This is worse than any pain I've ever felt before.

The burning pain threads through every nerve again, starting abruptly on my stomach and pushing down between my bloodied thighs, down my legs and back up my spine.

I try to hold in the gut-wrenching scream, try to hold myself together for him, but I can't. It hurts so damn much and I'm so damn scared. And when I look at Deacon's face, all I can see is pain and worry, and I know that he knows this isn't normal—that this isn't anything like our other children.

He grabs my chin as I scream again, forcing me to look at him, forcing me to stare into his bloodshot, frightened eyes. I grit my teeth, holding back the pain, feeling a tooth at the back of my mouth crack at the effort I'm putting on it to stop my scream from escaping.

Deacon leans over and presses his lips to mine, and I feel his hot tears drip onto my cheeks, mixing with my own tears. He sobs loudly, and I join him in the misery, meeting him halfway, because we know—we both know—that this is it, the moment we've been dreading. Even if it is too early. Way too early.

We thought we would have more time, but then, don't you always?

"It'll be okay, baby. It'll be okay. I'm going to look after you," he whispers.

Pain begins to radiate again, and I hold onto it for as long as I can, trying to breathe through it, pant, goddamn it—anything to stop the scream that reaches up from my gut and throws itself from my swollen, bloodied lips.

I cough violently, choking on blood and phlegm, gagging as Deacon pulls me up to sitting and pats on my back to help me hack it all up and out. But he can't help. Nothing can help.

We knew this risk when we left. We knew there would be no medical help—we just prayed that we wouldn't ever need it. The pregnancy surprised us both.

"Deac," I cry out, coughing on more blood. It sprays from my mouth, dribbles down my chin and covers the bed covers that I lie on. "I can't," I sob. I feel the warmth of more blood gush between my legs and I scream again.

A loud, guttural scream filled with fear and pain and goodbyes.

READ ON FOR A SNEAK PEAK OF CHAPTER ONE OF
ODIUM 2.5 ORIGIN STORIES

ONE

MATTHEW

The car behind bumps me forward in my seat as it slams into the back of mine. I laugh and curse all at the same time, turning to glare at who it is, thinking it's probably Daryl, my best friend from high school and now best friend in college.

I turn in my seat. "Hey, asshole, get a life, will you? We're on the same . . ." I let my words trail off as I stare into the eyes of the most beautiful girl I've ever seen.

Brown, shoulder-length hair, deep brown eyes, and a sprinkling of freckles across a little button nose. I take all this in within seconds, my brain taking a mental picture of her perfect face. The multi-colored lights flashing around us do nothing to stop my gaze. She giggles at my stare—honest to God giggles at me—and I can't hold back my nervous smile.

"Sorry, I thought you were my asshole friend," I yell over the noise.

She looks at me, her forehead crinkling in amusement as she tries to work out what I'm saying over the thumping techno music. I realize that both of us have stopped moving, our bumper cars at a standstill right in the center of the ring while we stare at each other like idiots. I catch movement from the corner of my eye before a red car slams into the right side of mine. The air leaves my lungs as another car hits the left side of mine, and my body slams sideways with an *umph*!

The girl giggles again, a hand covering her mouth in a gesture that's both sweet and sexy all at the same time. I turn and grin, ignoring the sound of Daryl's hyena-style laugh. The music still blasts far too loudly, the annoying lights continuing to flash around us. And to think, I previously thought they were cool and retro; now I just find them annoying, and I want to get off this damn ride and away from all these distractions so I can talk to her.

I turn to Daryl as he backs up his car and rams me again, still hyena laughing. As he goes in for a third ram, the car stops and merely taps the side of mine as the ride finally comes to an end. He dives out and straight toward me with a huge grin, his bright orange hair flashing as it catches the multi-colored lights.

"Come on, dickface." He ruffles my hair and grabs the back of my T-shirt, still grinning as he practically lifts me out of my seat. At six-foot five and built like a college linebacker—because, well, he *is* a college linebacker—he outweighs me easily, but I'm no small guy either.

"Get off." I shrug out of his grip and turn to look at the girl.

But she's gone, and the weirdest thing happens: my heart skips a beat.

Daryl drags me from the bumper cars while he continues to chatter away. He heads toward the hotdog stand without even noticing my total distraction from what he's saying. We'd come to the fair with a couple of Daryl's football buddies—nice enough guys, if not a bit rowdy for my liking.

"Two chili dogs." He barks out the order to the bearded guy serving before turning to me. "'Sup with you, man? You got that goofy look on your face again."

My eyes scan the busy crowd of boisterous kids and irritated parents, looking for the girl from the bumper cars. "Nothing," I reply, still staring into the throng of people. "And what goofy look? I don't have a goofy look."

Daryl pushes me. "Sure you don't." He hands me my chili dog and we head off toward the funhouse. "Not like when we were in high school and you'd go all gooey-eyed whenever Stacey Le'Hewitt walked into class. Oh shit, is that it?" He punches me in the arm.

"Is what it?" I dive away as he tries to tackle me.

"You've seen a girl?" He chuckles and takes a massive bite out of his food, not caring about what an asshole he's being.

"No," I snap, embarrassed at the mention of Stacey Le'Hewitt. That was a portion of my life I'd rather forget—though in a town this size, it's hard to do.

Stacey Le'Hewitt was just a girl, and I was just a boy. We were kids, but I thought it was true love. I know now that it wasn't—it was just two kids who liked each other an awful lot . . . only one moved on before the other. I've always believed in true love—the sort that you read about in books. Maybe that's because I was brought up by my mom—she used to read me Shakespeare every night—or maybe it's just in my DNA. Either way, it feels as if I've spent my entire nineteen years searching for The One. I look around me for the brown-eyed girl. Could she be it? It sure felt like nothing I've ever felt before.

The sun is beginning to set, casting a warm orange summer glow over the fairground and forming shadows around us. The air is thick with heat and alive with little bugs. The constant chirp of things can be heard from the small clumps of bushes and trees around the tents. I hate bugs. I swat at a little fly that gets too close to my face, feeling the humidity on my clammy skin.

We finish our chilidogs, scrunching up the wrappers as we arrive at the funhouse, and both of us drop them to the ground, throw a dollar each to the bored-looking vendor of the ride, and head inside. It's dark and stuffy, the bad fluorescent paint job on the crappy plywood walls showing the age of this thing. We balance over wobbly floors and make dumb faces in the crazy mirrors before heading back out the other side of the ride.

"That was a bust. Wanna to go back to the bumper cars?" Daryl asks.

It's a little darker than when we went in, but not by much. However, strings of cheap lights have been turned on around the fairground. I scan the crowd for *her* again, but continue to come up short.

"Sure, if you want." I shrug noncommittally and look down as I stuff my hands into my jeans pockets.

We head back over to the bumper cars, kicking a couple of stray cans that people have dropped on the way and chatting about the summer so far. Daryl has been struggling with the extra workload of college, and his mom is making him get a tutor when we go back after the break so he doesn't fall too far behind. I haven't found it that bad, though I've had more of a social life than I normally like. I'm not a great one for meeting new people, but between Daryl's boisterous nature and what he calls my "boyish good looks," it's been difficult to try and blend into the background like I prefer to do.

I stare at my white sneakers as we walk, burping out my chili dog and regretting eating it as the taste is regurgitated back into my mouth unpleasantly. Daryl continues to chatter away again, once more unaware of me only paying half as much attention as I should be. It's always been like this with us—probably why we've been friends for so long. He is the fast-talking joker and I'm the quiet one. We complement each other perfectly without cramping each other's style.

"Did you see that? There's a fight." Daryl tugs on my T-shirt and I look up.

Sure enough, he's right: a fight's broken out between a couple of dudes. By the looks of the girls bitching at each other to the side of them, I'd say they were probably the cause. Parents are dragging their little kids away from the fight—not only because of the violence, but because of the cuss words flying around. The whole thing makes me groan and roll my eyes.

A crowd closes around the two guys fighting and I follow Daryl over as he laughs and whoops manically. Me, I'm a lover not a fighter, and the sound of fists hitting flesh makes my stomach churn. It's not that I can't fight, it's that I choose not to—not unless I have to. And when I do it's usually to back up Daryl, since he seems to attract trouble wherever he goes. I follow him into the throng of people, pushing aside a couple that with a polite "excuse me." I get some shifty stares but most people are too preoccupied with watching these guys beating on each other to really care. The shrill voices of the girls arguing close by echo throughout the crowd, and I'm pretty certain that it's only moments now before those two start pulling at each other's hair like only girls can do.

I finally push to the front and see that a dark-haired guy has a smaller blond-haired guy pinned to the ground as he lays into him, his fists repeatedly flying into the guy's face as the blond guy snarls up at him.

Daryl is still laughing and egging them on much like everyone else, but it does nothing for me in any way. The sight and smell of the blood is just gross, and I can't quite grasp what enjoyment people can get from watching this. I turn to head back out of the crowd and bump straight into Brown Eyes.

ACKNOWLEDGMENTS

This book would not be possible without the help, love, and support of so many great people, and I am eternally grateful to each and every one of you. You all know who you are.

A massive thanks also goes to the fans that filled in my survival questionnaires. As followers of the series will know, some of the characters in my books are loosely based around real people and their answers to a survival questionnaire I sent them. So a big thanks goes to...

Nova Huff, Michael Robertson, Mathew Dudley, Jessica Sturgill, Becky Stephens, Julie Rainey, Zee Rahman, J.C. Michael, Rachel Helen Wilkinson, Melanie Bingle Marsh, Hilary Lauren, Deacon Jastram & Susan Pigott.

As per the usual, I never promised you a long life...or an easy death, a large part or a small part. But know that there wasn't enough room in this book for as much expansion of some of your characters as I would have liked, and as such, some of you have been carried over into part three of the saga, and also Odium 0.2 ⊡

And a HUGE thank you of course, goes to you, my awesome readers. I hope that you continue to enjoy Nina's story.

ABOUT THE AUTHOR

Claire C. Riley is USA Today and International bestselling author. Eclectic writer of all things apocalyptic and romance, she enjoys hiking, movie marathon, & old school board games. Claire lives in Manchester England with her husband, three daughters and naughty rescue beagle.

She writes under C. Riley for her thrillers and suspense.

She can be found on Facebook, Instagram, TikTok and more!

For a full list of her works, head over to her Amazon author page.

CONTACT LINKS

Website: www.clairecriley.com

FB page: https://www.facebook.com/ClaireCRileyAuthor/

Amazon: http://amzn.to/1GDpF3I

Reader Group: Riley's Rebels: https://www.facebook.com/groups/

ClaireCRileyFansGroup/

Newsletter Sign-up: http://bit.ly/2xTY2bx

IG: https://www.instagram.com/redheadapocalypse/

Twitter: @ClaireCRiley

Tik Tok: @redheadapocolypse

Made in the USA
Monee, IL
06 July 2024

61329076R00225